Praise for *King of Shards*

"A surreal and exotic adventure in a unique mythological setting. Scary, exhilarating fun!"
—N.K. Jemisin, award-winning author of *The Inheritance Trilogy*, the *Dreamblood* series, and *The Fifth Season*

"A gripping trek across a unique desert world rich with Kabbalah-inspired magic and vivid demons builds to a whirlwind climax."
—Scott H. Andrews,
World Fantasy Award-nominated editor of
Beneath Ceaseless Skies Magazine

"Matthew Kressel's King of Shards is an imaginative, intelligent, and soaring debut that mixes Jewish folklore/mysticism and modern-day social politics. The result is a unique spin on epic fantasy that is both timeless and timely, and a hell of lot of fun."
—Paul Tremblay,
author of *A Head Full of Ghosts* and *The Little Sleep*

"With King of Shards, Kressel threads portal adventure through ancient mythos. His demons and demi-gods and his very human (or mostly human) characters have to work their way through the terrifying, violent, and often beautiful alternate planes he's built using his incredible imagination and traditional and Apocryphal knowledge as a tableau. You will emerge transformed."
—Fran Wilde, author of *Updraft*

"Kressel's rich landscapes sing with ancient resonance by the light of modern flair. He weaves compelling tradition with innovative high Fantasy; culture and creativity become foundations for new myths featuring heroes built to shine."
—Leanna Renee Hieber,
award-winning author of the *Strangely Beautiful* saga

"This is a world where the mysticism of The Kabbalah and Torah begin to seem like everyday commentary, where ordinary people attempt to live their lives despite the extraordinary turmoil of unending conspiracy, secret saints, scheming demons, and shattered universes. This novel shakes the foundations of everyday reality, and the ensuing chaos is pure pleasure."
—Christopher Barzak,
author of *One for Sorrow* and *Wonders of the Invisible*

KING OF SHARDS

KING OF SHARDS

BOOK ONE OF THE **WORLDMENDER** TRILOGY

MATTHEW KRESSEL

Arche Press

This is A004, and it has an ISBN of 978-1-63023-028-9.

This book was printed in the United States of America, and it is published by Arche Press, an imprint of Resurrection House (Puyallup, WA).

Es per-shemp Bedu.

Edited by Darin Bradley
Cover Design by Darin Bradley
Cover Art by Leon Tukker
Book Design by Aaron Leis
Copy Edit by Shannon Page

First Arche Press edition: October 2015.

www.resurrectionhouse.com

For Christine, Pillar of my World

KING OF SHARDS

The Legend of the Thirty-Six

There are thirty-six just people who sustain the world, thirty-six hidden saints who quietly perform small acts of kindness and righteousness. So concealed are these saints that you or I could be one and not know it. Each of their small acts serves to uphold the world, and it is said that if not for their merit the world would be destroyed. Because in Hebrew the letter *lamed* is 30 and the letter *vav* is 6, we call these righteous ones the *Lamed Vav*.

"O Lord, did you not pour him forth like milk? Did you not make him firm like cheese? Hear me, you covered him with flesh and skin, you wove him of bone and nerves, and now you have destroyed him."

—André Schwarz-Bart, *The Last of the Just*

CHAPTER ONE

DANIEL WAS GETTING MARRIED TODAY, BUT ALL HE COULD THINK about was work. In the musty Hebrew school classroom of Temple Beth Tiferet he pulled the black suit jacket over his shoulders and remembered the storm, how he had laid warm blankets over weary shoulders. He tightened the knot of his wine-dark tie and remembered wrapping gauze around swollen legs. Those folks didn't have homes—hadn't for years, and yet here he was, about to venture off to an island for two weeks of luxury and indulgence. And what about Gram, who would remain home, alone, with no one to call if she needed help? He wanted to keep Rebekah happy, but the truth was he longed to stay in New York and continue working for the Shulman Fund, where he fought for the city's homeless. He wanted to stay close to Gram, the one who had raised him. But Rebekah, as sympathetic and understanding as she could be, had said their honeymoon was non-negotiable. They would be leaving first thing in the morning.

Fully dressed now in his itchy black wedding suit, Daniel gazed out the window. Last week's hurricane—unusual for New York—had swept out the late-summer warmth, and outside the afternoon air was crisp and biting. The sun descended over a copse of tall Westchester oaks, and the light pierced the blinds, sending ladders of orange across Christopher's smiling face. Christopher managed the Rising Path shelter that Daniel had helped build, and as he turned, the sun illuminated the tattoo on the dark skin of his neck: a crucified Jesus, blood spilling down his face from his crown of thorns, gazing up at God, awaiting redemption.

"I've never been to a Jewish wedding," Christopher said. "You told me about some of your customs, but I'm excited to see them for myself."

Christopher turned, and the shadow of his neck darkened the sky above Jesus, as if storm clouds were rolling in. "The rituals are beautiful," Daniel said, "but sometimes I feel as if it's more about the performance than the meaning behind them."

"All rituals are performances," Christopher said. "That's the whole point, isn't it?"

Above the chalkboard a paper Hebrew alphabet had been stapled to a long cork strip. In the orange sunlight, the letters seemed to burn. The letter Ayin was missing. Ayin, the divine nothing. Ayin, the good or evil eye, depending. At least, that's what Gram had said. Daniel shook his head. Now wasn't the time for her silly superstitions. Outside, the branches of dead trees shivered in the wind.

"What do you see?" Christopher said, as if he were a philosopher-rebbe from one of Gram's Hasidic tales.

"Randomness," Daniel said. The forest outside looked as if it had been blasted in a nuclear attack. Most trees were bent, broken. But not all. "Why do you think the storm knocked down some trees and not others? The fallen ones seem no different from any other."

"Luck," Christopher said. "It's like people. Some are blessed with good fortune. Others, not so much."

Ainems mazel iz an anderens shlemazel, Daniel heard Gram say in Yiddish. One's good luck is another's misfortune.

He remembered the night of the hurricane. The wind had been blowing in ten different directions, and Manhattan's streets were empty, gray, and rain-choked. Like a mouse in a giant cemetery, Daniel had weaved under dark skyscrapers toward Rising Path homeless shelter. Open only six weeks, they'd received several summons for overcrowding. Another, and they'd be shut down for good.

But when Daniel saw the homeless people waiting outside in the storm, the diabetic with his swollen ankles and bloody socks, the schizophrenic who couldn't light her cigarette, the drunkard who had collapsed on the curb, the mother trying to soothe her colicky baby, he'd convinced Christopher, the manager, to let them all inside.

It hadn't been enough. Dozens of homeless throughout the city had gone missing after the storm. Washed away to be forgotten, their deaths remained untallied in the storm's official toll. Daniel sagged with the weight of the memory.

Outside the classroom, the sun dipped behind a broken tree trunk, and the light splintered into a fan of orange rays. "The storm hurt a lot of people," Daniel said.

"I know," said Christopher. "But this is a day of happiness, Danny. You work very hard. You deserve this. Make sure you pause to enjoy it."

But do I deserve this? he thought.

Five years ago, right out of college, he'd taken the job with the Shulman Fund. Through their nonprofit wing he'd worked on many humanitarian projects. But Rising Path was his from start to finish, and he felt a responsibility for it, like a father to his child. He had made arrangements for his absence, of course. Christopher was more than capable of managing the shelter. But the storm had shown him that there was no such thing as being fully prepared.

Christopher pivoted open one of the small windows and lit a cigarette. Cool air raced around Daniel's ankles. "You never told me how you got home that night," Christopher said, exhaling corkscrews of smoke. "The buses and subways had shut down by the time you left."

"I walked."

"All the way to Brooklyn? In the wind and the rain?"

Daniel nodded.

"You didn't have to check up on us, you know. You could've called."

"I did. Several times. No one answered." He had actually called more than thirty times. He could still hear the hollow space at the end of each long ring.

"That must have been some walk," Christopher said.

"It wasn't fun. But at least I had a home to get back to."

Christopher took a long, slow drag. "Yeah," he said. "Yeah."

Pelted by the cold rain, Daniel had walked over the Williamsburg Bridge. Cars honked, and seagulls cawed as the bridge swayed fitfully. He had tried to call Gram many times, but she didn't answer. It tore him up. He should have been there, with her. When he was a boy, she had leapt through a wall of flames into his burning bedroom, wrapped him a blanket, and carried him through hell to safety. And for this selfless act she had been burned so severely that she resembled a hideous monster to everyone but him. His parents had died that night, and Gram had raised him as her own.

But he had just fled the nest. Three months ago he had moved out of Gram's Babylon home and into Rebekah's small Bushwick apartment.

Gram had survived the storm, thank God. Her house had only minor damage. But like the trees in the forest outside, from sheer luck. Floods destroyed more than half the houses in Babylon. For Gram, it could have been much, much worse.

An usher stuck his head into the classroom and said, "Daniel, it's time. You ready?"

He took a deep breath as Christopher tamped out his cigarette. Daniel nodded, and out they went.

The wedding party stirred when he arrived in the lobby of Temple Beth Tiferet. The antechamber to the sanctuary was large and opulent, with murals of Moses, the zodiac, and the Twelve Tribes of Israel frescoed on the walls. A glimmering chandelier hung over ornate couches. Daniel shook hands and kissed cheeks. Almost all of these people were from Rebekah's extended family, people he'd met only last night at the rehearsal dinner.

At that same dinner Christopher had asked Daniel why he'd chosen him to be his best man, why not one of his school buddies? And the truth was that Daniel hadn't made many long-term friends. They had moved to other cities, to bigger jobs. And after a while, Daniel had lost touch with them. Perhaps the fault lay with him. Secretly he enjoyed the freedom of anonymity, because it felt, in a strange way, safer.

Rebekah was readying in a classroom down another hallway. She had requested to forego the bridal veiling, but thought it bad luck to see Daniel on the day of marriage. The ketubah had been signed in the presence of the rabbi the night before, so all that was left to do was to declare their vows before the public and God.

He remembered the first time he saw her. It was at a prep meeting for a City Meals event. Her striking eyes, brown whorls flecked with green, reminded him of an autumn forest blowing in the wind. Rebekah worked for another nonprofit, and as they spoke, he found her sharp and witty. She giggled whenever he made a joke. And several times after, they met for coffee, ostensibly to discuss the event, but it became obvious that their rendezvous had nothing to do with City Meals. He felt guilty about that, at first, but his feelings quickly shifted to excitement.

When he spoke about work, she listened with compassion and understanding, beyond what he thought possible in a partner. Her shoulder-length hair was so black it seemed blue, and he loved to run his fingers through it when they kissed. The freckles on her porcelain skin covered her body like a sky full of stars, and when he closed his eyes he could count them all. Her husky and feminine voice, inflected with occasional Slavic intonations, made him feel warm and at home. But it was her selflessness that he had fallen most in love with, the person who spent eighteen hours a day making sure others had enough to eat, or got the medicine they needed, or had a warm place to sleep. She was, as Gram might say, *a gute neshome*. A good soul.

His heart warmed as he thought of her.

"Take your places, please," the usher said as he dispensed wine-dark yarmulkes to the men. "We'll be starting in a minute."

Daniel wiped sweat from his brow as live music started in the sanctuary, Bach's "Largo" from the *Concerto for Two Violins in D Minor*. He wore no fringed tallis, and there would be no chupa swaying over the wedding couple. Rebekah's requests, two of many particulars, like the bridesmaids' dresses of emerald satin, brocade trim, and sparkling belts fit for twenty-first-century cowgirls.

He'd left all the wedding details up to her, like the groomsmen's traditional black suits and their ties, handkerchiefs, and cummerbunds—all the color of spilled wine. She had chosen this shade for the flowers too, the color of the sky twenty minutes after an autumn sunset. The same color, Daniel saw as he looked out the glass doors of the synagogue, as the sky was just now.

The wind gusted, and a spray of leaves tumbled past the entrance. And following the leaves stepped a white-haired man dressed in a long cloak. The man peered inside the synagogue as he walked quickly past the doors, his eyes white as moons, and a wave of sudden dread washed over Daniel. The night of the storm rushed back to him.

He had been just a few blocks from Rebekah's apartment on the night of the hurricane, soaked and miserable, looking forward to a hot shower, when a tall, white-haired man in a long cloak— the same man, Daniel was certain—leaped out from behind the scaffolding of a construction site. Daniel remembered him from Rising Path. Earlier that night he had been staring at Daniel from a stairwell. His Roman nose and a sharp jaw were distinguishing enough, but it was those white eyes, as bright as twin moons, that he recalled most vividly.

With schizophrenics he often felt as if they could peer deep into his soul, beyond the boundaries of his ego, to glimpse disapprovingly at his fragile self, because that was the hellish place where they lived. But this man's gaze delved fathoms deeper, down into his reptilian brain, plucking at his primal fears, like a fever dream concocting nightmares from his id.

The man said, "Don't marry that beast. The cosmos will collapse, and all the universes will shatter in a cataclysm to dwarf all cataclysms. And it will all be your fault, Daniel."

He likely had overheard Daniel on the phone back at the shelter and concocted this delusional fantasy. Daniel took a deep breath and slowed his racing heart. And as politely as he could in the sixty-mile-an-hour gusts and heavy rain, excused himself from the stranger and headed home. He didn't tell Rebekah about the encounter. There was no reason to scare her. Things like this happened sometimes. And in the chaos that followed the storm, he had forgotten all about the encounter until now.

The white-haired man vanished behind the synagogue wall just as Christopher tapped him on the shoulder. "You all right, Danny? You look a little pale."

Daniel forced a smile. "I'm fine. Just a little anxious, that's all."

My fear is playing tricks, he thought. *That was a different man.* No other explanation made sense.

The usher gave his cue, and Rebekah's first cousins entered the sanctuary through the heavy mahogany doors. The next couple followed, then the third, and the fourth, their steps in sync with the music. With each couple, his heart rate intensified.

Rebekah's relatives had flawless skin, professional haircuts, upper-class jawlines, and model's noses. Only a few cousins had shown up from his side. He wouldn't have called them good-looking. Besides Christopher and his cousins, there was only Gram.

He had asked her if she would walk him down the aisle, but Gram had refused. He had begged her to come, and she agreed only if she could sit, veiled and anonymous, in the pews. She wanted no part in this ceremony. This was not about her disfigurement, or embarrassment. Gram hated Rebekah because she had stolen Daniel from her. And so Christopher had happily agreed to walk Daniel down the aisle.

He closed his eyes and imagined his parents' faces. What would they have worn? What would they have said? Would Dad have imparted some inane marriage wisdom? Would Mom have asked veiled questions about grandchildren? If only they had been here to witness this.

As if reading his mind, Christopher put his hand on Daniel's arm. "Remember, this is a day of joy, Danny. God wants you to be happy."

Daniel nodded and thanked Christopher just as the usher signaled it was their turn to enter. To the beat of the music he and Christopher stepped into the sanctuary beyond the mahogany doors. Towering stained glass windows spilled multicolored light over all the guests as they all turned to look at him.

His cheeks grew hot. He disliked being the spectacle. Rebekah's family, on the left side of the sanctuary, beamed with celebrity teeth, photogenic in their tailored suits and glittering dresses. Their expensive jewelry winked brightly in the light.

His relatives sparsely occupied the right side. A few stocky, balding men—distant cousins of his mother—and their middle-aged wives. Two kids argued over a pocket video game. The girl picked her nose and stuck it into her brother's face.

Gram sat in the fifth row, hooded and veiled. As he passed her, she made a gesture to ward off the evil eye. She kissed her hamsa pendant and whispered, "*Kinayn'ore!*"

He smiled and hoped that under her veil she smiled back. He stepped onto to the bimah and took his place beside the groomsmen. Christopher positioned himself beside a row of tall, good-looking men from Rebekah's family. He was a head shorter than the shortest and the only African-American among them. The rabbi, his beard as orange as dried apricots, raised his well-thumbed prayer book as the orchestra changed tune to an intense, aggressive waltz. Daniel couldn't place the song. Was this Rebekah's choice?

His relatives grimaced, but her side smiled and swayed and turned their heads toward the mahogany doors in unison, as if Rebekah had entered, but the doors remained closed. Yet an instant later—had they known she was coming?—the doors opened, and in she strode.

Daniel held his breath as her parents led her in. They were as pale, dark-haired, and as graceful as she was. Rebekah wore a black, tight-fitting dress affixed with hundreds of small mirrors that sent a planetarium of reflections over the audience. She had wrapped her waist many times with a thin, patent leather belt, and its over-sized buckle, a shard of a broken mirror, reflected spots of light in front of her as she walked.

He had seen her wedding dress many times, a lacy white gown that had taken up half their shared closet. What the hell was she wearing now?

Her relatives smiled. They sighed and got teary-eyed and held palms over their breasts. His relatives turned bemused gazes toward him, and he shrugged. He had no idea why she had chosen this attire. He couldn't see Gram's face under her veil, but he knew he wouldn't like her expression. Rebekah had always been unusual when it came to fashion. But this was bizarre.

Her parents kissed her and took their positions on the bimah. Rebekah flashed her white teeth, then looped around him, once, twice, as her mirrors dazzled him with a thousand reflections. Each loop represented a day of Creation, and she would end on the seventh day, the Sabbath, their marriage becoming an echo of God's work. And though he was blinded and confused, he was certain he counted five and only five loops before she paused.

Her eyes were whorls of green and brown. Her pupils dilated as she met his gaze. He was transfixed. Her expression was joyous, yes, but underneath lurked something feral, wild. Was she drunk? It took immense effort to move his lips. He whispered, "What's going on, Bek?"

She smiled. "I gird myself with the fragments of the Cosmos, just as you, Danny, have girded this world."

He stared at her. "What?"

The music halted. She nodded to the rabbi, and he began officiating. Daniel felt the eyes of his relatives upon him. His cheeks were aflame. They couldn't stop now. He'd get answers later, at the reception, as soon as he and Rebekah had a moment alone.

He repeated the Hebrew prayers after the rabbi and took Rebekah's fever-hot hand.

Christopher presented the gold band, and Daniel placed it on her index finger, her nails the same wine-dark color as his tie. He repeated after the rabbi, "Behold you are sanctified to me with this ring, according to the Law of Moses and Israel . . ."

Then came the kiddush, the Concord grape wine dark and shiny in the silver cup. The rabbi wrapped a small, clear wine glass inside a napkin and placed it on the floor. He nodded to Daniel, and Daniel lifted his foot.

"*Stop!*" someone shouted.

The sound came from the rear of the sanctuary, and everyone turned. Daniel gasped and felt as if someone had shoved a sharp, icy needle into his heart, because there he was, the same tall, white-haired man with moon-bright eyes, the same man who had followed him home that night of the storm. He had just burst through the sanctuary doors and was sprinting toward them.

"Stop!" the man shouted again. "Don't break the glass!"

Rebekah said, "Break it, Danny. Hurry! Break the glass now!"

The man leaped for the bimah, when suddenly he wasn't a man anymore but an enormous black dog, eyes as white as milk. Daniel gasped, and the audience shouted in mutual astonishment. Their faces blurred as if water had been poured over his eyes. But blurred wasn't the right word. It seemed as if everyone had been formed from millions of tiny cubes of salt. And not just the guests, but the prayer books, the pews, and the stained-glass windows too.

Everything had become granular, discrete. Even time itself skipped forward in steps, as if attached to a cosmic escapement.

This is a dream! he thought.

Gram was shouting under her salt-crystal veil, her words slurred and slow. The salt grains grew, and the world pixelated into a thousand bright mosaics.

Rebekah shouted, "Break the glass, Danny! Break it now!"

Everyone had become writhing salt-monsters, except for Rebekah and the dog. Daniel screamed, and his voice stretched across time, back to Creation itself, perhaps eons before. The dog reached the stage and morphed into a man. He grabbed Daniel's wrist. "You treasonous bitch!" he said to Rebekah.

Rebekah grabbed the silver kiddush cup from the stunned salt-crystal rabbi and smashed it against the man's forehead. Wine flew into the air, and a gash zippered open on the man's scalp. A spray of blood-red cubes spun in the air, unaffected by gravity.

Rebekah howled, and her face withered like the roots of an ancient tree. Her eyes became horrid pools of black. Daniel screamed again as the man yanked him away. And he let the man pull him off the bimah, away from that hideous face—across the sanctuary, through the lobby, and out the glass doors into the night.

Cold air nipped at his skin as the man yanked him over a parking lot paved with salt. He pulled Daniel past cubiform cars and into a metropolis of crystalline gravestones. The rising moon was a crescent of salt that spilled pale light onto pixelated branches. The stars were each single salt grains.

I'm hallucinating! he thought.

Screams and shouts rose behind him as the man released Daniel's hand beside a towering oak. "Who are you?" Daniel said between gasps. He tried to rub this nightmare from his eyes.

The man muttered several phrases in a bizarre, guttural language, then squeezed his hand into a fist and slowly opened it. A spark of light floated in his palm, a flame without a candle. He let the spark fall, and it fluttered to the ground. When it touched the earth, the spark vanished and the ground shuddered.

The man turned to Daniel, his pale eyes more ancient than time. "Who am I?" he said. "I'm the savior of the Cosmos. Now stand back."

This is a fever dream! Daniel thought. *It has to be!*

The ground sank, and he leaped back as a hole formed and deepened. It grew quickly, and the earth erupted in an explosion of frigid air. Dead pixelated leaves vorticed into the hole. A hundred gravestones cracked, the Hebrew names of the deceased split in two.

"Danny!" Rebekah screamed. She was sprinting through the cemetery toward him. "Come back!" She held up the napkin-wrapped wine glass for him to break.

Christopher was running behind her. "Danny!" he yelled. "What the hell is going on?"

He moved toward them, toward sanity. But before Daniel had gone three paces the stranger grabbed him by the waist. He struggled to free himself, but the man was too strong. The hole was twenty feet wide and growing, when the oak tree groaned, snapped, and splintered into a million cubes that plunged into the pit. The man paused at the growing rim to look down, and Daniel, unable to break free, glanced too.

Monstrosity!

He wailed in terror and closed his eyes. It was too big! Impossibly big! A brief glance was all it took. Oh God—oh God—oh God! A million universes could fit inside that abominable hole. No, endlessly more! Oh, God—oh God! No words would ever convey how large and empty this hole was, nor how Daniel knew its ineffable size from one brief and terrible glance.

He wished he'd never seen it. He knew this vision would haunt him forever. He wanted to run and hide from that awful pit. But with Daniel tucked securely in his arms, the white-haired man leaped headfirst into the abyss.

CHAPTER TWO

THE DEMON HAD SAVED DANIEL, BUT THE FOOL DIDN'T KNOW it yet.

They fell.

They fell.

No matter existed in this place before places, not a single atom in this void of voids. If he had a mouth to scream, the demon would have, because he remembered this terror, remembered tumbling into the Abyss, when the Creator had ripped his world apart and tossed her screaming children into the Great Deep.

Our mother, the demon thought. *Our destroyer.*

The blind idiot tumbled beside him, a spark of unsteady light, flashing in panic as they went down and down and down.

They fell.

They fell.

Milton had it wrong. It wasn't nine days. It was nine eternities. Ages crept past them in a silence that had lain undisturbed since before the first universe. The demon was more ancient than the oldest mountains, older than Earth, but the Great Deep mocked such notions of duration. It could swallow all the years of his life a trillion, trillion, trillion times. When he had been thrust into the Abyss the first time, he had known only fear. But he had been a child then. Now, he fell with purpose.

They fell.

They fell.

Time passed. An eon or a nanosecond. All was meaningless in the breadth of eternity. An orange pinprick formed in the emptiness below, a miniscule spark of light. They fell toward it. Flowing out from its glare, in currents long and wispy, came ballads of forgotten kings, cries from the death of children, a dying man's last breath. Like smoke, the currents drifted into the vastness to be forgotten, the broken sounds of a broken people in a broken universe.

The spark was but an atom's width, and if they missed it, they would tumble in this Abyss forever, flotsam in its infinite sea. He pulled the idiot closer and they hurtled toward the infinitesimal dot. Closer now. Closer.

And they entered! By a hairsbreadth they squeezed through!

Then, light! Everywhere light, and time, and dimension. And, cursed be her name, his power had abated. He was mongrel again.

They tumbled through blue sky, falling toward an orange landscape of sand. Orange and blue. Orange and blue. The wind rushed by his canine ears as they hurtled sandward. The idiot screamed as the demon braced for impact.

They slammed into a dune, rolled down its face. The demon tumbled and gasped and laughed, because after an eternity of endless nothing, even pain was a miracle.

They came to rest at the base of a dune. The idiot wheezed and tried to catch his breath. He gagged and vomited, then gazed up at the yellow sun before retching again. The demon waited, and his black mongrel fur grew hot in the sun. Blood dripped into his canine eyes from the gash where the bitch had struck him. It was salty as he licked it away.

The idiot stared at him, eyes wide, hyperventilating. There would be no getting through until he calmed, so the dog scanned the landscape. An undulant sea of orange sand surrounded them. The dunes crept forward like slow moving ocean waves under a vexing yellow sun.

Luck is with me today, the demon thought. *We've landed in the Tattered Sea.*

Not safe, by far, but better than the other side of the world. The demon turned to the idiot and was about to speak, but then remembered he was a dog. He would not reduce himself to barks and grunts.

On all fours the dog was more than half the idiot's height. The idiot backed away as the dog approached him. He explored the strength of his muscles, stretched his back, then paused, inches from the idiot, savoring the man's fear.

You and I have a lot of work to do, Daniel, the demon thought.

"What's hap—happening, dog?" the idiot stuttered. "Where am I?" The sands seemed to swallow his words. Nothing lingered in this place of impermanence.

With his snout, the dog pointed twice to the south.

"Are you . . . ?" the idiot said. "Are you pointing?"

The dog nodded.

The man laughed maniacally. "Did you just nod?"

He nodded again.

"What the fuck?" The idiot smacked his hands against his head and gritted his teeth. "Wake up, Danny! Wake the hell up!"

The dog gestured again, twice more, to the south. They had to move quickly, before Mashit came for them. And she *would* come.

The idiot wiped sweat from his face and took off his jacket. His boutonniere had leaked a wine-colored stain onto his shirt, like a wound. "This isn't happening," he said.

The dog leaped onto the man, and he fell backward. He snarled and shoved his snout into Daniel's face, then dragged a paw across his chest, tearing shirt and skin until Daniel screamed.

How do you not sense what you are? the demon thought. *How do you not know your cosmic purpose? You've concealed yourself so well you don't even remember who you are!*

The dog released Daniel, and trotted away. He gestured south again.

Daniel pressed his hand to his new wound. Blood mixed with the purple-flower stain. "Okay," he said, trembling. "I get it. You want me to follow you."

The dog nodded. *Yes, you damn fool!*

"This is insanity," Daniel said. He wiped his mouth and picked up his jacket. "Holy mother fucker, dog, where the hell am I?"

Not where the hell, Daniel, the demon thought, *but which one.*

———

Leagues across the orange sands of the Tattered Sea, the workday was nearly over. Beside the sharp crags of the DanBaer mountain, a new tower rose brick by massive brick. Twenty masons labored on its peak, adding yet another level to the Ukne Tower's rarefied heights. The masons were young, wiry, taut-muscled men, except for one young woman, as strong if not stronger than any of the men. Her skin was as bronze as oxen leather and her hair was as black and straight as the giraffes of Karad.

The masons whispered that her eyes were as dark as the voids between the stars, and that if you stared into them too long the darkness would infect you with her madness. She was unhinged, the masons said when she was out of earshot, a lunatic full of wild dreams and insatiable creativity, and only survived because her father had once been the chief architect for King Jallifex. But now that her father had broken his back, her future was less certain.

Rana had heard all this gossip about her, but she didn't care much for rumors. What mattered was setting stone in patterns lovely and unique. She wiped sweat from her eyes as she led the masons in an old worksong.

The men swung hammer to chisel with her words, hefted stones to verse, spread mortar by stanza. And as she sang and set stone, she imagined their movements were brushstrokes, the tower walls her canvas. She moved the men with music, their eyes distant and untroubled by the heavy labors, as they danced the wall into existence. A group of beryl-winged hawks circled overhead as she sang, crying out in mournful arpeggios whenever she paused.

The sun neared the horizon. Soiled with mortar, their bodies spent, the masons slowed, drooped, and finally stopped. They took quaffs from canteens, lit pipes, or dozed. They'd been working since dawn.

Rana sat on the stone wall and dangled her legs over the precipice as the wind whipped at her hair. Azru's crooked streets and alleyways sprawled beneath them. From this height the scattered ruins of the city that Azru had been built atop was clearly visible. She traced the Ukne's shadow over the jumbled rooftops to its peak deep in the Tattered Sea. In the desert, a caravan made its way out toward deeper sands, stirring up a cloud in their wake.

Davo sat beside her and offered her a dried pomm fruit.

"What did they do to it?" she said.

"Nothing!" Davo shouted. "I swear to Mollai."

Sometimes the other masons spat or pissed on her food. Never Davo, though. She sniffed the fruit and it smelled fine, so she popped it into her mouth.

"Do you think it will ever rain here?" she said.

Davo laughed. "In the desert?"

"Last night I dreamed of thunder and lightning and rivers in the streets." The city shimmered below as the day's heat bled off, and the drooping sun turned Azru as red as the Fires of Korah. "A storm of storms."

Davo nodded. "When I was really young," he said, "it rained for a whole day." He released a fistful of sand over the precipice. "People danced in the streets. They sacrificed calves in the temples. My father made me stay indoors, said the storm was demon's work."

"I heard about it," she said. "It happened before I was born."

"You can't imagine it. Oceans falling from the sky. The oddest flowers bloomed in the desert, thousand-colored, big as houses. Giant sparrows came to eat the fruits. The flowers lasted a week before they wilted. I never saw anything like it before or since."

"Sounds incredible."

"It was awful! I hid under my bed. I thought the world was ending."

"'One world ending is another beginning.'"

Marul Menacha had told her that. The old woman had told Rana that a thousand other things before she left one day and never came back.

Rana picked up a loose stone and began carving a spiral pattern into the wall. She had glimpsed the shape in a dream and had never quite been able to capture its essence.

"Did you hear there was another shooting star this morning?" Davo said.

"I did. You saw it?"

"It was brighter than the sun. It didn't disintegrate like the others. It arced across the northern sky. Two fragments this time, so bright I saw spots in my vision. It's an omen."

"An omen? Can't a shooting star just be a shooting star?"

"Three in one month?" He shook his head. "Nothing is ever just what it seems."

"That's what Marul used to say."

"Not smelly old Marul Menacha again," he said, frowning. "Just when I think you've forgotten her, you dredge her up again."

She stared at him. "I'll never forget Marul. She was my best friend."

"She left, what, five years ago? Marul's not coming back, Rana. She's dead."

Rana closed her eyes and prayed to Mollai that it wasn't true.

"Oy!" a man shouted. The gruff voice of Chief Architect Jo startled her. "What the fuck is this? The sun ain't set yet!"

The balding, corpulent Jo, drenched in sweat, waddled up the wooden ramp to the high construction site. The cedar planks complained with his heavy steps.

"Hey!" He kicked two sleeping boys. "Get the fuck back to work!"

Rana and Davo stared at each other to share a moment of despair. The Ukne was ahead of schedule. There was no reason for haste. But Chief Architect Jo was new to his job and wanted to impress King Jallifex.

The masons dragged their exhausted bodies over to the basin of mortar. Davo lifted a heavy block of ashlar, and Rana spread brown cement with a trowel on the unfinished wall. The others crept back to work. She inhaled and began another worksong.

Chief Architect Jo got sleepy-eyed as he lit his pipe. He allowed Rana her songs because the masons worked faster when she sang. He watched them set a perfect row of ashlar before he waddled back down the ramp, as if lost in a dream.

When he was out of sight, Rana leaned back against the wall and slid down to sit. Everyone stopped working with her. "I miss your father," Davo said. "He was the best chief architect we've ever had. Any chance he'll come back?"

"I doubt it," Rana said, picking up the stone and continuing her attempt to recreate the spiral from her dream. "He can't get out of bed without help. I think his back's broken for good."

"May Mollai heal him."

Davo eyed her hungrily, and she knew his look. The masons gazed at her like this when she sang, something about the music throbbing in their hearts that turned them into animals. Davo got this look around quitting time, when his mind was spent and his desire took over.

Men and their pricks! she thought. Was fucking all they ever thought about? She turned away from his glare.

Smoke drifting from the houses below lofted mouth-watering scents of meat and grains toward them. Nearly suppertime. She sighed. Her father would have let the workers go home early to enjoy the remains of the day. But never Jo.

"I should've been chief architect," she said. "I was next in line after my father."

"One day. You just need a few more years experience."

Her face grew hot. "Experience? Ha! No, Davo, it's because King Jallifex can't have a woman design his glorious city. What would his enemies think?"

Davo spat over the edge. "The same thing his friends think, that he's an ugly lizard."

The other masons laughed.

"If I were chief architect," Rana said, "I'd build a city greater than Karad. I'd build the greatest city Gehinnom has ever seen."

Davo's mouth hung open. "Don't speak like that. You'll offend the Goddess."

"Mollai has more on her mind than my little fantasies." She frowned and kicked sand to the rooftops far below.

"You need more patience, Rana. A few more years apprenticing and we'll each get our own foremanship. You'll see."

"Apprenticing? Davo, I set the capstones on the Crypt of Umer when I was six. I dangled from ropes two hundred stories above the ground! I helped my father design the palace where the king sleeps. I was weaned on mortar. How much more apprenticing do I need?"

Davo frowned. "Forget it. It's not worth fretting about things we have no control over."

"But that's just it. Every day I choose to heft stone for that sweaty fool." She pointed down the ramp where Jo had fled. "I could leave."

"Leave?"

"You know, quit."

"And do what? You can't work in Azru without the king's blessing."

"Then I'll quit Azru too."

Davo scratched violently at his black stubble. "Where would you go? In the desert you'd drown in the tides, or get eaten by demons, or kidnapped by Bedu. And you'd need a guide, and guides costs money. And you can't trust a sellsword—"

"Davo!" She shook her head. "Forget it. It was just a dream."

He squinted at her. "Rana, if you left, who'd sing for us?"

She felt pity for him. One day, she knew, she'd have to leave this place. Leave him. "Don't worry. I'm not going anywhere." *Not yet,* she thought.

He bit his lip and stole a glance at the sun. "Micah and me are going to the fermentary on Ramswool Row tonight. Want to join us?"

"And get groped by drunk men again? No, thanks."

"I'll make sure that doesn't happen this time."

"Sorry, Davo."

"Maybe we can go someplace else, then?"

"We?"

He lowered his voice to a conspiratorial whisper. "You know, you and me."

She climbed onto the wall and swept her gaze across the cityscape, over buildings she had laid with her own hands. Once this view had inspired awe. But as her hair fluttered in the hot breeze she realized this city was no longer enough. Azru was too small.

"Not tonight," she said. "I've got plans." She jumped off the wall and grabbed her satchel and tools.

"Plans?" Davo said. "With who?"

The sun touched the horizon, the official end of the day. The masons grabbed their belongings and raced down the wooden ramp, and Rana followed.

"Rana!" Davo shouted, running after her. "Wait! Tell me, who do you have plans with?"

A few early stars shined in the east as she shouted, "With a paintbrush, you fool!"

CHAPTER THREE

SOMETHING WAS WRONG WITH THIS DESERT. DUNES ROLLED across the sands like slow moving ocean waves, lofting Daniel and the dog hundreds of feet into the air before plunging them deep into valleys. He grew dizzy, queasy, as dunes merged, collided, and vanished, all while humming like an orchestra warming up, an out of tune symphony, threatening to harmonize but never quite succeeding. He took many deep breaths to keep his panic in check, but the technique was quickly losing effectiveness.

The huge black dog led onward, and Daniel followed, because what other option was there? Things flitted across the sky. Birds? Bats? When he turned to look, they darted out of sight, and he only caught their dark silhouettes. A few hundred feet away, a huge yellow cylinder slithered across the sands and his hopes rose. A school bus on a road? A stationary building appearing to move by optical illusion? But this "bus," he soon saw, had pearlescent scales, huge white eyes, and opalescent fins that flashed rainbows in the sun. Neither fish nor whale, but something wholly different. This huge beast swam through the dunes, serpent-like, in and out, under and over, before it vanished.

"What the holy hell is that?" he said. But the dog just kept on walking. "I saw you change shape," he said. "And I remember you. You followed me home from Rising Path. You stopped me in the street. And you were at my wedding. And now I'm in a desert that

26

sings and some yellow serpent is swimming across the sands. I'm dreaming or I've gone insane."

The dog glanced at the sun and kept walking.

"Where are you leading me? Where are we going?"

The dog ascended a dune, and at its peak the dog paused to stare at something Daniel couldn't see. The dune sunk slowly with a gut-vibrating hum, dropping by degrees to reveal the landscape beyond. And then he saw the city.

At the base of an enormous plateau there was a crowded city, nestled like a babe in its mother's arms. Gilded spires reached into the blue sky, their shiny tips burning like candles in the sun. Many walls crisscrossed in dizzying, overlapping layers that followed crooked and haphazard courses. Their jumbled shadows made the city's true size difficult to discern. In the cliffside, an enormous palace had been carved in the rock face. A webwork of bridges linked the palace to the city. It seemed as if this city had been built on top of an older city, one with different architecture and aesthetics, and that had been built on top of one before it, ad infinitum.

He had never seen anything like it, not even in a dream.

The smoldering sun sent the city's shadows deep into the sands, all the way to his feet and beyond. This was where the dog was leading him. The animal was already running toward it.

———

By the time Daniel and the dog reached the outskirts of the city, night had fallen. A spray of stars lit the sky, more points of light than he had ever seen. He grew dizzy and disoriented under their pallid glow. There were no familiar constellations. And the moon, rising above the mountain, had a strange face. It looked smaller too. Wrong, somehow.

I'm on the other side of the world, he thought. *I've been drugged and abducted. But why?*

Wind blew across the sandy plain, and the temperature plummeted. His unprotected skin, sunburned in the day, gave him chills. He donned his wedding jacket, the wine-colored flower still pinned to the lapel. People moved on the edge of the city, figures winding through crooked streets. Light and shadows flickered inside row after row of stone homes.

People. Civilization. His mouth watered at the smell of grilled meat and baking bread. He hadn't eaten since breakfast. The dog paused to sniff the air, then led on.

The outermost streets of the city were buried in sand. These peripheral buildings seemed to have been abandoned ages ago. Most were filled with sand. Daniel and the dog hiked up a cobbled street that sloped into the desert. After hours on shifting ground, the hard stones felt wonderful under his feet.

An aged woman, brown-skinned and leather-faced, sat under a smoky oil lantern beside a tray of necklaces and charms. A crimson scarf wrapped her head, and her loose brown robe was filthy. She eyed him and the dog through narrow eyes.

"Hello!" he said hoarsely. "Could you please tell me where I am?"

She took off the lid of a large jug beside her, dipped a bronze cup into it, and handed it to him. When he saw the shimmer of water, he thanked her and took it. He offered it first to the dog. The animal had brought him to civilization after all. The dog drank prodigiously.

The woman dipped again and offered him the cup, and he drank it all in one gulp. "Thank you," he said, giving the cup back to her.

"Ee-nee pos-yi nyah-neh," she said and threw the cup into the jug.

Daniel said, "May I have another, please?"

She slapped his hand. "Nyeh! Pos-wer so-nud-neh, soub!"

"Do you speak English?"

She scowled at him.

He made the universal sign for a telephone. "Do you have a phone?"

She held out her fingers, mimicking his gesture. "Nyeh bur-dah me-owpt na! Feh zhu, feg! Nyah-nyah!" She waved him away as if he were a gnat, and the dog clamped onto his hand and pulled him up the cobbled street.

"Not so friendly," Daniel said.

People in loose-fitting robes and tunics carried smoky oil lamps up and down the narrow avenues. They moved hurriedly, furtively, and didn't pay too much attention to Daniel and the dog, as if afraid of them. He called out to a few, but they only walked away faster when he did.

The city's ten thousand flickering lights from lamp and candle flames formed a starscape of its own. But this starscape moved as people walked the streets with lanterns in hand. Through open windows and shutters he peered into stone and brick homes. The residents had tea-colored skin, long, narrow faces, and eyes dark and intense. At stone tables they ate meals of soup and bread using metal and stone utensils. In one house, a man prostrated himself before a large stone effigy of a full-figured woman. In another, a man berated a boy who had broken some kind of loom. Behind a shuttered window, he heard moans of people in the throes of sex.

Their fabrics were fashioned from canvas, linen, burlap, leather. All earth-toned, with a smattering of natural reds and blues. Not a single pair of jeans or a t-shirt on any of them. No phones or computers either, or for that matter anything that hinted at the past thousand years of human technology.

Even the most remote places on Earth couldn't have sealed themselves off to modern life as well as this city had. No electrical wires. No advertisements. Not even a stray cigarette butt. How had these people so assiduously avoided modern contamination? It was almost as if he'd been thrown back in time, into one of Gram's folk tales of biblical Canaan.

On a dark, dead-end street, they paused before an ornate stone door twelve feet tall, as if made for a giant. Spirals within spirals had been carved into the door by a skilled hand. With a gentle push, the dog nudged the door, and it swung open on a miniscule pivot, a marvel of precise engineering. He followed the dog into a walled-in courtyard, each wall a magnificent mosaic full of people, monsters, and desert scenes. Four palm trees and rows of potted succulents bordered a walk that led to the opposite end of the courtyard, where three buildings stood boldly beneath the stars.

The central one was larger than the other two. The buildings were all built of white and obsidian bricks laid in a complex, repeating pattern. The roofs were slate, gently sloped, and were silver-tinted in the moonlight. Above the houses the stars burned in many colors.

Voices came from the largest building, echoing against the walls. Daniel smelled bread and his stomach grumbled. He thought about knocking on the door, but the dog pulled him toward the smaller building. The animal pawed at the door, yet another masterpiece engraved with an image of a giant bird leaping from a cliff. The dog shoved his body against the door, but it was locked. He gestured at Daniel with his snout.

"How about we knock on the door of the main house?"

The dog shook his head and growled.

"You want to go in here?"

The dog nodded.

"What's in here that's so important?"

The dog growled again and bared his teeth.

Daniel didn't want another scratch on his chest, but neither did he savor the idea of breaking into someone's house in a city that wasn't keen on strangers. Perhaps there was an easier way inside.

He circled around back, where the air reeked of feces. A few tall and thin cacti tilted somberly. He found a small, high opening in the rear of the building. An alcove. It was beyond his reach, but he used a potted plant as a stepstool and squeezed himself through the opening. It was dark inside, and as he fumbled for footing he crashed to the floor.

He sat up. He had only bruised himself, but he couldn't say the same for whatever object had broken his fall. A rectangle of moonlight shined though the alcove, revealing shadows numerous and strange. Something chittered high in one corner. A bird? He limped toward the door, banging into unseen things, and fumbled the latch. The dog bolted in.

"Okay. Now what?"

The dog shoved the door closed, then pulled Daniel into a corner, down to the floor, behind a table. And there they sat.

"Enough of this. I'm hungry and I'm knocking on the door of that house."

Daniel rose, when the dog exhaled phosphorescent green smoke from his nose. The smoke floated into the center of the room, where it coalesced into the shape of a young woman. She was beautiful, taut and muscular. She had brown skin, black hair, and eyes as dark as the space between the stars.

Daniel froze as the smoke slowly blew away, taking the visage of the young woman with it. From outside came the sound of footsteps, a voice singing like a spring bird. The voice echoed against the courtyard walls, and Daniel thought this could be what those ancient sailors heard in the cliffs by the sea as their ships crashed into the rocks. His body thrummed, and he felt renewed and energized. He found himself moving for the door before he realized he had stood, but the dog grabbed his hand and pulled him back under the table.

Someone fumbled with the latch. Whoever was singing was coming in.

CHAPTER FOUR

BY THE TIME RANA HAD REACHED STREET LEVEL, THE STARS WERE shining by the thousand-fold. With her tools in a satchel slung over her shoulder, she skipped home, whistling a tune that had come to her late one night while she had been toiling in her workshop. The cityfolk, heading home themselves, gave her plenty of space as she walked through the crowded streets. Her songs had made men do crazy things, the rumors went, like disrobe and dance in the streets, or laugh maniacally at the stars. Sometimes children threw stones at her, and more than one witch had cursed her. She still sometimes pulled baby scorpions from her hair.

Once, when she had come home with a bleeding welt on her head, Papa told her never to sing in public again. But she couldn't stop singing any more than she could stop breathing. Songs arose in her breast with the regularity of the morning sun.

At Dusty Square, she paused to run her fingers over the sharp teeth of the stone lion statues, as she liked to do every night before turning toward home, for good luck. Papa had carved them, these stone sentinels.

When she reached the tall door that led into the courtyard of her house, she found it swinging. *Guests?* she thought.

She walked into the courtyard, past walls she had painted and tiled herself. Something was amiss here that she couldn't place, but the smell of dinner from the house pulled her home. Besides the pomm fruit Davo had given her, she hadn't eaten since morning. When she opened the door, Mama was holding baby Liu in her arms.

Rana beamed as she came inside. She kissed baby Liu and Mama. Papa sat in his special wheeled chair that Rana had made for him, grunting as she kissed him hello.

"Who's my Little Bean?" Rana said, grabbing Liu from her chair. Rana couldn't resist her sister's brown pebble eyes, her soft, round cheeks.

"Put her down before she throws up," Papa said.

Mama helped Rana settle Liu back into her high seat. Rana picked up a washrag from the table and folded it into the shape of a cactus flower.

Compared to most of Azru's homes, theirs was luxurious. "The late King Umer," Papa boasted when he got very drunk, "could not have me live in an ordinary house, no! He wanted his chief architect to live in a home worthy of the king! I laid these stones by my own hand." Then Papa would knock on the wall and laugh. But since his injury, his story had taken on a bitter tone, as did most everything else Papa said.

He had built the adjacent storehouse as a buffer against the frequent famines. And when he'd discovered Rana's fountains of creativity, he'd built her the workshop. Inside those walls she had taught herself mosaic, metalwork, tapestry, painting, music, woodcarving, and many other arts. Her sculptures of the Goddess appeared in every nook and on every shelf about the house. Her brass lamps with hawk wings and oxen horns hung from the ceiling by chains she had made. Mama's wrists glittered with jewelry Rana had crafted for her, inlaid with precious stones she had mined from the mountain. Mama seemed often suspicious of the ease at which Rana learned each new skill. Once, when she was angry, Mama had said there was dark magic in it. But Papa said it was only her inherited talent that gave Rana her skills in the arts. She was the offspring of the chief architect, after all.

At Mama's order, Rana set the table with bowls she had painted with scenes from the Books of Tobai. She had molded the bronze utensils to resemble small hands. The four sat at a stone table Rana had hewn and polished from a solid block until the flecks of copper shined like stars. Rana eyed her creations doubtfully. They were never as good as she'd envisioned.

The table set, food ready, they turned to the bronze bust of Mollai that Rana had made, and Mama said, "Goddess Mollai, giver of rain and succor, praise your infinite greatness. May the winds of your blessings blow upon our family."

"So may it be her will," they replied. Baby Liu watched with curious eyes from her chair. One day, her sister would be old enough to paint and draw and set stone, and Rana would teach her everything she knew. Liu smiled, as if she was privy to this beautiful secret.

They ate a stew of ox meat and beans, a loaf of hard bread, a feast compared to what most ate. Grains and legumes arrived infrequently from the wetlands beyond the desert. Water was scarce and expensive. Azru was always at war with one city or another, and the city's storehouses were perpetually low, buffered only by Papa's foresight and wealth. But since his accident, much of that wealth had diminished. He was always concerned with money now.

"How's the Ukne coming?" Papa said. "You obeying Jo?"

Rana huffed. "Jo's an ugly lizard."

"Rana, your tongue!" Mama snapped. She frowned as she removed a morsel of chewed meat from her mouth and fed it to Liu.

"Everyone misses Papa," Rana said.

Papa lowered his eyes. Since he'd broken his back, he couldn't pick up Liu, and it was only by taking a strong powder from Anya the Healer that he was able to sit upright at the table.

Papa gave Mama a hard look. "You mustn't speak ill of the king's architect. You can't afford to lose your income, Rana."

"All the masons speak ill of Jo."

"That's no excuse."

"He's a poor chief architect. But we're ahead of schedule because of me, and I've improved his design."

"Improved?" Papa said.

"Yes."

"With his permission?" Papa put down his spoon.

Rana shrugged. "Jo's design was too simplistic. And structurally weak. A strong sandstorm and it might crack. I added reticulation to the stone settings. It looks better and it will be five times as strong."

"But he'll see the design wasn't his."

"Yes, but he never checks until it's too late anyway. The mortar has already hardened."

"Rana," Mama said, grimacing. "He'll whip you! You'll be flayed in public!"

"They'll never hurt me. The masons work faster when I'm there, because of my singing."

Mama looked concernedly at Papa.

"And Jo will take credit for the work anyway," Rana said. "He always does."

Papa stared into his stew. "Rana, these comforts we enjoy, they won't last forever. You need to prepare for the future. You can't disobey the king's architect like a spoiled child. You're twenty years old now."

"Twenty, fifty, a thousand! If I see a way to build something that's never been built before, I have to try to do it."

"And that's what drives me mad." He reached for her, but shouted and dropped his arm.

"Ari!" Mama shrieked. "Careful!"

"It's nothing." But Papa's face grew red, like the cliffs at sunset, as he grimaced.

"Demons, nothing!" Mama said. "Get yourself back to bed. I'll feed you there."

"No!" Papa slammed his fist on the table and his face contorted in pain. "I want . . . to spend a few minutes . . . with my family!" A tear rolled down his cheek and plopped into his stew.

Once Papa could heft a hundredweight stone over his head. He had stood without fear on the highest ledge. King Jallifex had paraded Papa, his chief architect, around Azru every Feast of Mollai. Now he sat here a trembling, wincing cripple.

Rana cursed the Goddess. Papa had offered up sacrifices to Mollai every week. He had prayed to her daily. And this was how she had repaid him? Sometimes Rana wondered if the Goddess even listened to human prayers.

"Rana," Mama said, trying to spare Papa more humiliation, "have you given thought to what I'd said?"

"Not now, Mama."

"Then when? Davo's a strong man. He'll go far in the Stonelayers' Guild. If you marry him we'll get his family's water rights."

"Marry?" Papa said, suddenly oblivious to his pain. "My daughter is considering marriage?"

"No," Rana said. "Mama's talking ox-ass."

"Beware your mouth!" Papa said.

Liu, who had been watching with eyes bright as stars, giggled.

"Davo's as good as any," Papa said. "Assuming it's men you're after." He looked at Mama, and she coughed.

She eyed Papa hard. Men, women, whomever she liked was none of their concern.

"It's just that," he said, "we won't be here forever. You're not like other girls, Rana."

She knew what he meant. But she said anyway, "What do you mean?"

"Your *talents*," Mama said.

"Yes, because of your *talents*, Rana. Marriage will cement your future."

Rana stared into her stew. It reflected the metal eagle hanging above the table. "I don't care about marriage."

Mama put her fists on the table. "What's more important than your future?"

Liu was staring at her, eyes glistering brown gems.

"May I clear the table?" she said.

"And run to your workshop?" Mama said, shaking her head. "You can't hide there forever, you know."

"Rana," Papa said, "your mother and I, we only want you to be happy."

"I know. But what makes me happiest is building new things."

"Blessed Goddess," Mama said, facing the bronze bust of Mollai beside the table that Rana had smelted from ore. "Let Rana see the drought of her ways."

"Rana," Papa said, "you are twenty. Your childhood is now dust. You have to give up your toys." He flushed in another bout of pain. "The sooner you learn that life is but a long series of compromises, the better off you will be."

"When it comes to my creations, Papa, I don't compromise."

"One day, Rana, you'll have to."

And with that, the meal ended. Rana cleared the table and helped Mama scrub the dishes with sand. She collected the solid waste from the chamber pots, where it would desiccate outside in tomorrow's sun. Later, they'd use it as fuel. She helped Mama set Liu down, then powder their beds against nightbiters. Mama gave Papa a large dose of Anya's potion, and he was soon asleep.

There was still clothing to wash, but Mama said, "Go, flower. I know where your heart is. Not here, that's certain."

Rana frowned. She wanted to tell Mama, *No, I love you! I want to be here with you!* But that wasn't true. Her workshop tugged at her, and there was no escaping it. Mama didn't look up from the steaming cistern as Rana stepped outside.

That strange song came to her again, and she hummed as she crossed the courtyard. The door to her workshop was unlocked. Had she forgotten to lock it? She swung it open. Inside the dark space was lit with a sliver of moonlight spilling in from the alcove window. She dipped a candlewick into a vial of alcohol and struck a flint. The workshop blossomed around the golden halo of light. She smiled at the sight of her many creations.

"Hello, Lorbria!" she said to the small bird hanging in a cage beside the window. She gave Lorbria a morsel of ox meat she'd snuck from the table, and the sun-yellow bird with a massive beak swallowed it in one bite. She had been meaning to find out what type of bird Lorbria was, but hadn't gotten around to it.

Something shuffled behind her. Startled, she turned.

A painting crashed over, and a strange man rose to his feet. She shrieked. A large black dog trotted out from behind her stack of paintings and she shrieked again.

The man gestured with his arms as he spoke rapidly in a strange, nasal tongue. His skin was pink, like those of the north, but the shape of his face was rounder than those men. In fact, it wasn't like any face she'd seen before. She'd also never seen the likes of his black coat or the purple flower dangling from his chest. Blood stained his shirt from breast to waist. His shirt was ripped as if he had been stabbed.

She yanked out a silver dagger from a drawer, its jeweled hilt glinting in the candlelight. "What the hell are you doing in my studio?" She waved the knife at him.

The man raised his palms to her. He looked too well fed to be a marauder. Those men lived scrap to scrap. And he had all his teeth and hair, so he wasn't one of the Cursed Men, though she couldn't be sure because she'd never seen one herself.

"Stabbed while you tried to rob someone, is my guess. Well, I'll stab you again if I have to! There's nothing here for you. Get the hell out!"

She waved the knife at him, hoping he'd move away from the door so she could make a run for it. The man spoke quickly, nervously. He sounded as if there were sand in his nose. The dog walked before the man, then exhaled a cloud of glowing mist, the same ghostly green of the DanBaer mountain after a lightning strike.

When the mist abated, there on the sandy floor, as if written by a steady, expert hand, were the words, *Marul Menacha is alive. She is imprisoned. I know how to find her.*

Not a dog, a demon! Here, in her workshop! And it knew of Marul Menacha. She trembled as her feelings for the old woman came flooding back.

Marul Menacha had once frequented their family meals. She had laughed and regaled Rana's family with tales of bejeweled kingdoms and palaces in mountain clouds. She had spoken of violent demons she had dined with, of sojourns in strange dimensions far beyond this planet. And there was a time when Rana had loved Marul more than her own mother. But Marul had stopped visiting, and though her parents would not voice it, Rana had guessed the truth. One demon encounter was enough, but the hundreds that Marul had met? It was only a matter of time before one killed her.

"Marul is dead," Rana said, hands shaking. "Go away!"

The dog exhaled again, and the green mist formed new words in the sand. *No, she is alive, but only just. There isn't much time.*

Not possible, Rana thought, shaking her head. She waved the knife again. "What game are you playing at?"

The dog exhaled, and the man watched too, his mouth hanging open like a fool. *This is no game. It is most serious. I am a friend.*

"The kind that breaks into houses?"

The pink man had tan hair like a knotted goat, and his mud-brown eyes were sad and old, as if he'd lost someone he loved a long time ago. He watched her with a strange kind of knowing. But his face was childlike, as innocent as Liu's. Was he a demon too?

The dog blew the words, *Help us free Marul, before it's too late.*

"Help you?" she said. "Is this Bedubroadstreet? Am I your next rube?" They stood between her and the door. It would be difficult to stab them both before exiting, but she had to try. She readied herself, when the dog blew, *Rana, we came for you.*

She shuddered. A demon that knew her name? Did Marul tell this demon about her? It had been five years since she had seen Marul, five long years since the woman had smiled and held Rana's hand. Marul had always asked Rana to sing her new songs, to show Marul her paintings, her sculptures, her art. Her parents had never quite grown comfortable with Rana's talents, but Marul had praised them from the start.

"You have a fire burning inside you, child," Marul had said, "and no soul on Gehinnom will ever put it out. Even the Goddess may be impotent against such a force. I prophesy a grand future for you, my Little Plum, one of infinite possibilities."

Marul! Rana gasped at the memory. She missed her so much she felt as if she were suffocating. "So where is Marul then?"

Up the DanBaer, the demon wrote. *Hidden beside the Black Chasm.*

A dangerous and cursed place. "And how do you know this?"

I escaped from there. Only you can help free her.

"Why me?"

You and she are needed for a great task.

"And what task is that?"

The task of saving the world, and a million others besides.

She shuddered again. She had met a demon only once, when Marul had brought one to dinner. Mama had gotten into a furious argument with Marul and chased both of them away.

"What's your name?"

I am Adar.

"And who's this man?"

Adar blew into the sand, *His name is Daniel, and he will help us. Without your help, everyone you love will die.*

She shivered, but remembered what was written in the Books of Tobai, *A demon deceives as a man doth breathe.*

"I don't believe anything you say," she said. "Now go before I call the king's sentinels."

Adar gagged, and with a disgusting belch, vomited up a small scroll, tightly bound with a lock of hair. He pushed the charred and blackened scroll toward her with his snout.

"I'm not touching that."

Adar wrote, *It's a letter from Marul.*

Rana shook her head. This was foolish, but she couldn't resist. With her knife pointed at them, she crouched down, rubbed sand to dry the dripping scroll, and undid the knot of hair. It smelled like bile and soot as she unfurled the parchment.

She read, "My Little Plum, I would give my right arm to hear you sing your sweet, sweet songs one more time. This cave drives me madder by the day. I'm not sure how much longer I can endure these walls. Every day I . . ."

The middle section had been burnt away. Only the last few sentences remained.

". . . why I can never send these letters to you. I write then burn them, so that such suffering may never be visited upon you. Oh, my Little Plum, I hope your life is full of joy without me."

Rana stood. From a drawer she fetched a letter Marul had written her years ago, which she had saved and reread when she missed her friend. She compared the handwriting. The letters matched, even down to the little flourishes within the dotted letter yib.

Do you believe me now? Adar blew.

"A clever trick," she said.

Marul will die without our help.

Rana felt like smashing something. "I'm sorry. I can't help you."

Think on it.

"There's nothing to think about."

We'll rest here and leave before dawn.

"You're kidding? This isn't a boarding house for demons!"

We'll rest. You consider.

Rana took a deep breath. "Damn you! Damn you both to hell! I wanted to paint tonight!"

Adar clamped onto the man's hand and tugged him away from the door, leaving room for her to leave, if she wanted to.

"If you know Marul so well," she said, "what color are her eyes?"

Green, Adar blew into the sand, *as cactus buds.*

Rana stepped past them, out into the cool night, knife pointed toward them. *Yes*, she thought, *as green as Ketef, the summer star, which Marul said was five times bigger than Gehinnom, and filled with tall, strange demons who lived in cities of made of glass.*

With a tremulous voice she said, "I'm fetching my father. If you're still here when I return, he'll kill you both."

Adar pulled the door closed, leaving her alone in the courtyard with her racing heart. She stared up at the stars. "Goddess Mollai, what do I do?"

Her mother's singing voice drifted from the open window, and Rana longed for her embrace. She entered the house. Mama hummed an old and lovely melody as she removed laundry from the hot cistern and hung it on a cord draped across the room. This, Rana realized, was the song she had been whistling on her way home, the one that had been in her dreams. Mama was an artist too, Rana sensed, but instead of embracing her creativity as Rana had, she had chosen to suppress her urges.

"Back already?" Mama said. She did not seem happy to see her.

Mama was strong, but couldn't wrestle a demon. And Papa was drugged and snoring. She wasn't sure if she should tell them anyway. She knew how much they both despised Marul.

"What's wrong, flower?" Mama said. "You look troubled."

"Mama," Rana said, "do you think Marul cold still be alive?"

Mama frowned. "I thought you'd given up that nonsense."

"Do you think she could be trapped somewhere?"

Mama scooped out a tunic from the cistern with a wooden fork. "Marul was an interesting person, I'll give her that. But she was a danger to this house. You're probably too young to remember, but she once tried to bring a demon to eat dinner with us. A demon, in this house! I gave that woman a having to that day, let me tell you."

Rana remembered it well. "Are all demons evil?"

Mama stared at her. "Every one is a trickster and a thief."

"Have you ever met one?"

She considered. "Other than the demon Marul tried to bring here? No. But in the Books of Tobai there are hundreds of stories of demons."

"Do you think a demon could ever help a human?"

"Goddess, where do you get these thoughts?"

"Mama, please, just answer me."

Mama frowned. "I suppose if this human were beneficial to the demon, then, yes, the demon might want to help. But demons are always selfish, Rana. Hang on—" Mama's eyes went wide. "I see what's going on here."

Rana held her breath. Mama would never forgive Rana for not telling her there were demons in the courtyard.

"You've started a new project, haven't you?" Mama said.

Rana exhaled. "Yes. You guessed it, Mama."

Mama nodded. "You always get that troubled look when you start a new project."

Rana hated herself for lying. She glanced out the window, afraid she might see the demons walking across the courtyard. But there were only cacti and stars. What if the demon's words were true? What if she chose not to help them, and everyone she loved died because of it? She shook away the disturbing vision. It was a demon's trick.

"Mama, do demons always lie?"

Mama sat down on a stool and put finger to lip, fully committing herself to the exercise. "In the Third Book of Tobai, the goddess Sunset falls in love with the demon Croon. And look how it worked out for them."

Rana hadn't thought about the story since she was a girl, when mother had pointed out the dancing lights of each star shining through her bedroom window.

"A demon doesn't know balance like humans do," Mama said. "It is born with too much judgment, too much wrath. Croon's corrupted love destroyed Sunset's light, and her many fragments formed the evening stars."

"Marul said the stars are just like the sun, only very far away. Around some of them spin worlds like Gehinnom, where creatures live."

"That woman had a great imagination. I see why you two got along so well. So, what are you making?"

"A copper statue." The shame of lying burned her stomach. "Of Mollai."

Mama smiled. "Maybe the king will like this one enough to display it in his palace. Who knows, he might parade *you* around the city the next Feast of Mollai."

Rana thought of Davo and their conversation at the top of the Ukne. She imagined hauling herself up the hundred flights to set yet another layer of stone for fat Jo. She sighed. How could she return to work knowing that Marul might be alive, trapped in some cave, needing her help? The mystery would tear her apart. She had to find out if it were true.

"Mama, I need to go away for a few days."

Her smile faded. "To where?"

"To the Smelter's House," she said. "Across the city." She had mastered the art of smelting when she was twelve, but Mama didn't know this. "To apprentice there. For two days. Maybe three. I'll stay with the Yuris." And she added, "There are eligible men there too."

Mama stood to hang a pair of dripping trousers on the clothesline. "And what about your job at the Ukne?"

"I told you. We're ahead of schedule."

Mama gave her a tender look. "When you were three, I was hanging the wash, just like now, and you'd drawn all over the floor with a piece of charcoal a picture of a woman, with wings. You said, 'It's you, Mama.' It was so beautiful. I didn't wash the floor for weeks."

Mama reached out and stroked Rana's cheek. "That little girl is all grown up now." Mama seemed tired, old. "I'm sorry, Rana, but the answer is no."

Rana felt sick. "But, why?"

"Do you think I didn't dream too? I wanted to visit the southern seas and sail in a great ship. Papa wanted to be a camel racer. But I've never been to the sea. And Papa hasn't ridden a camel in a decade. Rana, in the end, we have to let go of our dreams and do what is right for our future. That means keeping your job. Now help me hang these shirts."

CHAPTER FIVE

Through a crack in the door, Daniel watched the young woman walk into the adjacent building. He overheard her softly speaking to another woman, possibly older, in their strange language of silken words, like sand sliding over glass.

"That was writing on the ground," Daniel whispered to the dog. "Wasn't it?"

The dog nodded.

"So, can you write in English?"

The dog exhaled a green mist, and the sand formed perfectly shaped English letters, as if a printing press had just imprinted its large Roman typeface into the sand. The words read, *I warned you, and you did not listen, and now my power is nearly gone. We are in Gehinnom.*

"Gehinnom? Is that like Gehenna?"

The dog nodded.

Daniel laughed nervously. "We're in Gehenna? Where the dead go to burn off their sins?"

Do these people look dead to you? the dog blew into the sand. *Not dead, but stunted. They cannot rise above the Bronze Age.*

"Gehenna?" Daniel said. "So who are you? The angel Dumah?"

Here, they call her Mollai. No, I am Adar.

"So what are you, Adar? Not a man, and not quite a dog either."

A demon from Sheol, the oldest of Shards.

"A demon?" This was quickly growing insane. "So why are we here?"

To save you from the one whom you call Rebekah.

His heart panged at the mention of her name. "To save me from my fiancée?"

She is a demon, like me.

Daniel sat on the stool beside the table, feeling sick. "This is too much. I think I'm losing my mind." He rubbed his face. "I'm supposed to be on my honeymoon."

Conserve your strength. You will need it.

"For what?"

We will soon go up the mountain to rescue a woman, a powerful witch. She has the power to return you home.

"A witch? To New York?"

To Earth.

This was all so damned absurd! "Right, because we're not on Earth."

I told you. We are on Gehinnom, a broken world.

Daniel was weak, thirsty. He didn't want to believe any of this, but how could he deny what he'd seen? He looked around the crowded space. Dozens of paintings leaned against the walls, vistas of bizarre cityscapes, jagged mountains, elderly faces, cactus flowers, storm clouds, and dozens more. Though they had been painted using different techniques and in different media, each had a vivid, almost photographic quality. Whoever had painted them was astoundingly talented.

A squat black furnace protruded from the corner. Its chimney rose through the roof. Blacksmith's tools leaned against it. On crowded hooks hung metal bracelets, rings, belts, charms, and knives, sparkling with gems. Stacked in a corner were several stringed instruments similar to lutes and psaltery. Some were half-built, unstrung. Drums and flutes of various sizes lay about the floor. On a stone slab, an assortment of awls and chisels lay next to the busts of nine women's heads. Half had been painted in life-like detail, the others waited.

In rickety wooden boxes sat a stack of painted bowls. In the far corner, the upper half of a voluptuous woman had been chiseled away from a block of white limestone.

"Who made all of this stuff?"

Rana, the girl who was here. She will come with us.

"To rescue this witch who will get me back to Earth?"

Yes.

Daniel shook his head. "You're the man from the shelter, the one who followed me?"

Adar nodded.

"You warned me not to marry Rebekah, or, how did you put it, 'The cosmos will collapse and all the universes will shatter in a cataclysm to dwarf all cataclysms.' What did you mean by that? Rebekah has nothing to do with any of this!"

I am weak, Adar wrote. *I need rest, and you should too.*

"Rest? Here?" But despite Daniel's protests, the dog curled into a ball and would write no more words in the sand.

He was exhausted. He thought of Rebekah's smile, her understanding eyes, her laugh. A demon? She could barely cook two eggs without burning them. He giggled at the absurdity of it all. This was all a kind of horrible joke, a bad dream, a hallucination. It had to be. He removed the boutonniere from his lapel and turned it over in his hands. It had begun to desiccate in the dry air. The candle the woman had lit flickered as a wave of exhaustion crept over him.

Old memories danced within the tiny flame.

———

Danny wakes from a bad dream with a pounding heart. His body drips with sweat. He lies in bed as the buzzing streetlight outside spills pallid orange light into his bedroom. A poster of the solar system and this year's Yankees line-up adorns the wall. By the window, bathed in streetlight glow, his cockatiel, Isaac, flutters against the bars of his cage. His black shade lies in a loose heap on the floor.

A creak in the hallway. Danny blinks sleep from his eyes. Mommy always pulls his door closed after she tucks him in, making sure to leave a crack of light around the frame, the way he likes it. But his bedroom door is now open wide, for anyone to enter. The shadows in the hallway seem to push against the orange light, seeking entrance.

Another creak. Isaac slams against his bars, again and again. It's Mommy or Daddy or Gram, up for a late-night pee. That's all.

Baby powder dusts the floor. Mommy always tells Danny to powder himself in the bathroom, but Danny likes the way it falls across his bedroom floor like a dusting of snow. There are footprints in the snow. His, but also others, clawed prints, as if a chicken has circled his bed.

A dark shape slips past the door, a shadow's shadow. Even the orange light cannot grasp it, though it tries.

And its eyes! As sharp and bright as winter stars. They scan the room, but like the blind, they do not really see. The shadow stares right at Danny, then looks away.

The figure walks down the hall. Danny throws the covers over his head. The creaking pauses. The streetlamp hums. Sleep pulls at him. Just a bad dream. He closes his eyes, thinks of toast. The smell gets stronger, more real. Who's toasting bread this early? He peers out again.

The hallway is bright, and the air smells bitter. Wrong.

"Oh god! Oh god, Danny!" Mommy's voice, frantic.

The hallway glows brightly, as if all the lights are on. The walls roll with orange waves, like reflections from a luminous pool. A hundred fiery tendrils spill into the hall. They twist around his bedroom door like growing vines, devouring his walls. The solar system is incinerated. All the Yankees burn. Isaac lies leg-up on the bottom of his cage, as the flames reach him. As a thousand tongues of fire reach for Danny, he screams.

"Danny!" Daddy, howling.

Danny calls for Mommy and Daddy and Gram and God. The fires glower maliciously. They know him, and he knows them. These flames were there when he was born, mocking. This is a reunion, of sorts.

With a terrifying scream, a twisted monster leaps through the burning doorway. Its head is charred and its shoulders trail flames and smoke. The monster grabs a blanket and throws it over Danny. "Pray to God, Danny! The *Shema*, pray it!"

He feels like vomiting. This is no monster. No, this charred thing is Gram.

Gram picks him up. Even with closed eyes the flames blind. He will explode, like an egg in the microwave. She wails and stumbles as she hauls Danny through burning hell.

I'm too young to die, he thinks.

"*Shema yisroayl, adonai elo—*" Gram begins, but doesn't finish the prayer. He is too scared to pray with her.

The flames roar. His parents scream behind him. But the worst sound of them all is the one that doesn't make sense, the deep and throaty voice of a woman hysterically laughing.

CHAPTER SIX

IN THEIR COMMUNAL BEDROOM, RANA SAT IN THE DARKNESS, pondering the demon's words. Between Papa's snores and the chorus of singing locusts outside, she could have shouted and no one would have heard. Mama's lips were thin, like a mortise joint, and her breaths had become long and slow. Even so, it was difficult to tell if she was truly sleeping.

Liu lay awake in her crib, wrapped snugly in blankets, and stared out the alcove at the waxing crescent moon rising slowly above the DanBaer. The moon spilled white light all over her face. Liu pointed to the moon and said to Rana, "See the light?"

Mama smacked her lips and turned on her side.

"Hush," Rana whispered. "Hush now, Little Bean."

Liu smiled mischievously.

Mama snored. Along with Papa, the two harmonized an impromptu snorting rhythm.

I have to leave, Rana thought. *Mama will hate me for disobeying her, and Papa will skin me alive when I return. But I have to do this.* If there was a chance that Marul was still alive, however small, Rana would never forgive herself if she didn't go.

She whispered to Liu, "Promise to be good while I'm gone?"

Liu pointed at Rana's chest and said, "See the light?"

"Yes, the moonlight spills on me."

"You," Liu said, pointing adamantly. "The light!"

Her parents stirred, but their snores soon harmonized again. She kissed Liu on the forehead. "Dream well, sister," she said. "And go with Mollai." She rose from the bed and quietly collected supplies from the far corners of the house. It took a while, because she considered bringing every knickknack she stumbled upon in the house, until she eventually thought better of it. Perhaps she was saying goodbye to them all. Then, with two large satchels heavy on her shoulders, she snuck out the door into the night.

What Mama could never understand, what Rana could never tell her, was how much Marul meant to her. To tell Mama the truth would break her heart. Marul Menacha was the promise of a grand tomorrow, of untold lands and distant adventures. While Mama, as much as Rana loved her, was the paragon of an unfulfilled life.

She opened the door of her workshop, half expecting the demon and his friend to be gone, that she had dreamed the whole encounter. But the man was dozing on a stool with his arms crossed, looking watersick. She found herself oddly relieved that he remained. He stumbled awake when she entered, and the dog climbed to all fours.

She threw a water bladder to the man and said, "I assume you two have a plan?"

The one called Daniel fumbled to open the bladder valve as the dog nodded.

"Well?"

Adar exhaled green smoke, the mist faint, tenuous. The words barely left an impression in the sand. "*My power weakens. I'll tell you more, after I rest.*"

Daniel was drinking rivers from the bladder. "Easy with that!" she said. "That has to last a full day."

Daniel looked befuddled. Was he a pebble-head? She looked at the odd cut of his clothes. Instead of protecting the neck from the sun, a black collar folded back down the neck for no good purpose. And black fabric in the desert? He'd quickly suffocate in the sun. Perhaps his clothes were a thief's cut, made for slinking through the night like the Cursed Men. Whatever they were for, he couldn't go traipsing through Azru dressed as he was, with blood on his shirt. He'd be stopped by the sentinels and hanged on suspicion of thievery.

But Rana had prepared for this. She offered him new clothing, items she'd taken from her father's wardrobe. Beige pants and a leather belt of camel-hide she had cut and tanned to a deep ochre. She took pleasure in dressing him, as if he were one of her creations, delighting how the clothes changed his aspect from stranger to, well, less strange. She helped him out of his bloodied shirt and into a loose-fitting white tunic, also Papa's. The cut on Daniel's chest looked as if an animal had clawed him, three slices just about the size of Adar's paw. When she glanced at Adar, the demon dog blinked stolidly at her.

The clothes fit, though poorly. Daniel was taller than Papa, but not nearly as broad. "Well, Daniel, you might pass for a trader from the north," she said, "though your complete lack of Wul will be a problem."

He frowned and raised and lowered his shoulders, said something. She wasn't sure what the gesture was supposed to mean, but it calmed her.

"Keep your shiny shoes, Daniel. They'll fit you better than anything I have."

As she was shoving his old clothes into a satchel, he grabbed her arm. He said something short, gestured into the satchel, and pulled out his black jacket. From the front breast flap, he removed the violet flower, held there with a perfectly fashioned metal pin. She'd never seen a flower or a pin quite like it.

"From the wetlands?" she said, examining the unusual color, the delicate petals. It was deliciously mauve, like a sunset after a sandstorm. A few petals fluttered to the floor as Daniel slid the flower into his pocket.

"Do you know any Wul at all?"

He said something unintelligible.

"How did you grow to be a man and not learn a single word of Wul? Even folk on the other side of the world know basic Wul. Where have you been living, Daniel?"

He frowned.

"Well," she said. "It'll be dawn soon. We should get going before the Horns of Wakefulness. Best we keep a low profile."

She gave Daniel three water bladders and a satchel of food. She carried the rest, as there wasn't a satchel small enough for the dog.

Then the three of them walked into the courtyard. Above, the stars were fading behind the faint morning light painting the eastern horizon, beyond the DanBaer cliffs.

She gazed at her sleeping house. *Mama, Papa,* she thought. *I'm sorry. I hope you'll forgive me.* "Come on," she said. "It's time to leave." She led them through the stone gate onto the sleeping streets.

They walked up Bricklayers Lane, Daniel on one side and Adar on the other. In the pre-dawn light, the city was serene, save for the occasional gust of wind stirring up sand. When they reached Dusty Square and its four stone lions, she rubbed their sharp teeth just as the Horns of Wakefulness blew from the King's palace. Damn, was it dawn already? She had dawdled at home for too long. The blast echoed from the city walls, when a second and third set of horns joined the first. The sound ricocheted through the streets, until the whole city seemed to yawn and stretch at the sky.

The horns faded, and the day had officially begun.

Children kindled fires in hearths. Chimneys belched black smoke and came alive. Livestock wailed from slaughterhouses. Shop windows opened, exhaled scents of kneaded dough. The air carried the night's chill as censers released wartseed- and spice-oil-scented smoke from the Temples of Mollai, their priests intoning prayers to the beat of the waking city.

Rana was energized. She loved Azru, every living stone of it, the ones she had laid, and the ancient ones that predated Azru's current incarnation by centuries. Azru was a living thing, magical, unable to be killed by war, famine, earthquake or fire.

They reached the market quarter as the first light of day touched the DanBaer, and the mountain peaks turned as gold as molten glass. On Bedubroadstreet she waved to Emod, her old friend. The wizened hawker smoked his pipe in the shadow of his tent. He sat behind a table filled with rings, pendants, charms, belts, statuettes, and a thousand other crafts. Rana had given Emod most of these items to sell, quietly of course, since few people were willing to buy creations from a girl whose insatiable creativity meant she might have a touch of demon in her. Emod, the good man that he was, passed them off as trinkets imported from foreign lands.

Vendors were still setting up shop; few people traded so early. But Emod was ready. He'd never admit it, but she knew he slept out here, in the cold, under the stars. She never judged him for that. He was one of the few people who treated her as a person, not a cursed demon. If he accepted her for whatever she was she would do the same for him.

"What do you have for me today, my sunshade?" Emod said, his voice roughshod from too many years sucking a pipe.

"Sorry, Emod. I'm traveling today."

"And with company, I see." Emod sized up Daniel as he sidled up beside the table to examine the items laid upon it.

Two vendors away, Adar swiped a sundried camel flank from a man who was too busy setting up his table to notice.

"Damn him!" Rana snapped as Adar slinked under another table to devour his meal. The dog's theft could get them all killed.

"Shiny shoes," Emod said to Daniel. "Oiled ox leather, yes?"

Daniel gazed at his shoes then at Emod, said something in his weird tongue.

"He doesn't speak Wul," Rana said.

"Plesk-ni bom-wak du-fer?" Emod said.

"Not Ytrian either," she said. "Nor Bedu-Besk or Demonsbreath. I don't think he speaks any common tongue at all. What do you make of that?"

As Daniel gazed at the items on Emod's table, leaning into it, the table rattled. Rana had always wanted to build Emod a new one, but never got around to it.

"Where'd you find him?"

"He found me."

Emod took his pipe from his mouth and pointed it at Daniel as if the man were a trinket he might consider buying. "He's got the ghost-flesh of the north, but the shape of his eyes, the cliff of his nose, they're unusual."

"Do you think . . . ?"

"Yes?"

She leaned in and whispered, "Do you think he's a demon?"

Emod laughed and shook his head. "Hardly. More likely the bastard son of some wetland king who fucked his own sister."

She blushed. "Emod!"

"Well . . ." He gave her an apologetic look. "Just look at his hands. No calluses. He's not a laborer. My guess is he's a man with servants. A king's son."

Rana grabbed Daniel's hand. She examined them, and he stared at her. It was true. Daniel's hands were as soft as a baby's cheek. She dropped his hand and Daniel cocked his head at her, perplexed.

"He's a puzzle, indeed. But a puzzle for tomorrow." Emod sucked his pipe. He scratched his beard and exhaled a gray cloud of smoke. "Rana, did I tell you? A Massap trader bought one of your rings. The tall woman called it—how did she say?—'A fine knickknack.' I thought that was a good compliment, don't you think? Do you have any more like it?"

"A knickknack, eh?" Emod had a particular way of telling stories so the financial outcome always fell in his favor. "How much did she pay for my *knickknack*?"

"Oh, she haggled, that woman! Here's your share." He offered her three Jallifexes. Not half enough to buy the metal to craft it.

She glanced at his rolled up blanket, his rheumy eyes. "You keep it, Emod."

He didn't object. He never did. "That's very generous of you, Rana! Very generous. So where did you say you were headed?"

"Up the DanBaer."

"Up?" He frowned. "What for?" He sized up Daniel again.

"To see an old friend, I hope"

"This friend lives up the mountain?"

"Not quite 'lives.'"

"Then quite what?" He stared at her.

"How about I tell you about it when I get back?"

He took a deep quaff from his pipe and exhaled slowly, temporarily obscuring his face with smoke. "Then make sure you *do* get back. You mind your bones, Rana. I don't know what I'd do without my sunshade."

Starve, she thought. Or beg on the street corners like a skin-peeler. "I'll be back in two days. Three at most."

"Three? I'll pray to the Goddess for you." He relit his pipe as Daniel fiddled with a copper ring that had a six-pointed star signet.

"That's from the Sons of Ebraim," Emod said, "an ancient Bedu tribe. Original. Worth fifty Jallifexes. It's yours for thirty."

"I told you he doesn't speak Wul," she said.

"Every man speaks the language of trade."

"Let's go, Daniel," she said, grabbing his arm. "That's camel shit."

"Camel shit?" Emod exclaimed. "But, my flower, you crafted it!"

"That's how I know what it's worth!"

"Rana," Emod said, his voice slow and serious, "nothing you make is ever shit."

She pulled Daniel away from the table. "Let's go, Daniel. We've got a long trip."

"That's odd," Emod said.

"What's odd?"

"The table." He pressed against it with his palms. "It's rattled for years, and I could never quite get it to stop."

"I know. So what?"

"It's stopped rattling."

And indeed it had.

"It seems the stars are in your favor," she said.

"And yours, I pray," Emod said, bowing his head. "You mind those crags. And Goddess willing, come back to me, my sunshade."

"I will. Goodbye, Emod." And with these words they left Emod to the hot morning, and traveled on. Adar licked his chops as he trotted beside them.

"Is this how you rest?" she said. "By theft? You might have gotten us all killed! One more act like that and I'm putting a leash on you."

Adar huffed and lifted his snout, as if proud.

They walked up the sloping street as the rising sun struck the top of the Ukne Tower. Right now she would have been climbing the tower's thousand steps to begin another long day at work. Would Chief Architect Jo send a boy to fetch her? What would the masons do without her worksongs to take their minds off their hard labors?

She imagined Jo's disgruntled face, Davo's disappointment, and it felt as if a stone had been lifted from her heart. She was free. Free of work, free of responsibility, and it felt glorious! She skipped along the street.

A shriveled, aged woman sat against the husk of a dead cedar, which had long ago risen through cracked stone. The woman held her palms out and pleaded, and before Rana could stop him, Daniel had given her two dried pomm fruits from his satchel.

Rana grabbed his arm. "What the hell are you doing? Those are for us, not scavengers!" She spat on the ground before the woman.

Daniel said something, but it didn't matter. Rana had no patience for useless people.

"Lazy fucking waste," she said to the woman. "You have two arms, two legs. But you choose to beg instead of build. Disgusting."

The woman smiled to reveal rows of rotten teeth. She flicked Rana the demon's curse with her fingers.

Rana shivered. This was the third time someone had cursed her this month. To nullify the curse, she'd have to make yet another animal sacrifice to Mollai.

"Let's go, Daniel," she said, pulling him away from the hag. The woman smiled again as they turned the corner.

The sun was bright as workers tossed heavy sacks over shoulders. Muscled boys shoved seed-filled wheelbarrows up slopes. Teenaged girls led sleepy camels down the crooked avenues. The streets twisted to avoid the ruins of the city's previous incarnations. Where roads were impossible, footbridges led over the remnants of ancient and long-abandoned buildings.

From one bridge, Rana gazed into the crevices below. There were at least three subterranean levels, and dark corners hinted at even deeper ones. Long ago, she had tried to descend into those ancient tunnels and nearly died when the ceiling had collapsed. Since then, she preferred to observe from above. As the desert encroached, the city always grew up.

The air in the Qarrio district, a group of crooked thoroughfares in the southern quarter, smelled of sweat and shit, both human and animal. Bound in cages, pens, chains, and rope were camel, oxen, goat, eagle, hawk, and sundry other animals shipped from distant lands. A juvenile she-camel caught Rana's eye. About three-quarters the size of a mature adult, the animal was tied to a fence post and eyed passersby solemnly. Partly, it was the animal's calmness that attracted her. If they were to ascend the steep DanBaer, they'd need a steady beast. But mostly it was its juvenile size that she hoped would be reflected in its price. After making Daniel and Adar wait in the shade, she sidled up to the camel's owner, a short, thin man in boiled leather, sandworn from journeys across the Tattered Sea, and tried her best to charm him.

Rana had many skills, but haggling was apparently not one of them. The man would go no lower than ninety-five Jallifexes, even after she threatened to take her business elsewhere. She reached into her satchel and pulled out her bag of coins. She had spent most of her earnings on supplies for her studio, so the bulk of the coins in the satchel were Papa's.

As she handed over the coin, she thought, *I swear to Mollai, I will pay you back, Papa.*

This was borrowing, nothing more. She felt a pang of guilt, of course, but if Marul were sick or hurt, she would need to be carried. Plus the satchels were already heavy on her shoulders and they hadn't even begun their ascent up the mountain.

The camel seemed all too happy to be free of her owner. From the looks of her filthy fur and rope-burned ankles, he hadn't treated her well.

Rana was leading the animal back to Daniel and Adar, who waited under an awning, when a long-haired man in torn clothing stepped in front of her, so close she could smell his breath, and he said, "Give me the bag of coin."

He held a rusty knife to her stomach, panting his sour breath into her face. She glanced over at Daniel and Adar, who were distracted by a woman trying to sell Daniel a caged bird.

"Hey!" the man said. "Give it quick and I don't cut you!"

Using Papa's money to save Marul was one thing, but giving Papa's money away to this filthy thief was another. She pretended to reach into her satchel, and as she came up she elbowed the man in the jaw. He yelped, then slashed at her, slicing her forearm with the knife's rusty edge. Rana screamed.

"You little bitch!" he said. He lunged for her chest with the knife and would have killed her, but Adar suddenly appeared, a huge black silhouette. He leaped onto the man and knocked him over. The man screamed as Adar tore a chunk of flesh from his arm.

"Sentinels! Sentinels!" the vendors shouted. "Call the sentinels!"

"Adar!" Rana shouted. The dog had sawed deeply into the man's arm. "Let's go!"

Adar turned to her, fangs bloody, his white eyes huge and wild. The thief beneath him cried and grabbed his shredded arm, the bone visible under flesh and blood.

Rana leaped onto the back of the camel, smearing its sides with her own blood. She kicked it into motion, and it was all too happy to flee this scene. With her good arm she reached down to grab Daniel, hoisting him across the beast's neck. He lay there, looking terrified as they sped away. Adar, his jaw dripping red, ran beside them.

Her heart pounded as the blasts of the sentinels' horns came from behind them.

CHAPTER SEVEN

Daniel lay across the camel's neck, the wind nearly knocked from him at every bump, and they turned through two dozen streets, maybe twice that number, until the smelly street with its odd menagerie of animals seemed a distant memory. Rana looked around, then stopped the camel. Daniel slid off it gratefully.

It had happened so quickly. One moment Rana seemed to be buying a camel from a short man in leather, and the next she was screaming on the ground while Adar was chewing on another man's arm. And Rana was still bleeding from the deep gash in her forearm. Not life threatening, but serious. Hands shaking, he searched in his satchel and found a tunic.

Against her protestations he tore the tunic into several strips, and used them to bandage her arm. He felt queasy. The grotesque image of Adar chewing that man's arm down to the bone had been seared into his mind.

"You need a doctor," he said as he knotted the bandage. Blood spread quickly through the fibers. He rubbed his temples. The cut on his chest from the day before itched and stung, and his legs felt weak. "I might need one too."

Rana looked up at the mountain beside the city, pointed at it, said something in her silken tongue. She made the camel kneel, then climbed back onto it. She offered to help Daniel up, but he paused. Adar gestured for Daniel to get back on the camel.

Daniel shaded his eyes. A few passersby gazed suspiciously at Rana's bloodied clothing before moving on. *Perhaps*, Daniel thought, *I should get some new friends.* He considered running away. But to where? He wasn't sure he was ready to face this city without a guide. And Adar said he could get him home. It wasn't much to go on, but he had little else. So he took Rana's hand and climbed back onto the camel.

She kicked it into motion, and they trotted up the street. Adar kept pace at the camel's heel. The camel had no saddle, and Daniel's groin bounced painfully against its spine. He shifted as best he could, when his hand found the boutonniere in his pocket.

Rebekah, he thought, *wake me from this nightmare. You're no more a demon than I'm in Gehenna.* He shifted, holding Rana's waist as if grabbing at answers.

Could this really be Gehenna—*Gehinnom*—the realm where sins were purged? Gram swore Gehenna was a real place, as real as Earth, that hidden doors all over Earth, especially in cemeteries, led down to its world of suffering, that all the wicked passed through Gehenna, brought by the angel Dumah. That five evil men burned there for all eternity. But Daniel had argued with her. "The name comes from the Valley of Hinnom," he had said. "A place outside of Jerusalem. They sacrificed children to Moloch there. It was a scary place, and through the centuries the name morphed into Gehenna. It's not real, Gram."

"Gehinnom," Gram had said, using the Hebrew name, "is as real as your nose! At night, when I dream, my soul departs my body, and I travel to realms you cannot imagine. I've seen the suffering of Gehinnom. Be grateful you never glimpse their sorrowful faces."

"Dreams, Gram," he'd said. "Just vivid dreams."

But now, as he bounced on the back of the camel, his fingers around the wine-colored flower, he wondered if he should have listened more closely to her. Was he one of the dead, fated to suffer in this place of burning? Did he die at the wedding? Before? In the storm?

He shook his head. *Madness!* he thought. *This is all madness.*

As they approached the mountain, the streets became steeper, narrower, while the city behind them grew hazy with dust. Huge towers glittered prismatically in the sun, their sides bedecked with jewels, and the visage changed colors as the sun rose. It was all so breathtakingly beautiful. If this was Gehinnom, it wasn't all suffering and torment.

They turned the corner, and the mountain wall loomed before them, sudden and steep. A million strata of burnt orange stone reached high into the clear sky. On a promontory above, six rotundas had been carved out of the rock face. Fat vines drooped from balconies. Palms and leafy plants grew in lush gardens. The steep walls had been engraved with depictions of demonic beasts in battle with a large sword-bearing army. Above them a hundred arched windows looked out from high walls, their stone frames baroque wonders of masonry. They were traveling beneath the palace, the one that had been carved out of the mountain. He had glimpsed the palace when he first saw this city, but up close its walls seemed different, intimate. If only he had a camera, to prove that such a marvel existed.

Under the shade of one rotunda, five young women in flowing white robes smoked ridiculously long pipes. They laughed and their voices bounced among the folds of stone.

A woman leaned over the balcony and said, "Me-nee, wah, dom-tu?" Her companions burst into hysterical laughter.

"Pes-hu per-apt ba!" Rana snapped back. She glared up at the women and spat.

"Mu-mu!" the woman replied, waving her hand dismissively. "Mu-mu, feg!" Her companions guffawed, their echoes like cawing birds.

The laughter faded as they turned around a bend. They came upon a black pond a hundred feet wide, its calm waters vanishing inside a natural cave mouth. A spring? An elderly woman sat cross-legged on the ground, hands clasped in her lap, eyes half-closed with the far-away look of a meditating monk. A man in leather armor and a sheathed sword at his waist dozed against a tree. The tree's pink flowers were in riotous bloom and its petals littered the ground like confetti. It was the first tree Daniel had seen here, and its sudden pink beauty made him gasp. The man's hand squeezed the hilt of his sword as his chest rose and fell.

Rana grumbled, reached into a pouch, and tossed a coin into a bucket at the woman's heel. The woman formed a triangle with her fingers, sang a brief tune—her heart didn't seem to be in it—and pressed her forehead to the ground. Rana bowed and elbowed Daniel a few times before he realized she wanted him to bow too. Throughout this brief exchange, the guard didn't move, but Daniel knew the man only pretended to doze.

Toll paid, they trekked on, and the city vanished behind tons of rock. To their right, the cliffs rose steeply for hundreds of feet. To their left, beneath a precipitous drop, an orange expanse of sand spread to the horizon, the rolling desert he and Adar had crossed yesterday.

Parallel dunes marched across the desert like slow moving ocean waves. They were miles away, but their distant hum, like a giant bow drawn across a cello the size of a city, shook his belly. Every few minutes a dune crashed into the cliffs below, sending up sprays of sand. With a loud hiss, the sands drained back into the desert, as if they were standing on the rim of an hourglass a thousand miles wide.

The immensity of it all was too much, and he took slow breaths to calm himself. Their camel teetered on scree, and he held more tightly onto Rana's waist. The young woman was taut, muscular, stronger than him. As they climbed further up the mountain road, under the pestering sun, he began to wish he had stayed in the city. At least there he had shade and solid ground.

Rana hummed, softly at first. Her tune was baroque, a fugue of sorts, but with a tonal complexity unmatched by any classical piece he had heard before. There was perfection in it, a bird-like artistry he didn't think was possible from the human mouth. He closed his eyes and listened. The porcelain, freckled face of Rebekah smiled at him from behind his closed lids. They sat in her small apartment, candles flickering on the dinner table beside the second-floor window, the box with the engagement ring sitting open before her, her smile in the candlelight.

No malice, he thought. *There was never malice from her. She's no demon!*

Rana stopped humming, and Daniel blinked and awoke from the dream. It was disconcerting how easily he had drifted into reverie, almost as if her music had some kind of hypnotic influence. He shivered.

Rana was pointing deep into the desert. "Bedu she-way-lan," she said.

Many miles away a cloud of dust floated just above the sands. Within the cloud were hundreds of ash-colored specks. People, he realized, and camels and cargo, a desert caravan. A dune rose and obscured them from view, and when the sands descended again the caravan had jumped miles across the desert.

"Holy shit!" he said. "How the hell did they do that?"

Rana laughed. "Es per-shemp Bedu!"

Daniel shook his head. "What?"

Adar stared at Daniel, his moon-white eyes bright and steady, before he bounded on ahead. The caravan, when Daniel looked again, had leaped another mile.

———

The sun beat upon the demon's black fur as he trotted ahead of the camel. *Though you walk on two legs like a man*, the demon thought, *you might as well walk on all fours, like me. You are as ignorant as a mule, Daniel.*

"Es per-shemp Bedu," Rana had said. No translation in Daniel's patchwork English could have matched the native poetry. In Daniel's language, one might have crudely said, "Thus go the Bedu." The phrase implied the uncertainty of life, the nature of the universe to surprise, as the Bedu ever astonished with their ancient magic and knowledge of forgotten things.

The ever-creative Rana had made a pun.

The Bedu knew the rhythm of the sands and the seasons of its tides. They rode its eddies as a ship might navigate the sea. They knew the course of this broken world through the heavens and the motions of planets unseen by the naked eye. They possessed ancient magic that Daniel, in his puny existence, couldn't conceive of. They were men who walked like gods.

Men whom he needed to survive. The Bedu would save them from annihilation. With luck, the Bedu would help them save the Cosmos.

But first the witch Marul Menacha had to release him from this four-limbed shackle. What irony that she was the only one who could help him now! Normally, he could alter his shape at whim. Now he was but little more than flesh, his mind deteriorating with each second. Mashit had dethroned him, cast him out of Sheol, depriving him of his power; he'd used the last of that power to bring Daniel here. If he didn't reach Marul soon, he would wither and die, and the Cosmos with him.

They had to hurry.

Deep in the desert, a dune rose and obscured the Bedu from view. When it descended, the Bedu were gone, surfed away to some far-off city. Thus go the Bedu.

I will join you soon, the demon thought. *I must not tarry.*

Rana paused under the shade of a rocky overhang to drink. The demon didn't welcome the pause, but hydration was necessary. Before drinking himself, Daniel dribbled water into the dog's mouth from his bladder. The act was degrading, but the demon dog had little choice.

"So how will this woman get me home?" Daniel said. "Who is she?"

The dog needed to conserve his strength, but he allowed a brief answer. He inhaled deeply, forming the words in his mind, and blew them onto the sand. In English, the words read, "An old friend. She will make me man again, and then I will explain."

"Man again?" Daniel said, shaking his head. "All this is so . . . strange."

Rana was stacking a pile of stones into a miniature spiral stair. Daniel sat nearby, crossed his legs, and watched. He said, "If Gehinnom is a place of suffering, I don't see it. Dry, yes, and full of, well, *magic*. But torment? Torturing angels? This is not my grandmother's Gehinnom."

You privileged fool! the dog thought. How ignorant he was! But maybe that was for the best. The demon didn't want Daniel getting wise. Not yet, because he wouldn't like what the demon would propose, but it was the only way to save them all.

Daniel removed the flower from his pocket and spun it in his fingers.

Do you think that woman loves you, Daniel? the dog thought. *If you only knew what your "Rebekah" truly is you'd stomp that flower to tatters.* How many souls had Mashit slaughtered, how many demons had she sent to the bowels of Abbadon's palace to suffer for eternities? The human Daniel knew was a mirage, a fantasy.

Rana, building her spiral stair, began humming a tune, and he shivered with delight. Her melodies were creation itself, each note kindling fires inside distant, newborn stars. Daniel's eyes dilated as he fell under her spell.

Do you sense her power yet? the demon thought, giddily. *Do you feel what she is?*

"Goddess, would you look at that!" Rana said in Wul. She had stacked the stones in a spiral that began as a small circle and widened gradually as it rose. On Earth it would have been called a Fibonacci spiral. But this shape didn't exist on Gehinnom—couldn't exist—because the laws of *this* universe would not allow such a compact agglomeration of form. Her structure looked precarious, as if it might be toppled with a strong gust of wind, and yet as Rana placed the final stone on its peak it seemed steadier and more ancient than the mountain beside them.

"I've been dreaming this for weeks," she said. "It was haunting me. I knew it was possible, but no matter how hard I tried, it always collapsed." She leaped to her feet, excited. "I wish I could show Papa this. Or Chief Jo. I could build a life-sized one, a garden terrace or a private stair for the king!"

Daniel studied the curious shape. *You, Daniel,* the dog thought, *are the reason her structure doesn't fall. You are the hidden pillar. Do you know it yet?* Daniel was the reason Emod's table had stopped rattling too. His presence alone was enough to uphold universes. What was a loose table or a pile of stones?

The demon's hopes rose. Daniel, the sustainer! Rana, the architect! And he, the demon, with the wisdom to bind their trinity into something never seen in all of history.

The demon's hackles rose, his skin tingling with an electric charge. Another demon was near! He could not let whoever it was see him like this, a helpless mongrel. If they recognized who he was, things would not end well.

He leaped behind a crop of stone as a large shadow descended over the mountainside. A giant black eagle alighted on the cliff's edge. Larger than an elephant, the eagle spread her wings to block Rana and Daniel's escape.

The dog knew this demon. She was Chialdra, his brother's faithful servant.

Rana pulled a bejeweled dagger from her belt as Chialdra cocked her head. The bird's glittering topaz eyes blinked twice.

"What have we here?" Chialdra said in a voice like grinding millstones. Her sharp teeth glimmered with saliva. "Two fools and a camel?"

She has not sensed me? the dog thought. *Is my power that weak?*

"Leave here!" Rana shouted. "Or I'll slice off your wing!"

The dog had to stop this madness. Rana was brave, but no match for Chialdra. She'd snap Rana's spine like a twig. And he would not let his brother's idiot servant thwart his grand plans.

On all fours, he slunk low between the stones, weaving between their sharp edges. Daniel picked up a stone, ready to throw.

Chialdra cocked her head again. "No talisman, charm, or rite? No swordsman flashing his might? But a girl with a miniscule blade and a man who threatens with shade? How brave of you both. How bold!"

"We've nothing you want," Rana said.

"How do you know what I want?"

"We've no gold or jewels. And we swallowed devil's bane this morning. If you eat us you'd sicken and die."

"Devil's bane? Hahaha!" Chialdra cackled and cawed, hopped closer. Her wings smelled of blood from a recent kill. "I've not heard that one in awhile. No, child, I heard you hum! You're the Crooner they tell stories of, aren't you?"

"The Crooner?" Rana said.

"The no-things that dwell in the wastes of the Jeen speak of a girl from Azru who sings while she lays stone. The ones that fear none, fear you! I have long wondered, what could a girl possess that scares demons so? Her songs, the no-things say, are zephyrs of bliss. I was drifting in a thermal when I heard you now. The veil was lifted, and I glimpsed the ninth heaven."

"You aren't worthy of the first," Rana said.

"No doubt," Chialdra said. "But what need have I of heaven when I have the Crooner?"

"I think you've mistaken me for someone else."

"Have I? Rumors of your music float across the desert."

Chialdra is a simpering fool! the dog thought, listening from behind a nearby rock. *Rumors of Rana's power drift across Creation down to the lowest depths of Sheol.*

Rana raised her knife. "What do you want?"

"To hear you sing again! To hear that which makes demonkind tremble! Sing for me, and I promise I won't eat you or your brave friend. Your camel, however . . ."

"A demon's promise is emptier than air."

"How little you know of demonkind." Chialdra flapped her wings once; the gust knocked Rana and Daniel over. "And less of air!" Chialdra chuckled, a sound full of air and phlegm. "Besides, what choice do you have?"

A shadow fell across Rana's face as Chialdra raised her wings. The dog crept closer. Rana glimpsed him crouching low in the rocks. They exchanged glances, and for a moment he feared she would give him away. Instead Rana turned to Chialdra and said, "Let me think of a tune."

After a pause she hummed a new song. Her voice was honey waterfalls cascading down sunlit stones. Oh the ecstasy!

Chialdra retracted her wings and spun in wild dervishes on the cliff's edge. Her movements were careless, precarious. She teetered, caught herself, and spun again. As Rana sung, the dog dreamed of balmy nights in Abbadon's towering palace, the giraffe-necked Kokabiel beside him in bed, the hot breeze from Lake Hali blowing through the curtains.

Oh, Koko, how I miss you! How he missed running his hands over the demon's white fur.

Lost in dream, he nearly forgot to act. He sprung from his hiding place and chomped into Chialdra's knee. Chialdra screamed and flapped her wings, knocking Rana and Daniel off their feet again. Chialdra leaped into the air, and the dog hung on, biting hard, dangling beneath her body. He bit deeper, tearing into meat as she swung wildly, trying everything to fling him off. Hot blood spilled down his canine lips, across his body, splattering on the rocks below.

Chialdra screeched, and stones tumbled from the mountainside. Daniel leaped away. Chialdra pecked at the dog with her beak. Tossed about, he sawed into her leg until he found bone, then ground harder. With her free talon, she stabbed at him, piercing his side.

He yelped and released his bite. A mistake!

He fell for a horrifying second, then slammed into stone.

Pain! Not since the Shattering had he known so much pain! He gasped and spat blood as Chialdra righted herself in the air.

Her injured leg dangled limply, spilling blood onto the rocks. "My leg! My leg! I'll return to devour you all, I swear it! I swear!" she squealed. "And then you'll know a demon's promise!"

Weeping, she sped off into the desert, raining red onto the sands.

"Goddess!" Rana shouted, after catching her breath. "Adar? Adar! If he's dead we'll never find Marul!"

Foul pain throbbed with every beat of his canine heart. It hurt so much he could not tell which part was injured. Unconsciousness threatened, and he fought to stay awake.

"Adar!" Daniel shouted. "Adar?" His voice bounced across the rocks.

"Hush!" Rana said in Wul. "You'll cause a rock slide!"

Rustling above him. Someone was climbing down. Daniel, calling out.

Groaning, he rose to his feet.

"I see him!" Daniel said. "Adar! We're coming! Rana, he's badly hurt. He's bleeding."

The dog hopped toward Daniel. His left hind leg was broken, his right rear hip torn open and bleeding onto the stones. Three ribs were broken, perhaps more.

Daniel tried to pick him up, but he growled and leaped away.

"Let him up!" Rana said. "Oh, Goddess!"

He fumbled onto the path, limped three paces, and collapsed.

Rana covered her mouth. "You should have stayed hidden! Why would you do such a stupid thing, Adar?"

With his last bit of power, the dog exhaled green smoke. Except his power was too weak. The smoke blew away before the words found their way to impress the sand.

"Es per-shemp Bedu," he wanted to write.

CHAPTER EIGHT

WITH THE SAME SHREDS OF FABRIC DANIEL HAD USED TO bandage her own injury, Rana wrapped Adar's wounds. A sob formed in her throat. She felt like a helpless child, afraid she might explode with tears. If Adar died, there would be no way to find Marul, and this whole adventure would be for naught. Adar groaned as she bandaged him, whimpering with every fold.

"Be still now. Be still."

That was the largest bird she'd ever seen. The largest animal too, and a demon at that! The eagle had said rumors of her song drifted into the deep desert. Was that true? She recalled the look on the masons' faces when she sang, how they labored twice as hard under her melodies. Sometimes while singing, she felt as if the masons were extensions of her body, two dozen muscular arms bound to her through ligaments of music. She had thought it a mere vision, just another image that came to her like the vistas that haunted her dreams. But what if her music did have power?

She remembered the beryl-winged hawks that circled overhead when she sang, how they cried out whenever she paused. And the implacable Chief Jo always calmed like baby Liu snug in blankets when she sang. She was different, possessed of a creative spirit that terrified most men. But demons knew of her? Perhaps the cityfolk were right. Maybe she was cursed.

She finished bandaging Adar in a knotted weave she hadn't realized she had been making, an abridged version of the blanket she had knitted for Liu. A natural dog would have died from these wounds, but the demon Adar still lived. For how long?

"You can't walk," she said. "We'll carry you."

Adar defiantly climbed to his feet. His bright eyes had lost their luster, now rheumy and red like Papa's. She reached for him, but he hopped away.

Daniel had a worried look on his face. He too was lost without Adar, she realized.

"We'd better go," she said. "Before another demon visits. I'll refrain from singing, this time."

They mounted the camel, and Adar limped pathetically beside them. The faint moon rose above the DanBaer like a half-lidded eye, and she felt as if it wasn't the only thing peering down at them. The rocks seemed to whisper ancient secrets as the wind brushed around their sharp corners. Rainbow lizards skittered between the cracks, laughing.

The encounter with the eagle had left Rana with a lingering shiver, but under her fear was a curious elation. She had faced a demon and lived! Was this why Marul was always so full of life, because of how frequently she had skirted death?

Adar limped, tenaciously leading them onward, and she was impressed with his demon stamina. They reached the top of the DanBaer just after peak sun. A sand- and wind-blasted plateau spread for a full parasa to the south and east. A long time ago a city had stood here, but now only scattered rubble and faint marks that hinted of ancient foundations remained to speak of it. No one remembered the city's name; most called it Old Stone.

The ruby-tiered Araatz mountains, flat-topped, wind-blasted, extended to the eastern horizon, a stunning view. A long time ago Rana had asked Papa why their tops were flat as tables. "Did some great hand chisel away their peaks?"

"No, flower," Papa had said. "Time has flattened the Araatz."

"Time?"

"Time is the greatest of all masons," he'd said. "She lifts mountains and grinds them to dust, and the strongest men and the richest kings always succumb to her hand."

The memory filled her with nostalgia. She hadn't been on this plateau since she was six, when she had helped Papa build the Crypt of Umer for the dead king. She remembered working with stone, the excitement of wielding her first tools, Papa's strong hands guiding hers, pounding hammer to chisel, the peal of metal against rock. The joy after a day's work, sitting on his knee, looking out over Azru, much smaller then, listening to his stories of cities destroyed by war or cataclysm, rebuilt by heroes like her, one stone at a time. She knew she'd follow in Papa's footsteps, become a great mason like him.

"I'm quite sure," Papa had said, "you'll be much greater than me."

And she had rebuilt Azru, laying stone in nearly a thousand storehouses, towers, homes, and palace courtyards in her life, more than any other living mason. She could have taken Papa's place as chief architect. But King Jallifex did not want a woman in that role. Rana would have to wait until the king died or was overthrown. And even then there was no guarantee his successor would feel any differently about women in power, never mind that they all prayed daily to Mollai, the most powerful woman of them all.

She sighed. No, Azru, despite the late-night hopes of Mama, had always been a place ruled by men, and it would always be.

Azru was hidden below the cliff's edge, where the late King Umer's tomb clung. Hundreds of featherless gray birds had long ago made a nest of it. She wished she could see Azru from its vantage point now, how it had grown in those long years, but they were headed in the opposite direction.

She ached to hold baby Liu in her arms, to hear Papa's voice, even if he were to admonish her to wash her hair. She longed for Mama's nagging. And, Goddess, she even missed Davo's lustful stare. They weren't even a full day from Azru. What the hell was happening?

The answer came as she passed a toppled wall of stones where a tiny scorpion, its diamond pincers glittering in the sun, skittered away. This was the farthest she'd ever been from home. Her whole life lay behind her, in one small city she couldn't even see. It had taken her twenty years to come this far.

Why have I waited this long? she thought. She stared at the Araatz's immensity. *The world is enormous and I have only seen such a small part of it.*

Silently she recited a prayer to Mollai for Adar's health. The limping demon continued to lead them across the plateau. His steps slowed and became languid in the brutally hot sun.

"Please," she begged Mollai. "Please don't let him die."

They reached the far side of the plateau and followed Adar down between two large boulders. The sun vanished behind a rock wall as they dipped into the descending path, barely wide enough for a single man to walk. The path twisted crookedly alongside the mountain, bordering an immense canyon. She'd heard of this dreaded place. The Black Chasm was as terrifyingly wide as it was deep. Vertical black lines ribbed its slate-gray walls. The distant cliffs winked at her like flecks of diamond in coal, while the chasm bottom slept in shadow, save for a scattering of fires that belched noxious smoke that fouled the air.

Her lungs burned as she inhaled ash.

The Gates of Korah, she thought. She'd heard stories of travelers slinking down to their dark crevices and returning mad, if they even returned at all. The Cursed Men, it was said, held evil bacchanals among the smoldering fires on moonless nights. They feasted on the newly deceased and played piping music that struck men dead if they heard but a single note.

Was Marul down there? She wasn't sure if she could go there, if that were true. And her she-camel seemed to agree. The beast stopped. Daniel, grasping her waist, said something nervously behind her.

Rana kicked the camel's flanks. "Hey, girl! Come on! Don't stop!" The thought of stopping here seemed worse than whatever awaited them below.

The canyon walls whistled as if wind were whipping over the stones, but the ashen air was calm. She kicked the camel again, and with a groaning bleat the animal crept forward.

They rounded a knob of sharp stone, and before them appeared an enormous black obelisk. It was tilted at an angle, but leaning it still stood almost four-stories tall. It seemed to be cut from a solid piece of obsidian. Its surface was dull and featureless save for an engraved metal plaque on one side. She read the Ytrian inscription, severely sandworn. The words were written in a strange grammar and unusual script.

"The mountains and sky shake in fear of King Diasamaz," she read. "On this ninth day of Ev, in the 82nd year of Eshpeth, great Diasamaz defeated the armies of Zidad and took their daughters and riches. None will surpass his glory."

The names and dates meant nothing to her. Here stood a monument to a once-great king. And what was he now but a fading memory? The thought filled her with despair. She remembered what Papa had said, how Time makes dust of us all. Once a monument to a great king, the obelisk was now a tombstone.

Fine black ash blew up from the chasm as Adar limped down the crooked path. Her throat burned, and she took a drink, offered some to Daniel. In the canyon, vortices of black ash spun in tight circles like a flock of sparrows, except there was no wind to move them. As the black dust caught the light, it sparked like sun on water.

Adar teetered, drooled, and paused.

She dismounted and ran to him. "Do you need water? What do you need?"

Daniel came running behind her.

Adar gagged, then vomited a torrent of blood and bile. She winced as Adar vomited rivers. How could so much liquid fit inside him? She felt helpless as he vomited again and again.

"You're watersick," she said, fighting back panic. "Drink." She held her bladder open for him. "Before you faint."

He vomited again. "Adar, you can't die. We're lost without you."

Daniel petted Adar. He put his ear against the dog's chest, checking his heart. He frowned and shook his head.

With much effort, Adar scrawled in the sand beside his puddle of vomit. The letters were poorly formed and it took Rana a moment to read them.

"Key," it read. Adar fainted, and the spreading puddle swallowed the letters.

"Adar?" Daniel said. "Adar!"

The soot-filled air burned her lungs. The rocks beside the path were sharp as razors. Her injured forearm throbbed. Panic threatened to bury her alive. They couldn't remain here, in this dreadful place. Nor could they go back to the plateau. The bright sun was the worst place to be if you were watersick. "I should have packed a tent," she said. "Why didn't I pack a tent?"

Daniel tapped her and pointed into the vomit.

"What?"

He reached into the puddle, using the hem of his sleeve as a glove, and pulled out a round object. At first she thought it was a simple stone. But as the slime dripped away she saw that Daniel held an emerald sphere.

"What is it?"

He turned the sphere over, gave it to her. It was heavier than lead, and its weight surprised her. It fit snugly in her palm, its surface covered in raised symbols of an alphabet vaguely familiar.

"Is this the key he meant, do you think?" she said. "Perhaps to Marul's prison?"

Daniel's eyes opened wide, and he gestured at the sphere. She gave it back to him. He turned it over again and exclaimed, "Heebroo!"

"You know this?"

He said some more, but it was useless trying to communicate.

She took the sphere from him. "Okay, suppose this is a key, why would Adar give it to us here? There has to be a door close by. Adar said that Marul is trapped in a cave on the DanBaer." She scanned the mountainside. "The cave must be here!"

The cliff face rose steeply behind them. The stones were black and sharp, and there was no obvious cave. She put the sphere in her pocket and climbed the wall, avoiding the sharpest rocks. She paused when she reached a full story above the path.

"It must be here. It has to be here!"

"Rana!" Daniel pointed into the chasm, where a cloud was approaching.

The swirling cloud of ash engulfed them, depositing a thick layer of soot over everything. For a moment, all was black. But the tornado blew off as fast as it had come, twirling down the path. And there, for an instant, beyond the cliff's edge, a thin layer of soot hovered in the air, as if the mountainside extended three paces beyond the visible ledge. But the soot vanished like water draining into sand.

She leaped down, ran over to the ledge. Smoke obscured the floor of the chasm as she peered down. "You saw it too, didn't you?" She tossed a handful of sand over the edge. It hovered in the air, as if resting on an invisible shelf.

"Look!" she said. "Look, Daniel!"

A few seconds later the sand vanished as if swallowed. But there was no wind. She felt around the space beyond the ledge with her fingers. She felt sand on top of hard stone, but her eyes saw only smoke and empty air.

She turned to Daniel and smiled. "A hidden ledge!"

She filled her pockets with sand, then carefully stepped onto the transparent ledge. Nothing visible lay beneath her, but she did not fall. "By the Goddess, I hope I'm right."

Daniel stood by the ledge, eyes wide.

She dropped sand before her, revealing several flat ledges that fanned downward in a tight right-hand curve. A spiral stair! She caught its shape before the sand evaporated. She took another step, and a third, tracing out the curving path, until she had descended a half-turn. Daniel, watching her from the edge, said something nervously. A warning, it sounded like.

"Marul?" she whispered. "Marul, are you here?" She decided it best to keep quiet, if her jailers were close.

She took another step, and Papa's words came to her. She had once asked him how he walked without fear on the highest ledges.

"A mason," Papa had said, "never loses her fear of heights. She only learns how to manage it. One way is to, as much as possible, avoid looking down." But there was no way to move now without looking down. With every step she felt as if she would plunge to her death. And with a pang of dread she realized her pockets were empty. She was out of sand.

Like a blind person, she felt for each step with her outstretched foot. Ten more and she faced the ash-colored cliff. The invisible steps ended. She ran her fingers over the pits and scars, searching for a crevice, an opening, a keyhole. Daniel shouted and pointed down at her.

"What?" He was pointing to a recessed symbol in the rock.

"Heebroo!" he said. "Ayin!"

She removed the sphere from her pocket and twirled it slowly until she found the identical symbol. A letter? The raised symbol on the sphere was the same size as the recessed letter on the wall.

"The keyhole and the key," she said, smiling.

With the symbols aligned, she pressed the sphere into the rock—

And nearly fell forward as the wall swallowed her hand. It looked as if the wall had eaten her hand, that it had been sliced off at the wrist. But there was no pain. In fact the air was refreshingly cool wherever her hand was. Her arm moved through the wall easily. And so with a deep breath to steady herself and one last glance at Daniel, she stepped into the mountainside.

She found herself in a cool, dimly lit tunnel. Pale emerald light filtered into the tunnel from the chasm behind her. From this side, the cliff wall wasn't rock at all, but an emerald film, like tinted glass. The cliffs beyond were as dim as twilight.

Her eyes slowly adjusted to the darkness, and she took another cautious step. The tunnel walls were jagged and chipped, as if hewn in haste. Twenty paces down the corridor several tall door-ways led to other places. It was too dark to see what lay inside them. Rana moved slowly, afraid to venture too far from the exit and the light. She peered into one chamber. Dusty containers lay scattered on the floor. A high ceiling vanished in shadow. Otherwise, this place was empty.

Something rustled in the darkness, and she froze. Someone was approaching from the dark end of the corridor, breathing heavily. An aged man shambled into the pallid light. One of his legs twisted grotesquely, as if set poorly after a break. With each step closer, more hideousness was revealed. He was as skinny as a decaying corpse. Large gray eyes peered from hollow sockets, glowing with a faint yellow light, as if candles burned inside his head. He had few teeth, long and sharp; most had fallen out. Sparse threads of thin, white hair fluttered on his scalp as he shuffled forward. He was naked, save for a loose-fitting belt and a maroon cloth over his groin.

She retreated quietly, unsure if the stranger had seen her, when something glinted in his hand. She gasped. The sound she'd heard wasn't breathing, she realized, but the scrape of his sword along the floor.

"How did you enter this forbidden place?" he said in a voice like sand and gravel mixing violently. "You should not be here."

Rana reached for her dagger. In a trembling voice she said, "I've come for Marul Menacha. Is she your prisoner?"

"Not mine. I'm just the guardian, not the master of keys." He crept closer.

"But Marul *is* here?" The hope in her heart almost pushed out her fear.

"This is her eternal resting place, as it shall be yours." The creature, stepping fully into the light, was hideous. Once, he might have been a man. Now he was a grotesque shadow of one.

As he lifted his sword, Rana raised her dagger. She backed toward the door, toward the lighted world, reaching for the wall. Her hand pressed against the green glass, but did not pass through. She tried the sphere, pressing it randomly on its surface. There was no Heebroo letter keyhole on this side.

"No!" she said. "No!" Her voice echoed down the tunnel.

"A shame," the creature said, "that your last words will be so unoriginal." He lifted his sword. No, she couldn't die, not like this! But there was nowhere to go. She thought of Mama, of Liu's glistering eyes. But instead of striking, the creature plucked the sphere from her hand.

"Where did you get this?" he said.

It took her a moment to find her voice. "A . . . friend?" she said, swallowing.

He retreated two paces and sheathed his sword. "I am Grug, guardian of these caves." He turned on his heels and shuffled down the corridor, his sword scraping the ground behind him. He wore no shoes, and his hairy feet were heavily calloused. His testicles hung below his loincloth like two eggs in a shriveled leather sack.

"Come with me," he grumbled.

Rana straightened herself. "Is Marul here?"

"Here? I suppose in a manner of speaking, she is present."

"But alive?" Her words seemed to linger in the air.

"That depends on your definition of life." He disappeared into the shadows.

She sheathed her dagger. Marul! Goddess, Adar was right! She was here!

"Are you coming?"

"Yes, yes!"

The tunnel grew dark as she walked. "Where are you?" she said. "I can't see." Her voice tumbled into the darkness, and she grew afraid.

"Right." Grug grumbled a few bitter words in a harsh language, and sconces in the walls flickered to life with a hundred little tongues of orange flame.

Rana blinked, astonished.

"Sometimes I forget," Grug said, "what it was to be a man."

"I couldn't tell you," Rana said.

The walls seemed to shiver and dance in the firelight. Strange symbols and long columns of numbers had been scratched onto the walls by a nervous hand. None of the scratchings made sense, though here and there she did recognize the Heebroo letters from the emerald sphere. The farther they walked the more numerous the scratchings became, so that after a few minutes the walls were covered from floor to ceiling.

"You're a Cursed One?" she said.

"We call ourselves the Mikulalim."

"Is it true what they say about your kind?"

"I don't know. What do they say?"

"That you . . . eat dead people."

"My, you're a bold one," Grug said. "Most men lack the courage to ask such questions."

"As I said, I am not a man."

He snorted. "Yes, we do."

"Do you want to eat me?"

Grug laughed. It was an awful sound, like the sound of the eagle's leg being torn open by Adar's teeth. "We eat the flesh of men as you eat the flesh of beasts, only after death. Do you plan on dying soon?"

"Not if I can help it."

"Then not yet."

Despite her fear, she found herself oddly warming up to this Grug.

They stepped through an arched doorway and entered a circular chamber thirty paces across. Hundreds of candles spread about the chamber burned brightly, filling the room with golden light. Even so, the walls glowed with an illumination beyond what the candles provided, like a halo around the winter moon. The walls here were also covered with strange writing, but in even greater density than the corridors. A queer tree-shaped diagram had been drawn on the floor. And in the very center of it, as motionless as a statue, crouched a small woman.

"Keter is the crown, the havdole, the dividing line, beyond which no mind may pass unscathed," the woman muttered. "Beyond Keter lies Ein Soph, the unknowable. Gehinnom is the same. Forever unknown to me now!" Her words were ragged, like an overworn shawl.

"Did you know?" the woman said. "Four entered the heavenly orchard? Azzai looked at the Shekinah, and boom! He died. Poor sap! Zoma looked, and he went mad. The insanity! Elisha killed all the plants. He denied what he saw, fool! Only Akiba left in peace. How? How does a man glimpse the divine and not lose sanity? Tell me!"

Her long gray hair was natty, and a filthy brown robe hung over her shoulders. Could this raving, filthy woman be Marul?

"You have a guest," Grug said.

The woman snapped her head toward Grug. Her pupils were tiny in the candlelight, but her eyes, those were green as cactus buds, green as Ketef, the summer star. A line of snot dripped from her long, curving nose. A familiar nose. Rana's heart filled with a glut of emotions—relief, fear, excitement, terror.

"A guest?" Marul said. "One of your brothers?" She scratched her cheek with a long-nailed finger.

Rana stepped into the light. This was not the Marul Menacha she had known five years ago, the woman who had conquered demons and traveled to dimensions she could explain only in crude metaphors. "Marul?" she said, shyly. "Marul, it's me, Rana."

Marul stared at Rana for a moment. Then she turned her eyes to the floor, where a tree of circles and lines had been drawn, labeled with the same Heebroo symbols that were on her emerald sphere.

The woman pointed to a circle on the left of the diagram. "Do you see this sephirah, Grug? This is Din, sphere of judgment. That is Ashmedai's nature, to judge."

"Yes," Grug said.

Marul pointed to a second circle. "And this is Chesed, sephirah of mercy. To a demon, Chesed is poison, weakness! This thing that calls itself Rana cannot be real. It would be too merciful. Ashmedai would not allow it. It is an apparition. Send it away!"

"Marul," Rana said. "I know it's been years. I've grown. But it's me. Rana Lila." She stepped closer.

"Stop!" Marul shouted. She pointed an accusing finger at Rana but did not turn her gaze from the floor. "She's a phantasm! A trick. Where are you hiding, beast? Oh, you must get so hard watching my agony, you vile demon!"

"I'm no ghost, Marul." She glanced at Grug. "And I've come to free you."

"Freedom comes not from a mirage. Oh, the evil king must be pleased, watching me squirm! But I'll not fall for his tricks."

"This is one of her good days," Grug said. "Mostly she rocks in the corner, holding her knees, moaning."

Rana crouched beside Marul and took her hand. It was small, frail. Not the strong hand she remembered. "You used to call me your Little Plum, do you remember?"

"He could have learned that," she said. Her voice echoed back from the tunnels. "Enough torment. Please, Grug, please, make it go away."

"I'm real, Marul."

"Lies!"

"Marul, feel the warmth of my hand. Hear the sound of my voice. Forget your eyes. What does your heart tell you?"

"Stop!" Marul screamed. She ran across the room and buried her face in her hands. Sobbing she said, "Make it go away, Grug. Make the ghost leave!"

"She's no illusion, mistress. And she came with this." He held up the emerald sphere.

Marul eyes widened. With a stooping gait, she approached Grug and snatched the sphere from his bony hand. "Where did you get this?"

"It's hers. A key to the upper door."

Marul spun the object in her hands, examining its sides. "Twenty-two Heebroo letters, dancing, aflame. All keys to many doors."

"A dog called Adar gave it to me," Rana said. "A demon. Do you know him?"

"A dog, you say?"

"And a demon."

Marul scratched her head. "Could one of Ashmedai's enemies have come to rescue me? Mashit herself? Rana, is that really you? My heart will shatter if it's a lie."

"I swear to the Goddess it's me."

"Vows mean nothing. Prove you are Rana."

Rana lifted one of the candles and carefully poured its hot wax into her palm. Years of working with stone had calloused her hands; she felt no pain. She collected the wax and formed a small ball in her hands. With a pinch here, a nudge there, and a little coercion from a candleflame, she formed a round shape between her fingers.

"Here," Rana said, holding her creation up. "Do you recognize this?"

Marul stared at the sculpture in Rana's hand. "A plum?"

"I had never seen one before. You told me they were from another world. You brought me a bag of them. They were so delicious. I ate so many I got sick. You said if I wasn't careful—"

"You'd turn into a plum yourself. Oh, Rana." Marul stepped closer. She took the wax sculpture from Rana's hands as her eyes glimmered in the candlelight. "I wrote you dozens of letters. Grug could have delivered them for me, if I had asked him to. But I burned them all."

"Why?"

"I didn't want you to be a part of this. And also so he couldn't read them."

"So Grug wouldn't read them?" Rana said.

"No! Grug is just his slave. And my only friend. Here." She sighed as if she had long ago given up all hope. "Rana, my Little Plum, if it's really you, you must leave, now! If Ashmedai finds you here . . ."

"She cannot leave by the upper door, mistress. Her particular key is one way only."

"Then which way can we leave?" Rana said.

Marul shook her head. "Rana, you should never have come. How on Gehinnom did you find me?"

"I told you. Adar led me here."

"The dog?"

"And demon. He's dying outside, on the mountain path. An eagle demon attacked us. It was terrifying." She didn't add that it also felt exhilarating.

"You were attacked?"

She nodded. "And there's a pale man called Daniel who looks like no one I've ever seen and doesn't speak a word of Wul. We came here to free you."

Marul glanced at the circles on the floor and seemed suddenly ashamed. "I wish you hadn't come, Rana. You've no idea what you've gotten yourself into."

"Then tell me!"

Marul shook her head. "Later. Grug, can enter and leave these caves at will." She held up the emerald sphere. "Grug, can you bring her companions down here with this?"

"Yes, but that will just entrap them here with you."

"If this dog has come to rescue me, if he has given Rana the key, then he must know how to escape. And if he's dying, we have to save him! What other options do we have?"

"Darkness is the abode of my kind," Grug said, "not yours, mistress. I will fetch them, so you may find your way home."

"How I wish it to be true!" she said. "I've been here so long, it feels as if I've never been anywhere else."

"I'll need the key."

Marul tossed Grug the sphere, and the Cursed Man retreated into the dark corridor.

When he was gone, Rana said, "Grug is not your friend, Marul. You've been here so long you've befriended your jailer."

"Grug has sustained me all these years. And at times, he has been more than a friend to me. We are close. He's been a comfort in my moments most dire."

Rana shivered. She didn't want to envision what that truly entailed.

"Come here, Rana!" Marul said. "Let me see the woman you've become."

"Marul." Rana's chest felt like it was splitting open. "I've missed you so much. I'm sorry. If I had known you were trapped, I would have come sooner. Everyone thought you were dead."

"I *was* dead." She turned the wax plum over in her palm. "But no longer." She came over to Rana and squeezed her tight. Rana squeezed too, afraid to let go.

"Goddess, you need a bath," Rana said.

"I need much more than that." She placed her hands on Rana's shoulders, examining her body. "By Mollai, you've become such a beauty! The boys must be jumping at you."

Rana felt her cheeks flush. "Most are jumping away."

"Don't be silly."

"It's true. Many people think I'm evil, because of the things I can do."

Marul looked askance at her. "Your sparks of creativity, you mean?"

"My sparks have become a raging fire, Marul."

Marul put her finger to her lip. "We soon may need your creativity again. Things might get . . . complicated."

"Marul, I've missed you so much."

"I've missed you too, Rana."

Rana took her hand. "Promise you won't ever leave me again."

Marul sighed, and her eyes shone in the candlelight. "You better not turn out to be an apparition. I promise, child, I won't ever leave you again." Her voice echoed down the hollows of the empty caves, slowly fading.

CHAPTER NINE

Two weeks after Daniel's parents had died in the fire, he visited what was left of his house. The air reeked of spent campfires, heavy with soot and carbon ash. And where his house had stood was now a dirty splotch of black. His bedroom, the living room, den, kitchen: all were destroyed. Though it was only September, an autumn chill nipped at the air, and the first leaves had begun to fall from the trees. He stepped onto the foundation, over burnt rafters, past charred dressers with clothing still inside. Isaac's cage lay tipped, the cockatiel's body missing, eaten or rendered to ash. He found his parents' room. Only the singed metal frame of their bed remained.

He sat on the frame, the metal weave hard on his backside. Memories came to him. Mom running her hands through his hair as she read him *The Hungry Caterpillar*. Dad beside him on their bed as they watched *Star Trek* reruns together. A thousand boring dinners, stupid fights about taking out the garbage or making his bed or leaving too much baby powder on the floor. He'd promised himself he wouldn't cry. He'd cried too much over the past two weeks. But it was hard, because everything was gone.

He sat on the singed bed frame in the cool air, letting the memories come, until the sky turned red. Lights went on in adjacent houses. He had peered into their homes from his bedroom countless times, wondering what lives they led. They would live on without him. People walked their dogs, drove by in cars. None noticed Danny sitting on the burnt frame. The first stars shone in the sky, and he felt as if he too had become ash.

Gram had been barely conscious in the hospital, moaning and wailing, covered in bandages. The doctors said she would survive, but her life would be filled with disfigurement and chronic pain. He wasn't sure yet what that would mean for her, but he knew her future would be worse than his. He'd had enough of self-pity for a lifetime.

So he rose from that dead place and biked back to his great uncle's house, and he asked his great uncle to take him to the hospital. And when he got to Gram's intensive care room, he took her hand. She opened her eyes and gazed at him, her eyes were drugged and far away.

"When you were a baby," she whispered—he leaned in to hear— "we put you in a crib by the window on *erev shabbes*. The sun was going down. It turned the room a brilliant orange. It cast a shadow of your crib onto the wall. It looked like a menorah, Danny, with seven dancing flames." She squeezed his hand. "From then on I knew what you were."

She closed her eyes, whimpered, and the nurses came to give her more morphine. Then she slept. She never mentioned this story again, and later he wasn't sure if she remembered telling it.

But he remembered it, now, as he sat beside dying Adar and the canyon belching ash. The memory burned like the air in his throat. Rebekah, Gram, his job—had he lost everything, again? And what had taken their place? Demon dogs. Giant talking birds. Invisible staircases on mountainsides. Was this really Gehenna? He had worked so hard to build himself a life, and it was gone, again. He felt sick.

Gehenna was a place of suffering, the sins of the wicked burnt away like dross. So perhaps this was his cleansing. His parents were burned, and now it was his turn.

Perhaps that's how Gehenna works, he thought. *it takes your pain and tosses it out onto the viewscreen of the world, projects it back to you.*

The canyon smoldered. He sipped from his canteen, a stitched leather bladder made from some poor animal's hide. Daniel hadn't eaten meat since the fire. Thereafter the smell of meat had turned his stomach. Adar whimpered beside him. Daniel put his hand on him, just like he had done to Gram, in the hospital. The camel groaned and spat at the black clouds. Suddenly, the ash caught the sun and made a glorious rainbow of light. It was beautiful, for an instant.

Rana had been gone for twenty minutes at least, and Adar was fading. If Rana didn't come back, what then?

"Ten more minutes," he said, "then I'm going back to the city." At least they had food and water and clean air. But he wasn't sure he could leave Rana out here alone.

He dribbled water into Adar's mouth. He didn't know if it would do any good, but he had to do something. The ash over the canyon grew suddenly thick, as if hundreds of new fires were being kindled below. He got to his feet as biblical-sized pillars of smoke and fire rose to swallow the sun. If this was his moment of reckoning, he would stand to greet it.

Darkness closed over him as clouds darkened the sky. His heart pounded. The air grew so thick with smoke that the camel, only paces away, vanished. He covered his mouth with his shirt, but it didn't help. He was suffocating.

The horror of the night of the fire came burning back. He had to get out of here! He bent down to pick up Adar, when someone said, with a voice like sloshing mops and crinkling plastic, "Is the dog dead?"

A hideous figure shambled out of the smoke toward him. It had sagging, dead skin, hollow eyes that glowed faintly with yellow light, missing teeth and thin white hair. It was less a man than a walking corpse.

Daniel stood his ground. "Are you my torturing angel?"

"Eh?" said the corpse. "Many have called me a torturer, but never an angel. You must be Daniel."

He felt chills at the mention of his name. "I am." No point in hiding from his fate. He coughed, rubbed his burning eyes.

"We must hurry," the corpse said. "The smoke will only block the sun for a spell, and I cannot abide the sun for very long."

Only now did Daniel realize that the corpse was speaking English in a heavy accent he couldn't place.

"Who are you?"

"I am Grug," the creature said, "and you are not strong enough to lift the dog." With a brush from his bony, long-fingered hand, he pushed Daniel aside. In one swift motion, he swung Adar's limp body over his shoulder. Adar moaned, and green bile dribbled from his mouth.

Grug put his ear to Adar's side. "Not dead, but just only," he said. "Come, Rana and Marul await below."

Marul, was that the woman Adar had said would get him home? "*In* the mountain?"

"Yes. Now hurry, before the light returns and I become ash too."

Grug walked out past the cliff's edge onto the invisible stair. He leaped fearlessly down the unseen steps with Adar slung over his shoulder. The blowing ash revealed the stair's outlines, but only faintly.

"What about the camel?" Daniel said.

"Leave it."

"But it will die."

"It's a better survivor than you are."

Daniel sighed. He shouted to the camel, hidden behind the veil of smoke. "I'll come back for you! Hang tight!"

The camel groaned.

"Hurry!" Grug shouted.

Daniel took a cautious step out into the abyss. The smoke was thinning and the orange disc of the sun peered through the haze. He took another step down, another. At any moment he feared he would fall.

Bile and blood from Adar's dripping mouth left a slippery trail on the stairs. Daniel descended slowly, avoiding it. Grug paused before the mountain wall and Daniel crept up beside him. He dared not look down.

Grug revealed the green sphere with its raised Hebrew letters that Adar had vomited up. He pressed one side to the mountainside. The letter ayin on the sphere met a recessed ayin in the cliff wall. Ayin, the nothingness from which all things sprung, ayin, which preceded the Ein Soph, the unknowable endless. Gram's Kabbalistic lore swirled in his mind.

Grug's hand vanished into the wall as if it weren't there, then he stepped through. But before he had slipped all the way in he grabbed Daniel's arm and yanked him through too.

Daniel found himself inside a refreshingly cool, dim cave. The air was stale and dry, a welcome respite from the burning air outside. It smelled sad, somehow, like a lifetime of snuffed candles.

"This way," Grug said, and Daniel followed close.

Flickering torches in high sconces lit the way as they walked deeper into the cave. They passed many rooms. He peered into them all but saw only dust and shadows. Whoever lived in this place didn't tidy often. With chalk and stone someone had written Hebrew letters—and many foreign ones too—onto the walls. Some of their shapes he'd seen in Gram's Kabbalistic books. The four-letter name of God, the Tetragrammaton, fanning out in a Fibonacci pyramid. Stars of David inside circles, inside complex zodiacs. Crudely drawn pictures of amulets and scrolls, with tidal waves of words crashing over them. Once, at one of the homeless shelters, a woman had written all over the walls in an all-night fugue. She had been taken to a hospital and put under heavy sedation. She said God had commanded her to write until she was dead.

"Where am I?" he said. His voice echoed from unseen corridors.

"You're inside the DanBaer."

"The DanBaer?"

"The start of the Tremble, what the humans call the Araatz."

"But you are *not* human, I gather?"

"Once. Now, I'm Mikulal."

"Mikulal?"

"A Cursed One."

"Cursed? With what?"

"Your kind usually don't want to know."

"What if I do?"

Grug turned to face him. His eyes glowed with unholy light, two ghostly candles burning deep within his skull. Daniel swallowed. Perhaps he'd been too forward.

"You come from America, yes?" Grug said.

Daniel straightened. "Yes."

"The land of teeth whiteners and no-fat barbeque sauce and reality television."

"There's quite a bit more to us than that."

Grug scowled. "You're a sick people. You're richer, healthier, and have more luxuries than trillions of beings across the Cosmos, and yet you find yourselves perennially unhappy. To salve this unhappiness, you acquire endless material possessions and numb your minds with tawdry entertainments. But in the end they only echo back to you how empty your existence is. The truth is, though you make appearances to the contrary, your sole purpose is tending and caring for yourselves."

"You sound like my grandmother."

"She must be wise."

"Wiser than I realized. Are we in Gehenna?"

"Gehinnom," Grug corrected. He continued walking.

"Am I dead?"

"Do you feel dead? Death visits Gehinnom like any other world "

"Is this where my sins are burned away?"

Grug harrumphed. "If only we could burn our sins so easily away."

They entered a large, round chamber. Hundreds of candles filled the room with bright golden light. Rana and a decrepit, middle-aged woman sat on a stone bench in fevered conversation. They didn't notice that Daniel and Grug had entered.

Was this the woman who Adar had promised would help him get home? Or was this another of Gehinnom's punishments? Either way, the woman's natty hair, soiled clothes, and crooked posture didn't inspire confidence. Grug coughed, a disgusting, broken sound, and the women stopped talking and turned their gaze to him. Their eyes flickered in the candlelight; the woman's eyes were a startling green, bright as a tropical leaf.

Grug rested Adar on the ground in the center of the room, and the animal sighed. Rana stood, and she and the woman spoke heatedly in their lilting language. The conversation grew so intense that at times it seemed as if they were arguing.

Adar lay on a pattern of circles and lines drawn on the floor. Ten circles, connected by twenty-two lines, each line labeled with a single Hebrew letter. Inside the circles were Hebrew words. It was a familiar diagram. "The Sephirot," he said.

The woman stopped in mid-sentence and said, "Besu bri-ti! Mesu om-pay ti?"

"I'm sorry," he said. "I don't understand."

"She wants you to repeat what you just said," Grug said.

Finally! he thought. *An interpreter.* He'd get some much-needed answers. "I said those are the sephirot."

She responded, and Grug translated. "Mistress wants to know how you know this?"

Mistress? he thought. "It's the Tree of Life," he said, "the ten divine emanations, the aspects of God from which all things emerge. My grandmother has a painting of them hanging on the wall right next to a Chagall and a photo of my parents." He'd seen the figure many times in Gram's Kabbalistic books, which she had scattered all over the house and consulted whenever trouble arose in her life, which seemed pretty much every day.

Grug translated. The woman and Rana conversed heatedly.

Adar lay on the floor, his breath fading.

"Can this wait?" Daniel said. "The dog is dying. We have to help him."

"Mistress would like to know how you have such knowledge of the sephirot," Grug said. "I told her you're from the Upper World, where such knowledge is easily accessible."

"The Upper World?"

"Your reality sphere. Your universe. Earth moves through the Upper World like a bubble rising in molasses." Grug looked at the woman as she spoke slowly, solemnly. Daniel wasn't sure, but Grug looked as if he might have been digusted with what she was suggesting.

The woman looked Daniel up and down, bit her lip, and nodded.

Grug sighed, a sound like cities crumbling into the sea. "I need to ask you some questions," Grug said. "Are you circumcised?"

Daniel coughed. "Pardon?"

"In the ritual performed by the Abrahamic faiths, the prepuces of male infants' penises are removed on the eighth day to symbolize the eternal covenant between man and the unitary God."

"I know what circumcision is. How is this relevant?"

"Are you a Bar Mitzvah? Were you Baptized? Did you ever engage in the Fast of Ramadan or commit large portions of the Qu'ran to memory? Did you participate in the Ceremony of the Sacred Thread? Wash the feet of a Shiavist guru? Light candles for Diwali? Did you ever meditate on the nature of emptiness for more than forty-five consecutive days? Have you ever had an experience of satori?"

Daniel shook his head. "What the hell is this about?"

"I need to know what religious rituals you practiced."

"What for?"

"What I'm about to do defiles them all."

Daniel retreated from the corpse-man. "And what exactly are you about to do?"

"Cheat the Cosmos."

"I don't understand."

"It doesn't matter if you understand. Well? Have you?"

"What does it matter if I'm circumcised?"

"You've had the Covenant of Circumcision?"

Daniel swallowed. "Yes."

"You're an Israelite?"

"I'm from Babylon. The Long Island Babylon. The only thing biblical that happens there is the number of boring people who live there."

"You're a Jew?"

Hesitantly he said, "Yes, so?"

"Were you Bar Mitzvah'd?"

"Yes. Why is this important?"

"Rituals are power, protection against curses. This may not be possible. This will either work or it won't. Only one way to know for certain."

"What will work?"

Grug closed his eyes and began chanting in a language that seemed to be full of curses and imprecations, even though Daniel didn't understand the words. Grug's voice oozed despair, like the moans of someone stuck in a nightmare. Quickly, too quickly to be possible, Grug grabbed Daniel's head and yanked him close. Daniel winced as Grug leaned in, as if to kiss him. The man's breath was foul, his face rotten, and Daniel screamed.

That's when the corpse-man bit off the tip of Daniel's tongue.

Daniel screamed again, but now his voice made no sound. Instead a column of air flowed out of his mouth. A terrible, empty hiss.

"Quickly!" Grug said. "Bite off the tip of mine!" He held out his tongue, a shriveled, wormy, pus-white thing.

Daniel winced and fell back against the wall.

"Hurry, you fool, or you'll lose *all* language, forever!"

Daniel screamed silently, trying to wake up from this nightmare. Grug unsheathed his sword and with a deft motion sliced off the tip of his own tongue. Black blood spilled from his mouth onto the stone floor. He leaned over and grabbed Daniel's neck.

"Open your mouth!" he said. "And swallow this!"

Daniel tried to break free, but Grug was too strong.

"Open it or you'll gzyxqmlzbyp! It will qthcfaplmitf if you zswqnjkzyehf!"

Grug's words made no sense. And Daniel's own thoughts dissolved into gibberish before they were born. He knew what he wanted to say, but the words wouldn't come. Grug kicked him in the stomach, and when Daniel gasped, Grug flung the piece of meat into his throat, pressed his jaw closed, and said, "hnzaqwiu-llow, swal-low! Swallow!"

The corpse-man was right! This defiled all faiths! Daniel didn't eat animals, but this was infinitely worse! Human flesh! He gagged as the meat lingered in the back of his throat. Grug held Daniel's nostrils closed, and when Daniel gasped for air he choked on the meat. Oh, hell of hells, he had no choice! He had to swallow the vile thing!

And down the lump went, that heinous thing, down into his stomach. Grug released him, and Daniel retched against the wall. A terrible, high-pitched whine echoed down the corridor and after a while he realized it was his own scream.

He tried to make himself vomit, but the meat would not come up. "Oh, God," he said, his head against the wall. "Please, God, I want to go home."

"Are you done yet, Grug?" the woman said. "Because we need your help."

Daniel rose from the wall, sensing a curious shift in the air that he couldn't place. Something was profoundly different.

"What the hell did Grug just do to him?" Rana said, grimacing.

The woman put her hands on her hips. "We had no choice! We had to give him Azazel's Curse, to speed things along."

"We?" Rana said. "I didn't choose to do *that* to him."

The realization came to Daniel like a punch to the gut. He understood Rana. And the woman too. A moment ago they might have been speaking Urdu, for all he knew.

"You speak English?" he said as he staggered toward them.

"No," the woman said. "You're speaking Wul. Can't you tell?"

He felt the tip of his tongue. There was no pain, no evidence of injury.

"We shared flesh," Grug said. "Now we are brothers."

"Get away from me, freak!" Daniel said. The lilting words that flowed from his mouth felt strangely familiar, and yet, as far as he could tell, he had never uttered these arrangements of syllables in his life. "I'm not speaking English, am I?"

"No," the woman said. "You're speaking Wul."

"But I thought he didn't understand Wul?" Rana said.

"I don't," Daniel said. "I mean, I didn't. What the fuck?" He felt his lips and heard the strange sounds echoing down the tunnel. "You . . . who are you?"

"I am Marul Menacha, The Witch Who Gives Demons Pause," she said with a smirk. "And you're Daniel, I presume?"

"Daniel. The man who has no idea what the hell is going on."

Marul squinted. "You seem familiar. Have we met?"

"I don't think so."

"Rana says the dog led you here, that he was impaled by an eagle demon and fell to the rocks. Why are *you* with the demon dog?"

"I've no idea why he brought me here. Adar is the one with all the answers. He will die unless we help him. Can you do something?"

Marul squinted at the dog. "I know a ritual to heal a demon. It requires human blood and near total darkness. We'll need a black candle. Grug, will you? Rana, my Little Plum, may I see your blade?"

Grug leaned into a pile of candles, his arm across the flames, and pulled out a squat black one. He tossed the candle to Marul, who lit the wick with another. Grug muttered something brief and waved his hand, and all the candles winked out, save the black one and its ruby flame. The room turned bleak, blood-hued, and their shadows haunted them from the walls.

The smell of snuffed candles reminded Daniel of the mountainside, of charred houses. He shivered, reeling from his new fluency, as Marul sliced her forearm with Rana's blade. The blood dripped into a copper cup.

"What the hell are you doing?" he said in English, then in Wul.

She eyed him sharply while holding the knife. "Do *you* know how to heal a demon?"

"No."

"Then kindly shut the hell up! Rana? I'll need your blood."

"Are you sure?" Rana said.

"Blood is life. Please, I'll do it quickly."

Rana frowned and offered her injured arm. It didn't take much to reopen the wound. Marul sliced it, and Rana gasped as her blood spilled into the cup.

"Now you," she said to Daniel. "Give me your arm."

He shook his head. "No fucking way! I've had enough blood-letting for one day." The words of this new language poured from his lips as if he'd spoken Wul his whole life. It was utterly astonishing.

"Two may not be enough," Marul said.

Daniel retreated from her. "It will have to be. You're not cutting me."

Marul shook her head and pointed the knife at him. "If he dies, we may all be trapped. This dog holds the key to our escape."

"Sorry," Daniel said. "Try Grug. He seems happy with cutting himself."

"Grug is a Mikulal. His blood is tainted." She spat, just like Gram did whenever she mentioned evil.

"You mean the blood that I just swallowed?" He wanted to vomit.

"Your blood hasn't quickened. You're still not . . . I think we can still use your blood."

"Quickened?"

"Forget it! We'll make do with what we have. Now, give me total silence! If any of you interrupt me for any reason, disastrous consequences could result. Do you understand?" Rana nodded. He swallowed and nodded too.

She danced around the candle, all showy and ridiculous, like a budget magician about to pull the wool over the eyes of her audience. She enjoyed this immensely, he sensed, having people to dazzle and impress.

She held the cup of blood over Adar as she chanted, "We freely offer our blood to you, demon, as a symbol of healing. Take it and rise!"

She wasn't speaking Wul, but an older language, one that called to mind Druid temples and planetary occultations and huge effigies of long-forgotten gods. But Daniel understood this language and knew the power in its words as if he'd spoken them his entire life.

Marul poured the blood onto Adar's wounds and it sizzled like water on a hot skillet. "We offer our blood to you as strength against wards." She poured it onto Adar's tongue. "We offer our life-essence to you, so that you may rise. Accept our offering, demon, and be whole again!"

She flicked blood into the candle flame. It flared, and the flame brightened after she drew her hand away. Like a beating heart, the flame throbbed, growing wider with each beat. It grew into a miniature sun, expanding outward, a red giant, spinning faster and faster. The sound of the crackling flames was deafening.

Daniel backed away from the intense heat as the ball grew. Tongues of flame swam across its surface. They formed fiery letters, burning words. Hebrew words.

Minupatz. Shattered. *Shavour.* Broken. *Afelah.* Darkness.

Their meaning came easily, even though he didn't know the Hebrew words before this moment. But they were more than words. Each was meaning itself, conveyed in thought forms, wordless gestalts.

Minupatz, and his soul dissolved into atoms. *Shavour*, and he was a continent, crumbling into the sea. *Afelah*, and he plunged into a black hole.

Words, the root of all thought. Thought, the root of reality. Gram's teachings burned in his mind.

Marul's eyes grew wide, seas of flame reflected in them. She shouted above the din, breaking her own admonition for silence. "Something's wrong! It's drawing too much power! Stand back! Get back!"

Adar's skin crawled, as if a thousand insects inside him were probing for a way out. His limbs bent against their joints, snapping like tree branches. Adar howled as his long snout shrunk into his face. His fangs vanished, and his coat of black fur dissolved into bare skin. He became a lump of quivering pale flesh. Five arms spilled out slowly from the lump, like leaking streams of milk. Four long arms, plus one short and fat. The arms resolved into the vague shape of a person, four limbs, a head.

The milk hardened into a skeleton, calcified hands and feet, vertebrae like dragon's teeth, a large human skull. The hands opened and closed without muscle or sinew to coerce them. Ribs reached up from the spine like claws. Blood dripped into the skeleton from the flaming ball, hardening into muscle and sinew, lungs and bowels, a reverse dissection. Last came a suit of skin, white as chalk, wrapping itself around the figure.

Where the dog had been, now lay a naked, muscular, middle-aged man with a cap of snow-white hair. A familiar man. The one who had abducted Daniel from his wedding, who had brought him here, to Gehinnom. The man smiled, opened his eyes.

Marul screamed.

The ball of flame exploded. Sparks slammed into the walls, bounced. They glowed like a sky full of orange stars before winking out, one by one. The room plunged into darkness and silence. His ears rang from the echo of the miniature sun. He blinked away spots, hoping to find purchase on something besides the impossible darkness.

He heard slow, deep breathing from where the man lay. A few paces away, Grug muttered a few words, and a constellation of a dozen candles blinked to life. The room filled with their weak yellow light.

A tall man stood before them—the stranger from his wedding—and the horror of that moment came flooding back.

In a deep and calm voice, the man said, "It's good to see you again, Marul. Have you been well?"

Marul screamed so loudly that Daniel had to cover his ears. "It's him!" she wailed. "The demon who imprisoned me! And I just saved his worthless life!"

CHAPTER TEN

AWAKE! ALIVE! HE WAS MAN AGAIN! OH, THE LOVELY SINEWS of human flesh, the blissful nectar of masculine form. The demon stretched his arms, twisted and craned his neck as Marul, that self-aggrandizing witch, screamed at him.

"Shut your damn screeching!" he said.

Marul—what a hag she had become—wailed as she pointed at him. "I've saved the life of this beast! The one who imprisoned me!"

"Marul, Marul!" Rana said, trying to calm her. "I don't understand?"

Marul stared at him, her eyes full of hate and malice. "This beast that stands before you," she said, "is none other than Ashmedai, King of Demonkind."

"Please," he said, holding his hand over his heart and bowing. "I much prefer Caleb. Ashmedai is so Old Testament, don't you think?"

"No," said Daniel as he walked around him, as if he were examining a statue. "Apocrypha, actually. The Book of Tobit."

"Impressive, Daniel," the demon said.

"You're Ashmedai?" Daniel said, squinting.

He smiled and nodded. "Caleb, please."

Rana pulled out her dagger, a lovely bejeweled thing, and threatened him with it, while Grug fell to his knees and bowed in deference. A few lonely candles burned beside him. In the oldest language, which could not be heard by human ears, nor spoken with any tongue, conveyed by thought alone, Ashmedai commanded Grug to light the other candles. Grug's lips weaved a song of fire into the fabric of reality, and three hundred more tapers awakened with light.

"The Mikulalim," Caleb said, "do have such a lovely courtship with fire, don't you think? Come now, Rana, there is no need for violence."

Rana examined him in the full light. Her eyes scanned his naked body, and there was a hint of blush on her tawny cheeks, a subtle dilation of her eyes. Though she might hate him, some deep part of her, he guessed, was curious of what she saw.

"Please," Caleb said, "I'm not here to hurt anyone."

Rana furrowed her brow and frowned. "Did I really bring your jailer to you, Marul?"

"You were amazing, Rana," Caleb said. "Far braver than I'd imagined. You confronted the eagle demon without pause. I'm proud of you!"

Rana lowered the knife a fraction.

How often, he thought, *has Rana heard praise for who she is, instead of criticism or fear?*

Marul shook her head over and over. "No, no, no, no, no, no!" she stammered. Her eyes flitted around the room as she gibbered. "I could have destroyed him. Just had to let him die, and my cage would have opened. I would have been free!" She clutched her head and tugged on her greasy locks.

"If he dies, you're free?" Rana said.

Marul screamed, "Yes!"

Caleb sensed from her body language what Rana was about to do. She lunged at him with her knife, but he easily parried the blade, snatched her wrist, and raised her arm high. Blood from her wound dripped down her forearm as he squeezed. She swung at him with her free hand but he grabbed that too. He dug into her wrist with his fingernails and she dropped the blade. She squealed, two bracing notes.

By Sheol's suns! There was music even in her cries! So much power within this small creature. But hers was feral power, in need of taming.

"You are brave, but impulsive, Rana," Caleb said. "You must think before you act. Marul is wrong. If I die, the three of you will remain in this mountain until the last star burns out. And, besides," he said, "you would never find out why I've brought you here."

"Yes," Daniel said. "We need answers. Let Rana go. You're hurting her."

Daniel spoke in Wul. Curious. When had he learned that? "Look at you, Daniel," Caleb said. "As ignorant of your nature as a newborn is of his one day being able to walk and run and even fly." He released Rana's hand, and she fell to the ground. She retreated to Marul's side, rubbing her wrists.

"I was this close to letting him die," Marul mumbled.

"Enough!" Caleb said. "I'm alive, and that is that."

"If he's a demon king," Rana said timorously, "then is Daniel his prince?"

"Of a kind," Caleb said. "Daniel, tell Rana and Marul how we met, if you please."

"All right," Daniel said. "I first saw him the night of the big storm. I was checking in on a homeless shelter . . ."

Daniel told his story, beginning on the night when Ashmedai followed him home, to his unexpected entry into Daniel's wedding, where the guests turned into, as Daniel put it, "giant cubes of salt." Rana stared at Caleb, blushing. Though she tried to hide it, she kept glancing between Caleb's legs as if she'd never seen a naked man before.

Caleb smiled as he listened to Daniel's interpretation of events. *Cubes of salt!* he thought. *What a reductive metaphor!* In the last major redaction of the coded scrolls that had been eventually compiled into the Five Books of Moses, the scrivener Samuel ben Eliyahu described the death of Lot's wife in much the same way, as "pillars of salt." But Caleb supposed comparing Daniel's experience to seeing "cubes of salt" was easier to imagine than trying to explain explosive sensory decoherence as a result of one's consciousness matrix being forcefully separated from its long-time world-vessel. But humans always preferred metaphors to the truth.

". . . and then this girl—Rana—walked in and found us hiding on the floor," Daniel said. "Rana knows the rest."

"Goddess," Marul said. "You leapt into the Great Deep without a vessel?"

Caleb smiled proudly. "Only you comprehend what could have happened if we missed the infinitesimal doorway to Gehinnom."

"You would have fallen through the Abyss for all eternity," she said, "without respite of sleep or death, with nothing to occupy your minds except your stillborn fantasies that would slowly drive you mad."

"Not so different from the fate that awaits us all if we don't act now!" he said. "Daniel, will you tell us about your lovely wife, Rebekah?"

He shook his head. "She isn't my wife. I ran out before we finished the marriage ceremony." He reached into his pocket.

"Go on," Ashmedai said. "Pull out that shriveled flower."

"This?" He revealed the desiccated boutonniere. Its petals hung like dead skin.

"Hear me, Daniel. Rebekah's true essence is like that flower. A wilted, shriveled corpse. Cut short before its prime, left to fester. Like my brothers, who were scorned by the Creator. But there are ways of making things appear beautiful again."

He waved his hand over the flower, and it blossomed back to vibrant life. A waste of his power, but Daniel needed to understand. Its wine-purple petals, like the dual sunsets of Sheol, glowed of their own light.

Daniel's eyes grew wide.

"Rebekah is no different. A dead thing revivified. Ultimately, a mirage." With another wave of his hand the flower reverted back to dead skin. "Daniel, your Rebekah doesn't exist. What lies beneath is horrid. Her name is Mashit, an ancient and cunning demon."

"Mashit?" Marul said. "You were about to marry Mashit?"

"He was," Caleb said. "She usurped my throne, robbed me of my power, and cast me out of Sheol. Her love for you is a ruse, Daniel, for once I believed she loved me too."

Daniel squirmed. "Rebekah works for a charity. She's helped countless people. I've seen her work. She's no demon. You're lying."

"I won't deny I have a tendency toward falsehood. As king, it was not easy to maintain power without dissembling. But I swear by

Great Abbadon, the first king of Sheol, that Rebekah is as much a demon as I am."

Daniel shivered once. "What would a demon want with me?"

"A profound question. Why, among billions, did she choose you, Daniel? Marul, you should guess the answer to this one."

Marul scowled. "I'm not playing your foul games."

"This is no game. I'll give you a minute."

"I don't know," she said. "He looks like any boring Upper Worlder to me."

"Exactly!" he said. "Look at how *ordinary* he seems. A common man, easily forgotten. But there's a spark of wisdom in Daniel's eyes, is there not?"

Marul stirred. She approached Daniel cautiously, as if he were a caged beast. "It wasn't his face that was familiar. It was his name! I knew I recognized it! It's been so long, I'd nearly forgotten! Is he Daniel—Daniel Fisher?"

Caleb smiled.

"Goddess Almighty!" Marul said. "Damn you, Caleb, have you brought one here? Is that possible? How did you cleave him from the Earth?"

Caleb nodded. "Mashit did all the work for me."

"What are you talking about?" Rana said.

"Daniel," Marul said, "is a *Lamed Vavnik*."

Caleb laughed, his voice careening down the corridors of stone. "Now there's the Marul Menacha I remember! The Witch Who Gives Demons Pause indeed. Behold, Daniel Fisher, one of the thirty-six anonymous people who sustain the Cosmos. But anonymous no more."

Daniel cocked his head. "A Lamed Vavnik? Me?"

"What's a Lamed Vavnik?" Rana said.

"A Jewish myth," Daniel said. "In the Hebrew language, letters are numbers. The letters *lamed* and *vav* mean thirty-six. The *Lamed Vav* are thirty-six just people who sustain the world. If any of them should cease being righteousness, the world would be destroyed."

"I'd hardly call them righteous," Caleb said. "Privileged, perhaps. Naive."

"What would you know of righteousness?" Marul said

"Mashit was about to destroy Daniel," Caleb said. "I *saved* him. Is that not just?"

"Saved?" Daniel said. "From what?"

"From *whom*. Mashit used the wedding ritual to cleave your soul from Earth, Daniel. This is why you saw, as you put it, 'cubes of salt.' It was your perceptual system losing its attachment to Earth. Had you stomped on that glass, Daniel, Mashit would have gained full power over your soul. Separated from Earth, she could then destroy you. It was her separation that let me bring you here, safe from Mashit's evil, for the moment. But she will come, I can promise you that."

"Nonsense!" Marul said. "Demonkind have spent millennia seeking to slaughter the Lamed Vav. You want us to believe you've had a change of heart and you want to save him?"

"Not just Daniel," Caleb said. "I hope to save them all."

Marul shook her head. "I've heard many absurd things, but this is madness!"

"The Earth is a fountain, overflowing with energy, the water of life that sustains all the worlds," Caleb said. "It spills down to water the broken worlds of the Shards. The thirty-six Lamed Vav uphold the Earth like pillars. If the Lamed Vav were removed, the water comes splashing down in a great flood upon all the Shards. But soon after, Earth will dry up, and all the Shards will wither and die."

"What are the Shards?" Rana said.

"Are you speaking of the klippoth?" Daniel said. "The husks of failed worlds?"

"I am," Ashmedai said. "The Shards are broken universes, shattered eons ago, by the Creator, she who exists beyond all ken. There are countless Shards. Most are uninhabitable. But on many of them live sentient beings—demons and humans—who live torturous lives. Were it not for the waters of life dripping from the Earth, the Shards would dry up. If you destroy the Lamed Vav, as Mashit hopes to do, the Earth shatters, and the Cosmos will die.

"This is why I've gathered you all here! Mashit commands the Legion of the First, a fearsome demon army. She and her allies have killed two Lamed Vav. They will soon destroy a third. One by one, they remove the pillars of Earth. There is an order, and it must be followed.

"If they kill enough, soon the foundations of the Earth will crack, and the water of life will pour out. The Upper World will crumble, destroying the Earth. The sustaining waters will cease, and the countless Shards that depend on Earth for life will wither and die.

"But that won't be the end of you and me. Though all the worlds will dry up, our souls will persist. We will be conscious long after our bodies turn to dust. Trillions of lost souls will drift across the Great Deep, a sea of limitless nothing. And after a trillion, trillion, trillion years of untold suffering, the Great Deep will close, swallowed once and for all by the Creator's light, finishing the cycle of creation forever.

"This will happen. It is a certainty. Unless we stop Mashit from killing the Lamed Vav. And if we work together, we *can* stop her. If you help me, together we can save the Cosmos."

"After what you've done to me," Marul said, "you dare ask for my help?"

"By any reckoning, you owe me nothing, Marul," he said. "I made you suffer in ways few have. But would you let Rana suffer for your hatred of me? And what of the countless human souls in all the Shards who will suffer horribly if the Legion succeeds? I know your heart has not room enough for so much pain."

Marul took a deep breath. She squinted at him. "There's treachery here, but I can't see it yet. What game are you playing at?"

"This is no game! I am fighting for life itself. But I understand the irony. Here stands the former King of Demonkind, hoping to save the Earth. But like all creatures, I do not wish to die. I need your help, Marul. I need to get back to Earth to protect the remaining Lamed Vav."

"Why did you leave in the first place?" Marul said. "You could have stayed to protect them while you were there."

"Mashit would have killed me, once I showed myself to her. I had to protect Daniel from her. Now that I've upset her plans, I've given us precious, needed time. "

Marul shook her head, but he knew he'd piqued her interest. "You want to travel all the way to Earth? I was a powerful witch, but have you seen me lately? I need Grug to light my candles now. Besides, the one time I traveled to Earth, I got the power I needed from your brother. Go ask him!"

"He and I are not on the best of terms."

"I'm not surprised," she said.

"The Quog Bedu possess such power," Caleb said. "They will help us."

"Ha!" Marul laughed. "It's said the Bedu can move stars in their sleep. But stories are like mirages—they disappear if you look too closely. Besides, the Bedu despise demonkind. Why would they help you?"

"They don't have to know I'm a demon."

"Oh, they'll know."

"Chialdra didn't sense me. The Bedu won't either. With your spellcraft, Marul, and their power, we can form a vessel to bring us back to Earth. Help me, and I'll release you from your bonds, forever."

"What if I don't?"

"Then you can rot in this cave, and I will find someone else."

Marul frowned as she considered his offer. "What about Rana? You don't need her for anything. Rana goes free, if I help."

Caleb needed Rana more than she could know. Without Rana, he was a carpenter without an architect, an engineer without a design. Yet to reveal his goal to them now would be too soon. "Very well," he said. "Once we leave these tunnels, she's free to go."

"You're not really going to help him, are you, Marul?" Rana said.

"If it means you can go home, I will."

"But he's lying!" Rana said.

"About something, I'm certain of it," Marul said. "Without him, there is no leaving these cold walls. We have no choice."

"There are always choices," Rana said.

"Indeed," Caleb said. "So best make sure you pick wisely."

CHAPTER ELEVEN

ALL THIS TALK OF SHARDS AND LAMED VAVS AND DISTANT worlds beyond Gehinnom made Rana feel as if she were spinning in a sand devil. But when she saw Marul's cactus-green eyes under the nap of tangled hair, her heart warmed, and her confusion faded.

Goddess—Marul was alive. She was here!

The demon—Adar, Ashmedai, Caleb, whatever his name was now—stared at her as he said, "Grug and I need to fetch supplies for our journey into the desert. I'm sure while I'm gone you'll want to discuss with each other how I am deceiving you. I'd expect nothing less. But I speak the truth. All existence is in danger, and we are the only ones who can stop Mashit."

All existence? Rana huffed. His cocksure swagger irritated her. Did he feel no shame at being naked in front of women? "Fetch some clothes while you're gone," she said.

He smiled at her, and she blushed. Then he and Grug left the chamber. Something in Caleb's gaze made her feel awkward, exposed, as if he'd seen something inside her that she couldn't quite see. She hated the funny little quiver it made in her belly.

Daniel sat on a stone bench against the wall and looked as if he were deep in thought. How could so few people hold up a whole world, especially one as flaccid as Daniel? Surely it wasn't by strength.

Marul gazed at the floor, shaking her head.

"I'm sorry," Rana said. "When the dog told me you were alive, I knew he was probably lying. But I had to know. I had to see if it was true."

"No apologies," Marul said. "I'm the one who should be sorry. If it wasn't for my arrogance, you wouldn't be in this cage with me."

"Arrogance? How so?"

Marul swept her foot across the dusty floor. "I've had too much time to think in these caves. I'm not the person you think I am, Rana. I've done terrible things."

"We've all committed sins against the Goddess we wish we could forget."

"Not like mine. Rana . . . you should have stayed home. This world you've stepped into is full of terrible dangers."

"Better danger than another day of drudgery working on the Ukne Tower. Besides, I *had* to come, Marul. For you."

Marul rubbed Rana's cheek, and Rana closed her eyes to savor her touch.

Daniel walked over, and in a gentle voice he said, "Are you hurt, Rana?"

She rubbed her wrists, her forearm. The bleeding had stopped but the cut was still raw. She felt exposed, helpless. "I'll live."

Daniel stared at her. "Do you really believe that I'm a Lamed Vavnik?"

Rana imagined Daniel holding up a world over his head, the way Papa used to heft stone. Then she imagined Daniel dropping it.

"How would I know?" Rana said.

"There are specific traits a Lamed Vavnik has," Marul said.

"Like what?" said Daniel.

"Selflessness, empathy," said Marul.

"Plenty of people have those traits."

"Humility, another sign."

He shook his head. "You're reaching."

"There are subtler signs," Marul said. "It's in the gaze, the body language, and something that could best be described as a feeling of quiet support in your company."

"Or maybe," Daniel said, "Caleb is lying. Maybe I'm no more a Lamed Vavnik than you're a demon." He looked back and forth between them. "You're not demons are you?"

Marul snickered, and Rana smiled at the familiar sound of it. "We're human," Marul said. "But Caleb is telling the truth about you. Daniel, you're a Lamed Vavnik."

"How can you be sure?" he said.

Marul closed her eyes. "It's complicated. Let's just say your name is known to me."

"You believe his story about the world collapsing?" he said. "This demon army coming for us? The Legion of the . . ."

"First," Marul said. "I've seen the horrid ranks of the Legion, and that vision still haunts me. I've visited many Shards, and I've seen many beings living tortured lives upon them. As for Mashit—" she made eye contact with him— "your almost-wife, she and her ilk have been trying to destroy the Lamed Vav for millennia. But the Lamed Vav are expert concealers. You are the *Tzadikim Nistarim.*"

"The hidden righteous ones," Daniel said.

"Yes," Marul said.

"If this is true," he said, straightening, "then we *have to* help Caleb. We have to save the Lamed Vav before—" he swallowed— "before Mashit kills them."

"Or," Rana said, "Caleb is using you for something else."

"Like what?" Daniel said.

"Why did he save you, Daniel?" Marul said. "Why bring you here to Gehinnom? And your story of the perverted wedding ritual sounds just like what Mashit would need to do in order to cleave you from Earth. Caleb's story makes a lot of sense, actually."

Rana shook her head. How were they so gullible? "Let me take you to Bedubroadstreet," she said. "A thousand hucksters there would make a fortune off the two of you. He's a demon, you idiots! Lying is his blood."

Marul winced, and Rana regretted her outburst. But Marul had been alone for too long and had lost her wisdom. "Marul," she said, "I thought you were dead, and now here you are, alive. You'd have me leave you in the arms of your jailer and just go back home?"

"Rana, you're a child. You've so much life ahead. This world you've entered is not a game. You could die. Now settle down and let the adults handle this one, all right?"

Rana felt as if she had just been slapped. Did Marul share the same sentiment as King Jallifex? As Chief Jo? That she was just a child, incapable of self-determination? By Mollai, why wouldn't anyone ever let her try?

"Maybe I was a child when you left," she said, "but I'm a woman now."

Marul's eyes came to rest on Rana's bust. "In shape, perhaps. But in wisdom?" Marul waved her hand dismissively. "Hardly."

Rana squeezed her fists. She felt like smashing something. "You think you know me, but you know a child. That child has died, and a woman has replaced her. I have lived a thousand days without you. While you were gone, I built towers a hundred stories tall. I set the capstone on the Great Arch at the King's palace. I designed the bridge over Olam's Gap, which uses no mortar and supports the weight of a thousand loaded camels."

"So you've moved stones," Marul said, "but the heart is heavier than stone. You know nothing of suffering."

She squinted at Marul, as if seeing the woman's face for the first time. How had Rana not seen it before? Marul was entirely impressed with herself, even in this dark cave.

"Suffering?" Rana said. "I fell in love with a mason. I hoped to marry him. Then I saw him splatter on the cobblestones when he fell from a construction site. Papa used to lift stones over his head no man could carry, but he broke his back and now he can't sit up without screaming. I was supposed to succeed Papa as chief architect, but King Jallifex gave that job to his nephew, who doesn't know slate from shale. The greasy king declared war with Guernia because he could, and I saw the sad, scarred faces of the men returning from the first and only battle, having witnessed things too ghastly to mention. The city lost half its males in that pointless war.

"And I've seen wonderful things, Marul. I've known the joy of a new sister, whose eyes sparkle like stars. I've seen the avatar of Goddess Mollai descend over the desert at night, bright as the moon, her nacreous light fanning out like a star-bird's tail. I've known the love of a man and shared a bed with a woman. And while you were gone, I made things. Wonderful things. I taught myself more arts than you can imagine. You say I haven't lived, and I say you don't know a damned thing about me!"

Marul's mouth had opened in a little circle of shock. "Fat Jallifex is still king? I didn't expect him to last a week after his father died."

"He outlives everyone's expectations, in girth as well as in rule."

Marul smiled. Then she blinked, as if taking in Rana anew. "I'm sorry," Marul said, "about the boy you loved. It's not an easy thing to lose a loved one. And, Goddess, you have a sister? Why didn't you tell me that first thing? How old is she? What's her name?"

"Liu. She's eighteen months, and she's the most beautiful thing in all the world, and maybe a thousand others."

"I hope I can meet her," Marul said.

"So do I," said Rana.

Marul beamed, and the tension between them vanished like smoke. "It seems we have a lot of catching up to do. But I'm afraid we haven't time."

"For five years I thought you were dead, Marul. Now that I've found you, I'm not going to let you vanish again."

"Rana, you cannot come. It's too dangerous."

"No," she said, "you'll be coming with me." Then she whispered, "I plan to kill him."

"Goddess, no, Rana! Put such foolish thoughts out of your mind."

"But Caleb *is* mortal, yes? And weak. We've seen him bleed."

"We can't kill him," Daniel said. "We need him. How else will we stop—" He swallowed again. "Stop Mashit from killing the Lamed Vav?"

"Don't believe his lies," Rana said. "Marul, you said if he dies, you'd go free?"

"I believed that the magic binding me here would be broken if he died," Marul said. "But he says that's not true."

"Only to keep you under his thrall," Rana said. "We should kill him as soon as possible."

"And what of Grug?" Marul said.

"What of him?"

"Grug is my friend," Marul said. "His companionship was all I had to keep me from insanity. Rana, this is foolish talk. You are no more a killer than I'm a mason. Keep your knife. We'll let Caleb take us out of the cave, and once we're free, you will go home, and

Daniel and I will take care of this Lamed Vav business. My decision is final."

"What decision?" Caleb said as he and Grug strode into the room. To Rana's disgust Caleb was still naked. Grug carried a large container in his arms. Several heavy satchels were slung over Grug's shoulders. He deposited everything onto the ground.

"I will help get you and Daniel back to Earth," Marul said.

"I'm glad you see it my way," Caleb said.

"Not all of us agree," said Rana.

"Some dissention in the ranks is to be expected." He smiled at her, and damn it, she blushed again! Couldn't he put on some clothes? "We've a long journey ahead," he said. "We need to build up our strength."

So demons need to eat and rest too, she thought. Could he die of starvation or poison? She stole a glance at Marul, who glared at her, as if to discourage her malevolent thoughts.

Caleb flipped open the container. It had been stuffed to the brim with large cuts of bloody meat and smelled of a fresh slaughter.

"Where did you get meat?" Marul said. "There's nothing but rats down here."

"On the mountainside," Caleb said.

"Outside?" said Marul.

Grug's hands were stained with blood, as was the hilt of his sword.

"The she-camel," Rana said.

"You killed it?" Daniel said, shocked. Rana felt sickened too. She had set the camel free only to see it die. She vowed to herself she would not let the same thing happen to Marul.

"Make us a fire, Grug," Caleb said.

Grug tore apart the container with astonishing strength. The rusty nails squeaked like rodents as he yanked the boards apart. Echoes scurried down the tunnels. His movements were quick, repugnant, offensive to the senses.

"Why did you have to kill the camel?" Daniel said.

"We need to eat to build our strength," Caleb said.

"Well I don't eat meat," Daniel said.

Caleb picked up a bloody cut and peeled off the hide in strong, quick jerks. "I'm afraid you'll find, Daniel, that Gehinnom isn't kind to vegetarians. When the choice is between meat or death, what will you pick?" He threw the bloody cut to Daniel, who leaped out of the way. The meat rolled to a stop on the floor.

"You don't eat meat," Rana said, "and you have the strength to hold up a world?"

Daniel stared at the flesh. "Sometimes it takes more strength *not* to do something than to do it."

Rana's knife lay on the floor. She turned to Marul. "I couldn't agree more."

———

Daniel sat away from the flames, elbows on his knees, staring at the ten circles of the sephirot that Marul had painted on the floor. He was inside the central sephirah, Tiferet—Beauty. But there was nothing beautiful about death, the total destruction of being. Once, it had been a camel, and though it didn't know much of the future or past, didn't plan for birthdays or pine for the days gone, it did savor its life, as all creatures do. Now it was just meat.

The smell of it cooking, the grease dripping onto the flames of a roaring fire Grug had kindled, reminded Daniel of Gram's brisket. She had roasted one every Sunday when he'd lived with her, though he'd long since stopped eating it. He suddenly missed her nagging, her Yiddishkeit, the way she could be comforting even as she harangued. All those stories she told him growing up, those *bobe-mayses*. They were true, weren't they? Dybbuks possessing the bodies of young brides-to-be, *shedim*—demons— leaving cocks' footprints at the foot of a dreamer's bed. Dumah and her thousand eyes, waiting at the sinner's grave to crack it open with a flaming rod and drag the unfortunate down to Gehenna.

Was Gram saying Kaddish—the mourner's prayer—over his grave now?

The fire flickered with memories. Rebekah's face formed in the flames; perhaps he'd imagined it. He remembered that hot summer day as they held hands and walked along the sculpted High Line Park in Manhattan. She took his photo beside a cluster of black-eyed Susans, then they sat on a bench and shared a cup of coffee.

"Cargo trains," she'd said, a drop of coffee on her upper lip, "used to come through here, right where we're sitting."

The crooked boardwalk, built over the rails, went right through a dozen skyscrapers, following the old route. "Yeah, it's pretty cool," he said, feeling inane. His tongue always tied in knots around her.

"This was a thriving trade route," she said as the hot breeze fanned her hair. "But the route wilted, decayed." She looked wistfully down the boardwalk, as if peering back in time. "The trains stopped. The rails rusted. Weeds grew tall. It was a graveyard. Now look at it, Danny. It's been reborn."

Crowds of people had walked past them, entranced by the flowering plants, the modern skyscrapers leaning over the path. Daniel was happy. Human life was mostly suffering, true. But for the moment the world seemed at peace.

"It's beautiful," he said.

"It gives me hope," she said.

"Hope?"

"Because it shows that dead things can be beautiful again." She stared at him, her eyes two more hazel flowers in the edenic scene.

"This wasn't dead," he said, "just abandoned. There was plenty of life here."

She nodded. A brave bumblebee navigated the crowds to dart between the black polka dots of the black-eyed Susans. "We've been given a garden," she said. "And what have we done with it? A few live in luxury while millions suffer. We're destroying the world."

He nodded. "I see us as confused adolescents," he said. "We stand on the precipice before a vast, strange universe and are utterly terrified of the view. So we cower and hide in consumerism, in the mindless purchasing of products. We don't realize our creative power, our absolute freedom to build the kind of universe we want."

She let slip a smile. "Yes! We can turn the abandoned places into gardens again. You and me, Danny. We will make great things together." Her hand held his, warm and welcoming. They sat on that bench for a long time, letting the world and its potential speak for itself.

A timber popped in the fire, and Daniel awoke from the memory. Was Rebekah a fantasy? A charade played by a demon? What of all the charity work he'd seen her do? And what of the nights under the moon and the orange-lit city, when they lay in bed, grasping each other and forgetting the bleak world? Were those lies too? He remembered Rebekah's face at their wedding, how it had withered like an ancient tree, how she wasn't perturbed at all by the shape shifting man-dog leaping toward them, but kept insisting that he break the glass. An act, Caleb had said, that would have allowed her to destroy him.

He stared into the fire. Maybe he had been a fool to believe such a person could exist. Or maybe he was a fool to believe Caleb now, as Rana had said. He felt queasy with ambivalence.

"You'd better eat," Caleb said, and the singsong Wul consonants tickled Daniel's ears.

"I'm not hungry," he said, even though his stomach was rumbling at the smell.

The smoke from the fire blew out of the chamber, whisked off by currents of air. Strips of meat hung on a spit, and the fire flared as grease dripped. He hadn't eaten meat in seventeen years, not since his parent's death. But the meat smelled delicious, tempting.

Caleb had covered himself in a draping, sand-colored linen robe tied with a brown leather belt. As he poked and prodded the fire he resembled a stately Roman senator.

"We've a long journey, Daniel, and you won't find any fruit or edible plants for hundreds of parasot."

Parasot. The plural of *parasa*, a measure of distance, which he now understood to be roughly three miles, another curious artifact of this new fluency.

"There will be only water and meat," Caleb said, "and little of either."

Daniel stared into the flames, searching for hints of Rebekah's face. "Are there any of those pomm fruits left?" he said.

"No," Rana said. "You ate them all."

His stomach rumbled, but he couldn't bring himself to eat the camel. Grease and blood smeared their cheeks as they ate. Soon, little was left but bone and gristle. Where was its head? Had they left it in wide-eyed terror on the cliffs above? He imagined scavenger birds pecking at its eyes. He grimaced as Grug cracked open a bone and sucked out the marrow.

"I have a treat," Caleb said, holding up a wooden box.

"You're going to kill yourself?" Rana said.

Caleb laughed. It was a haughty sound, as a king might make at the antics of his jester. "Tobacco. From Earth. I hid this box here ages ago. Let me roll us each a tube."

In Wul there were a hundred words for "pipe," but not a single one for "cigarette." Paper, he supposed, was not easily acquired in a desert, and certainly not something to burn. Caleb offered Daniel the first. He was never a smoker, but he took it, if only to stave off the hunger.

Caleb gave "tubes" to the others. Rana studied hers, opened it, and dumped the tobacco into her hand.

"You broke it," Caleb said.

"No," she said, quickly refashioning her cigarette so that it was as well formed as a Marlboro. "I perfected it."

Caleb smiled. His gaze was predatory, more animal than sexual. Whatever Caleb saw in her, he savored it.

The demon lifted a brand from the embers and offered the glowing tip to Daniel. Daniel puffed, inhaled. His head spun and his body tingled as the nicotine surged through his body. He laughed at the absurdity of it all.

"What's so funny?" Rana said. She sucked her cigarette as classily as Lauren Bacall in *Casablanca*. In the firelight, Rana was stunning.

"Here I am," Daniel said, "smoking with a corpse-man, a demon, and two women from another world, while speaking a language I'd never heard of yesterday. That's what's funny."

"I'm no corpse," Grug said.

"Sorry," Daniel said. "I didn't mean to offend." As more nicotine entered his body, the words scratched on the walls seemed to shake and glow. They were written in Hebrew and Aramaic and cuneiform and other scripts, rambling on about exits, portals, escape.

Caleb sighed and leaned back, exhaling a gray stream of smoke. "My energy returns like Ora rising above Abbadon's cliffs at dawn."

Rana squinted at him, in malice or perhaps curiosity. "Ora?" she said.

"One of two suns that spin about each other in Sheol's sky."

"Sheol?" Daniel said. "The realm of the dead?"

"Dead in spirit, perhaps, but things live there. Sheol is a realm quite distant from Earth, furthest from its sustaining waters. The oldest demons have dwelled there since the Shattering. Twin suns burn in Sheol's crimson sky. At night, giant red stars infest the sky like a pox. By day the air is too hot, by night it's too frigid. The land is barren, mostly granite and basalt cliffs. Eons ago Great Abbadon built the first kingdom there. From the dust, under his leadership, we lifted ourselves up. From the ashes, we built a home. We renamed the palace after him when he died. I took over his throne, and ruled Sheol for twenty-five hundred years. Until Mashit betrayed me and cast me out. Sheol is my world. My home. And I have been exiled from it."

"My heart bleeds," Rana said.

Caleb seemed not to notice Rana. His eyes were glazed, as if lost in memory. "It's not just my world. All the Shards will die if we don't act."

"The husks?" Daniel said.

"The Shards are shattered worlds, universes that the Creator destroyed because they had too much judgment, too much wrath, and not enough mercy. Their myriad fragments float in the Great Deep like potsherds in a field. Sheol exists in but one Shard of millions."

Rana spit into the flames. "Who cares? Why should we risk our lives for cosmic debris?"

"Because," Caleb said, "those shattered worlds are not empty! Trillions of beings dwell within the Shards, leading bitter lives. Their worlds are ragged, broken things. They sip the water of life from Earth in drips and drops, like a dog begging for scraps from his master's table. The little life force they receive from Earth bleeds out like water through a cracked jar."

"Better that they all die," Rana said. "Why should we give a damn about a bunch of broken worlds filled with demons like you?"

"Because," Caleb said, "Gehinnom floats within a Shard too."

—

"Lies!" Rana said, leaping to her feet. She wanted to strangle Caleb and wipe that persistent smirk off his face. "Marul, tell me these are all lies!"

Marul hung her head and closed her eyes. Almost imperceptibly, she shook her head.

Rana felt a sob grow in her throat. "So Gehinnom is, what? Broken? How?"

"It is like a painting you become unsatisfied with," Caleb said, "and have torn to shreds. The Creator was not satisfied with this universe, and so she smashed it."

"Marul," Rana said. "Say something!"

Marul opened her eyes. They were rheumy and tired. "I'm sorry, Rana. His words are true. Gehinnom floats in a Shard."

Rana shook her head. "That doesn't make sense. If our universe is broken, how do we walk and breathe? How does the sun rise and the moon set? How do the stars twirl across the sky if everything is broken?"

"Fill a jar with water," Caleb said, "and smash it. Most of the water spills out, but a few drops remain on the shards. Gehinnom is like one of those drops, clinging to the surface."

"Until we evaporate!" Rana said.

"My point exactly," Caleb said. "It's only Daniel's Earth that keeps the Shards from drying up. Which is why we must preserve it."

Rana felt as if she were suffocating. Yesterday the world seemed so small, circumscribed by a compass and a rule. She could have built anything she dreamed if she'd had the stone and tools. But what kind of tool would one need to repair a universe? Daniel stared at her, his eyes as haunted as the boys who had come home from the war.

"I must rest," Caleb said. "You should too. Grug, will you?"

Grug muttered four harsh words, and the fire winked out, except for a single candle guttering near the wall. The sudden absence of heat made the room feel cold, and Rana shivered.

"Grug has blankets for you," Caleb said. "Tonight we sleep with rock above our heads, tomorrow we sleep under the stars."

Marul said, "Oh, how I miss the stars."

Caleb took a blanket from Grug, laid it flat in a corner, and spread himself upon it. He closed his eyes and lay as still as the dead. Rana eyed her knife, which remained on the floor where she had dropped it.

Caleb added, "I'm a light sleeper. Don't waste your time trying to kill me."

"Yes," Marul said, eyeing Rana. "I suggest we *all* rest."

Rana trembled with rage. If Marul had always known Gehinnom was a failed work of art, smashed and discarded, why hadn't she told her?

Was it because, Rana thought, *Marul believed I couldn't handle the truth? Well, Marul, I can! I can!*

But even as she thought this she trembled. She felt as if the ground might crumble into a million pieces, flinging her soul across eternity, with no Lamed Vavnik there to catch her.

Grug offered her a blanket. "Don't curse your lot," Grug said. "Be thankful for your portion, however small. Endless scores live far worse than you ever have. Compared to some worlds, Gehinnom is a paradise." His unholy yellow eyes peered into hers, and she shivered. She took the blanket and sat upon it, next to Daniel.

"What's your world like, Daniel?" she said. "What's different about Earte?"

"Ear-*th*," he said, stressing the hiss. "There most people don't believe in demons. I definitely didn't. They don't have giant eagles or talking dogs. But I guess the most obvious difference is that we have more . . ." He seemed to struggle to find the right word. "*Tools*. So many tools to help us get through the day. We have one tool where we can talk to each other even though we're hundreds of . . . parasot away from each other. We have giant metal ships to fly through the air and metal wagons that whisk us across the ground. There are these . . . boxes that show scenes from far away. But the people aren't all that different. The humans at least."

"I think you will find, Daniel," Marul said with closed eyes, "that humans on Gehinnom are much less forgiving of being kept awake at night. Now the two of you, listen to your elder and go the hell to sleep!"

Rana frowned. How could Marul sleep now? Daniel lay on his back, staring at the ceiling. In the weak light, Rana quietly picked up her knife. Daniel watched her slip the blade into its sheath. Her hand squeezing the hilt, she looked at Caleb. Grug was staring at her. He averted his eyes and, without a word, left the chamber.

The white-haired demon lay still, three paces away, as she considered what to do.

CHAPTER TWELVE

"THE SUN WILL RISE IN TWO HOURS," GRUG SAID, ROUSING THEM from sleep.

Caleb sat up, blinked away the horrid dream—a recurring one; he had been tumbling through the Great Deep, helpless, screaming for the Creator—his mother. And though she had created him and a trillion others, she decided to destroy their universe. Billions had fallen through the Abyss at the Shattering. Few had survived. Far fewer had fallen *twice*.

All that emptiness, Caleb thought, sitting up. *And the Creator had not enough room for us demons, even in the Abyss's farthest corners?* He spat into the ashes of the fire. *Curse her.*

Rana sat on a stone bench, awake. A hundred little waxen soldiers were arrayed on the bench beside her. *Was she up all night crafting them?* he wondered. Her creativity truly was insatiable. She looked exhausted.

Grug prepared their supplies, and Daniel, eager to move, helped him pack. But Daniel was pale and paused often to rub his blood-shot eyes.

"You need to eat," Caleb said, offering Daniel a strip of dried ox meat.

Daniel shook his head. "Maybe later."

Grug handed each of them a bag, and Marul said, "I can't believe I'm going outside! To smell fresh air again! To see the sky! I've forgotten what the sky looks like."

"The sky," Caleb said, "certainly hasn't forgotten you." She scowled at him as they left the chamber and entered tunnels covered with Marul's endless scratchings. Caleb felt smug knowing that none of Marul's spells had worked. His prison had held this powerful witch for five long years. He smiled to himself as they walked. To light their way, Grug kindled sconces high in the walls with his Mikulalim magic. "We'll be taking Kipod's Stair," Grug said. "It's the fastest way to the desert."

"A stair?" Marul said. "Here? I've searched these caves a thousand times. There's nothing but dust."

"You saw what you were supposed to see," Caleb said.

"Grug?" Marul said, turning. "You told me there were no connecting passages, that you traveled through the upper door that leads to the invisible steps."

"I'm sorry, mistress," Grug said. "I had my orders."

"You see Marul," Rana said. "Do you still believe this jailkeep is your friend? He held you under lock and key for five years."

Marul paused to catch her breath. "Grug is under a compulsion. Isn't that right, Grug?"

"I must obey Lord Ashmedai," Grug said. "He whom you call Caleb."

"You see, Rana?" Marul said. "You see? My Grug had no choice!"

"*My* Grug?" Rana mumbled. "Yes, I see clearly now."

Caleb saw it too—he should have guessed it sooner. In the long, empty hours in this cave, Grug and Marul had become quite a bit more than friends. This pleased him; it had proved just how far Marul had fallen from her days seducing young beauties by the dozen. There was no limit to how low Marul might go.

They entered a dark, unadorned room a dozen paces wide. A few worn containers lay heavy with dust and time. "Like the vanishing stair," Caleb said, "a spell here keeps the dust thick, the footprints hidden. Now kiss the floor."

"Excuse me?"

"You heard me. Kiss the floor. Did I not say that the exit was right under your nose?"

"My lips," Marul said, touching hers. She closed her eyes. "Ten thousand spells. Ten thousand rituals, incantations, and here my freedom waited, a stone's throw from where I slept."

"As it was meant to be," Caleb said.

Marul fell to her knees, swiped away a layer of dust, and kissed the floor. Like a giant sighing beast, a rift opened in the stone and a stale gust of air sprayed her hair. A black portal ground noisily open, a rectangular door in the stone floor. Marul stared wide-eyed into it.

"Oh, blessed Mollai," she said. "Giver of rain, it's beautiful."

"Kipod's Stair leads to Yarrow," Grug said. "The city of my brothers."

"And out to the sky!" Marul said.

"Yes, mistress."

Obsidian steps descended into darkness. Caleb grabbed a dusty torch from the wall and had Grug light it with three harsh words. The room brightened, and Caleb stood over Kipod's Stair, stale air blowing in his face.

The staircase itself was less than three paces wide. It spiraled into the dark, turning at vulgar angles. On the right an irregular wall followed the steps down. On the left, down the center of the turning stair, was a hollow pit, its bottom lost in shadow. There were no railings, no holds, and Caleb's torch, what weak light it cast, revealed only the first landing, a small platform fifty-five steps down.

"It's a precipitous descent," Grug said. "So stick to the walls. Do not look over the edge. If you grow dizzy, lean toward the walls, but do not touch them. They host a pernicious fungus. It attaches itself to the skin and will devour you over weeks."

"So why are we going this way?" Rana said.

Caleb stepped down into the darkness, illuminating further stairs. He had no time for hesitation. "Because this is the fastest way to the desert," he said. Marul followed him, eager. Then came Rana, Daniel, and finally Grug.

The torchlight made their shadows shiver along the walls as they descended. Marul and Daniel moved slowly, cautiously, but Rana moved quickly, unperturbed by the sheer drop. Mikulalim glyphs and their translations in Wul and Ytrian, greeted them at each landing, warning trespassers away with threats of dissection and slaughter. The echoes of their footfalls plunged into the deep, warning of what might happen if they lost their step and fell.

An animal suddenly moaned from the pit below. The moan rose in volume, until the walls resonated with the sound, as if they were inside a gigantic pipe organ.

"Goddess, what the hell is that?" Rana said.

"My kin," Grug said. "It is a warning."

"Against what?" Rana said. "I thought they're your brothers?"

"I've read the writing on the wall," Daniel said. "They feast on the organs of trespassers."

"Don't worry," Grug said. "We're not trespassing as long as the king is with us."

They continued their steep descent. Every fifty-five steps, the stairs turned sharply left, and after dozens of such landings, the effect was dizzying. Before the next landing, Rana screamed. A glistening swarm of black scorpions was racing up the stairs toward them. Their many pincers glowed in a thousand flickering shades of ultraviolet.

"Grug!" Caleb shouted. "Hurry, use your fire!"

But Marul had already stepped forward. She raised her hands and weaved a spell in the stagnant air. The black scorpions moved even more quickly.

"Stupid witch!" Caleb said. "You've made it worse!"

But the scorpions began bunching up at an invisible barrier, reaching for them in sped-up time. Their movement was a blur, and the animals soon lost their ultraviolet glow. They turned grey, then white, like burning wood becoming ash. And there the white creatures remained, inches from their feet, becoming a thousand scorpion-shaped piles of dust.

Marul lowered her hands.

Rana stepped closer, kicked the pile of dead scorpions. The pile collapsed to a fine powder that blew over the edge. "What did you do?" Rana said.

"I sped up the flow of time for them," Marul said, hands on her hips. "They died of old age, trapped inside their own bubble of time."

"How horrible," Daniel said.

"Horrible?" Marul said.

"They starved only inches from their food."

"I should let them eat you next time!" Marul snapped. "You should be more grateful! I just saved your damned life."

"Sorry," Daniel said. "Thank you, Marul."

"Don't thank her yet," Caleb said. "One problem has been replaced by another. Look at the walls." The landing where the scorpions had lived was now overgrown with giant lumps of fungus that hadn't been there minutes ago. Gray-green fungal shelves oozed from the wall in staggered, overlapping layers, blocking their descent.

"Not good," Grug said. "If we touch the fungus with even the barest scrape, it will explode, releasing dangerous spores. If they get in your lungs or touch your skin, they'll slowly digest you. It's a most painful death."

"Can we burn them?" said Daniel.

"No, they'll explode," said Grug.

"Then we'll just have to go around," Caleb said.

"Where? There's no room!" Marul said.

"There's plenty of room," Rana said, "near the edge. I've worked on ledges that had far less walking space than that."

"But you're a mason," Marul said. "I'm an old woman."

"Who just defeated an army of scorpions," Rana said. "You don't look so old from here."

Marul tossed back her hair with a hand and smiled. "Why, thank you, Rana."

"We have no choice," Caleb said. "We have to go forward."

"We could go back," Daniel said. "To the cliff."

"There's no time," Caleb said. "Come with me or rot here. It's your choice."

"Goddess help us," Marul said.

Caleb made the crossing first. He would show them they had nothing to fear. Up close, the fungus resembled moldy bread. Its surface was pitted, crusty and covered with pastel rainbows of dust. White crystals glimmered on its surface. His nose came within inches of it as he walked perilously close to the edge. Carefully, he made it to the other side.

"There!" he said. "See? It's easy."

Rana came next. She crossed the landing in three quick steps. How graceful she was! But Daniel was more timid. He skirted the edge slowly, and his hand nearly brushed the fungus.

"Daniel!" Marul said. "Watch your hand!"

"Quiet," Grug whispered. "Even a loud sound can release the spores."

Daniel made it safely across. "Now you, Marul," Caleb said. She took a deep breath and approached the fungus. Her movements were slow, awkward. She was short enough to avoid the tallest fungal shelves, but the waist-high ones were much too close.

"I can't go on," she said, frozen halfway across.

"You have to," Rana said.

"Come," Caleb said. "Your freedom awaits."

Her legs wobbled.

"Careful!" Caleb said, "Your arm—"

Marul slipped and fell. But Grug—with the speed of an insect—snatched her hand. Marul screamed. She dangled over the precipice, and only Grug's strength kept her alive. Caleb commanded Grug in the silent tongue, *Don't drop her! I will cut you to pieces if you drop her!*

The fungus above Marul shivered, threatening to pop. Grug, with Marul hanging from his arm, walked past the mold and deposited Marul safely on the far side.

Rana ran to Marul and hugged her. "Oh, thank Goddess!"

"Thank *Grug*," Caleb said. "He's the one who saved you."

"Thank me later," Grug said, "before this fungus decides to burst."

They continued their descent, turning and turning, down into that neverending darkness. Marul wheezed, while black circles, exacerbated by the shadows, grew under Daniel's eyes.

"You look tired," Caleb said. "Let's rest."

"How much farther?" Marul said, wiping sweat from her brow.

Grug glanced at a glyph carved into the wall. "One thousand and forty-five steps."

"So many?" she said, then shook her head. "No, I won't rest until I see the sky."

"Daniel?"

"Let's keep going," he said.

"You look tired," said Caleb. "You must eat."

"I'm fine."

He didn't look fine. He was pale and sickly and needed sustenance. The stubborn fool would learn soon enough. Caleb said,

"Very well. We continue." They continued their descent, their footfalls the only sound in the darkness.

"Grug," Marul said, "why didn't you tell me about Kipod's Stair? Is it because you were compelled to lie?"

In the silent tongue Grug asked Caleb, *May I answer her, my Lord?*

Caleb replied, *You may.*

"Yes, mistress," Grug said. "I was compelled to lie."

"Then I don't begrudge you for what you had no control over."

"That pleases me," he said.

"Tell me, did you use these stairs often?"

"Twice per day."

"Why so much?" she says.

"It was my duty as your caretaker to see you well."

"So many things I had you fetch for me! Candles! Meat! Water! And chalk! So much chalk! What a terrible burden that must have been, carrying those things up and down this dreadful staircase, day in and day out."

"As far as burdens go, mistress, walking Kipod's Stair is the least of mine. And if my king commands, I obey. It is useless to fret over something I have no power over."

"And what is the nature of his power over you, Grug?" Daniel said.

"It is the same power he has over all my kin. He is our king, and we are his servants."

"Does he have power over your mind?" Daniel said.

"I cannot disobey."

"Not even in thought?"

As they spoke, it struck Caleb that Daniel was speaking perfect Wul, and without an accent at that. It was a spell, for certain, yet something about it was still raw, unquickened.

Grug? Caleb asked in the silent tongue. *Did you give Daniel your curse while I lay unconscious?*

Yes, my Lord, Grug replied. *I was against it, but Marul insisted.*

Damn that witch, Marul! If Daniel became a Mikulal, he'd fall under Caleb's power. That might be helpful. But if the poison quickening in his blood meant Daniel was no longer a Lamed Vavnik, his plans would be ruined, and he'd never forgive Marul for that! He studied Daniel. *Are you still a Lamed Vavnik?* he thought. "Grug will die for me," Caleb said, "if I order him to." *And what will you do for me, Daniel?* he thought.

"He has no free will?" Daniel said.

"Of course he does," Caleb said. "He moves unmolested within his sphere of influence."

"But you control the boundaries of that sphere?"

"Grug's needs are met. And he is content, because he knows his place. How many people in this wretched Cosmos can say that?"

"*Are* you content, Grug?" Daniel said.

"Yes," Grug said.

"Are you sure?" Daniel said. "Or did Caleb order that response too?"

Something screamed from the pit below, as if a mammoth creature had just been speared in the dark. Another Mikulalim warning, and likely the last.

"Grug," Caleb said. "Tell them who it is that approaches Yarrow, so they may prepare."

"Yes, my Lord."

Grug took a deep breath, then let loose a deep bellow. The sound grew into a howl, then a shriek. His voice shook the walls. Dust from above rained on their heads, when Caleb remembered the fungus, hanging so precariously.

Rana was holding her ears. "Stop it!" Rana shouted. "Please, please, stop!"

"She is right!" Caleb said. "Stop now!"

Grug stopped wailing immediately, but the echoes lingered.

"That was the worst sound I've ever heard," Rana said. She looked as if she might be sick.

Caleb stared up, into the darkness from where they'd come. "So? Did it burst, Grug?"

"I'm afraid so, my Lord. I'm sorry. I had forgotten. Spores are raining down."

"How much time?"

"We should run."

CHAPTER THIRTEEN

THEY SPRINTED DOWN THE STEPS, AND AT EVERY LANDING Daniel peered up into the darkness. At the farthest reaches of Caleb's torchlight a faint cloud glimmered, like ashen snow. It was coming down.

Daniel panted as they descended. Marul was the slowest of them all, and they often had to wait for her to catch up. Caleb looked up at the cloud and said, "Will we make it Grug?"

"Marul!" Grug said. "You must walk faster!"

Caleb was still gazing up at the cloud when Rana leaped for him, knife drawn. She was quick, but Caleb was quicker. He spun away from her jab, Rana lost her footing, and she flew out over the edge—into the pit. She screamed and fell.

"No!" Caleb howled.

Rana shrieked, a horrid sound, as she plunged into the dark.

"Rana!" Marul screamed. "Ranaaaaaa!"

"Damn her!" Caleb said. "*Damn her!*"

Grug dropped to the ground and stuck his head over the edge. Above them the fungal cloud inched closer. Grug moaned so loudly that Daniel had to struggle to hold in his bowels. The walls rattled, dust shook free, and rained down after Rana.

"Rana!" Marul cried. "Ranaaaaaa!"

Grug kept moaning. The fungal cloud, gray and scintillating, roiled a hundred feet above. Sound waves rippled across its surface as it slowed, stopped. Grug kept up that horrid sound, and the cloud began to ascend back into the darkness. Daniel dreaded the other sound that he knew was coming. Rana splatting against stone. But it never came.

Rana's scream abruptly ceased. Grug stopped his dreadful sound. The echoes faded, and but for their sharp panting the air was quiet. Daniel felt sick with fear.

Marul faced Grug. "You saved her?" she said, shaking him. "Didn't you? *Didn't you?*"

Caleb pushed Marul away and grabbed the corpse-man. "Well? Does Rana live or not?"

"I'm not sure, my lord," Grug said, peering over the edge. "I hoped to cushion her fall with my voice. The shock may have knocked her unconscious, or . . ."

Marul tugged at her hair. "Oh, Rana . . ."

"You idiotic, impetuous, girl!" Caleb shouted over the edge. "You foolish, naive child! Why would you do such a stupid thing?"

"Goddess," Marul said, looking up, "Great Mollai, Giver of Rain and Succor, I beg you, bring Rana back to me! She's just a girl." Marul leaned over the pit and shouted, "Rana? Are you there? Can you hear me?" Only echoes returned. She turned and punched Caleb in the arm. "Beast! Vile demon! Why did you leap out of the way? Why did you let her die?"

"Instinct," Caleb said, letting Marul punch him. "She came for me and I just . . . it was not meant to happen this way."

Marul spat in his face. "Always your life above others! A knife wound for you is but a scratch to a human. You could have let her stab you!"

"I know," Caleb said, letting her spit dribble down his face. "I know."

"We need to move," said Grug. "I have pushed the spores higher, but they are falling again. I may have given us a few minutes, that's all."

"Rana," Marul said, rubbing her bloodshot eyes. "My Little Plum. Why did you come for me?" She stared at Caleb, and her murderous gaze slowly shifted to Daniel. He shivered and looked away.

They descended again, as quickly as before, and said little. In the silence, Rana's scream lingered in Daniel's mind. Every time he blinked, he saw the look on her face as she flew out over the edge.

Marul suddenly stopped. She turned to Daniel and said, "You're supposed to sustain worlds, and you couldn't even save one life?"

"I'm sorry," Daniel said. "If I could have, I would have saved her."

"Mistress," Grug said, "we have to go. The fungus is coming!"

Marul shoved a finger into Daniel's chest. "You just stood there. Did you know she was planning to stab him? Did she tell you last night? I know you saw her pick up the knife."

"No. No, I swear."

"Liar!"

"Mistress! Come!"

"I'll tell you why the Lamed Vav hide," Marul said. "It's because they're all cowards! Every one!"

Daniel hung his head, thinking, *And what secrets did you hide from Rana?*

Marul resumed her flight down the stairs, mumbling curses. Down they went, step after black step. Three times he caught himself looking ahead for Rana, only to recall with a pang of dread that she was gone.

Grug led them down, wary of the approaching cloud, when at last they reached the bottom of Kipod's Stair. Daniel thought they would see Rana's broken body here, but there was only a flat obsidian floor. It reflected the flickering torchlight, but curiously not their bodies. No crumpled mess lay here, thank God. Daniel sighed. Perhaps Rana was still alive.

"No blood!" Marul said. "So where has she gone?"

"I told them our king approaches," Grug said. "They may have . . . cleaned the space."

"Is she alive, Grug," Marul said, "or not?"

"We will find out soon enough."

Despite Gram raising him rigorously Jewish, Daniel wasn't religious. He saw too much misery in the world to put his faith in a "just" God. But he prayed for Rana anyway. It seemed like the right thing to do.

The fungal cloud dropped into the torchlight above their heads, rapidly descending. Grug shouted, "Hurry!" He beckoned them through an immense doorway and into a vaulted antechamber. He recited five words in a syllabic tongue that Daniel understood.

"The dead make no music."

Two mammoth stone doors began swinging closed, grinding as they moved. The fungal cloud hit the first landing, bounced, and rushed for them. The doors banged shut with a great clamor, but not before a trickle of dust slipped through the crack. The golden flecks twinkled as they approached, as fast as a running man. Grug leaned forward and sang a deep note, a sound like a chanting monk, when the cloud flew back against the wall and dropped like a pile of cigarette ash. At last, it was still.

They breathed a sigh of relief, and Daniel took in this huge antechamber. On the opposite side of the vaulted space was an enormous arched door, framed with translucent emerald blocks. The arch surrounded a dark void. The torchlight penetrated but a few feet in before dying. Grug entered the darkness, and they followed.

The air reeked of spoiled meat and dead animals and other foul things. As they walked the torch revealed blurred shapes in the dark. Things scuffed, scraped, and skittered like rats. Daniel felt a sudden urge to run. Whatever lay hidden in this cavern was not meant for human eyes. He steeled himself as they walked ever deeper into the dark.

The reek intensified as the torch revealed a swarm of shriveled faces, huddled together. Taut skin stretched over large skulls. Long, scarce teeth glistened with saliva. Yellow eyes peered from deep sockets. Wisps of white hair protruded from scabrous heads. Hands rested on sword hilts or on a brother's shoulder. Knuckles gnarled like ancient trees. Hundreds, maybe thousands of them amassed in the dark like rats.

One stepped forward. A geometric bronze emblem was pinned into to the leathered skin of his chest. It flashed in the torchlight. A crown of blood-red rubies adorned his head, winking maliciously in the firelight. He lifted a golden chalice, its smooth luster alien to this fetid place. He fell to one knee, bowed his head, and offered the chalice to Caleb.

Caleb took it, and black, syrupy liquid spilled from its rim. "My children," Caleb shouted, the delayed echo announcing the great distance to the unseen chamber walls. "Let my companions see you in your full glory."

Mutters of assent arose in the darkness. High in a distant wall, a sconce flashed to life. Then another was lit, and another, a circle of illumination, growing. The space grew bright, and Daniel shielded his eyes. The cavern was huge! A stone ceiling hundreds of feet high arced over their heads. The far walls were so distant they were fuzzy with haze.

"Behold," Caleb said, "The Mikulalim."

Ten thousand corpse-men thronged in serried ranks, filling the cavern. They overflowed into giant tunnels and wide avenues that led into darker places. Even more corpse-men crowded on tall bridges that spanned the avenues, leaned from a thousand terraced windows, or stood on gilded balconies. Caleb raised his chalice.

The entire throng—every last creature—took to one knee, a sound like a clap of thunder. Caleb drank heartily, and the black liquid dribbled from his lips. He lifted the chalice again, and they bowed their heads low.

The crowned one lifted his head and said, "Welcome to Yarrow, my lord. Our city is yours. Our blood is your blood."

Caleb's skin glowed, as if a candle burned inside him. He licked his lips. "Not as powerful as human blood, but a welcome meal, Havig."

"You drink the sacrifice of thousands, my lord."

"And what a good sacrifice it is. Havig, my friend, you look frail. Have you been eating?" Caleb chuckled, and the many thousands of corpse-men erupted in laughter. It was a wretched sound, like a million crows cawing. And when their laughter abated, and the air grew still, Daniel said to Havig, "Where is Rana? Have you seen the girl called Rana?"

"Yes," Havig said. "We have."

———

Her scream was the only thing in the whole world. Then it had stopped, everything had stopped—all but her heart, which hammered like chisel on stone.

Am I alive? she thought. *Or is this the netherworld?* She lay on her back. It didn't seem to be broken. *Breathe. Breathe.*

Except for her fear, she felt little pain. Perhaps the pain would come. She slowly opened her eyes. A dozen corpse faces stared down at her, a circle around her head, like the constellations of

Mazzaroth belting the night sky. Their eyes glowed as if candles burned within. Their presence should have frightened her, but she felt oddly calmed by their silent breathing. The chiseling of her heart slowed by degrees.

"I am Yig," one said, his voice like hide being stripped from flesh. "You are safe."

Yig's face came into focus. He looked much like Grug, but Yig's cheekbones were higher. A relation, perhaps?

"As a friend of the king," Yig said, "you are welcome in Yarrow." The others nodded and mumbled their agreement.

"King Jallifex?" she said, her voice hoarse from screaming.

"No, not that engorged human. I speak of our lord, King Ashmedai."

"Oh, you mean Caleb."

Yig shook his head. "In his presence, you must call him, 'My Lord.'"

They helped her sit up. "Never." She thought it best not to reveal how she'd just tried to kill their "lord." She rubbed her temples. "What happened?"

"Grug broke your fall with his voice. The sound knocked you unconscious. We brought you here to let you rest."

She felt sick as she remembered the hideous moment of freefall. While falling she'd had a vision. She was older—it was years from now—and her sister Liu was weeping at Rana's empty grave. The vision had been more horrific than her impending oblivion.

I almost let my sister grow up alone, she thought. *I abandoned her, without thinking.* But by some miracle, Goddess be praised, she had survived. Because of Grug, no less. Rana decided to rethink her hatred of the Cursed Man. "Where are the others? The people I was with?"

"The king and his companions have arrived in Yarrow. They are heading to the Lev as we speak. Mistress, drink this." He offered her a stone cup. A dark liquid sloshed inside.

"What is it?"

"A wine fermented from the fungus that grows in these caves."

"The same fungus that grows on Kipod's Stair?"

"You know the greyel?"

"Not by name. I thought it eats you from the inside out?"

"It does. But fermented, the greyel is medicine. Like all things, its nature is manifold."

She stared into the cup. If they'd wanted to kill her, she wouldn't be here. Plus it was rude to refuse a drink from those who'd given her succor. She took a sip. It was as bitter as kak root, but she felt her spirits lift. She took another sip as they watched.

Her head began to clear, and she examined her surroundings. She sat on a stone plinth in a circular chamber. The walls were black granite, with veins of obsidian and calcite. Torches burned in the four corners of the room. The orange-yellow light darted haphazardly about the room's odd angles, like furtive sparrows. Arching doors led off into other chambers.

"If you're well enough to walk, mistress," Yig said, "we'll escort you to the Lev. The king will meet us there."

"Does he know I'm alive?"

"He requested your presence as soon as you were able."

"I see," she said. Doubtful she would escape these caves without a map. Besides, Marul was still with Caleb. She had to return to them, rescue Marul, and take her home.

Yig gestured toward the door. "Our lord awaits."

She frowned, wiped dust from her tunic. "Let's go see your lord."

They entered a tunnel wider than the broadest streets of Azru. The two walked ahead, while the other Mikulalim followed a few paces behind. Torches along the walls blinkered to life with spell-laden whispers as they moved. From high, recessed windows shivered furtive shapes of Mikulalim peering down at them. The walls echoed the steely sounds of their desolation.

They walked through a labyrinth of crooked avenues. Stone stairs led into strange corners, buttresses bent at vulgar angles, and steep walls leaned oppressively over all. Distantly, a flute was piping some maddening, indefinite tune. She shivered and remembered the legends of the Black Chasm, of the Cursed One's dreadful bacchanals, whose music drove men to madness.

"What is this place?" she said.

"This is Yarrow, mistress. Our city."

"A city? How many of you live down here?"

"A hundred thousand Mikulalim, give or take."

More than twice the population of Azru. She shook her head in awe. "I've lived in Azru my entire life without knowing another city sits just under my own." What else, she wondered, was so close that she could not see it? She drank in the city with thirsty eyes, afraid to miss the littlest details.

Ornate stone bridges arced across the streets, doorways appeared in unexpected places, and corners met at unnecessary angles. At first the city seemed haphazard, random, but she began to sense a subtle artistry in it, a purposeful disjointedness. "My father taught me to set stones in a predetermined order, to know your destination before you begin. I hadn't realized that I could embrace chaos and still craft something marvelous."

"All things are born from chaos," said Yig.

"I don't see any joints or seams. Your stonework is incredible. How did you mortise the blocks so well?"

"There are no mortises. There are no seams."

"But that would mean—"

"Yarrow was not built like the cities in the sun, with stone piled upon stone. It was built by taking stone away."

"You *excavated* Yarrow?" She let loose a little yelp. She'd always assumed that art was crafted by combining simple forms to build complexity. "I've freed statues from marble and chiseled the Crypt of Umer out of the side of the DanBaer. But an entire city, loosed from stone? It's beyond words." Ideas for projects unfurled spectacularly in her mind.

The frenzied piping grew louder as they stepped into an enormous cavern. Rana stopped, struck by the gargantuan size of the space. Azru's tallest towers could fit inside this cavern with ease. Stalactites, wider than King Jallifex's palace, reached from ceiling to ground in obese columns. Strata of beige, magenta, amber and emerald marked the eons of their formation. These stalactites had been hollowed out, made into homes. Thousands of Mikulalim peered from many windows, parapets, and golden bridges, their glowing eyes affixed on her as she walked.

Torches and fire pits burned everywhere, making the gold and feldspar in the distant rock walls flicker like stars. Yig walked toward the largest of the stalactites, a colossal formation hundreds of paces wide. Perhaps a trick of the firelight, its surface looked soft and wet and seemed to throb with the grotesque music.

Though she searched, she could not find the source of that demented piping. A thousand eyes peered down at her, searching, hungry.

"Why are they staring at us?" she said.

"They stare at *you*, mistress."

"Me?" She slowed her pace and felt herself blush. "Why?"

"Because we are creatures of sound. We know a thousand languages, but music is our mother tongue. In you, we see ourselves reflected."

She stared at Yig's leathered face. "I'm not like you."

"No, not a Mikulal. But music animates your bones. We know who you are, Rana. Forgive me, but it's an honor just to walk with you."

So the Mikulalim know of me too? she thought. *But why do they know of me?* Was it because she could sing better than their demented flutist? King Jallifex had a hundred psaltists in his palace that could perform better than that madman. Did these Mikulalim revere those musicians as well?

They passed under a low-spanning bridge, and a crowd of Mikulalim leaned over its alabaster railings to watch them pass. "And what am I," she said, "that you know of me, when before today, I knew nothing of you?"

"You are not like the mass of humankind, Rana, who toil without purpose or mission. Your energies are directed. Your thoughts sublime."

Was he speaking of her art, her creations? "But *how* have you heard of me? I've never left Azru until yesterday."

"When you sing, Rana, the whole Cosmos listens. You are Gu."

Gu? Was this a term of respect, or something else? The masses were staring at her. She fixed her eyes on the granite path. It was thickly veined with gold, and they walked upon it as if it were common sand. How strange these people were who treaded upon gold!

They reached the base of the monstrous stalactite, and the mad piping exuded from its every orifice. "This is the Lev," Yig said. "The Heart of Yarrow."

The piping was not music so much as madness, a flurry of notes hurled at the abyss to stave it off. But its attempts were futile, as all attempts were.

A large doorway into the stalactite lay between two golden plinths. Their smooth surfaces reflected the firelight, playing devilish tricks with her eyes. She grew sleepy, watching the flames. Yig picked up a cedar branch from a stone bucket, lit it with magic, and they entered.

The air was rank with death and decay as they wended up the twisting stairwells. They trudged across honeycombed rooms decorated with leather tapestries and bone furniture. And Rana saw female Mikulalim within these rooms. Their bodies were as lean as the males, their breasts small and sagging. Long white hair flowed down their backs like drifts of sand. Some tied their hair into braids. They wore gold necklaces, hematite rings. From their large ears dangled amethyst gems. Like the men, their eyes flickered with subtle flames. But in the women these cold fires hinted of some unutterable desolation. She did not see any Mikulal children.

The piping grew louder as they ascended, and so did the pounding of her heart. What would Caleb do to her when she returned to him? She fought against her desire to run. She had to see Marul again, to free her of this dreadful place.

They entered a spacious chamber bedecked with gold. A raucous banquet was in progress, and many Mikulalim crowded the space. Five men played bone flutes, the source of that demented piping. Upon a checkered floor, tiled with blood jasper and smooth hematite, male and female Mikulalim danced sickening jigs.

The far side of the room lay open to the stalactite city, a great open-aired window, and a hot breeze blew in from the cavern. Giant tapestries on the wall fluttered in the steady gusts.

Her heart skipped when she saw Marul, Daniel, and Grug sitting at a long banquet table. Mikulalim pried them with dried meats and cups of wine. Only Grug indulged. At the center of this banquet table, on an immense golden throne, sat Caleb. His cheeks were stained with animal grease as he laughed and pointed at the twisting dancers.

"My lord," Yig announced, his voice almost buried under the music. "I present to you the Gu, as you requested."

Caleb abruptly stood, raised his hand. The piping stopped. The dancers froze in mid-jig. Everyone turned to Rana, and her face grew hot.

"'Who is that,'" Caleb said, "'who, without death, goes through the kingdom of the dead?'"

"Hello again," Rana said.

"My Little Plum!" Marul shouted. She leaped from her seat, ran around the table, and embraced Rana. "Blessed Mollai!"

They hugged, and Rana didn't want to let go. Daniel, smiling, came over to welcome her back. He took her hand, squeezed it. "I'm happy you're all right. You scared us pretty good."

The demon king sauntered over, and his servants followed him like hungry dogs. "Do you want something to eat?" Caleb said.

"I'm not hungry." She stared into Caleb's moon-white eyes, searching for malice, but found only an unexpected compassion.

"Had a little slip there, did we?" He wiped his mouth with a leather napkin, then let it fall. A servant caught it before it hit the floor. "One must be mindful, when walking the Stair."

"I'll try to remember that next time I travel it."

He put his large hands on her shoulders and peered deeply into her eyes. He was huge, bigger than Papa, and his presence was unexpectedly soothing, just like when Papa used to put his arms around her when she got sad. She hated herself for linking the memories, because how could she take comfort from the monster who had locked away her best friend? Was this part of his magic? But she couldn't find the strength to pull away from him.

"Rana," Caleb said. "I feared you were gone forever." His voice resonated inside her chest. She closed her eyes. Damn, why did he have to be so soothing? "The Cosmos would have mourned your loss. There are none like you in all the Shards."

A Mikulal approached the king. A curious metal brooch of interlocking shapes was pinned in the flesh of his chest. A gold crown with glittering rubies sat crookedly on his head. "We are deeply honored by your presence, my lord. Your servants have but one request, if it pleases the king."

"Yes, Havig?"

"We wish to hear the Gu sing."

That word, again, Rana thought. *Gu.*

"She will not!" Marul snapped. "We'll have none of that!"

"None of what?" Rana said. "Song?"

Caleb smiled, revealing his large and healthy white teeth. "Would you deny our gracious hosts the pleasure of your voice, Rana?"

Marul grabbed Rana's wrist and squeezed hard. "Rana, you don't want this. Trust me."

Rana recalled the hungry gazes of the Mikulalim on her walk to the Lev. "I don't understand. What's so special about my music?"

"When you sing," Havig said, "for a short time, we forget our pain."

Murmurs of assent spread throughout the room.

"You've heard me before?"

"As I told you," Yig said. "When you sing, the whole Cosmos listens."

The Mikulalim stared at her. Eons of suffering hung heavy on their faces.

"Grug," Caleb said, "what say you? Do you desire Rana's song?"

"Yes, my lord. Very much. But only if the Gu wishes it."

"So," Caleb said, "would you deny the one who saved your life?"

Their gaunt, eager faces surrounded her. "I suppose not," she said. "I don't see the harm in one song, if it makes them happy."

Marul squeezed her wrist even harder. "Rana, you've no idea what you are saying!"

"What's wrong with singing? What happens if I sing?"

"Something profound," Caleb said. "You'll discover who you really are."

Rana was trembling. "And what am I?"

Caleb smiled. "A little goddess."

"Only a girl!" Marul said. "Just a girl. Rana, please. Don't."

Rana yanked her hand from Marul's grasp. "I'm not a girl anymore, Marul. I make my own decisions now, and I choose to sing for these Mikulalim."

Marul turned her gaze up to the ceiling. "By the Goddess, why does she not see?"

Caleb clapped his hands in anticipation. "She will see," he said. "Who she is."

Havig gave Rana a broken-toothed smile. "Please give us a moment to prepare." He walked toward the open-aired side of the chamber that peered out at the cavern. A stone ledge extended several paces beyond the walls, a black terrace with no railings. Two golden plinths, like the ones at the door below, reflected the firelight in curious dancing waves. She stared at them, mesmerized.

Havig stepped onto the ledge and chirped several staccato notes. His echo returned moments later, amplified by a thousand walls below.

"Goddess," Rana said. "The echo!"

"This is our Pedestal of Lamentation," Havig said. "There is no better place to sing in all of Gehinnom." His voice fanned out gloriously over the city.

"You want me to sing *out there*?"

"We want you to sing to all the people of Yarrow, mistress."

The Mikulalim in the chamber were hurriedly sitting themselves in concentric circles. They made complex gestures with their hands, then bowed heads to floor, over and over, their murmuring like wind against the DanBaer.

"I can't sing for a whole city," she said.

"Of course you can," said Caleb. "Let Yarrow hear you, Rana. And for the first time, you might truly hear yourself as well."

"What am I," Rana said, "that others know of me before I know of them? What is it about my songs that travel to places I've never been?"

"Sing," Caleb said. "And you will know."

Marul was shaking her head, Daniel was staring, and the Mikulalim were chanting. She stepped out onto the Pedestal of Lamentation and gazed down. Many thousands of Mikulalim filled the interstices below. More were pouring in from adjoining tunnels.

"What should I sing?" she said.

"Anything, mistress," Havig said. "Anything at all."

Her legs felt weak. What if she disappointed them? What if her voice broke? What if this was a demon's trick? But she had to know what she was.

She cleared her throat, and a note slipped out of her unbidden, as if it had waited eons for her to open her mouth so it might fly away. Its echo returned moments later, amplified by its journey across the cavern. Goddess, it seemed as if this place had been made for music. Even the susurrus of her breath was carried to the far reaches of the cavern and beyond. If her songs in Azru had resounded through the Cosmos, how far, she wondered, would her music travel here?

She took a deep breath and began.

A note flew from her mouth, a bird spreading wings. It lofted in the air, free. It swooped past the distant walls, dived into the tunnels, spinning and frolicking as it traveled. It whooshed over the masses of Mikulalim, down Yarrow's crooked streets and around its odd corners. It flew up Kipod's Stair, circled Marul's prison before escaping through the emerald door. It climbed up the invisible stair, hopped over the Fires of Korah, and leaped past the lizards of Old Stone on the top of the DanBaer. It raced down the mountain path to the heart of Azru. It skipped through the city streets like a she-camel, turned at the four stone lions in Dusty Square, and raced toward home. It slid under the door-frame, rattled the hanging pots, shook the clothing on Mama's lines. It slunk into the bedroom to curl itself snugly around baby Liu's ear. The Little Bean opened her eyes and giggled. "Rana!" Liu said.

And all this from the first note! When she began the second, she felt as if all of Gehinnom were listening. The Mikulalim stared, slack-jawed. They were extensions of her body now, invisible sinews connected to her. With the third note she thought that if she wished it, the masses would drop to their knees. With a fourth note they did just that. The clap of their kneeling made the Lev shudder. With a fifth note, a surge charged through her, a stampede of oxen in her blood. She was inexplicably and terribly aroused, filled with a sexual urge greater than any she'd known. Because she felt it, everyone felt it too. Whatever consumed her while she sang dove deep into their ears and wrapped around their brains, wringing out all other thoughts. Anything at all that she wished, they would do.

And this was all so utterly wrong. *No one*, she thought, panicking, *No one should ever have such power!*

She stopped in mid-note. Her voice lingered in the cavern, afraid to vanish. Eventually, it faded. The women were weeping. The men held their chests and bowed. Marul's pupils were wide and dark.

Daniel's mouth hung open, drool falling from his lips. The white of Caleb's eyes shone like winter moons.

Caleb blinked awake and applauded. The sharp sound broke the spell. As everyone awoke, murmurs filled the room. Jumbled voices floated up from below the ledge.

"I have never, in my long existence," Caleb said, "been treated to such aural bliss. Rana, you have outdone even the Creator herself."

"Praise the Gu," Havig said, bowing. "Praise the Gu, forever."

Rana felt so weak she thought she might fall. The energy that had surged through her seemed to vanish like water down a basin drain. "I need to go," she said. She was still on the Pedestal. Her voice spun out over Yarrow for small eternities. The masses nearly fell into a trance again. "I need to go. Now."

Great Goddess Mollai, she thought, *I'm a monster. A demon like Caleb. Or something worse.* Marul rushed to her, took off her cloak, and placed it over Rana's shoulders.

"Come, Little Plum," Marul said. "Let's leave this accursed place."

Rana let Marul lead her down the twisting stairs of the Lev and out into the hot air of the vaulted cavern. "I warned you," Marul said, holding Rana close.

"What am I, Marul?"

"You are Rana Lila, my Little Plum."

"But not only. I'm something else."

"You've been given a precious gift. But you've always known that, haven't you?"

"I felt . . . something." She dared not voice its dreadful magnitude, which like a sandstorm came to swallow her. "Am I a demon?"

"No! The furthest from it. What you felt is Caleb's cunning and the eagerness of a million cursed people to end their suffering. Their emotions were as much of that experience as yours. Don't let it confuse you! That's not what you are. When we leave these tunnels, you run straight home to your parents, to your baby sister, Liu. I will survive. I always have. This world of demons and shadows isn't yours. You're not meant for all this."

And for the first time in her life, Rana agreed with that sentiment.

The others spilled quietly out of the Lev, led by Caleb and Havig. A crowd of Mikulalim formed around her, but kept their distance. They stared at her as if she were a precious gem.

"We leave *now*, Caleb!" Marul said.

"Calm yourself, witch," said Caleb. "First, Havig has something for our treasured guest."

Havig approached her. Rana flinched as he held up a silver chain, its small links sparkling in the light. On its dangling pendant, Rana recognized the symbol from Havig's chest. A triangle inside a square, inside a circle, inside another triangle. The pattern repeated, a receding tunnel of concentric shapes. At its center was a scintillating eight-pointed star of yellow stone. The shapes seemed to breathe as the pendant spun, left and right. A hole remained on Havig's chest where the pin had been.

"Take this gift," Havig said, "in return for yours. It is not nearly as great as that which you have given us, but it is the greatest thing we possess."

"What is it?" Rana said.

"Protection," Havig said. "You have given us, however brief, a respite from our daily hell. For that we are eternally grateful. This pendant was one of a small number given to us by Azazel, who lies chained in Dudael, beyond the Mountains of Darkness. It will protect you from harm and hide you from evil. Wear it, and we will rest easy, for we know the Gu is safe."

He took her hand and placed the necklace inside her palm. Rana nodded her thanks, then Marul led her away. "Caleb," Marul said. "*Let's go!*"

"Havig," Caleb said. "Alas, the witch is correct. It's time for us to leave Yarrow."

"We regret to part with your glorious company, my lord," Havig said. "As you've requested, I have provided ten of my best men. They know the tides of the sands and the habits of its creatures. They will see you across the desert to the Quog Bedu. We've given you supplies for three weeks. May you reach your destination long before then, my lord."

Ten Mikulalim stepped forward. Swords hung from their loose-fitting belts. Together they hauled four black trunks, large as coffins. Grug and Yig, Rana saw, stood among them.

"The loyalty of the Mikulalim," said Caleb, "will be rewarded when our task is done. This I vow by Great Abbadon."

The throng took to their knees and bowed to their king. Then they turned and bowed to Rana, and in a flash she was back on the Pedestal, the sickening power coursing through her blood. She felt the need to sing again, to command their minds and make them dance.

Dance, puppets! Dance! she thought. She closed her eyes. *No, no! This was sickness! It had to stop!* She pulled Marul close, and buried her head in Marul's bosom like a child.

Marul patted her. "It will all be over soon, Rana." Then she said, "Caleb, I beg you, let Grug stay in Yarrow"

"But Grug wishes to join us," Caleb said.

"By compulsion?"

"By his own choice, Marul, and you know it."

"Grug," she said, "you must remain here. It will be dangerous."

"I do not fear my death as much as I fear yours," Grug said.

"You never know when to turn away, do you?"

"And you never know when to be quiet."

She sighed. "A truer statement has never been uttered." She took Rana's hand. "Come, child, it's time to go."

They walked toward the gold-flecked cavern wall, where a narrow tunnel led into the rock. Rana clasped Havig's necklace. The metal was cool and soothing in her palm. She wanted to throw it away, to forget this place. But she found herself slipping the chain into her pocket.

They entered the tunnel. Quickly, the light grew dim as Yarrow vanished behind them. They turned through narrow tunnels, led by a taut-muscled Mikulal carrying a torch. From the distance, growing louder with each step, came a deep, resonant throb, as if she were hearing the DanBaer's slow-beating heart.

"What is that sound?" she said.

"The sand break," said Grug. "Waves of sand flow in from the Tattered Sea and break against the mountainside."

A point of light appeared ahead, its brilliance alien to this dark place. With a start Rana realized this distant star was daylight. She longed to bask in the sun, to escape these bleak walls of stone. And if she felt this after just one day, what was Marul feeling after five long years?

Marul squinted into the light, her pupils smaller than mustard seeds. Daniel stepped up beside them both.

"Yesterday Grug cut off his tongue and force-fed it to me," Daniel said, looking especially pale. "From what I gather, this is so I could understand your language, Wul."

Marul stared at the light. "Hm? Oh, yes, that's correct."

"Grug's people are the Mikulalim," Daniel said. "In Heebroo, that means 'cursed.'"

"Yes," Marul said.

"Will I . . ." He paused. "Does that mean I—"

"I didn't know who you were, Daniel," Marul said, eyes fixed on the exit ahead.

"But you didn't answer my question. Will I become—"

"Enough!" she snapped, "I haven't seen daylight in five years! Can't you let me enjoy this moment in peace?"

Daniel frowned. "I guess. Sorry." He walked on ahead toward the Mikulalim, until he was out of earshot.

"Grug gave him the Mikulalim curse," Rana whispered to Marul. "Daniel will become one of these Cursed Men, won't he?"

Marul stared into the light, and the green of her eyes brightened by shades. "I thought he was just another fool from Earth, a nobody, in over his head."

"But he's not, is he? He is a Lamed Vavnik, a pillar of the Cosmos. But if he's cursed, what does that mean? Can he still hold up the world? Will he fall under Caleb's thrall, like Grug and all his people?" *As they nearly fell under mine?* she thought with a sickening twist of her belly.

"I don't know. He's not yet a Mikulal. But his desire for human flesh will grow to consume him. And when he finally tastes it, his quickening will be complete. Then the curse is irreversible. But if he doesn't taste human flesh, he will remain a man. Mostly."

"But if you knew this would be his fate, why would you do that to him?"

"Because, Rana, I've been locked in this mountain for years! You've no idea what that has been like! You came with a promise of freedom, and I needed answers. What was I to do?"

"Grug protested," Rana said, "Now I see why. It's because you asked him to poison an innocent man!"

"Oh, hush, child," Marul said. "When you're locked in a cave for five years, *then* you can judge! This is my moment of freedom. Let me enjoy it."

Rana gazed at the woman beside her. Her natty hair, wild eyes, and soiled clothes. Imprisonment had changed Marul, and not for the better. Daniel, glanced back at them. He must have known they were speaking of him. His eyes were sunken, his skin pasty. Would this pillar of the Cosmos soon become a walking corpse man? Marul had condemned him to a life of hell and seemed to care not one bit.

CHAPTER FOURTEEN

WHEN LIGHTNING STRUCK THE BLACK CLIFFS OF ABBADON, ITS thunder echoed for hours as it wound its way through the folds of stone. In the same way Rana's voice resounded in Caleb's heart. How glorious was her music! How sublime was her sound! She had tasted the power; Caleb had felt its surge. The poor girl had lived her entire life in a cage the size of a city, and for the first time she glimpsed the immensity beyond its walls. No wonder she cowered now. But his little fledgling bird would soon overcome her fear and spread her wings.

The cave mouth approached, and the desert blinded them with daylight. His Mikulalim servants donned heavy black cloaks woven from human hair. The cloaks concealed their faces under large hoods. They slid on gloves of brown human leather. They checked each other for absolute concealment. Without such protections, the sun would draw what little moisture they had from their bodies and leave them as desiccated lumps of living tissue.

Light shone from the opening a hundred paces away. Grug, in the silent language, reminded Caleb to warn the others of the sand break. Rana and the humans quickened their pace, their shadows long and shrinking in the tunnel.

A sand wave crashed against stone. The walls rumbled, and for a moment daylight vanished behind the wall of sand. A rush of air blew through the tunnel, and the party paused.

In the silent tongue, Grug said to Caleb, *Please, my lord, instruct them now. Marul will be slow.*

Grug, Caleb replied, *this place you have in your heart for the witch will be your demise.*

Grug stared at Caleb. *You may be right, my lord*, Grug said. *But it's not a choice.*

Caleb said aloud, "There are always choices, Grug." He turned to face his human companions. "Rana, Daniel, Marul, listen to me! The sand recedes as I speak. Soon it will reach its trough. Things will appear calm as we reach the cave mouth. Do not let the serenity deceive you. We have nine minutes to reach the far side of the break, a thousand paces away. You must run. If you don't reach the far side in time, the next wave will swallow you alive. There is no margin for error."

The humans eyed him gravely.

"Wait until Grug gives the word," Caleb said. "If you venture out too soon the undertow will suck you under."

They approached the opening. The bright daylight split into three shades. Blue sky, orange sand, and the brown shadow of the DanBaer.

Marul stared at her freedom. "Oh my," she said. "Oh my."

They waited at the cave mouth. Below them a steep hill of dark stone sloped down to the sand. Sharp, thin columns spiked up from the rock like stony swords. The sand hissed as it receded down the slope, leaving behind remnant puddles of orange dust.

"Seconds, my lord," Grug said.

"Prepare yourselves!" Caleb shouted.

"Wait." Grug said. "Wait . . . *Now!*"

They burst from the cave mouth and leaped onto the black stone as sand slithered down its steep bank. Marul, Rana and Daniel slipped and stumbled as they weaved between the knife-edged columns, while the Mikulalim, laden with cargo, descended easily over the terrain.

"Hurry!" Grug shouted as he reached the sandbank. Caleb followed close behind, but the humans were timid and lagging.

"Ignore the damned rocks!" Caleb shouted. "What's a small cut if you're buried under sand?" Marul stared at the sky, mouth agape. "Marul, you witch! Enjoy the fucking view later!"

She nodded and shuffled down, while Daniel and Rana helped her descend.

"Marul is too slow," Grug said. "Always too slow. I'm going back for her."

"Do it," Caleb said, "and hurry!"

Grug ran up the steep cliff, while the other Mikulalim dropped the heavy containers to the sand and began tugging them forward with heavy straps. The trunks left deep furrows behind them as they went. Grug shoved Rana and Daniel out of the way and hoisted Marul onto his shoulder. The witch shouted as Grug leaped with her down the black slope.

"Leap over the sandbank!" Grug shouted to Rana and Daniel. "It will suck you under if you step on it!"

Timidly, Rana and Daniel jumped over the slowly rising bank.

Grug, Marul on his shoulders, stopped when he reached Caleb. "We're too slow!" he said.

Caleb shouted to the Mikulalim dragging trunks, "You two! Go fetch the stragglers!"

"But what of the trunks?" one of them said.

"Leave them!"

Obeying, the two Mikulalim abandoned their cargo. Rana yelped as they hoisted her up. Daniel seemed no happier.

"You two!" Caleb shouted. "Grab the trunks!"

Two other Mikulalim, already pulling trunks of their own, paused beside the abandoned cargo and doubled their load. Their pace slowed dramatically with the added weight.

They all pressed on toward the dune at varying speeds. Time was not in their favor, but the fresh air brought new life to Caleb. The warm sun kissed his skin. The dune's crest rose into the sky, a massing tidal wave of orange sand. The ground groaned like rending metal.

Grug ran beside Caleb, Marul on his shoulder. She was gazing up at the sky.

"How long?" Caleb said.

Grug's face was hidden under his cloak as he looked first at the mountain and then at the rising dune. "Three minutes," he said.

The first Mikulal crested the dune and vanished over the far side. The sand shook as it pushed them skyward. A second Mikulal crested the dune, then a third. They vanished on the other side. The two carrying Rana and Daniel leaped over the edge to safety.

"Marul!" Rana shouted, her voice muffled by the wall of sand.

Grug and Caleb paused at the dune crest. Grug let Marul down and she stumbled down the slope toward Rana.

Behind them, the rising sands had almost obscured the mountainside. "Under a minute, my lord," Grug said. The ground beneath them heaved ever upward. Soon the dune would break. But the two Mikulalim carrying double trunk loads were hundreds of paces from safety. One was ahead of the second, but not by much. The furthest one suddenly dropped his straps and began sprinting for the dune.

"What in Abbadon is that creature doing?" Caleb said.

"My lord," Grug said, "if he doesn't run, he'll die!"

"Stop!" Caleb shouted to the man. "Go back and fetch those trunks!" The desert air muffled Caleb's voice, but the Mikulal had heard him, because he stopped running and looked back at the trunks.

"My lord," Grug said. "Please!"

"We need those supplies, Grug."

"Do we, my lord?"

"Go!" Caleb shouted. "I gave you an order!"

The Mikulal bowed to Caleb, to all of them. It was slow and deliberate. Then he turned and ran for the two trunks. The dune crest rose so quickly that Caleb grew dizzy.

"My lord, let me help him!" Grug said.

"No, Grug. You stay here."

"But my lord, Yig is my—"

"Shut up, Grug!"

The Mikulal reached the trunks, picked up the straps, and began dragging them.

"Pull! Puuuuuull!" Grug shouted, his voice desperate, despairing.

The dune surged beneath them. They had to move. "Forget him," Caleb said. "He's lost."

Grug hesitated. The dune was about to overtake them, so Caleb yanked Grug toward the safe side of the break. They fell down the slope and came to rest on their backs. Behind them, a monstrous wave of sand lurched toward the mountain. It smashed against the rocks with a great clamor, sending up a huge spray of dust. And when the noise abated, and the sands receded, there was no sign of Yig or his cargo.

"Why, my lord?" Grug said. "Why did you order Yig to die?"

"He abandoned his cargo," Caleb said. "His one and only task." To the other Mikulalim Caleb said, "Let Yig's sin be remembered by all. Such shall be the punishment for anyone who abandons his duties."

Grug turned his hooded face toward Caleb. Perhaps it was a reflection, but the light in Grug's eyes was as bright as a bonfire. "My lord," he said, "Yig was my brother."

Caleb wiped sand from his robe. "Then let it be known that my judgment is not biased toward those who believe their proximity to me incurs special favor."

Marul bounded toward him. In the full light of the sun her wild gray hair glistened with a half-decade of grease. "The demon shows his true colors!" she spat. "You sent that man needlessly to his death!"

"Is this how you thank me for your freedom?" Caleb said.

"Freedom?" she said. "I would have remained in that cave forever if I knew it would have spared Yig's life!"

Caleb laughed. "What a joke! Is this little show of compassion for Rana's behalf? You can stop your sanctimony, witch. I know who you really are."

"You're a beast!"

"Not the worst that I've been called." The sun beat on his face, hotter by the second. "Grug, have your men hand out water bladders to everyone. Make sure the humans drink often. Now, tell me, which way to the Bedu?"

Grug stared at Caleb for a long moment. If there was malice in the gaze, he hid it well. Grug glanced up at the sun, then at the DanBaer. Another sand wave rose to shield the mountain, crashed into it, and threw up sheets of sand. Quietly, Grug said, "The Bedu use the tides as birds use wind. In this season, the tides flow to the northwest." He pointed deep into the desert.

Caleb strode past Marul, past Rana and Daniel, past the Mikulalim and their trunks, and began walking northwest. "Let's move," he said. "We've a long trip ahead of us."

"You're forgetting our deal," Marul said. "We take Rana back to Azru first."

Caleb turned to face Grug, and in the silent tongue, he said, *Rana cannot leave me, Grug. I need her. You mustn't let her out of your sight. Do whatever it takes to keep her here.*

Yes, my lord, Grug responded.

"She cannot get to Azru from here," Grug said.

"Why the hell not?" Rana said. "Azru's just on the other side of the DanBaer. I can see the city's dust beyond the western peaks."

"To safely reach Azru," Grug said, "You must approach via the traders' route, a full parasa from here. Otherwise you'll be swept into the desert."

"Is this true?" Marul said to Rana.

"I don't know," Rana said. "Maybe. I don't know the currents on this side of the DanBaer. I know there are strong currents on the other side."

"Then take us to the traders' route," Marul said, squinting in the light.

"When we reach that corridor, mistress, I'll inform you."

"Will you, Grug?" Marul said.

Grug glanced at Caleb and said, "I will, Marul."

Why do you love her, Grug? Caleb said in the silent tongue. *She'll betray you when it suits her, just as she betrayed the Cosmos.*

You and I see things differently, my lord, Grug said.

You were just a blanket to keep her cunt warm in the dark. Now that she's in the sun, watch how quickly she discards you.

You are my lord, Grug said, *and I shall obey you. But you are not our rightful king. Our true master lies chained in Dudael, bound upside down beyond the Mountains of Darkness. You are only a placeholder king.*

Grug's words were meant to barb. They might have even been a death wish. Caleb—Ashmedai—and his brother Azazel hadn't spoken in centuries. Caleb only ruled the Mikulalim now because Azazel had lost the throne in a bet a long time ago. One day, the Mikulalim secretly hoped, Azazel would command them again.

You're angry, Grug, Caleb said, *so I'll forgive you your outburst. But I'll have you know, I plan to liberate your bound king.*

Grug gave him a surprised look.

Yes, Grug. With your help I plan to free the Mikulalim as well. If I succeed, one day soon you will walk in the sun without need of a cloak. You will become a whole man again.

And you, my lord? If you succeed, what will you become?

Caleb looked into the deep desert and smiled.

<hr />

The sun was an oppressive yellow ball that taunted Daniel with every step. The sands smelled of baked cement, and every now and then, cinnamon. Was it from Yarrow? From Azru? Elsewhere? Daniel sipped water, knowing this bladder had to last days. The gnawing in his stomach had vanished, replaced by an impossible fatigue.

Yig, he thought. *Poor, helpless Yig.* Caleb was taking them deeper into the desert. Was he the only one who could save Earth? He hadn't even given Grug time to mourn his dead brother. And still Grug walked steadfast beside his king. Was he even allowed to feel?

As they headed northwest over the shifting sands, the DanBaer plateau receded. Swirling smoke rose from an adjacent canyon, the one that burned beside the invisible stair. Specks of windblown ash tumbled in the air. In all other directions rolled an undulating sea of orange sand. Mammoth dunes lumbered across the desert, lifting the party up, dropping them stories. Daniel was always dizzy, and whenever he looked back, the mountains were not where he expected them to be.

Grug and Caleb led on, and Marul gazed at the sun, pausing often to sigh. The black-robed Mikulalim crept behind the party, hooded like a mass of grim reapers. The only sound was the slithering of the trunks across the sand, the occasional gust of wind.

The Mikulalim seemed to be watching him, though he couldn't see their eyes under their hoods. He felt as if they had been walking straight, but the furrows behind the trunks weaved like a drunkard's path.

"You're wavering," Rana said. She wore a curiously patterned scarf over her head, interwoven with lines of crimson, yellow, and blue in fractal-like complexity. Another one of her creations? "Have you drank?" she said.

"*Buckets*," he said in English.

"Huh?" She sidled up to him. "Daniel, tell me about your Earth."

"What do you want to know?"

"Are there cities?"

"Many."

"What do they look like?"

"They're all different."

"What are the buildings made of?"

"Wood, concrete, and metal, mostly."

"Which metals? Bronze? Copper? Hematite?"

"*Steel*, mostly."

"Stee-ul?"

"An alloy of iron. Super strong. They use it to build towers over a hundred stories tall. The biggest cities are filled with them. We call them sky scrapers."

"Because they scrape the sky." She stared up at the cloudless blue. "Yes."

"Daniel," she said, moving closer, "do you really think you're going back to Earth?"

"I sure as hell hope I am."

"I miss my parents, my sister so much. But I keep thinking, if I go home, I'll never get to see your Earth. I'll never get to see another world."

"I have family back home too." He thought of Gram, waiting for him. And Rebekah? She was still family too. "If I could go back this instant, I would."

"Oh, I still want to go home," Rana said. "*Eventually*."

A train of wild camels, nearly the same orange shade as the desert, crested a dune. Hundreds of them sped past the party, stirring up a huge cloud of dust. Everyone stopped to watch, and the scene was breathtaking. And then, as fast as they'd come, the camels vanished over another dune. The dust settled, and all was quiet again, save for the whistling of the dunes as they crept across the desert, like wind over glass bottles.

"Yesterday, you were an ordinary man," Rana said. "And today you're a Lamed Vavnik."

"It's still hard to accept."

"Yesterday, I was a mason," Rana said. "And today . . ."

"What are you?"

"A Gu, they called me."

"Your music," Daniel said. "It was . . . *intense.*" The feelings had overwhelmed him, as if he had taken bad acid or had smoked weed laced with chemicals. His ego had shattered, and what was left was a conscious thing, aware but without will. And Rana's voice—her energies—had stuffed that void. Daniel, in that moment, had ceased to be himself and had become part of something greater. The feeling was terrifying and wonderful. Total liberation, but also death. He wasn't sure if he wanted to experience that again.

"Did you feel . . . my power?"

He shivered, trying to suppress the memory. A rush of emotions shuddered through him, pleasurable and terrible and total. With all this new knowledge, his sense of self was fragile enough as it was. But with Rana's prodding, his psyche teetered toward dissolution.

She must have sensed this, because she said, "I'm sorry, Daniel. Don't answer that. If it was anything like what I felt, it couldn't have been pleasant."

"No," he said. "Parts of the experience were amazing. But it was like having my soul erased and replaced by, well, a tidal wave of emotion. I felt your spirit, Rana. It was a force emanating from you like . . . like heat from the sun. Intense and inescapable."

Rana let slip a nervous laugh. "And to think that had I listened to my mother I'd be setting yet another row of stone on the Ukne Tower at this moment, oblivious to all this."

Marul was walking a distance ahead when she stopped and shouted, "Look, Rana! Look!"

Four narrow stone towers peeked up past the western edge of the DanBaer, their tops sparkling in the sun. Hazy with dust, a nest of jumbled buildings bulged from the mountain base. He recognized the view from when he and the dog had approached it.

"Azru!" Marul said. "Oh, beautiful, lovely Azru! How you've grown!"

"Do you see the three eastern-most towers?" Rana said. "The one with the minaret and the two with the connecting bridge?"

"I do!" said Marul.

"I built those," Rana said. "Not alone, of course. But I added my own designs. The amethyst and quartz inlay was my idea."

"Oh, they're splendid! Marvelous and splendid, Rana!"

Though Azru had frightened him before, Daniel missed the comfort of its walls, the shade of its roofs, its edible fruits.

Rana sighed. "Mama's probably setting Liu down for a nap right now. Papa's probably sitting by the window watching the Ukne rise, cursing Jo's ineptness. They're probably worried about me. But I've gone off like this before. And I always come home."

Daniel thought on what Rana had said. "Rana, there's your home," he said. "Go to it."

The jeweled city flashed in the sunlight, wavering. When he squinted, Azru and its towers resembled a woman, in a vague way. The mountain became her curving bust. The jeweled domes became her shimmering hair. The woman swayed in the heat, a slow dancer gliding closer. He blinked his eyes, and the vision grew sharper.

The figure drifted closer, a pale-skinned goddess, naked, her long black hair almost blue in the sun. A pearlescent cape fluttered behind her, attached to a white band at her neck. A golden metal band wrapped her waist and shone with solar reflections. She reached for him, and the sky turned wine-dark, a night without stars. She glowed as bright as the moon as she approached, and he knew her.

Rebekah!

She drifted toward him. "Danny!" she moaned, her voice faint, torn into shreds of sound. Tears poured from her eyes, and they turned to shards that floated into the purple sky. "Where are you, Danny? Where have you gone, my love?" Her eyes searched but could not find him.

"Rebekah!" he shouted, but his voice made no sound. "Rebekah, I'm here!"

Wolf-like, her head snapped toward him, a beast pointing toward its prey. Her pupils dilated, grew huge, as she found his eyes. Her brown eyes, swirling with green, were an autumnal forest. Each was enormous, a banded Jupiter across the sky. Lips the size of universes floated up to his ear. She whispered, "Where are you, Danny?"

She touched a giant finger to her golden waist and brought it up before his face. Her finger glowed with molten gold, like dripping honey. She touched his forehead and rivers of delicious warmth entered him. It warmed his brain, flowed down his neck and shoulders, relaxed his torso, calmed his waist, settled in his legs and feet. He was cocooned, a swaddled baby. He wanted to sleep so badly.

"Where are you, Danny?"

The wedding—her horrid face! Falling through the Abyss—its impossible size! The desert, Azru. Yarrow and the DanBaer. They rushed through his mind like a fast-forwarded film.

"Gehinnom," he mumbled. "Gehinnom. Gehinnom."

Rebekah smiled.

Her voice faded, her Jupiter eyes receded into the blackness of space. The wine-dark sky became blue again. Rana and Marul stood over him. It took him a moment to realize that the world had shifted ninety degrees. His head had slammed into the sand.

———

Everyone stared down at him, their faces backgrounded by azure sky.

Caleb helped Daniel sit up. His mouth was as dry, and his skin felt as if it were on fire.

"You were mumbling to yourself," Rana said. "You didn't hear me shouting at you?"

"I just hallucinated," he said.

"What did you see, Daniel?" Caleb said. His moon-white eyes probed into his.

He remembered everything, vividly. But he said, "Nothing. I mean, I don't remember."

"You're watersick," Marul said. "And sunburnt. You need to eat. If you don't eat soon, you'll be just as dead as Yig." She turned to Grug and said, "Apologies, Grug."

"It's true," Grug said. "How can Daniel hold up the Earth if he cannot stand." Grug looked at the Mikulalim for a long moment, when they nodded and picked up one of the trunks. They positioned it behind Daniel, while the other Mikulalim began hoisting a tent.

Rana handed Daniel a piece of dried meat.

"What is it?" he said.

"Oxen thigh, spiced with cinnamon, turmeric and salt, sun cured."

"I don't eat meat."

"Then die," Marul said. "It's your choice."

He stared at the flesh.

Caleb said, "It's but one meal of many we must take if we are to make it home, Daniel. When you are back on Earth, you can become vegetarian again."

A shadow fell over their heads as the Mikulalim hoisted the tent cloth. Grug took off his hood and sighed. The shade was a blessed respite for them all. Daniel took the meat from Rana. He turned it over in his hands.

"Just eat it," Rana said.

It smelled like shoe leather. When he licked it, it was salty and bitter. He could taste the animal fats. His mouth would have watered had he had the moisture.

"*Est gezunterheyt*," he said.

"Huh?" Rana said.

"Eat in good health. What my grandmother says before meals."

He took a bite, swallowed. It traveled down his esophagus like an invading army. The taste took him back more than a decade, when Gram had stewed her brisket all afternoon until the meat was so tender it melted in his mouth. The flavor would linger on his tongue for hours afterward. His parents had been alive then, and he savored the memory.

"Well?" Rana said.

"It's decent," he said, taking another bite.

"Decent?" Rana said. "My mother made this!"

He smiled. "In that case it's delicious."

She smirked. "Nice try, pebble head."

As the food entered him, he felt his energy returning. He tore at the meat with his teeth. It was good. Why had he been so repulsed by this?

"Slow down," Marul said. "Have some water too."

Soon everyone was eating and drinking, including the Mikulalim.

"Caleb," Marul said, "what happens when we reach the Bedu? They revile the Mikulalim. And as for demons? Loathe is too weak a word."

"Our Mikulalim guides will depart before we reach the Bedu," Caleb said.

"And what about you?"

"I will pass as a human."

"They'll know you're a demon."

"I'll hide my powers. They won't sense me."

"They'll see through your lies and flay us all alive."

Daniel listened as they discussed their plans, but the vision of Rebekah still haunted him. Was it just a dream, a hallucination brought on by fatigue? Or was that truly her, Mashit, reaching out across universes? And what had she said?

Where are you, Danny?

"I will handle the Bedu, Marul," Caleb said. "You need to focus on readying your spell to get Daniel and me back to Earth."

A Mikulal poked his hooded head into the tent. "My lord," he said. "Something has just appeared above the city."

"*Something?* What is it, fool?"

"Best my lord sees for himself."

Rana leaped out of the tent, and everyone followed her. In the air above Azru a small thunderhead spun within what looked like a dark hole in the sky.

"A rain cloud?" Daniel said.

"Not in the desert," Caleb said. "It's her."

"Her?"

"Who do you think, Daniel?" Caleb said. "Your lovely wife comes for you."

He remembered the dream. "Rebekah is coming?"

"Mashit!"

"What is that cloud?" Rana said. "What does it mean?"

"Pack the tents!" Caleb shouted. "We move, *now*!"

"But what is it?" Rana shouted over the growing wind.

Caleb said, "It's a door. And we don't want to be here to see what comes through."

CHAPTER FIFTEEN

THE MIKULALIM HASTILY PACKED THE TENT, WHILE RANA STARED at the growing cloud. It spun like the water in Mama's cistern, round and round. With each cycle it grew a little larger, a little darker. The desert wind picked up, blew sand in her eyes.

She felt a hand on her shoulder. Startled, she turned to face Daniel.

"Your home is there," he said. "Go while you have the chance."

But she couldn't leave now. She had only just begun to learn who she was. If she went home, she'd just be another ordinary person, working til her back and her dreams shattered.

"Rana! Daniel!" Caleb shouted. "Move, now!"

"On Earth," Daniel said to her, "there was a storm just before I came here. I wasn't there to protect my grandmother, and I've regretted it since. If something's coming through that door, then you should go and protect your family. It's where you need to be."

She nodded. Daniel was right. How could she leave her family alone? What if they needed her help? She turned and shouted to Caleb, "I'm going home!"

Caleb dropped his satchel and ran to her. "You'll do no such thing."

Marul came over. "What's all this?"

"I'm going home, Marul," Rana said as a ball of emotion welled up in her throat. "I'm sorry, but I can't go on with you."

"What's there to be sorry about?" Marul said. "Azru is where your life is."

"It's too dangerous," Caleb said. "You'll be safer here, with us."

"I'm going home to my family."

"I forbid it!" Caleb said. The Mikulalim surrounded her.

"So," Rana said, "will you kill me if I try to leave?"

"Not kill," Caleb said. "Subdue."

"If you don't let her go," Marul said, "I won't help you get back to Earth. Shove me back in that cave or kill me here, but I won't help you."

"Same for me," Daniel said. "I'll stop here unless you let Rana go home."

Rana was strengthened, knowing she had such allies.

"Imbeciles, all of you!" Caleb said. "Don't you understand what's coming through that door? Mashit will kill you all, the Earth will crumble, and the Cosmos will fall asunder. All because of your pathetic human sentiments!"

"It's our sentiments that make us human," Daniel said. "Let Rana go."

Marul crossed her arms and stared at Caleb. "You know where we stand."

Caleb turned to Rana. "Are you willing to give up the knowledge of who you are? Who you can be? If you go home, you'll be just another forgettable human."

Rana was torn. She wanted to know more than anything. But Mama, Papa, and Liu needed her. She had to return, to see them through this demon storm. "I'm going home," she said.

Caleb shook his head and shouted, "Fools! If Rana dies, do you know what the Cosmos loses? Do you? Grug, give the idiots their wish. Escort the baby home."

Caleb's words brought Rana no relief. How she wished she could stay!

Marul approached her. "So now it's you, Rana, who leaves me."

Rana was about to speak when Marul pressed a finger to her lip. She put her hands on Rana's shoulders "No, my Little Plum," she said. "No sad goodbyes or wet eyes. Save your water. Just go and hug your sister for me."

"I will," Rana said.

"Well? Go!"

"There's one more thing I have to do." She strode over to Caleb and unsheathed her knife. Grug stepped to block her, but Caleb said, "No, Grug."

Rana grimaced with the pain as she dragged her knife across her palm. She wringed her blood onto the sands. "By the Great Goddess Mollai, giver of rain and succor, with my blood on her desert, I vow that if any harm comes to Marul or Daniel, I will kill you."

Lightning flashed behind her, and thunder rolled across the desert. She shivered. *The Goddess*, she thought, *must be listening.*

"You don't need to vow to your worthless deity," Caleb said. "I want them alive as much as you do, Rana. The Cosmos needs their help." He held up his hand. "You have my word, by Great Abbadon. I shall let no harm come to them."

"A demon's word is . . ." Marul trailed off. "Go, Rana! Leave while you can. Demons are fickle creatures."

"We are also," Caleb said, his eyes fixed upon the storm, "the most single-minded."

———

Caleb had been born eons ago, had seen myriad creatures rise and fall in glorious, fleeting symphonies. He had tumbled through the Great Deep not once, but twice, plunging through the Abyss where Eternity rested her weary head. He had endured countless forevers. He had become a patient sort. But Rana's parting felt as if he were losing his right arm.

Bring her back to me, Grug, Caleb commanded in the silent tongue. *Alive and unharmed. Lead her in circles across the sands. Pretend to be lost, adrift on tides. Have her don the necklace Havig has given her. It will hide her from the Legion's eyes. And when Rana is weak and watersick, bring her back to me. We'll delay long enough for you to catch up to us. Be as quick as you can! Time is not in our favor.*

Yes, my lord, Grug said.

Marul approached Grug. "Promise me you will be safe," she said. "Both of you."

"You will see me soon enough," Grug said.

"I hope so, Grug," Marul said. "I really hope so."

Remember! Caleb commanded. *She must survive, at all costs! Even of your own life.*

Grug frowned and nodded once. And with swift farewells, Rana and Grug sped off toward Azru. Caleb watched them for a moment before he directed the party on again. They ascended a dune, and at its peak Marul stopped to watch Rana and Grug until another dune rose to obscure them. It obscured the city too, and the cloud hung like a stain above it.

How did Mashit know we are here, on Gehinnom? Caleb wondered. *Does she know we are in the desert now, racing for the Bedu?*

They treaded over a landscape of orange sand, the tides helping them along. No course seemed wiser than any other, but the knowledgeable Mikulalim led them forward.

They crested a dune, and Marul shrieked. A cyclone of man-sized scorpions watched them, ready to attack. But the Mikulalim whispered fire into the fabric of the world and the scorpions burned. Daniel averted his eyes as they screamed. Marul stared at the dying creatures, fascinated. Smoke rose from their carcasses, betraying their position as the few squealing survivors scuttled down the dune's far bank. Hawks circled above, and when the party moved on, the birds flew down to peck at the carcasses.

They walked for hours, mostly in silence. Daniel sidled up beside Caleb as the sun was getting low. Long shadows exaggerated the dark circles under his eyes. Was this exhaustion, or was his Mikulal nature growing?

"I have questions," he said.

"I may not have answers."

"When we go back to Earth, what happens?"

"We stop Mashit and her Legion from killing the Lamed Vav."

"How?"

"By warning them. Hiding them, if we have to."

"You know where they are, then? *Who* they are?"

"In a manner of speaking." The truth was that Marul knew their names, and he didn't, but Daniel didn't need to know this, yet.

"I don't get you," Daniel said. "You sent Yig to die to serve as a lesson for the others. If you have no compassion for one man's life, why do you care about the Lamed Vav?"

"It's purely selfish, Daniel. I don't want to suffer for eternities when the Earth shatters and the Shards wither. Nor do I want to everything I know to crumble to ashes. Mashit needs to kill one, perhaps two more Lamed Vav, and then—" He slapped his hands together. "We're dust."

Daniel gave him a curious glance. "So why does she want to destroy everything? Where is her sense of self-preservation?"

"She is a short-sighted fool. She always has been."

"But not you, king of demons?"

"What do you see when you look at me, Daniel? A cold-hearted beast? A monster? Do you think I'm brutal for brutality's sake? I am merely being honest about the nature of reality. I did not make the predator kill its prey. I did not create the scorpion's sting or the snake's venom." He gestured up at the sky, which was steadily filling with gray clouds. "Our glorious Creator fashioned the world that way."

"But you yourself said we always have a choice," Daniel said. "Nature may be brutal, but we don't have to be. The choice between good and evil, that is the beginning of morality."

"Are you quoting Deuteronomy to me?" Caleb said. "'I put before you life and death, good and evil. Choose—'"

"'Choose life so that you may live.'"

"I *am* choosing life, Daniel. For all. If some have to die so that the rest may live, then by any moral equation, I am correct. The fault with humanity is that you're too focused on your immediate social groups. You fail to account for the great tapestry that weaves its threads through the Cosmos. From a distance, one death is minor when compared to the fate of all."

"My grandmother says that each man is a universe. Kill a man and you destroy a world."

"Kill a Lamed Vavnik," Caleb said, "and you destroy a trillion worlds."

Daniel had no answer for that. *Soon*, Caleb thought, *you will learn the truth, Daniel. You will see that my course is the only path, as all others lead to ruin.*

With your help, Daniel, Caleb thought, *we will make the Creator tremble and awaken from her eons-long sleep. And when she does, it will be too late for her or anyone to stop us.*

———

The sun hovered above the DanBaer, as if afraid to set. Their shadows stretched for hundreds of paces behind them as Rana ran toward home. Grug kept a steady pace beside her. The traders coming in from the Tattered Sea never ran to Azru, not even when marauders were hot on their heels. But she wasn't a trader, and her family was waiting.

The storm had doubled in size in the last hour. With every moment the vortex spun faster. Bleak clouds raced around the wide rim, as if its giant mouth might swallow Azru whole.

"Mistress," Grug said, "the best route is this way." He pointed away from the city, deep into the desert.

"You're trying to get me lost, aren't you?" she said.

"I'm trying to protect you."

"You think I'm a fool. I've seen traders coming in from the Tattered Sea ten thousand times. This is how they come."

"When the tides flow south," he said. "Now they flow west. We'll be swept into the desert if we don't turn now."

"Ox-ass, Grug! I know Caleb doesn't want me to leave him. He's no different from the sweaty drunkards at the fermentaries. I'm not a person to him. I'm a thing to be used! Go back to your king, Grug." She reached for her knife, in case he objected.

Grug's hideous lips were the only things visible under his hood. "Please, mistress. This is the way to safety."

"What will you do if I don't go with you?" she said. "Knock me unconscious and drag me back to him?"

"I have orders to see you to safety."

"I'm sure," she said. "As you saw to Marul's."

"I cared for her. I gave her what she needed."

Rana had a vision of the two naked, locked in each other's embrace. She suppressed a shiver. "You gave her everything but her freedom."

"If I could have freed her, I would have. The king would not allow it."

"Your *king* killed your brother. How are you still faithful to him?"

Grug sighed, a sound like the final breaths of a thousand dying men. "I have no choice."

On Bedubroadstreet she had met charlatans who used mind-witchery to charm people out of their pockets. A man had once compelled her to undress before she had awakened and reported him to the king's sentinels. Of course they subsequently hired the man to work in the king's harems. "Is it a magical compulsion?"

"A powerful one. Azazel's Curse of a Thousand Tongues courses through my blood, directing my being. Azazel is our true king, but Lord Ashmedai rules over us while his brother lies chained at the bottom of a chasm in Dudael. Azazel is very different from his brother."

"Azazel is Caleb's brother?"

"Lord Ashmedai's brother, yes."

"So your loyalty is passed from one hand to the next, like a tool?"

Grug did not answer. Maybe he couldn't.

She gazed at his sorry spectacle. Underneath his black cloak, his ugly shell, Grug was a prisoner too, locked in an invisible cage. She found herself pitying him.

"I'd lived so long in darkness," Grug said, "I'd forgotten what kindness felt like. Marul was kind to me."

"She was kind to me too," Rana said. "A long time ago."

Grug glanced up at the growing storm. "For her sake, mistress, put on the necklace that Havig gave you."

"Why? Will it put me under a spell? Make me your slave?"

"It will keep you hidden from them. Please, mistress."

She took the necklace from her pocket and held it up. In the fading light its facets sparkled like stars. The pendant leaned away from the storm as if blown by a strong wind, though there was, for the moment, none.

She dropped the necklace to the sand and stomped on it. "I'm going home, Grug. Will you stop me?" She held the hilt of her knife.

Grug sighed. "No, mistress. I will protect you to my dying breath."

The sun touched the DanBaer, and its cool shadow spilled over the desert. The storm crackled with blue lightning, and the thunder echoed for minutes after. A stiff wind whipped up, throwing sand into her eyes, but she pressed on, and Grug stayed beside her.

In the growing twilight she reached the outskirts of Azru, where the Csilla Homes, long abandoned, leaned steeply into the desert.

"Seems you were wrong about the tides," she said.

"We were lucky."

The watermaids had abandoned their posts, which was rare. Across the city, the palace flickered with lamp- and firelight. Her parents and Liu were just minutes away, across the city's center, and she felt a pang in her heart as she longed for Mama's arms.

Crimson rays fanned over the DanBaer in a glorious sunset. The Ukne Tower scintillated in the reflected light, but the rays vanished as quickly as they'd appeared. The sun had set, and night had begun.

There was a curious shift in the air. Grug threw back his hood. His face was doubly horrid in the ruddy twilight. He stared up at the cloud. Lightning flashed across its center, its two ends spinning within the vortex.

"I feel them," he said. "They're coming."

"Who's coming?"

"We need to leave this place, now."

"I'm going home," she shouted over the wind. "I have to see my parents."

A circle of darkness formed in the cloud's center. It widened into a pit blacker than a moonless night. She felt as if it were pulling her soul from her eyes one sand grain at a time.

A four-legged beast came spinning out of that hole, and Grug shoved Rana down beside a large cracked stone. An enormous giraffe floated down. It had spiraling ram's horns and a vicious rat's face. Skinless, it was a blood-red mass of muscle, sinew and bone.

"What the hell is that?" she said.

"Kokabiel!" Grug said. "We need to go!"

The skinless giraffe landed on its hooves ten streets away. This beast named Kokabiel raised its enormous head, and thundered, "WHERE IS THE RANA?"

Her blood turned frigid. "Me?" she whimpered. "Why the hell does it want me?"

Kokabiel's voice shook the city, echoing like thunder from the mountain.

The giraffe used his cloven hoof to skewer a man running beneath him. The demon held the bleeding, weeping man before his eyes, turning him left and right. A scintillating stream of blue smoke floated from the man's mouth into the demon's, as if he were drinking his essence.

"YOU ARE USELESS TO ME!" Kokabiel shouted. The skewered man fell limp, and the giraffe tossed him away.

The palace horns blew the staccato call to arms. Soldiers began gathering by the western palace wall.

"GIVE US THE RANA!" Kokabiel shouted. "OR YOU SHALL ALL PERISH!"

Rana dared not breathe, lest that hideous beast turn his gaze toward her. Grug, in one swift motion, threw back her hair and clasped the necklace around her throat.

"What the hell did you—"

"Hush!" he said as a tingle began in her neck and quickly enveloped her whole body, as if she wore an invisible robe. "It will hide you from them!"

Multicolored beasts began spiraling out of the storm's black center.

She held the pendant as Kokabiel skewered a fleeing woman. Scintillating blue smoke floated out of the woman's mouth into the demon's. Then she collapsed, dead.

"USELESS!"

Motion, everywhere. The whole city was bleating like frightened goats. In some windows, fires were lit. In most, they were snuffed.

"I have to get home!" she said.

"It's too dangerous!"

"I know a secret way." She leaped away from him, climbing up steep cobblestones.

"Stop!" Grug said, sprinting after her.

Panicked people slammed into Rana as she ran. "Just give the demon what it wants!" someone said. "Goddess, give them the mad bricklayer!" shouted another.

Rana bumped into an elderly woman and knocked her to the ground. She paused to help the woman up, when a flash of recognition passed before the woman's eyes.

"*You!*" the woman said. "You're Rana Lila, the—"

"No! I'm—"

"Yes, it's you!" she said. "The demon girl!" she shouted. "She's here! Rana is here!"

Rana sped off. Behind her she heard the woman shouting to others.

As she ran people shuttered windows and doors, snuffed out lamps. Animals wailed as she wended through the streets. She sped onto Ramswool Row just as three enormous snakes fell from the sky as if a giant's intestines had just been eviscerated.

The snakes swallowed people ten at a time. As the still-living victims struggled to get out, the snakes' translucent skin bulged. A stream of blood and bone flowed from its rear.

"Rana?" they slithered. "Where isssss the Rana?"

One snake turned, dashed for her. *I'm done!* she thought, shrieking. But the snake turned at the last moment and devoured a young man beside her.

Grug leaped from the shadows. "Come!" he said, grabbing her arm. "Hurry!"

They ran through the streets as bats with sword-like beaks swooped low over houses. When she glanced at their dull-silver eyes she was struck with a wave of despair that nearly stole her breath. With twisting dives the bats lanced dozens around her with their sharp beaks.

But not me, she thought. *They do not see me.* She touched the pendant. It was hot as burning coal, but strangely did not burn her hand.

She crested a hill, where she could see the upper districts. A gigantic ram was knocking over buildings with its coil of horns. The Kelilah Tower toppled into the DanBaer, collapsing a corner of the king's palace. The whole word shook and thundered.

The king's army was mounting a resistance at Azzan Square. Arrows flew up from their serried ranks, when a phalanx of black boars as big as houses barreled through the archers and the arrows ceased.

Acrid smoke filled her lungs as fires began to spread. The smell of charred human flesh turned her stomach. Quickly, the smoke grew opaque. She gagged and retched as she lost her way, stumbling randomly. "Grug?" she said. "Grug, where are you?"

She slammed into something hard. She felt its shape and recognized what her hands had stumbled upon. She had rubbed these sharp teeth a thousand times. This was Dusty Square, and she was beside the stone lions Papa had carved. Just a few hundred paces from home.

A bull emerged from the smoke, standing upright on its hind legs. Three stories tall, its eyes were milk-white, like a blind man. Inside its womb, clear as glass, five fetuses writhed. Their malicious eyes searched hungrily as their blind mother groped onward, rocking the ground as it walked. It paused paces away, sniffing the air, before groping on.

She crawled through more smoke. The storm cloud above was shrinking. The stars were coming out, little diamonds of promise. Screams and moans leaped from every corner of the city. A thousand homes burned, many she had built with her own hand. Gasping, she found the walls of her house. The huge stone door she had painstakingly mounted on its tiny pivot lay shattered. The rubble formed a heaping pile.

"Mama!" she shouted. "Papa!"

She climbed over the rocks and into her courtyard. Bloody footprints of man and beast covered the ground, as if a herd had been slaughtered here. When she passed a severed human ear, her fear grew to a fever pitch. All the plants had been toppled, their basins shattered. She ran into the house. On the table was an open satchel half-filled with supplies. The cistern sighed a cloud of steam, the paddle slowly spinning around the rim.

"Mama! Papa! Liu!" she called.

No sound but distant screams, the close crackling of fire. The house was empty. How far could they have gotten with Papa's broken back?

She ran into her studio and found only paintings, busts, statues. Suddenly she hated them all, these inanimate things. They had stolen time from her family. Lorbria, her pet bird, lay unmoving at the bottom of her cage. A trail of bloody footprints led around to the rear of the house, and she followed them, her heart feeling as if it might burst from terror.

Something whimpered, a sound as faint as a feather brushing a harp string. Behind the house two oxen hung from slaughtering hooks. *Why oxen, here, now?* Rana thought.

And then she understood. These weren't oxen.

She screamed. Mama and Papa hung upside down from hooks. Bound and flayed, their skin lay on the ground like shavings of wood. Blood dripped from their gently swinging bodies. She froze, struck by the horror of it. Then she ran to them.

With three quick knife strokes she severed the ropes. She lifted Papa off the meat hook—she pretended not to hear the repulsive sound—and nearly slammed his head, he was so heavy. She took Mama down next. Rana's arms dripped with her parents' blood. She let out a scream so loud she thought it might crack the world.

"Mamaaaaaaa! Papaaaaaa!"

Mama's eyes fluttered open.

"Mama? Oh, Mama! Mama I'm here!"

". . . p-p-please . . ." Mama's voice was more tenuous than the wing beat of a moth. "No more . . ." Mama said. Blood rolled from her mouth as she turned her head. "Please, no more. I told you. I told you!" Mama's eyes were glued shut with dried blood, and Rana tried to wipe them clean, to open her eyes.

"Mama, I'm here! I'm right here!"

"Goddess, forgive me," Mama said. "I told you, my daughter went to the Smelter's House. To the Smelter's House! Now, please stop. Please! Let me down. Goddess, forgive me. Goddess forgive me . . . I'm sorry, Rana. I'm sorry . . ." Mama's mouth fell open. Her eyes stopped.

"Mama!" Rana screamed. "Wake up! Wake up!"

But she didn't wake. And Rana sat there for a while, beside her parents, weeping, until the flies had begun to peck at their faces.

Liu! she remembered, after a time. *Goddess, where is baby Liu?*

The stink of blood was strong on her as she searched under the beds and in closets. Where was she? Where was she? Rana tore through the canvases in her studio, toppled statues by the dozen. Maybe Liu had crawled into a nook to hide?

She searched everywhere, but Liu was gone.

She heard footsteps. Grug appeared at the top of the rubble, covered in ash. "Are you hurt?" he shouted. He ran to her. "Are you bleeding?"

"It's not my blood," she said weakly.

"It's not? Then whose—Oh. I'm sorry, Rana. I'm so, so sorry."

"My sister is missing."

"Perhaps she has fled to safety."

"She's just a baby."

Rana gazed at her studio, its contents upturned. "This is where it all began," she said. "If I had told Daniel and the dog to fuck off, as I should have, if I had called the king's sentinels, if I had told Mama or Papa—" her voice cracked "—that a demon had come into my studio, I'd be sitting down for supper with them now. It's all my fault. I did this!"

The world spun, faster than the demon vortex, and she bent over and threw up.

Beyond the pile of rubble that had been the courtyard door, someone was shouting. "Here! It's just inside here!"

She knew that voice. She wiped her face and stood, but Grug grabbed her arm. "No, we should hide." He led her to the rear of the house and they crouched in the shadows. Her parents lay nearby, attacked by flies. She closed her eyes and thought she might be sick again.

"Here, just in that small building!" the familiar voice said. She knew it from another time, another place, a world as far away as Daniel's Earth.

"A king's treasure!" Emod said. "Worth as much as the palace gold!"

Emod, the hawker from Bedubroadstreet. Emod, the homeless man who sold her creations for small fortunes and gave her a pittance. Emod, the only one in Azru who wasn't scared of her. Her only true friend.

Another voice, gruff and low, proclaimed, "If you lie, my sword takes your tongue."

"No lies!" Emod said. "Come see! Come see!"

More voices echoed from her courtyard walls. At least three others, maybe more. "Why aren't we looting the palace?" one said.

"Because there's nothing left, maggot!" said another.

Grug gestured for Rana to remain still and reached for his

sword. But she had to see them, whoever these men were. She peered around the edge. Five shirtless men, their chests covered with tattoos, stood beside her studio, wielding huge scimitars. Their unruly dark beards hung to their breasts, and many scars crossed their bodies like distressed stone. A thin man with long white hair waited alongside them. He wore a colorful robe and a gem-encrusted belt that seemed more apt for a bride than a man.

Three men came out of her studio, each carrying stuffed sacks. The other men yanked the sacks to the ground and the contents fell out.

"What's this shit?" one said. "Wooden heads? A rusted flute? How is this treasure?"

She wanted to bite their heads off. Those were hers! As if sensing her intentions, Grug pressed her down.

"There are jewels too!" said Emod. "Rings, bracelets, necklaces, charms! You name it!"

Emod, she thought, *how could you?*

"You see?" Emod said to the largest of the men, a beast of a man with a scar that ran down his left arm and ended with a missing finger.

"Yes, I see," the beast man said. Taller and stronger than the others, they all faced him. Probably the leader. "I see that we don't need you anymore." He lifted his sword.

"Wait!" Emod said. "I'm worth something to you too! I speak the Chthonic tongues. I could be an interpreter!"

The man guffawed like a choking camel. "We have no need for an interpreter."

"Then a slave! I'll do whatever you ask of me."

"Heh. You're not my type."

"The witch queen of Ektu El," Emod said, "pays a hefty sum for interpreters! And her harems are world renowned for the beauty of their women!"

The man scratched his chin. "Very well, interpreter. You live, for now, but only because I'm in a good mood." He sheathed his sword. Then to this men, he said, "Check the buildings. Take anything you can carry. We'll leave this festering city before Onai's fifth star rises."

The men charged into her house. They flipped beds, knocked

over tables, shattered the cistern. Water flooded through cracks in the foundation, pooling at her feet. Emod waited in the courtyard, guarded by the leader, while the white-haired man rifled through a bag of jewels.

"Impressive cut," he said in a high-pitched, effeminate voice. "Hand polished, I think."

She held her knife to her chest, breathing heavily.

Inside her house, a man said, "What the fuck is this?" His voice came from the window just an arm's reach away. If he stuck his head out he would see them both.

"That's the Goddess, you goat! Ain't you never seen an idol of Mollai?"

"Yeah, but never like this."

It must have been the bronze bust she'd made for Mama. The one that had sat next to the dining table. The idol they prayed to before every meal.

"Well, oxface, toss it in the bag!"

Rana wanted to tear them to bits. She let slip a grunt of rage.

"Hey!" squeaked the white-haired man in the bridal belt. "I think I just heard something from behind the house."

Grug gestured for her to stay low as the men ran out of the house.

A man stepped into the shadows close by, just five paces from where Rana and Grug were hidden. The man hovered over the bodies of her parents. "Whoa!" he said. "Guess somebody ain't coming home tonight."

"Not there," the robed one squeaked. "The sound came from the other side!"

Before the man turned to investigate, Grug leaped from the shadows and sliced the man's head off in one stroke. The head plopped to the ground beside her parents, eyes still flitting around in horror. His body collapsed in a quivering heap.

"Kill him!" the leader shouted.

Scimitars held high, they charged Grug. Their swords clanged and echoed as Grug parried their blows, while Rana crouched and held her knife. Grug fought like no one she'd ever seen. He evaded their blows in movements swift and sudden. A man spotted Rana and came for her. She stabbed him in the leg. He screamed, snatched her by the hair, and yanked her up. He raised his sword, about to swing, when blood spilled from his mouth. Grug's sword emerged from his stomach.

She slid from the man's grasp as another man hooked his arm around her neck. His breath was fouler than camel shit.

"I got the bitch!" he said. He held his sword to her chin.

The leader shouted, "Don't kill her!"

The man's fetid breath made her retch as Grug speared another man through his eye, and he went down.

"Drop your sword!" the leader said to Grug. "Drop your sword, you cursed wretch, or we kill the girl!"

The blade pressed against her neck, her captor's breath hot in her ear. Grug leaped onto a stone bench. The men panted like dogs as they circled him.

"I said drop your sword, or the bitch dies!"

Grug glanced at Rana, and the same eons of utter desolation she had seen in the Mikulalim women spread across his face.

"Don't, Grug!" she said.

But it was too late. Grug threw down his sword, and it clanked against the stone. The men yanked him down from the bench and shoved him to his knees. The leader approached, his swagger cock-sure and offensive.

Rana struggled to free herself of the man's grip, but his blade was pressed sharply against her neck. "Be still now, my calf," he said. "Be still."

The leader pointed his sword at Grug's heart. "You are a maneater, aren't you, you vile thing."

"Yes," Grug said. "But I have no choice about it. You are vile because you choose to be."

The man laughed. "As vile as they come!" His men laughed with him. And while they were chortling like pigs, he drove his sword deep into Grug's heart.

"No!" Rana screamed.

Grug's candleflame eyes guttered as he looked up at her. "Sing . . ." he wheezed. "Sing, Rana, sing . . ." Blood, black as tar, poured from his chest. The light in his eyes winked out, the candles snuffed as Grug's head lolled forward.

"Goddess! Rana?" Emod said. "Oh, Rana, forgive me!"

She sagged in the arms of her captor. Mama and Papa, butchered like animals. Liu missing and likely dead. And Emod, her only friend, had betrayed her. She had nothing left, nothing at all.

The leader, the beast of a man, grabbed her chin with an enormous callused and dirty hand. He turned her face left, then right. "What's a pretty thing like you doing with a maneater?"

She spat in his eye.

He slapped her hard, then wiped the spittle away. Her cheek stung as his dark eyes considered her. "Clean the bitch up. We'll sell her to the queen of Ektu El for her harem. Tazo, do your magic."

The white-haired man approached Rana. During the fight, he had cowered like a child. Now he strutted over, his colored robes sweeping across the ground. His eyes were slate blue. One stared right at her, the other peered off at the DanBaer. He clapped his hands and raised them skyward.

"*Sleeeeeep!*" he droned. "*May the winds of sleep descend upon you, so that you will know dormancy of thought and body, as the gods do sleep in their eternal repose.*" He spoke Bedu-Besk, the trader tongue, and she knew enough to understand this was no magic spell, but a show for these brutes. He was no magician. He was a charlatan.

She laughed, because laughter was all she had left.

He frowned, then took a small vial from his pocket. He opened the stopper and waved it before her nose. She held her breath, but he kicked her in the stomach, and she gasped.

A curious scent entered her nostrils, like stale tea, baking bread, and strong alcohol. A cold exhaustion spread over her. She was tired of running, tired of hurting, so tired of watching everything she loved be destroyed. The cool ground rested against her cheek as strong hands laid her down. The world grew dimmer, Grug's eyes stared back at her, and her parents gazed up at the twinkling stars.

"Mama," she said. "Oh, Mama."

CHAPTER SIXTEEN

A THOUSAND SHADES OF INDIGO SWADDLED THE SKY AS THE sun went down, and Daniel remembered his wedding night, when the sky had turned the color of dark wine. What had Gram done after he had run out of the synagogue? Had she been frantic? How had she gotten home? Was there a search on for him? It had been three days since he'd left Earth. He wished he could send her a message, let her know he was safe—as safe as one could be walking with Ashmedai and his cursed slaves across Gehenna—and that he was coming home.

When he closed his eyes he imagined the smell of Rebekah's hair, the lopsided curve of her smile. They had once eaten at an Italian restaurant in the West Village. At a corner table a young couple's baby had been crying for most of the meal. The patrons were growing frustrated and gave the parents angry looks. They asked the waiters to intervene. But the waiters were too polite, and the parents of the screaming baby seemed oblivious to all but their meal.

Daniel had said, "I wish I could soothe the kid somehow."

Rebekah had smirked. "I know a little trick," she said. She wiped her lips with the napkin, got up, and walked over to the parents. He didn't hear what she'd said, but soon the parents were laughing with her. Rebekah leaned over the crying baby and swirled her finger before his eyes. She touched the finger to the baby's forehead and immediately he stopped crying. Rebekah smiled, said something to the parents, then sauntered back to Daniel.

The other patrons thanked her as she sat back down.

"What did you do?" Daniel said, smiling. "Hypnotize him?"

She smiled back at him, eyes bright and dilated. "I cast a spell on him. And if you don't eat your broccoli rabe, Danny, I'll turn you into a newt!"

He had laughed, and was even a bit turned on. But now, as Daniel walked across the purpling sands and the sun dipped low, he realized that it actually had been magic. And if she could charm strangers so easily, what had she done to him over the weeks and months, while he had slept beside her, dreaming? Maybe everything he'd felt for her—everything he still felt, despite what Caleb had said—was false.

I was under a demon's spell, he thought. *And maybe I still am.*

The heat of the day blew off with a western gale. The sun had been cruel to his skin. His body burned, and he welcomed the night's cooling air. A furious number of stars blinkered to life above him, and a rising crescent moon spread eggshell light over the sands.

When it was too dark to see clearly, Caleb said, "Let's camp for the night." He would not permit fire or lamplight, which might betray their position. So they set up camp in the darkness.

Daniel worried about Rana. Had she made it home? And what about that storm that Caleb said was a door? What had come through? Mashit? He asked Marul, but she said, "Better if we don't think about such things, Daniel."

"Aren't you worried about Rana?"

"Of course," she said. "But it makes me ill to think of it."

The Mikulalim pitched four tents and fastened them together with coils of rope. Daniel was curious as to why, when Marul approached and said, "They fasten the tents together so they don't drift apart in the night. The sands of the Tattered Sea shift like an ocean. If we don't tie the tents together, one of us could wake a thousand parasot from the other."

The Mikulalim retreated to their tents, while Marul, Caleb and Daniel sat in another tent under the dim light of a shaded lamp hanging from a rope. They offered Daniel dried strips of ox meat, and he ate it without argument. His stomach wasn't yet used to the animal fats, but he was beginning to crave the taste.

After the meal, Caleb rolled cigarettes. "Smoke your tobacco. Relax. Then get some sleep. I need to speak with the Mikulalim."

He left for the other tent, leaving Daniel alone with Marul.

"Let's go outside," Marul said. "It's been ages since I've glimpsed the stars."

They smoked their cigarettes while lying on their backs outside the tent and staring up at the spray of stars. The nicotine made him giddy, and he sighed often. It was so dark the dusty lane of the galaxy was visible. A shooting star flashed across the sky and Marul gasped.

"Oh! How I've missed this," she said. Her voice enhanced rather than diminished the silence, as if she were the desert sighing. He didn't want to disturb this moment, but he had too many questions.

"Marul?"

"What is it, my love?"

Her love? "If demons are real, are *angels* real too?" He used the English word, since there was no cognate for angel in Wul.

"Do you mean the Malachim?"

"The Malachim, yes, I think so," he said. "'Malachim' has so many meanings. In Hebrew it means *angels*. In Wul it means a bystander. Someone who—"

"Someone who watches, but does nothing."

"So angels exist too?"

"Of course they do."

"What are they like?"

"There are the Malachim, the angels," she said, "and the Shedim, the demons. Caleb is a Shed, a being born long before our universes were created. The Shedim are creatures with too much Din, too much wrath. Where you and I see cause for mercy, they see cause for punishment.

"The Malachim are the opposite. They have too much Chesed, too much mercy."

"How can you have too much mercy?"

"The Malachim would share tea with a murderer of children and not think it strange. They accept the torturer and saint alike. Our human notions of justice are alien to them, because they do not judge. The do not see good and evil. All to them is cause for mercy."

"But what do the Malachim think of Mashit's plan? Do they know she is trying to kill the Lamed Vav? Could they help us?"

Her face glowed as she puffed on her cigarette. "I'm not sure how much they know, but I'll tell you this, I lived on your Earth once, in a city called Shanghai."

"I didn't know that you'd been to Earth."

"Yes. I lived there for several years. And I once encountered a Malach there, and I begged him to help Gehinnom. I told him about our famines, our wars, our disasters that keep this planet forever in the dark ages. He knew about Gehinnom, but he told me he would not interfere, that none of his kind would. It was against their nature as non-judgmental beings. We were walking in the street once when a car hit a mother and her baby. They lay there dying. I tried to save them, but hadn't enough power. But the angel did, and could have saved them. And he let them die, because he said it was not his place to interfere in the natural course of events."

Daniel swallowed. "That's horrible. It's not the view of angels most people have."

She harrumphed. "Most people are stupid."

They stared at the stars for a while, and Marul sighed often, even when there were no falling stars, as if she were making love to the sky. "It's staggeringly gorgeous," she said.

"It is," he said. "Which is why I'm confused. We're inside a Shard, a fragment from a shattered universe, right?"

"Yes."

"There are millions of stars out there. So how is this universe broken?"

The silhouette of her head rose before the sky like a dark mountain. "Do you have any idea how *big* Earth's universe is? How many billions of galaxies? This Shard is but the tiniest fraction of that size. There is only one galaxy here, and it's very, very old and tired. Don't let yourself be fooled by this fleeting vista of beauty. Appearances aren't what's broken."

"Then what is?"

"The foundations."

"Foundations of what?"

"Civilization began on Earth, when? Ten, maybe fifteen thousand years ago?"

"I think so."

"On Gehinnom, people have been building cities for fifty thousand years, and some artifacts suggest civilization here may be millennia older. We should have reached those stars by now, but we still have cultures that sacrifice their children to appease angry gods and humans who see no sin in owning another person from birth to death like property. A few of us try to raise this world up, to create a moral and just society. We build cities and make laws. But in a few years, two decades if we're lucky, it comes crumbling down again. It's always the same, Daniel, though it wears a different face each time. War, famine, earthquake, plague. We've seen them all. We are thrown back into a primitive state. We cannot grow, no matter how hard we try."

She sighed, a sound like a cinder burning out. "So, you see, Daniel, the sky isn't what's broken. It's the ground under our feet." She put a hand on his forearm and turned toward him. Her hand was warm and rested lightly, a bird on a branch, about to fly off. "But I'm not broken," she whispered. "In fact, I'm quite agile, for my age." She ran a finger down his cheek, making his body tingle. "You've been through much recently. So have I. We both could use release." He hadn't noticed until now that her other hand was hovering above his groin. And though she wasn't touching him, he felt soft, delicious waves of warmth caressing him there.

She whispered to him. He couldn't decipher the words, but the sounds made his thoughts as slow as dripping honey. She rolled him onto his back, climbed on him, and unbuckled his belt.

"Marul, what in Sheol are you doing?" Caleb shouted. "Get off him now!"

Clarity returned, and Daniel blinked away the fogginess in his mind.

"But he wants this!" Marul said.

"No, I definitely don't!" he said. He shoved Marul off of him. "I'm not your goddamned plaything! I'm, not anyone's! I'm Daniel Fisher, Lamed fucking-Vavnik!" He stormed away onto the moonlit sands.

"Daniel," she said, "don't go far! You could drift—"

"Fuck off!" he said. "All of you, just fuck the hell off!"

"As if you haven't poisoned the world enough, witch!" Caleb said. "You had to sully Daniel too? Is this cheap magic how you got Grug to sleep with you?"

"Beast!" Marul said. "Daniel wants me!"

"You couldn't pay a whore to want you!"

They exchanged insults as Daniel walked away. He stopped only when the tents were faint shapes against a sea of black, afraid to go any further. The sands wavered beneath him, making his gait unsteady. Under the pale moonlight he waited for his erection to subside. But it lingered, painfully so, for minutes. Was this a remnant of Marul's magic?

He had had enough of being led around like a dog on a leash, yanked this way and that. Under the distant stars he felt free, freer than he ever had. But he had also never felt more alone.

Caleb was walking toward him, calling his name, when he abruptly stopped. In the northern sky, six bright points of light appeared, as bright as phosphorescent flares. The lights fell slowly, and dozens more appeared, each with long, scintillating tails, as if a tremendous firework had exploded in the stratosphere and was raining down.

A sudden wind whipped up, blowing tent and sand. Thunder rolled across the desert, and the ground shook. A low and deep reverberation throbbed at the edge of hearing, vibrating his gut, loosening his bowels.

Each light was a miniature sun. And as he looked he longed for something he couldn't put to words. Home, perhaps, but not his physical home. The air crackled as a white-hot fragment crashed a hundred yards away and sent up a spray of sand. Glowing pieces were crashing all over the desert.

"What is it?" Daniel shouted. "What are they?"

Caleb's eyes seemed unnaturally bright as he approached Daniel. "Fragments," he said. "Pieces of your universe, like mortar. They're raining down over all the Shards."

A wave of terror shuddered through him. "Is the Earth gone?" he said. "Is this the end?" He thought of Gram, of Christopher, and of all those countless billions, tumbling into the Abyss, suffering for eternities.

"No," Caleb said, to Daniel's great relief, "but your lovely wife has killed another Lamed Vavnik. She is one step closer now."

Daniel tried to sleep, but Marul's snoring made it difficult. She had promised she wouldn't try her tricks again, but he didn't trust her. He slept on the opposite side of the tent, as far away from her as the space allowed, while Caleb slept like a corpse between them.

Afterimages of the fragments streaked through his vision whenever he closed his eyes. What kind of person had this Lamed Vavnik been? Was she old or young? What country was she from? Did she fall in love, only to be smashed like a glass at a Jewish wedding?

The sand hissed as it blew against their tent. For the last few minutes, someone had been whispering outside. At first he had thought it was the wind sweeping over the dunes. But the whispers lingered even as the wind went still. Eventually he mustered enough courage to creep over to the opening and peer out.

The ropes that bound the tents together were taut and straining. He thought this might have been the sound he'd heard, when he spotted all the Mikulalim sitting in a small circle a short distance from the tent. They murmured as they joined hands. A fire burned in their center, red as a summer's sunset, its flames licking the air much too slowly.

Daniel had thought Caleb ordered them not to make a fire. So what was this?

The Mikulalim raised their hands skyward and produced a sound like a foghorn bellowing over an empty sea. His stomach shook with the sound, but Marul and Caleb didn't even stir. How could they remain asleep with such noise?

A column of light, pale as the moon, leaped up from the fire into the moonless sky like a spotlight. A swarm of red sparks corkscrewed up after it. The Mikulalim continued their bellowing horn, when some thing the color of rotten eggs flew through the column of light. Daniel didn't catch its full shape as its bleak silhouette drifted across the stars. It dipped into the light again, revealing a tangle of hairs on a belly mottled yellow and brown. The object played with the column of light like a moth to a lamp, never revealing itself completely.

A second silhouette joined the first, then a third, and a fourth. Soon hundreds of shadows blotted out the stars. The Mikulalim kept up their dreary note, when a gigantic bird landed at the threshold of the fire's glow and dragged itself into the light.

It was vile! A huge featherless chicken, twenty feet tall, with red, pupil-less eyes, each like a single drop of blood. A body dangled in its long, sharp beak. A Mikulal in a black cloak.

The ground shifted, the tent ropes groaned, and Daniel lost his footing and fell.

The featherless-chicken cocked its head. Its red eyes focused in on him. It dropped the body and leaped into the air with a flap of its awful wings. The other silhouettes vanished like startled pigeons, and the stars blinkered back to life.

The Mikulalim stopped their singing. They were staring at him. He knew he had intruded on their private ceremony. He wanted to run back into the tent and hide. But that was the old Daniel. The new one would be a pawn no longer. He got to his feet.

A Mikulal waved Daniel over. The others went to fetch the body.

Daniel's legs wobbled as he crossed unsteady sands. The Mikulal wore nothing, save for a loincloth and a large gold earring hanging from his right ear. The slowly burning fire made his shadow squirm as if alive.

I am Junal.

The words had been shoved into his mind.

"Hey! Did you just—"

The man held up his palm. The others stared angrily at him.

Now is not the time for crude oral speech. Again, the words were thrust into his mind, loud and unwelcome. *Think your thoughts to me, Daniel. Do not speak them aloud.*

He's talking into my head, Daniel thought.

This is the ancient language, the oldest language. Think in images, not words. It will take time to master.

You . . . you can hear my thoughts? he thought.

Not hear, Junal said. *I can sense them, if you project them. You have been given Azazel's Curse of a Thousand Tongues. You are becoming a Mikulal. One of us.*

God help me, Daniel thought, and then realized that Junal had heard. *What were you doing, just now?* he thought. *What were those flying things?*

Offspring of the great Ziz, Junal said. Daniel received a vision of a mammoth bird, its feet spanning continents, its head touching the stars. *The Children of Ziz serve us, and we serve them. You interrupted the obsequies.*

The obsequies? The others were removing the dead man's cloak, and Daniel recognized the corpse's face. *Yig?*

Grug's brother, yes. They found his body on the sands and returned him to us. We would have thanked them with a song. They love our music. But you scared them away. Now we owe them a favor.

I'm sorry. Your sound woke me.

Only Mikulalim can hear it. Will you dine with us?

Dine? He heard a crunch. *Now?* The other men were cutting off Yig's ankle with a blade, and Daniel winced. Another was carving Yig's flesh with his sword, then handing pieces to the others. When they all had the flesh of Yig they collectively thought, *May your song rise again through us.* They bit into Yig's flesh together.

Daniel gagged. *Oh, God, that's disgusting!*

It's not disgusting, Junal said. *Yig will not be lost. He will remain with the tribe. You are but half a man now, Daniel, and half a Mikulal. Taste him, and complete your quickening.*

No! Daniel thought. "No!" he said aloud. The others eyed him again as he retreated toward his tent. "I'm sorry, Junal," he said. "I'm sorry."

Inside the tent he fell onto his blanket. Caleb and Marul seemed to still be asleep. *Is this what I've become?* he thought. *Eater of the dead? And I'm supposed to be the righteous one who upholds the world?*

That night he slept fitfully, if at all. He thought it would have been better to have let Marul have her way with him than to have seen the Mikulalim eating Yig. When light dabbed the horizon with orange-blue light, Junal thrust his head into the tent, and Daniel sat straight up.

"It'll be dawn soon," Junal said.

Caleb woke immediately, but Marul needed several hard shoves before she stirred. The Mikulalim packed the camp with impressive speed. They had a light meal, and Caleb told Daniel to conserve food. "It might be days," he said, "before we reach the Quog Bedu."

The sun crested the horizon, and a blaze of yellow light spread over the sands. As the desert warmed, it gave off a pleasant stony smell that reminded Daniel of the summers of his childhood, playing games in the paved street. Marul turned her face sunward. Her irises, the pupils tiny pinpricks, were the green of rainforests. How old was she? He'd guessed around sixty, but in the light she looked younger. Forty-five? Less? He thought that, with a bath, some shampoo, she might be quite attractive. But after last night, he didn't trust his senses around her. This might be more of her magic. She caught him looking, and he turned away.

He felt no pleasure in the rising sun. The light hurt his eyes and skin, and it would only get hotter and brighter as the day wore on. He was trying to reposition his shirt so it better shielded his body, when Junal came over holding a black cloak in his hands.

Wearing his own cloak, Junal looked like the Grim Reaper. "For you," Junal said. He offered the cloak to Daniel, identical to the one he wore. The finely weaved fabric shimmered in the sun. "Put it on."

"Thanks, but I'll be fine," Daniel said.

"Your Mikulalim nature grows." A chill rolled down his spine at Junal's words. "Your skin is milk-white." And into his mind, Junal said, *I have my orders to protect you.*

Daniel dreaded the idea of resembling one of these Cursed Men. But the sun hurt, biting his skin as it rose. He couldn't go another day unprotected. Reluctantly, he took the cloak.

He stripped to his boxers, while Marul watched. At the last moment he remembered the wedding boutonniere and retrieved it from his pocket. The cloak's material was soft and silken, cool and comfortable against his skin. He slid the boutonniere into his new pocket.

What is that? Junal asked.

A memory, Daniel said.

Junal reached into a pouch at his belt and pulled out a lock of auburn hair. *This was my wife's. She died four hundred and nineteen years ago. It still smells of her.*

Daniel thought, *Were you married, before . . . ?*

Before I was cursed, yes. Her name was Daarni. We lived in a city called Gelecek that does not exist anymore, and no one remembers. There had been talk of forming a system of laws determined not by king's decree but by popular vote. The king said he was open to the idea, and invited us to a forum in the city square.

Hundreds of us assembled, hoping for a better world for our children. But once we were inside the king locked the gates. We were trapped as the archers picked us off, one by one. I lay near death when the Mikulalim came after dusk to feast on the bodies. They offered me their flesh, so that I might live. And I cared only about seeing my wife again, so I ate. But it was too late for Daarni. An arrow had pierced her heart.

I'm sorry, Daniel said.

You may think our habits vile, Junal said, *as I once did. But among the Mikulalim, we have no strife. Our king Havig is just, our laws are fair, our women are equals, and we treat the stranger as a brother, so long as he respects our customs. No city of men on this world can boast that.* Junal glanced at the lock of hair before tucking it safely back in his pouch.

"The cloak befits you, Daniel," Caleb said as he and Marul came over. "Though perhaps a bit too large." Caleb smiled, and it was beautiful and horrid, like the jaws of a shark. "Listen up," Caleb said. "There will be strong currents today, my guides tell me. The Bedu use these currents to travel faster than a bird. But their channels run parallel to each other. If we enter the wrong one we could be sucked into an eddy or flung across the continent. Stay alert and follow the Mikulalim closely."

With this they walked northwest, chasing their shrinking shadows. The sands shifted with every step, scuffing the black leather of Daniel's shoes into a featureless gray. The ground heaved as if he were on a boat, and it was disconcerting to think that, on a whim, its currents might fling him across the world.

As the sun rose, the day grew hot, and Daniel pulled his cloak more tightly about him. Wind blew over the dunes, whistling high-pitched tunes, like wet fingers run over wine glasses. Dunes rolled across the desert, lifting and dropping them hundreds of feet. Sometimes the sand collided and the desert screeched like metal sheets tearing.

He was always dizzy, ever thirsty.

A row of cumulous clouds appeared in the north, quickly evaporated, and left behind a shower of yellow dust that reeked of sulfur. Hordes of black worms rolled in the sand beneath their feet like tumbling seaweed. "Don't step on them!" Junal warned. "They'll eat through the soles of your shoes!" As a dune lifted them up, Daniel and Marul hopped and skipped, trying to avoid stepping on them. When the wave rolled past the worms were gone.

Nothing on Gehinnom seemed to linger for long.

They walked for hours, pausing only to let the Mikulalim correct their course, or to take meal breaks. Twice the hooded men lost their way. They argued with each other, while Caleb defiled the air with ancient curses. As they walked, Caleb looked back the way they'd come, as if expecting Mashit at any moment. Great waves of sand, hundreds of feet high, crossed the desert miles off. They all fell silent, as if the dunes might hear them and turn to swallow them.

"Is the whole planet a desert?" Daniel said to Marul.

"No," she said, panting. She had been slow all day. "There are salt-water oceans in the south. Far to the north, beyond the mountains, there's a tiny belt of jungle. Go even further and there's ice. Most of this planet is desert, though."

"How do they grow food for everyone?"

"With great difficulty. In rare regions of temperate air and half-dead soil, they use slaves to haul water for hundreds of parasot."

"Why not build a pipeline?"

"A pipe wouldn't last a month. The ground is always shifting."

"I wish there were a way to help them."

"Get yourself in line."

"What do you mean?"

"Demons provide the cities with food, technology, and lost knowledge, in exchange for worship, favors, and loyalty."

"My grandmother said that demons gave the sciences to humankind. I laughed at her."

"*Give*," said Marul. "Present tense. Without demons' help, Gehinnom would be a dead world."

"Really?"

"It's like this across all the Shards. Without demon intervention, the myriad worlds would be barren."

"So they help the helpless? Like what I do, back on Earth."

"And what *do* you do, Daniel?"

"I work for a charity."

She harrumphed. "Do you ask for favors in return?"

"Never."

"Then what you call charity I call slavery."

"There must be a way to help them."

"I tried, and look where it got me."

"Just because you failed doesn't mean others can't succeed."

She stared at him. "It's your nature to want to repair things. That's what makes you a Lamed Vavnik." Her green eyes tugged and toyed with him, and he looked away.

"It's my *job*," he said. "To help the suffering. I don't see why I can't do it here."

"I'm not the only one who's tried, Daniel. In every generation, a few special ones are born. People like Rana. She has no need of demons' help. She is astounding all on her own. To someone like her, the limits of this world are visible with every breath. She rails against the void with each creative act. But those that rattle the cage too loudly always end up dead, their ideas buried under waves of sand. That's why I never told Rana that every brick she lays, every bust she molds will be dust before she reaches forty. But I will tell you before you waste your time on a fool's errand. You can't change the Shards, Daniel. Suffering and transience are the natural order of things here."

He thought about what Rana had said to him. "Three days ago, I was just a man," he said. "And now, I'm a Lamed Vavnik, poisoned with Azazel's Curse, trying to save the Cosmos. From my point of view, Marul, the natural order of things is pretty malleable."

"I once thought so too," she said. "I traveled widely, searching for knowledge. I hungered for power. Instead, I found my own weaknesses."

"Yes," he said, suddenly. "You cursed me, Marul. You gave me Azazel's Curse." The anger bubbled up from within his belly.

She blinked at him. "Yes."

"I understand why. You wanted your freedom more than anything. But you condemned me for it. You thought I was ordinary, expendable. If it was necessary to sacrifice one life for your freedom, so be it. That makes you no different from Caleb."

She stared at him, and there was vulnerability in her gaze, as if Daniel had pierced through her outer, protective shell. "If I could take it back, I would."

"So," Daniel said, squeezing his fist into a tight ball, "is this change inevitable? Can I undo this curse?"

"Have you eaten human flesh?"

"Other than Grug's tongue, no."

"Then the quickening is not yet complete. If you don't eat human flesh, you will remain a man, mostly."

"Mostly?"

"Your craving for human flesh will grow with each passing day."

"So how do I undo this curse?"

She stared at him. "I don't know. I'm sorry, but I don't think you can."

He wanted to shove this arrogant witch to the sand and choke her. This wasn't like him, such violent thoughts, but this new Daniel wasn't the same person who had left Earth. He took a deep breath and said, "Will I fall under Caleb's thrall? Am I even a Lamed Vavnik anymore?"

She eyed the horizon. "I really don't know."

"I'll never eat human flesh," he said. "I'll never be Caleb's slave."

"Best to hold onto that," she said, "for as long as you can."

He was beginning to hate her. The sun changed course, or maybe it was the sands. The crystalline whine of the dunes grew louder, so that Daniel thought he heard whispers just beyond the ever-moving peaks.

In the noonday heat the party slowed to a languorous crawl. Lulled by the singing dunes, the rolling ground, he slipped into a stupor. He wasn't sure how much time had passed when he saw a man standing on the crest of a dune, looking down at them.

Daniel rubbed his eyes, but the figure remained. The man leaned on a tall staff, the wind tugging at his long white beard. Bushy white hair sprouted from his large head. His tea-colored skin was a few shades darker than his beige robe.

Caleb raised his arm, and the Mikulalim reached for their swords.

"Name yourselves!" the bearded man shouted. His voice was small, child-like, but they stood in a bowl-shaped valley that greatly amplified the sound.

Caleb stepped forward and said, "I am Caleb, leader of this party."

The valley had the opposite effect on Caleb's voice, reducing it to a whimper. The sands had stopped moving too. Something was wrong here.

"From which city do you hail?" the man said.

"Azru," said Caleb.

"How many days out are you?"

"Less than a day."

"You flee the destruction?"

Daniel glanced at Marul, in time to notice her flinch.

"Yes, brother," Caleb said. "What a dreadful sight was the sundering of Azru's walls. But as they say, *One city's rubble is the next city's foundation*. We left before the worst. My party and I are inexperienced desert walkers, but by the favor of the Goddess, you have found us!" Caleb made a triangle with his fingers, the same gesture the sitting woman made by the blooming tree just outside of Azru. "Will you help us, friend?"

"We have watched you," the man said.

We? Daniel thought.

"You have followed the tides as a desert roamer would," he said.

"We have turned with the winds as the constellations of Mazzaroth spin with the seasons," Caleb said. "The stars must favor us!"

"In Azru, there lies a square where four stone lions surround a basin. What is its name?"

"Such fine stonework! My wife adores those lions. She is a seamstress. I have a great story about—"

"What is the square's name?"

"Brother, our home has been attacked. We are weary and watersick. Let us break bread in shade together."

"Demons have ransacked dozens of cities across the world. Marauders scavenge the desert like vultures, preying on refugees. You claim to be of Azru, yet you cannot name a street that any child there would know. But your greatest sin of all is that you walk across the Tattered Sea with abominations."

Daniel shivered, because he knew by "abominations" the man meant the Mikulalim.

Caleb said, "Brother, friend, I beg your forgiveness. As the saying goes, *There are no friends on the sand, only survivors.* We are not from Azru. We come from the Araatz, the mountains beyond the DanBaer. We have hired these hooded men for escort because we feared the demon horde would storm our conclave and fled."

"You speak falsehoods by the bushel."

"Do you not welcome the stranger?" Caleb said with a hint of malice. "Do you not water the parched?"

The man considered Caleb, then tapped his staff twice.

Hundreds of people suddenly crested the dune, and Daniel recalled the furtive whispers he had heard. There were young, taut-muscled men in leather garb, wielding swords and daggers and slingshots. They carried shields of leather, wood, and metal. Behind them came older men, with long beards and fluttering robes. And behind these walked a parade of young, beautiful women, bedecked with jewels, twinkling like distant suns. Children clasped the hands of bright-eyed mothers. Babies dangled from slings and suckled on breasts. And behind this throng walked a train of solemn-eyed camels and a tribe of curly-haired goats, all heavily burdened. There were hundreds, maybe thousands of people. Banners on long poles whip-cracked in the wind. But all the people were quiet. Even the animals went still.

The Mikulalim's swords flashed in the sun as they drew them.

"Sheath your weapons!" Caleb ordered. "Raise no arms against them."

"My Lord," Junal said. "They will slaughter us!"

"Sheath your swords," Caleb said, and the Mikulalim obeyed him. Caleb turned to Marul and said, "Witch, why are you so coy? Speak to them, before we're all killed!"

Marul glanced at Daniel before she said, "You'd soon have me become a demon too."

"You're half one already," Caleb said.

In a language different from Wul, Marul shouted, "Good people of the desert, I am Marul Menacha from the city of Ilia. Many years ago I slept under your tents. I shared a hundred sunrises with your fathers. Give us your favor in these dark times. We mean you no harm."

This language was harsh, raspy, more suited to the desert than melodic Wul. And Daniel understood every word.

The bearded-man consulted a stout man at his side. Then he strode down the steep dune, his legs thick and powerful.

Caleb opened his arms wide and said, "Good friend, we welcome you—"

The man ignored Caleb and walked up to Marul. It seemed as if his astoundingly blue eyes, the color of the sky after a summer rain, could pierce through all subterfuge.

"You've changed much," the blue-eyed man said.

"Haven't we all," said Marul.

"I remember you, Marul Menacha of Ilia. I sat on my father's knee as you regaled us with stories of worlds beyond Gehinnom. You spoke of hollow metal birds that fly men from city to city and brave souls who traveled to the stars on pillars of fire."

"Who is your father?" she said.

"Alazar ben Olam, blessed be his memory."

"His *memory*?"

"The sands have taken him."

"Alazar, gone?" Sadness wrinkled her face, but she quickly composed herself. "How did he leave us?"

"The forty houses suffered an execrable curse. At every sundown, we turned into boars and scorpions, returning to our human bodies at dawn. Many died each night, until my father made a deal to save us. He bargained with Chialdra, the eagle demon. Though Chialdra helped us remove the curse, she betrayed my father and ate him alive in front of our children. May her name forever be a curse." He spat.

Marul winced. "A tragedy of generations. You are Jesse, then?"

He shook his head. "Jesse was my brother. He died of malnutrition three years ago during a famine. I am Elizel ben Alazar."

"Little Elizel?" Marul exclaimed. "The boy who raised an orphaned calf and raced it around the camp, making your mother crazy with fright?"

"Zissl mothered more than half our camels."

"Oh, Elizel, how you've grown! So much time has passed."

"And with time comes change. The desert sparrows bring rumors from across the world. Demons are ransacking cities everywhere. They hunt for a demon named Rana."

Marul's face twitched. "Rana's no demon. She's a human girl!"

Elizel eyed her suspiciously. "You know this Rana whom they seek?"

"Distantly," Marul said. "We were friends many years ago." She eyed Caleb. "I have been away from many things for a long, long time."

"The cycle of destruction returns to Gehinnom again," Elizel said. "Demons return to seduce the distraught with their poison knowledge. They foul the minds of our children and plot our slavery for a thousand generations. We must be ever vigilant. Tell me, Marul, why do you walk with these abominations?" He gestured to the Mikulalim, and—Daniel realized with a start—himself.

"They are our guides. We were looking for you. We need the help of the Quog Bedu."

"For what?"

"It's a long story, and—" she held her hand up to shield the sun— "best told in shade. Will you give us sanctuary?"

Elizel considered for a moment. "We will offer *you* sanctuary, Marul, and respite for the humans among you. But our law does not allow these maneaters to walk the sands and live. In the name of the Great Goddess Mollai, Giver of Rain and Succor, we must to destroy these abominations."

Marul shook her head. "Elizel, please! The Mikulalim have been nothing but kind to us. Allow them to return to their home!"

He frowned. "I sympathize, Marul. No one wants blood, and least of all me." He eyed his people crowded on the hill. "But you cannot ask me to flout the law while thousands watch."

"As a friend, as someone who slept in your father's tent, I ask you—no I beg you—make this exception! Send your people away, and allow the Mikulalim to flee."

"I'm sorry," he said. "But that cannot happen. I gave the order before I came to meet you. It cannot be rescinded." He tilted his staff toward them and fifty armed men charged down the hill. There was nowhere to run.

"Daniel!" Caleb shouted. "Take off your cloak! Now! Hurry!"

Daniel threw back his hood as the men ran for them. Stones whooshed past his ears. One hit a Mikulal in the head, and he wailed as he went down. A soldier came for Daniel and raised his sword. Marul shouted, "Stop! He's human!" The soldier knocked Daniel in the ribs with the butt of his sword. Daniel gasped and tumbled onto sand.

Soldiers surrounded Junal. He never lifted his sword. They sliced open his cloak and it fell to the ground. Naked and trembling, Junal screamed as his skin caught fire in the sun. Smoke and flames leaped from his body as Junal withered like a punctured balloon. Daniel watched, sickened, as the screaming Junal shrunk into a quivering lump of animal tissue. Junal's mouth had melted away, but his scream continued.

The soldiers tore away the cloak of another Mikulal, and another, until all were screaming. Caleb's hold on them was so strong they went willingly to their death. "Stop!" Daniel screamed. "Stop killing them!" He rose to his feet, but a soldier kicked him in the back of his legs and he stumbled again.

In a different language, Marul chanted, "*May your suffering be abated. May the cool waters of eternity salve your wounds.*" The Mikulalim whimpered as Marul's hands glowed the stark blue of ancient sea ice. The Mikulalim turned the same color, and their screams lessened. In less than a minute, all of the Mikulalim had been reduced to smoking lumps of flesh.

A soldier put his sword against Marul's neck and said, "Stop your magic, witch, and let the abominations die!" She lowered her hands. The glow faded, and their screams resumed.

Four soldiers surrounded Daniel. One raised his sword.

"Remove your cloak!" Caleb shouted.

Daniel yanked the cloak over his head and tossed it aside. He fell to his knees. He wore only his boxers, and the sun poured like boiling water onto his skin. He wanted to scream, but with great effort he held his voice, afraid they would kill him if he made a sound.

Elizel swept through the soldiers. He stopped before Daniel and demanded, "Why do you wear the cloak of maneaters?" His ultra-blue eyes bored into Daniel's head like Junal's words.

"Because," Caleb said, "he's a milk-skin, from the north! He cannot abide the sun."

"I asked him!" Elizel said. To Daniel he said, "Answer me!"

Panting, Daniel said, "I'm from . . . the cold north. The hot sun hurts me."

Elizel didn't seem convinced. He turned to his men and said, "Burn what's left of the abominations and salvage what we can from their trunks. Then burn those too, as it is said, *The cursed shall burn in your passing, so that not even the dust of their memory remains.*"

The soldiers hurried to execute his orders as Elizel climbed up the dune.

"Elizel ben Azar!" Marul shouted, her cheeks wet with tears, "You're nothing like your father!"

"I know," Elizel said. "Unlike him, I do not bargain with abominations."

The soldiers tore apart the Mikulalim trunks and kindled a fire with the wood. One by one, they threw the screeching Mikulalim into the pile. Daniel watched as a soldier picked up Junal's pouch, the one that held his wife's lock of hair, and tossed it in to the flames.

CHAPTER SEVENTEEN

THE DREAMS WERE ALWAYS THE SAME. RANA WAS LOST IN THE smoke, groping in the dark, as Mama called, "Rana, baby, where are you? I can't see!" Mama's voice was faint, just out of reach, and no matter which way Rana turned she never got any closer. A different voice, a man's raspy whisper, reached into her dreams. She opened her eyes.

She found herself in a small tent. It was light, but not bright. Maybe just before dawn. Her head throbbed painfully, and her tongue stuck to the roof of her mouth. Drugged, by that robed man's potion. She tried to move, but found her arms and feet were bound. Her body ached from lying too long in this position.

"Rana, are you awake?" Emod lay beside her, bound in thick leather belts. His face was heavily bruised, and blood stained his shirt.

"So, Emod," she said hoarsely, "how's business?"

"Quiet!" he whispered. "They're just outside the tent."

Heavy belts wrapped her, just like him. Straining, she brought her knees to her mouth, and reached for the belt with her teeth.

"Wait!" Emod said.

But when her mouth touched leather a sickening taste spread on her tongue. She gagged and retched.

"That charlatan pretended to charm these belts with magic," Emod said, "but I saw him sprinkle some powders on them."

She pushed through the waves of nausea, blinking away the visions of her parents' flayed bodies, the pecking flies. "Where are we?" she said. It hurt even to speak.

"A couple hours from Azru, I think. Somewhere on the Tattered Sea."

"You owe me money."

"Huh?"

"I gave you my works to sell. And you underpaid me, every time."

"Rana, *focus*! These men, they're going to sell us into—"

"I never asked for my fair share because I thought I was helping you. I thought I was keeping you from starving."

He blinked at her. "You were."

"I want my backpay," she said.

"Rana, these men, they would have killed me."

"You brought them to my house, Emod. *My* house." Her voice rose, and Emod glanced at the tent opening. "There were a thousand other houses to plunder, but you chose mine."

He closed his eyes. "Can you forgive an old fool?"

"You're neither old nor a fool," she said. "And I see you never were a friend."

He closed his eyes and shook his head. "I was hiding under my table when they came down Bedubroadstreet. They were slaughtering everyone along their path. They were about to kill me, when I blurted the first thing that came to my mind. I told them I could lead them to your studio, that they would find treasures there. I know how foolish that sounds now, but when you have a sword to your neck, you'd do stupid things too."

"It takes less than a sword for some," she said.

"There was death everywhere. I was terrified. We were just outside your house when we ran into this trembling woman. She was carrying a baby. These beasts were going to toss the baby into the flames and do unspeakable things the woman. But I said, 'Look, here we are! A treasure house sits just over this pile of rock!' And while the men looked, the woman fled with the child. You see, Rana, I saved not just my life, but two others as well."

Rana thought, *A baby girl, by my house?* "What color were her eyes? This baby's?"

"I don't know. It was dark."

"Her hair, was it straight and black?"

"I don't remember. Maybe. Yes, I think so. Why does it matter?"

"I never found my sister."

"Goddess, you think that baby was Liu?"

She paused. There was something in Emod's tone that made her suspicious. He had spent his entire life swindling people. Was he spinning a tall tale, one that made Emod the hero instead of the villain? Or had he really saved Liu's life?

Oh, Liu. Precious beautiful Liu.

How Rana longed to hold Liu in her arms. How she ached to stare into her sister's glistering eyes. Soon she would wake up from this horrid dream, and Mama and Papa would be waiting for her to sit down to dinner.

Emod stared at her. "Those demons who attacked Azru, why were they looking for you?"

She shivered at the memory. "Not me. Someone I was with."

"That pale-skinned man? The one who didn't speak Wul?"

"His name is Daniel Fisher, and he holds the world on his shoulders, but you wouldn't know it by looking at him."

"And here you blame me, when it was you who brought those beasts upon Azru."

She remembered the crumbling walls, the falling towers. The city she had built brick by brick—was it all dust now? "It's not my fault. That dog was the demon king Ashmedai. He brought this upon Azru."

"A lowly dog, the Great Ashmedai? Stealing steaks on Bedubroadstreet to eat?" Emod shook his head. "Rana, you've inhaled too much of that man's potion."

"But it's true. Mashit, a demoness, has cast him out of Sheol. She is looking for him."

Emod gave her a pitying look. "Rana, we're both exhausted. And there's something important I need to tell you before they come back. While you were sleeping, the leader—the one with the scars across his face and arm—he tried to touch you." He paused. "I told him that you were a virgin, that the witch queen wouldn't buy a woman defiled with diseases. He beat me, but then seemed to grow entranced by your necklace. He stared at it for several minutes, as if dreaming, and then he grew sleepy and left."

The necklace, to her surprise, still remained around her neck.

"These men are beasts," Emod said. "He will try to approach you again."

"I won't give him the chance."

"Then we have to find a way to escape."

Rana remembered Grug's last words. *Sing, Rana, sing.* "Yes," she said. "I've an idea." She shouted, "Hey! Ox asses!"

"What the hell are you doing?" Emod said.

Suddenly the beast of a man, the leader with the missing finger, shoved his scarred, bearded face through the tent opening. With him came the smell of sweat and shit. Last night she had feared this face, but now she saw only a diseased animal that needed to be put down.

"Ah, the whore is awake!" he said. "You two ain't getting any food or water til tomorrow, so you best shut your little—"

"You want to sell me to the harems in Ektu El?" she said.

"That's the plan."

"You'd make three times more selling me as a performer than a whore."

"You dance?" the man said, scratching his beard.

"No, I sing."

"So can I!" he said. "With my ass!" He laughed and coughed up phlegm. "Now be a good whore and shut the fuck up. And you—" He kicked Emod in the ribs. "Keep your mouth shut!"

"What you doing with the bitch?" someone said outside the tent. "If you fuck her, then we get a turn too!"

"There's nothing but shit in here," the leader said. "Finish packing the camp!"

"Oh my Goddess!" Rana said in her best slatternly voice. "Your cock is so big and hard! Can I lick it? Please, can I?"

"Rana!" Emod said. "What the hell are you doing?"

The man raised his hand to hit her, but another man, even more ugly, strode into the tent. "You said we ain't to fuck the bitch because our pricks are dirty, but you said nothing about her sucking us off."

More of the men joined in. "Is he fucking her? What a demon!"

"He was going to show me his big cock," Rana said to the second man. "How about you take me outside so all you boys can have a go?"

"Rana!" Emod said. "What are you—"

The leader kicked Emod. "The bitch lies!" he said. "I got my fucking trousers on!"

"Yeah, but it's been weeks since we had soft lips between our legs," the other said. "Let's bring her outside and have turns at her, just for a bit."

"There will be no such thing!"

The men protested. "Bring the whore out! Let's see her titties!"

"Enough!" the leader said. "You want to see her?" With one huge arm he lifted her by a belt and carried her out into the bright sun. He threw her down to the sands.

"Hey!" one said. "Don't break her! She's worth a small city."

Rana coughed and blinked as her eyes adjusted to the brightness.

"There!" the leader said. "As you can see, she's tied, and my cock is in my pants. And if any of you dogs try to shove your pricks into her, I'll cut them off!"

Rana faced four dour-eyed camels, each overburdened with plunder from Azru. The bronze bust of Mollai she had made for Mama poked from one of the saddlebags.

There were six men, scarred, tattooed, hirsute, plus the charlatan in his colorful robe. This pale man smoked a long, thin bone pipe while one of his eyes leered at her. The other gazed at the men. All the men eyed her hungrily, except for the charlatan, and Rana sensed that he preferred their form to hers.

"I can sing," she said. "I can sing more beautifully than dessert sparrows. I'm worth more as a singer than a whore."

"Is that true?" one said.

"Don't know," said another.

"How much more?" said a third.

"At least five times," she said. "Maybe ten."

The charlatan's long white-hair blew in the wind as he lowered his pipe. "She's trying to trick you," he said. His mousy voice barely reached her ears.

"Back in Azru, you cowered when the men fought the maneater," she said to him. "You chant gibberish. You're no magician. You use cheap potions any fool can buy."

He scowled at her, then reached for a knife at his belt. It was her knife, she saw, the one with the bejeweled hilt. "I'll show you magic!" he squeaked.

The leader raised his hand to stop him.

"Let me sing," Rana said. "And judge for yourselves my worth."

The charlatan crossed his arms. "Let's hear you, then."

"Yeah," another said. "You can practice your song for when we spread your hips!" The men laughed and the robed one took a puff of his pipe. Rana's nose twitched from the cloyingly sweet scent of the smoke.

"I cannot sing while bound," she said. "How do you expect me to fill my lungs?"

"It's a trick," the charlatan said. "She wants to run away."

"We're in the deep desert. Where would I run off to?"

The leader stared at her for a minute, then ordered the charlatan to undo the "magic" of the bonds, which amounted to him putting on gloves while he unbuckled the many belts and chanted nonsense words in Bedu-Besk. As he unbuckled them, she whispered, "You're not half a magician. You're not even half a man."

His face grew red, but she knew he would not hit her, the coward. Her body ached, but it was wonderful to be free of the belts. She wiped sand from her clothes as she stood. The men crossed their arms and waited.

"Well?"

Teeth missing, lice crawling in their beards, panting like dogs, they watched her. Her parents were dead, and yet these vermin got to live? Justice had to be meted out.

In Yarrow, on the Pedestal of Lamentation, the acoustics had been superb. Here, the desert swallowed her voice like a hungry beast. She adjusted her volume, adding staccato, melody. She thought of Mama, Papa, Liu, using her feelings like kindling for flames inside her. She stoked them to a raging conflagration. Her voice rose in pitch, as patient as the rising sun.

Their pupils dilated. Their mouths opened. Their faces went slack.

The masons had labored twice as hard when she'd sung. Davo and the masons might all be dead now. The Ukne had been toppled. The kindling piled on.

Their eyes rolled up into their heads as they trembled like old men.

When she had wanted the masons to add reticulation or distressing to the stonework, they had obeyed her, even though Chief Jo might give them the whip. And now, while she sang, she understood why. They had no choice. They had become tools.

Drool dripped from their mouths, their arms dropped to their sides, and their eyes went as blank as the statues that had lined Azru's streets and stood no more.

The Mikulalim kneeled when she'd imagined them kneeling. And the same thundering arousal, that torrent of pleasure, shuddered through her again. The men dropped to their knees, faces bright red, their trousers tented and pricks throbbing. Their minds were gone, sung away. They were hers.

She imagined the charlatan walking into the tent and using her knife to free Emod. And the cretin did just that, his eyes spinning like stars as he walked.

As she sang, there came a shriek, then a gurgling sound. Emod emerged with her bejeweled knife, blood dripping down the blade. His expression was wild, manic.

She sang and Emod slew each in turn. He jabbed the knife into their backs, some more than once, because they were large, and it was only when the men received their fatal blow did they shriek. Emod slaughtered them all, but before he killed the leader, Rana stopped singing.

The beast man fell to his knees, shuddering. Emod awoke from her spell, gasped, and threw the bloody knife to the sands.

The kneeling man said to her, "Please, please don't—"

"Take off your clothes," she said.

"What?" he whimpered.

"Take off your fucking clothes."

"Yes, yes, whatever you say!" He got up and stripped to his undergarments.

"Everything," she said. "Take it all off." Naked, he stood before her like a scrofulous goat. He was potbellied, covered in curly dark hairs. She picked up her knife.

"Rana!" Emod said. "Don't."

"Get on your knees," she said.

The man dropped to the sand. "I have a storehouse in Blömsnu!" he cried. "Rooms full of treasure! It's yours! Every last gem!"

"Gems?" she said. "Will rubies bring my parents back? Will a bag of emeralds return my sister to me?"

"No," the man cried. "But they will make their loss easier to bear."

"He's right!" Emod said.

"No," Rana said. "Only one thing will make this right." She moved toward him, twirling her knife.

"Please!" he said. "Life is hard in the desert. We do what we have to. You know the rules of the sands!"

"Shhh," she whispered as she ran a finger down his cheek, as he had done to her last night. "Quiet now. It's time for the dog to go to sleep now."

"You dirty witch whore!" he spat as tears poured down his face. "I should have fucked you when I had the chance!" He lunged for her, but she thrust the knife into his crotch. He screamed as blood poured from the wound. Emod cried out and turned away.

Holding his bleeding crotch, the man screamed, "Please!"

"How many of your victims begged for mercy? How many women did you rape and kill? How many children did you slaughter? How many families did you destroy? Where was your mercy then?"

The man shook his head and whimpered. "Please!"

She pushed him onto his back and with a quick slice, she removed his genitals from his body. He wailed as she held the severed flesh above his face, letting its blood spill into his mouth. He coughed and choked on his blood and tears.

"Funny," she said, "how so many of the world's problems are caused by this little piece of flesh. And yours, I must say, *is* so very little." She tossed it over her shoulder. "Enjoy the fruits of your labor."

Emod was staring at her, mouth agape.

"What are *you* looking at?" she spat.

He retreated from her, as if she might pounce.

"Let's load the camels and get the fuck out of here," she said.

"Rana," Emod said, trembling, "*what* are you?"

"What am I?" The dead men lay quiet around her. The sands were stained with their blood. "I am judgment."

A tear rolled down Emod's cheek. "If you are judgment, then I shall be mercy." He picked up a sword and said to the leader, "Forgive me." Then he plunged the blade into the man's chest. The man gurgled and went still.

In the silence, Rana's heart calmed. She held her dagger up to the light, and its gems flashed with tiny rainbows. She wiped blood from the blade with her shirt, while Emod fell to his knees beside her. He made the Mollai Triangle with his fingers and said, "Goddess, forgive me! Giver of rain and succor and life, forgive me."

CHAPTER EIGHTEEN

WHERE ARE YOU, RANA, CALEB THOUGHT, YOU PRECIOUS, irreplaceable wonder? Do you lie broken under a heap of stone? Did Mashit find you, and is she at this very moment torturing you to find out where we've gone? Or did you escape and are now flying toward me like a sparrow over the sands? Grug, Caleb thought, *have you failed me?*

Time would reveal all soon enough. There was none like Rana in a billion Shards. With her vision and his guidance, together they could do great things. If she were dead, such a loss! Such a loss.

"Are you listening?" Daniel said.

The three of them, Daniel, Marul and Caleb, sat on a fine-tapestried carpet inside the Bedu tent, its walls adorned with golden and crimson filigree. A hanging censer misted the air with strong perfume. Bedu servants pried them with food and wine, and their many bronze bowls and silver cups shone.

"What happened to Azru?" Daniel said as a servant girl offered them a tray of dried fruits. He declined, but Marul helped herself to generous portions.

"Delicious!" Marul said to the yellow-eyed girl. "Where are they from?"

"Witch," Caleb said "are you cracked in the head? We are but one word away from sharing the fate of the Mikulalim, and you feast? Right now Elizel is meeting with the leaders of his house to decide our fate. This could be our last meal."

"All the more reason to enjoy it," she said. "Besides, it's been quite a long time since I've had a meal like this."

Daniel said to the servant girl, "Azru was attacked?"

The girl looked for another servant, who had just stepped outside to refill a pitcher. The gold on her wrists, neck, and waist could have bought a small city, and yet among the Bedu she was of the servant's house. Such was the Bedu wealth. She blinked her yellow eyes and said, "Thus go the whispers of the woodcock on the wind."

Marul pointed into her cup and a lithe young man refilled it with wine. She eyed his crotch as he poured.

"Tell me what happened," Daniel said.

"A hole in heaven opened up," the girl said, "and a horde of demons fell out." Underneath her fear was a hint of excitement. "It's said that King Jallifex's head rots on a spit, and his subjects scatter across the sands. You three are from the Araatz?"

"We're from many places," Marul said, giving Daniel a cautious look.

"Do you encounter many maneaters?" said the girl. "Or demons?"

An older girl entered the tent and said, "Aviva, go refill your pitcher in the store-tent."

The girl nodded, and her gold adornments flashed as she stepped out into the sun.

"Marul," Caleb said. "Isn't it about *time*, we had that talk?" He hoped she understood his implication. It took her a minute, when she finally nodded.

"Yes," she said, putting down her cup. She placed her hands on her knees, palms up, then brought her hands together, turning her hands so that one palm spun over the other, then reversed the gesture. In Demonsbreath she mumbled twenty-nine words. The older girl looked as if she was about to speak when the glimmer in her eyes froze like glass. The smoke from the censer stopped mid-rise, its curlicue poised like a question mark.

"What's happened?" Daniel said. "Why did everything stop?"

Marul kept her palms together. "We're moving in sped up time," she said.

Daniel sat back, eyes wide. "Like the scorpions on Kipod's Stair?"

"Except we're the ones moving faster now," she said. "They can't hear us."

"They've been listening to everything we say," Caleb said. "And reporting back to Elizel. They give us food and drink to make us slow and stupid, in the hope that we might reveal something. We are not guests here."

Daniel said, "They can't hear us at all?"

"They might hear a brief buzz," Marul said. "Like an insect passing."

Daniel leaned forward, scowling, as he said to Caleb, "You ordered the Mikulalim to die. You murdered them!"

"If you recall," Caleb said, "it was not I who sliced open their cloaks and tossed their bodies into the flames."

Daniel's face turned red. "Nine men were burned alive because you commanded them to lay down their swords and die."

"The Mikulalim aren't men," Caleb said. "They are fragments."

"Where you see fragments," Daniel said, "I see slaves."

"I'm not sure how long I can hold this spell," Marul said. "Can we get to the point?"

"Do you think they would spare you, Daniel," Caleb said, "if they knew the Mikulal poison swirled in your blood too? How quickly you forget that I saved you. Twice now."

"I should tell them you're a demon," Daniel said.

"Only if you are suicidal," Caleb said. "They'll kill us all if they discover who I am."

"They may have already sensed your nature," Marul said.

"Doubtful," said Caleb. "I've taken precautions. I am as human as can possibly be."

"Not from where I sit," Daniel said, staring at him.

"Are you as vulnerable as a human too?" Marul said.

Caleb looked into Marul's green eyes, searching for motive. A hint of her old power glinted there, under the surface, the part of Marul who once thought she could be a god. *What are you plotting, witch?* he thought.

"Enough of these games," he said. "We need each other as much as we need the Quog Bedu. Their priests are the only ones who have the power to get us back to Earth. If I had ordered the Mikulalim to fight, how would you suppose we curry their favor then?"

"Slaughter is *not* the only way!" Daniel said.

"Have you a better path?"

"Yes," he said. "Truth. Honesty. Once they understand what's at stake, they'll help us. We're trying to save Gehinnom too."

Marul shook her head. "We can't tell them the truth. Not all of it, anyway. Once we reveal ourselves they will only see us as a witch, a demon, and a maneater trying to deceive them."

"You don't know that for sure."

"I've lived with these Bedu," Marul said. "There is a reason why they've survived for centuries on this world where all things turn to dust. They trust no one, only Bedu, and sometimes not even then. They are a cautious people, for good reason. We cannot tell them the truth, but perhaps we can reveal just enough to get you home."

"So, what's the plan then?" Daniel said. "Keep murdering people until I get home?"

Caleb took a deep quaff of palm wine from his silver cup, and felt his stomach warm as it went down. "We first must convince Elizel to help us. To do that we must appeal to his self-preservation. Let me do the talking."

"My spell is faltering," Marul said. "Hurry! Everyone, back in your places."

The question mark of smoke began to rise, slowly at first, until it became a fading exclamation point. The servant girl blinked and looked bemused. She gave a curious look at Caleb's half-empty cup, which had been full a moment before.

"May I offer you more palm wine?" she said, adding a smile.

Every one is a spy, Caleb thought. *Well-trained to feign innocence.* "The Bedu have been more than gracious," he said to her with a broad smile.

Outside, a man shouted, "The Chieftain is coming!"

Elizel ben Alazar stooped as he entered their tent, and the servants bowed to him. Two strong men followed Elizel. Caleb and the others rose, and Caleb made the Mollai Triangle to greet him.

"Sit, sit!" Elizel said, pointing at the rug. "Be comfortable and serene. This is a tent of peace." But his hasty words betrayed his urgency. Beside him stood a tall, burly man with a square black beard. "This is Otto ben Zadok, general of our armies."

Otto bowed to them as his eyes stayed fixed on Caleb.

"And this is Uriel ben Temen." He was hard-jawed man with large, dark eyes unusually far apart, like a camel. "Uriel is our High Priest, master of Scriptures, and my right-hand. Otto and Uriel will hear your story." All of them sat and formed a circle. With a wave of Elizel's hand the servants fled the tent. Outside, Caleb saw, four guards stood with hands on sword hilts. Appearances aside, this was no friendly convocation.

"Have you eaten enough?" Elizel said. "Had your fill of wine?"

"The Bedu hospitality knows no limits," Caleb said.

"We have only a few minutes before the shift," Elizel said, referring to the tides of sand. "We must speak quickly."

Uriel's camel eyes warily observed them, as if Caleb and the others might strike at any moment. Otto meanwhile endlessly tugged at his beard, looking thoughtful.

"Well?" Elizel said. "Speak!"

Caleb took a deep breath. "Brothers of the sands, the Seventh Book of Tobai speaks of the Thirty-Six Pillars that hold the Kuurku aloft in Heaven. I shall presume all you learned men know the story."

Uriel looked to Elizel for permission, and Elizel nodded. "Yes, we know the tales of the Thirty-Six Pillars quite well," Uriel said. "And we know the myriad interpretations of the interpretations of the interpretations."

"Brothers, what if I were to tell you that those ceaseless fountains will soon cease? That the water of life will stop flowing?"

"Stop how?" said Uriel.

"Demons are murdering the Thirty-Six Pillars, one by one, in the Kuurku. Like a house with weakened columns, the Kuurku will collapse. When this happens, all of us will suffer horrible torments for eons until we die in a cataclysm so great the whole Cosmos will shudder."

Uriel said, "Are these demons who kill the Thirty-Six Pillars the same beasts who have attacked the cities across Gehinnom?"

"Yes, they are the Legion of the First, and under the command of Mashit, a demoness."

"We know of Mashit," Otto said, spitting to the side. "Word has come from afar that she's taken over the throne of Sheol from the cursed Ashmedai." He spat again.

"And now," Caleb said, "Mashit is using the Legion to attack cities across Gehinnom."

Otto whispered something in Elizel's ear, and Elizel nodded.

Otto said, "Why do they attack this world, now?"

"Have you seen the fragments falling in the night sky?"

Uriel nodded and said, "They are pieces of the Kuurku, the Seat of the Flowing Waters."

"The wisdom of the Quog Bedu is renowned," Caleb said. "In order to destroy a Pillar, one must break him from the Kuurku like chiseling a brick from a wall. You must remove the mortar to free the brick. The Legion has been killing the Thirty-Six Pillars, one by one, and these fragments of the Kuurku are evidence of their removal."

Uriel nodded. "Continue."

"Soon, brothers, there won't be enough Pillars to uphold the Kuurku. The waters of life will rain down in an unimaginable torrent upon this world and the myriad Shards. There will be an explosion of life like this world has never seen. But the waters will soon cease, the Shards will dry up, and our souls will wither in the Great Deep over timespans beyond imagining. It will be the end of this cycle of eternity."

Uriel took a long, deliberate breath. "This is but one interpretation of events. Our priests have debated the signs. Where you see portents of ending, we prophesy a new beginning for this world. As one cycle completes, another begins."

"Surely, you are joking," Caleb said.

"Blessed Mollai, Giver of Rain and Succor, redeems the souls of her faithful servants," Uriel said, "as it is written, 'At the end of every season, Mollai brings the fallen to her breast.'"

Was he playing the fool, to bait him? Or did Uriel really believe this drivel?

"Brothers," Caleb said, "if what I say comes to pass, even blessed Mollai, Giver of Rain, will perish too."

Otto scowled. "The Great Goddess is not mortal!" He jumped to his feet. "I think we've heard enough, Lord Elizel. The shift comes and—"

But Elizel pulled him back down. "Sit! We have more to hear from Caleb."

"Thank you, Lord Elizel," Caleb said, as Otto reluctantly sat.

"Marul says you need our help," Elizel said. "How?"

"A world of abundance drifts in the Kuurku like a grain of sand lost in the wind. Humans dwell on this world."

"The Land of Erte," Uriel said.

"Yes," Caleb said, "Terra, Gaia, Haaretz. Earth, with its blue oceans, its thriving cities, its fruitful fields and dense forests. Brothers, we need you to take us there."

Otto laughed. "We do not even ferry strangers to distant cities, and you would have us take you to this world among the stars?"

"Actually," Uriel said, "The Land of Erte lies far beyond the stars. It floats even beyond our universe."

"Your Bedu priests," Caleb said, "are powerful magicians. You can send us there."

"Why?" said Elizel.

"To stop the Legion from killing the Pillars. To prevent the Kuurku from collapsing. Dear brothers, to save you and your people and all the people on Gehinnom from a horrid death."

Otto crossed his arms and gave Caleb a hard, skeptical look. Uriel said, "Even if we believe your intentions are genuine, why do you think we can ferry you to the Land of Erte? We are powerful, but not omnipotent."

"Marul Menacha, the woman who has supped in your tents with your fathers, knows a spell to craft a Merkavah, the vessel that can ferry us across the Great Deep. But she needs power. This is why we've come to you. Your power is greater than any other on this world."

Otto tugged at his beard. "Lord Elizel, this man spins lies like the stars of the Jeen. We have fifty fothers of barley and two hundred jars of oil to haul to Blömsnu before the quarter moon. With the attacks, the cities will need the Bedu more than ever! We have no time for one man's delusions—"

Elizel raised his hand to silence Otto. "You are three," Elizel said, sweeping his hand before them. "How do three humans stop a demon army?"

"With speed and forethought," Caleb said. "We will seek out the remaining Pillars and hide them before they can be killed. And to give us even more time I will restore a Pillar who has fallen from the Kuurku to Gehinnom."

"And who might that be?" Uriel said.

"This man here," Caleb said, pointing to Daniel. "Daniel Fisher, Lamed Vavnik."

Daniel sat back, breathed in deep as the men took this in.

"Him?" Otto said. "A Pillar? He was wearing a cloak of the maneaters just an hour ago. Lord Elizel, this defiles our tent."

"Elizel," Marul said. "Lord Elizel. On the blood of my fathers, by the Great Goddess Mollai, I swear, Daniel Fisher is a Pillar. He needs to get back to Earth."

Uriel inspected Daniel, as if he were a beast for sale. "Daniel may be a Pillar, or he may be an imposter. How can we know what you say is true?"

"The demon army that attacks this world," Caleb said, "is looking for him."

"Which means they're now looking for us!" Otto shouted.

Elizel stiffened his jaw. "If this is true, then you bring great danger to the Bedu. And for this you want our help?"

"Lord Elizel," Caleb said, "the danger is already upon us. Your people are the last hope of Gehinnom. And you very well may be the last hope of the Cosmos. I know we're asking you to take a leap of faith. But if we do nothing, then we might as well throw ourselves on our swords now. The demons will have already won."

A ram's horn blew three bracing notes, and Elizel and his men exchanged glances.

"The shift comes," Elizel said as he climbed to his feet. "Prepare yourselves for travel." He took a deep breath and said, "Before I decide what to do, I'll convey your story to the Synedrium, so the houses can speak their views. This is too great a decision for one man."

"Lord Elizel," Caleb said, "the Legion won't wait for your politics."

"I agree," Otto said. "Hence why I vote we cast these foreigners into the desert before they bring hell to us."

"That would be a grave mistake," Caleb said, "for all."

Elizel paused at the tent opening. "The burden of leadership is weightier than lead. I wish it on no one. The Synedrium will meet as soon as we reach the next sandlull. Until I hear from the houses, I will make no decisions."

Elizel swept out of the tent, and Otto muttered, "Coward." Otto glowered at Caleb as he and Uriel left.

The servants ran into the tent and snuffed the censer, stowed the cups, and rolled up the rug. As they collapsed the tent, the yellow sun beat down upon them again. The dunes had fled since they'd entered the shade. The flat sands gave no hint that they would soon fling them across the desert faster than a jet.

The six thousand Bedu packed the camp—a small city—with uncanny speed. In minutes it was as if the camp had never been. A group of soldiers remained close, keeping their wary eyes on Caleb and the others. Their shackles, he saw, were subtle.

Daniel shivered in the sun. "I—I need protection. Where is the cloak?"

"They burned it," Marul said. "Let me go see what I can do."

In a few minutes one of the servant girls returned with a hooded gray cloak. It was ragged and soiled, but it was enough to cover most of his exposed skin. Daniel donned it eagerly. To Caleb's surprise, he watched Daniel shove his purple wedding flower into his pocket.

Had Daniel held it in his fist this whole time? That meant that even in the midst of the battle he had thought to save it.

Daniel, Caleb thought, *do you still cling to your fantasy that Rebekah was real, that all of this is a bad dream? You are in for a great shock.*

Daniel threw his hood over his face and said, "How am I supposed to hold up a world, when I can't even hold myself up?"

Marul helped him cover his skin. "Stop with your self-pity," she said. "It's very unflattering. Just think, by tomorrow, you'll be home, and all this will be forgotten."

"I'll never forget this," Daniel said.

The Bedu arranged themselves in serried ranks, and even the animals fell into line. A sparrow darted across the sky, chirping a song in a high key. Caleb could hear the bird, but none other seemed to notice. He listened as the sparrow sung a message from Havig.

Grug is dead, the sparrow sang, sweetly and quickly. *Rana's parents dead too. Rana is missing, location unknown. The Mikulalim scour Gehinnom, looking for her, my lord.*

Caleb shuddered as the sparrow flew away. Was Rana dead? What a dreadful, dreadful waste. A knot tightened in his chest. He needed Rana for his plan, but this emotion was something else, something unexpected. By Abbadon, he missed her.

A ram's horn blew, and the six thousand men, women, and children began their slow march across the sands. Toward salvation or death, they marched on.

———

A dune two hundred feet tall pursued them as they walked, and Daniel felt that at any moment it would crash upon them. The Bedu walked in separate houses, each several hundred people in number. Like soldiers in an expert march, they maintained formation even as the hills and valleys rolled steeply beneath them. Within each house marched standard-bearers, strong boys with biceps of stone. They hoisted banners of azure, crimson, and gold, and the name of each house was written in a flourishing script. Each house had a distinct symbol. Kissing hawks, cups of wine, a tent, entangled snakes, crossed swords. There were at least forty flags, but the moving sands made an exact count impossible.

One house drove a herd of camels, another drove goats. One house seemed to consist only of men. Daniel and the others walked with House Ravid, priests and soldiers and their families. Fifty paces ahead, Elizel, Otto, and Uriel were in a heated discussion. Otto cursed and shouted, but Elizel never reacted to his outbursts, and instead stared ahead at the horizon. Uriel shook his head, as if disappointed with them both.

The Bedu, Daniel saw, were a wealthy people. The hilts of their swords glittered with jewels. Golden belts and bracelets flashed from their women. Their gossamer clothing was finely sewn, and intricate threads of blue, yellow, and crimson weaved through elegant seams. Several of their camels bore cedar palanquins on their backs, knobs and finials carved into roaring lions. Prayers had been delicately inlaid in the wood.

Daniel had never seen these letters before, but he understood the words perfectly. A prayer curved over one nearby palanquin window: *May her Great Name be exalted and sanctified in the World which She hath created according to Her Will . . .*

The prayer was nearly word for word the same as the Kaddish, the Jewish prayer for the sanctification of God's name. And he remembered—it seemed ages ago now—that when Rana had conversed with that pipe-smoking salesman in Azru, Daniel had picked up a ring with a Star of David signet.

I'm not the first to come from Earth to this world, he thought. How many had come before him, trading ideas, beliefs, knowledge? And how many from Gehinnom had traveled to Earth, like Marul? *Maybe,* he thought, *the ancient Hebrews got their beliefs from this world and not the other way around. Or maybe it was infinitely more complicated.*

The titanic dune chasing them groaned and hissed like a creeping monster. For the past hour, many odd creatures had visited the wave. Mirrored worms, furry green caterpillars, skeletons as big as dinosaurs. They vanished soon after they appeared, returning to the sandy depths from which they had been churned.

Marul put her small hand on his shoulder. "Don't worry," she said. "The dune won't break. Not this far into the Tattered Sea. We're riding the wave," she said. "Every minute takes us parasot across the desert."

She looked back toward Caleb. The demon had ingratiated himself with a group of leather-clad soldiers, who chortled and belly laughed at Caleb's crude and bawdy jokes.

Marul turned back to Daniel and said something else. *Can you hear my thoughts? Nod your head if you understand.* Her words, just as with Junal, were thrust into his mind.

Surprised, he nodded. *You speak the Mikulalim language?*

Grug taught me the silent tongue, she thought. *But I can converse only when in physical contact. Answer me aloud before Caleb suspects something.*

"Where are we headed?" he said.

She glanced over her shoulder at Caleb, before think-speaking. *You were right, Daniel, back in the tent. There is another path.*

Without Caleb. Aloud she said, "We are headed to Blömsnu, I think, to deliver grain and oil."

And what is this other path?

We will pretend we were ignorant of Caleb's demon nature until now. That he deceived us into helping him. He is weak, vulnerable, in human form. I don't think I'm strong enough to kill him, but the Bedu might be. "The sun feels good on my skin," she said. "It's been so long."

"Perhaps you've had too much," he said. *I thought you said they'll kill us if they discover he's a demon?*

"I have only just returned to the light," she said. *If we knew he was a demon, and still befriended him, then yes, we would likely be killed. But if we play the unwitting victim, the Bedu might have mercy on us. If you stay close, I will do my best protect you when the time comes.* "Why would I shy away from the light so quickly?"

"Because excess of anything is never good." *We need Caleb, Marul! He knows who the Lamed Vav are. Without him, we can't protect them when we get back to Earth!*

Caleb is not the only one who knows, she thought. "'The road to excess leads to the palace of wisdom.'"

Who else knows then? he thought. "Or ruin."

She stared at him. *I know.*

He was confused. How could Marul, the witch who'd been trapped in a cave for five years, know where to find the other Lamed Vav? Had Caleb told her?

Does it matter how I know? she thought. *It only matters that I do. We don't need him.*

Daniel realized he had to be more careful of his stray thoughts. *I've never killed anyone before. I don't know if I can start now.*

You won't have to lift a sword. "Ruin?" she said. "How can I fall any lower than I've already been?"

He stared at her. "You could die." *Even if I don't strike the killing blow against him, it would be murder. The same as Caleb ordering the Mikulalim to drop their swords.*

Her face grew red. "For some, death is freedom." *Do you know how many millions Caleb has killed? How many suffered because of him? This is our chance to rid the Cosmos of him forever! Daniel, don't deny me my revenge!*

Daniel caught a stray thought from Marul, an image of her crushing Caleb's skull with a stone, his blood pouring over the stone floor of her prison. It was so vivid he knew she had imagined this a thousand times over the years.

Gram used to say, "If I could go back in time to strangle Hitler in the cradle—*emoch shmo!*—I would have! I would have killed that baby if I knew it would save millions." Behind them, Caleb still joked with the soldiers. Would his death be just?

Wait for my sign, Marul thought. Staring into his eyes, she lifted her hand from his shoulder. "It is a good day to think on things," she said.

He heard laughter behind him. Five children had been following him. They were pointing and whispering. Pushed by his peers, a dark-faced boy approached Daniel. His eyes were enormous blue orbs. He lifted a small knife and said in Bedu-Besk, "Hark, stranger! I'm a Shield of the Tribe. You break the twenty-fifth law. 'Thou shalt not defile your tents with the unclean.'"

Daniel put his hands up in mock surrender. "Apologies, little shield. It's been days since I bathed. I'm as unclean as they come." He smiled.

The boy glanced back at his peers and they urged him on. "The punishment for defilement is death," the boy said, nervously.

"In that case, lead me to your baths."

"Maneaters need to be destroyed."

Daniel frowned, remembering the Mikulalim screams, when something hard slammed into his head. His skull rang with pain, and it was followed by a severe wave of nausea.

"Maneater!" a girl shouted.

Daniel fell to his knees, holding his ringing head, when something hot and sharp pierced his side. Daniel gasped as the boy ran away, his knife flashing in the sun. He saw his blood pouring onto the sand, and only then did he feel the pain.

"No!" Caleb shouted. "What did that little bastard do?"

Daniel rolled onto his side, clutching the wound. Hot, wet liquid poured over his hand. Was this happening? Marul hovered above him, speaking, but he heard only the droning of bees. The dune rose behind them, an enormous wall made of blood. The skeleton of some long-dead beast floated up from the depths, split into pieces, and sank again, consumed in red.

CHAPTER NINETEEN

SHE RODE ON THE BACK OF A CAMEL, TOWARD AZRU, TOWARD home, and Emod rode beside her. Emod had said little since they left camp, preferring the stillness of a tobacco pipe taken from one of the dead men. With a short tether, they each pulled a second camel, and all of them were laden with the bandits' loot. Most of the items appeared to be from Rana's studio. The copper bust of Mollai she had made for Mama poked out from a bag at her heel, flashing in the sun.

"Azru's gone, Rana," Emod said to the sere plain, breaking hours of silence. Mournful dunes crept across the sands of the Tattered Sea like hungry ghosts. "There's nothing in Azru for us now."

"There's Liu," she said. "And my parents. I have to burn their bodies."

Emod sighed. "The king's armies have been defeated. No one guards the streets. Those bastards—" he swallowed "—won't be the only pillagers."

"You said you saw my sister alive, rescued by a woman."

"I'm not sure what I saw. Rana, we have jewels worth a small city. Let's go to Ektu El and build a new life. You can craft your art, and I can sell it again."

She gritted her teeth. "That would be death." She had to believe Liu was alive. What else was left? "I have to go back for my sister."

"You told me all about Liu," he said, his voice as shaken as the horizon. "But I never saw her myself. Maybe it was another child I saw."

"If you want to leave, Emod, then go. Ektu El is nine days north."

He dragged a hand through his dark, greasy hair. "I've crossed the desert many times, but always with a guide. I've no idea which way to go."

She pointed with her chin. "Forward is south. Backward is north."

"Are you sure? We've been walking south for hours. We should have seen the Araatz by now, the DanBaer." The bruises of his face had begun to fester and had turned as orange as the sands. "I see nothing but more desert."

"I know the sun," she said.

"So do I. I lived my days under it. But do you know the tides?" A small dune rolled beneath them, whistling a somber note as it passed.

"No," she said. "Do you?"

He shook his head.

"Then we head south until we reach Azru, or we die. I don't see any other way."

He mumbled, "There are always other ways." But he remained beside her.

Their camels slowed as the dunes grew steadily larger, when, like frightened rams, the dunes skipped away and the desert became as still and flat as water in a bucket.

"I don't like this," she said.

"We must be in a sandlull," Emod said. "Where the tides cancel." And he added, with despair, "There are none near Azru that I know of."

In the haze on the southern horizon a rectangular object wavered in the heat. Dark as an olive but flecked with brilliance, it leaned off-kilter like a brick set poorly.

"Do you see that?" Emod said. "Perhaps I was wrong. Maybe we are approaching Azru!"

"No."

"Are you sure? Maybe it's a piece of a tower that has fallen? Blessed Mollai, I hope it's so."

"I know every brick in Azru. That's something else."

The object grew as they approached, revealing its great size. It was three stories high and two hundred paces on its longest side. Its surface was dark but reflective hematite, though it had been severely sandworn and rusted. Carved in relief on its surface in many rows, demons and humans waged a brutal history along its sides. A tall name curved like a bow over the histories in an ornate Ytrain script.

"*The Stele of Yiskorel*," Emod read. "If we're here, then—"

"Then we're hundreds of parasot from Azru," Rana said. Mama had said so many times that the desert eats people like a lizard eats ants. She would die here. She thought of Liu, staring up into some stranger's eyes, wondering where Mama and Papa had gone.

She said, "I'm sorry. I thought we were headed south."

"The Stele once pointed the compass," he said.

She stared at its crooked alignment. "Now it's just a misplaced stone."

The camels looked up at the Stele as they passed, mesmerized by its reflections. The bas-reliefed demons stared at her from its surface, their metallic eyes glinting in the sun. The Stele had been crafted from a solid piece of hematite. What monster chisel could have hewn so much stone? What great hand could have hefted it here? She wished she could meet the artisans who had crafted it, but like most things on Gehinnom no one remembered their name. A few of its corners still shined with a mirror luster, but the desert had not been kind to the Stele. One side had been entirely sandworn to a blur.

"Yiskorel, the Memory of God," Rana said, "fades like an old man."

Emod sighed. "He isn't the only one."

"Emod," she said. "Back at the camp—"

"Please. Let's not talk about it."

"But there something I need to say."

"Rana, *please!*" His voice echoed from the folds of hematite.

"It had to be done," she said.

"Rana," His lower lip quivered. "I've never killed before."

"Those men deserved death, Emod."

"Did they? All of them?"

"Yes," she said, because the alternative was too horrid to consider. "Besides, you didn't kill them. I did. I just used your hands." She trembled at the power she wielded. To move men with song. When she found Liu, no one would ever stand in her way again.

"You're wrong," he said. "I was not an empty vessel, a puppet, which you moved. I was fully awake. Alive! And most of all, *inspired.*"

"Inspired?"

"I murdered those men, Rana, not because you moved my hands, but because I *ached* to kill them. Decades living on the streets, being beaten and robbed and cheated, were the tinder. Your song lit the match. Now my heart is a raging fire, and I cannot put the flames out."

"You want to kill again?"

He glanced at her. "Kill? My life was dull, full of long days and frigid nights. When you sang, I felt something I had long forgotten, something I hadn't felt since I was a boy. Rana, I want to hear you sing so I can feel that surge of life again. And that terrifies me."

"Life terrifies you?"

He shook his head as if shooing away demons. "What scares me is knowing that all of my days were shadows, that my life was dust. I can see now how much time I've wasted."

"We do the best we can with what the Goddess gave us."

"And what did I do with these calloused hands?" he said, releasing the reins. "Lie, cheat, steal? And now, I've killed. They are stained now."

She harrumphed. "I saved your life. You could at least be thankful."

He looked mournfully at her. "Thankful? Rana, I thought you were my friend."

"Were you ever mine?"

"Of course!"

"Really? How many times did you cheat me out of my earnings?"

"I was poor. I thought you were being kind."

"I was, but I thought you were a different person. Not a coward who betrays his best friend the instant someone points a blade at his neck."

"I was your best friend?"

"You were my only friend."

He rose in his saddle. "And now?"

"Now we are but two strangers in the desert."

"Yes," he said with growing confidence. Emod did have a way with strangers. "The Rana I knew didn't inspire men to slaughter." He shook his head. "Rana—if you remember anything of our friendship, then grant me one final kindness. Please don't ever sing to me again."

"Not every song must inspire murder. I could sing to make you feel joy, even pleasure, if you wanted it."

"I've no doubt you can. But your music is not what I fear most. It's the silence, after." He swallowed. "I've found a void inside myself I did not know was there."

"Then you should thank me for showing it to you."

"Rana, not everything should be brought into the light of day."

She looked at the sun. "In the desert, Emod, we have no choice."

He slumped forward, broken, ruined. And she had ruined him. But Emod didn't kill her parents, she thought. And Emod didn't kidnap her and try to sell her into slavery. Maybe she had been too harsh with him.

"It's all right, Emod. Rest assured, I won't sing to you, if that's what you want. We'll find Liu, and the three of us will travel to Ektu El, where it rains every day. I'm tired of this desert."

Emod lay desolate. Perhaps he'd always been this way and she'd never noticed. "I will eat and sleep and die in the rain," he said. "I will let the waters wash me away, until there is nothing left but silt and shame."

They continued south, until the Stele of Yiskorel vanished over the horizon. The tides returned with force, and the whistling dunes rolled beneath them in wave after nauseating wave. A black speck spiraled down the distant sky and darted back up into the air.

Ash, from Azru?

The speck whirled down and darted up again, and this time she caught a silhouette of black wings. She sat up on her camel.

"Rana, my eyes are poor," Emod said. "Do you see a black thing in the sky?"

"It's a bird, I think."

"A rather large one," he said. "It may mean we're near a city."

"I hope so."

They scaled a tall dune, and as they reached its peak the bird dove toward them. It swooped low across the sands a hundred paces away, its shadow rolling over dunes. With a metallic squawk, it banked on its enormous wings and came racing for them.

"Look out!" Emod screamed.

It darted over their heads, blotting out the sun for an instant. With the bird came an ashen smell of a thousand spent campfires. Men returning from the deep desert had smelled the same, and they had spoken of horrid things on a desert of black sand. The bird's dark wings, topaz eyes, and its festering, crooked leg were all familiar. This was the same bird she had met on the DanBaer, the demon eagle called Chialdra.

Rana said, "Oh, hell," as Chialdra arced into the sky.

"What do you mean, 'oh, hell?' What is it?"

"It's a demon. I've met her before."

"You shared tea and tobacco, I hope?"

"Not quite. She vowed to kill me."

"Oh, Goddess," he said, raising his hands skyward. "Dear Mollai, do you entertain yourself with our suffering?"

Wings spread wide, Chialdra circled above their heads. The camels eyed the bird, growing nervous. Chialdra squawked, her voice distant but audible, "A gift of my master, it must be, for the Crooner returns, the desert bird who beguiles with song!"

Rana touched her necklace. Why wasn't it working?

"I came to hear but one song," Chialdra said, spiraling down, "But you tricked me! My leg is ruined, beyond repair. Even my master Azazel will not fix me, for he says I get what I deserve."

"I'm sorry about your leg!" Rana shouted. "But the one who bit you was the demon Ashmedai. He gnawed your leg, not me!" And, she thought with rising bile, it was also Ashmedai who brought the demon horde here, who was responsible for her parents' death.

"Ashmedai, a lowly mongrel? Ha!" Chialdra squawked.

"Not any more. He walks like a man again. He crosses the Tattered Sea with the Cursed Men. If you have a quarrel, it is with Ashmedai, not me!"

"I have one leg left, and I'll not lose that too. Little worm, you were complicit in the attack. For that you must die."

Emod cleared his throat and shouted, "Great demon!" He bowed as if to a great king. "Rana has beguiled me too. I am her victim! Spare me your vengeance!"

"Emod!" Rana sneered. "Are you really this craven?"

Chialdra screeched, "Do you think us friends, that I have compassion for strangers? I am demon, and you are man. And your cowardice is repulsive to me."

Emod clasped his hands and whimpered, "Please!"

"Your song," Chialdra said, "was the most lovely I've heard. It still rings through the chambers of my heart! But now I hop like a toad to eat, I wince with every wing beat, and I must sleep on my side. In the morning I pick vermin that has crawled into my feathers! It is a shame, to destroy your oasis of a voice, but it's best to rid this desert of your guile. Hark now, Crooner, for your songs are not the only ones with power! For I am a bird of the desert, and you are in my realm now."

"Rana!" Emod wailed. "Forget what I just said to you. Sing to this demon!"

"You're incorrigible, Emod!" she said. But it was a good idea. Except that Chialdra was high again, and circling ever further away. She could never raise her voice to such a height.

"It's too late," she said. "She's too far."

"So what do we do?"

"We ride!" She kicked her camel. "Go! Go!"

She sped off toward a large dune, and Emod quickly chased after her. Chialdra circled higher, and began to sing a poem in a bizarre language. Rana didn't understand the words, but the melody was familiar, as if she had heard its tune whistling through the eaves of her house on windy nights.

"Goddess, what is that?" Emod said. "What the hell is that?"

Far to the south, a black barrier was quickly rising from the horizon, as if a curtain was being drawn across the sky. The wind picked up, blowing sand into her eyes.

Her camel hopped nervously. "A sandstorm! Chialdra's calling the winds!"

"What do we do?" he said.

"We have to find shelter."

"Should we pitch a tent? Bury ourselves in sand?"

"Not here. We're too exposed."

"Let's go back to the Stele!"

"It's too far."

They paused at a dune peak to look around. Their camels groaned at the approaching storm. Chialdra sang and sang and the black curtain rose over a quarter of the sky. Bleak, roiling clouds reached a hundred fat fingers toward the sun. Lightning struck in the south, and the thunder rolled across the desert. Her camel shuddered, and she struggled to hold on.

She clasped the Mikulal necklace and closed her eyes as the wind howled. "You helped me twice already," she whispered. "Help me one more time."

"We could bury ourselves at the dune's base," Emod said.

"No, the winds will make a vortex."

"Then where? Where do we go?"

She scanned the desert. Nothing but sand and more sand. It was hopeless. They were going to die. "Nowhere," she said.

Emod sagged. "I wanted to feel rain again," he said. "Pouring down my face."

"I've never felt rain," she said. She made the Mollai Triangle with her fingers. "Blessed Mollai, Giver of Rain and Succor, see Liu through the narrow path. Bring her to the house of peace and blessing, as you have promised the faithful."

In the half of the desert where the shadows had not yet reached, something flashed.

"Emod, did you see that light?"

He squinted. "Lightning?"

"No. There's something over that third dune."

The clouds swallowed the sun, and Chialdra vanished inside them. Her cackling song continued above the growing thunder. Half the sky was covered in murk, and the storm itself seemed to be alive, its gray folds the skin of some monstrous beast. Rana had never seen anything so large and terrifying, not even in the vortex above Azru. Lightning struck and thunder pealed. The camels brayed as sand pelted them. A parade of enormous dunes came marching up from the south like soldiers, while the sands beneath them bucked like angry animals.

"Cut your second camel loose," she said. "Let's make a run for that light."

"But there's nothing there!"

"Do it, Emod!"

"The camels hold our future, Rana! *My* future!"

"If we don't run, we'll have no future." With a slash of her knife she severed the rope to her second camel. The beast barked. From its saddlebag she grabbed a satchel of jewels, then cut the leather straps of the mount. It fell to the ground.

"What are you doing?" he said.

"Giving it a chance." She threw the bag of jewels to Emod. "Enjoy your riches in Sheol. I'll be over that dune!" Then she darted off toward the glare.

"Goddess!"

She glanced back a minute later. Emod had loosed his second camel and was speeding after her with the bag of jewels clutched to his chest.

Her loosed camel kept close, but Emod's camel, heavy with burdens, struggled to keep pace with them. It bleated heart-rendingly as it vanished behind a dune. The second camel turned back for its companion, and when the dune rolled past, the two animals were gone, though their bleating remained.

Darkness spread over the desert as the storm hurtled across the plain, swallowing what was left of the light. Lightning forked in blinding green flashes, and the whipping air grew acrid with the smell of molten glass.

Her camel barked as she kicked it. The wind howled, and sand tore into her skin. They crested another dune, when lighting struck twenty paces ahead. Her camel reared, and she hung onto its reins as the thunder shook her bones. The light winked again. A reflection? A thousand paces away, mostly obscured by windblown sand, hundreds of people were making camp.

"Am I dreaming?" Emod said. "Is that real?"

"Goddess, I hope so!"

They raced for the camp in darkness so thick that in between lightning strikes she could see no more than ten paces. When the green lightning flashed, she glimpsed a swarm of cackling birds swirling around her, birds of sand. They pecked at her with grainy beaks, but it was too painful to keep her eyes open, and for long terrifying seconds she kept them shut. Her fear was too much, and she screamed.

Chialdra's laughter echoed through the clouds. "Howl, song-bird! Wail! I shall suck the marrow from your bones! If any remain!"

A flash of lightning reflected from a transparent surface that arced into the sky. The desert went dark again before Rana could grasp its full shape.

"Rana!" Emod shouted. "It hurts!" He was near, but she couldn't see him. A monstrous dune hoisted them up and threw them down just as suddenly, rumbling like a falling mountain as it went, and she nearly fell from her mount.

"Keep going!" she screamed.

Her camel was bleeding. The reins were slippery from its blood. She rubbed her face and found to her horror she was bleeding too.

"Emod?" she cried. "Emod, where are you?"

The shape appeared over a dune, like a rising moon, a trans-parent dome covering a camp of hundreds. Men and women in long white robes stood inside its perimeter. Pale blue light flowed from their hands toward the transparent wall. She spotted an opening, a small, glowing circle large enough to fit a man. Two robed men struggled to keep the door open, and two women were waving Rana toward them.

"Hurry!" a woman shouted into the din. "We have to close the door!"

Rana raced toward the opening, but she had to close her eyes. The storm shredded her skin, her face, her eyelids. She leaned against the camel's neck. Suddenly the wind ceased, but the pain grew worse. Her camel groaned and fell over, and she tumbled onto sand.

A round-faced woman hovered over her. The storm roiled behind her head. "How many are with you?" she said in Bedu-Besk

In Wul she replied, "Just Emod."

"We saw no others," the woman said in Wul. "Be still. The healer is on her way."

Every pore in her body wailed in pain as she climbed to her feet.

"Are you mad?" the woman said. "Lie down!"

Two magicians held the door open, while a third peered into the storm. Before the woman could stop her, Rana ran through the portal.

The pecking birds, the excruciating pain, returned. "Emod!" she called. "Emod!"

Something bleated nearby, and she stumbled toward it, eyes closed, led by sound. She tripped over something big and opened her eyes. Emod's camel lay prone. A bone protruded from its hind leg. It was braying like a calf. Emod was trapped underneath, unmoving. She tried to free him, but the camel was too heavy.

"Mamu," he cried. "Mamu, help me!"

She screamed, and it sounded if the whole world was screaming with her. She fell onto her stomach and buried her face. The sands shredded her clothing, her back. This was the end. All would be over soon. She would join Mama and Papa in heaven.

Strong hands grabbed her, lifted her onto shoulders. With quick, heavy steps they carried her through the maelstrom and back into the dome. The silence that followed seemed louder than the storm. They set her on her back, and she was too shocked to speak. A second man lay a grotesque shape down beside her, a monster so bloody and torn she couldn't tell what species it was. But she knew who this was.

"Emod," she said, her voice as shredded as him. "Emod, look at me!"

He didn't move.

A husky man with a sharp jaw approached her and said in Wul, "Chialdra has left the Bedu in peace for twenty-two years. What did you do to arouse the demon's wrath? And why does the symbol of the cursed men dangle from your neck? I should throw you back out there!"

A woman pushed the man out of the way. "Step back, brute!" she said in Bedu-Besk. "Let me heal these men!"

Goddess, Rana thought, delirious. *Am I so damaged they cannot tell my gender?*

"Send a message to Lord Elizel," one said. "Tell him we have more guests."

A woman muttered a spell, a tuneless chant, beside Emod.

"We're too late," the healer said, after a moment. "He's too far gone."

The same woman approached Rana, and a soothing, blue light filled her mind. Her pain ebbed. She opened her eyes and stared at the bloody thing beside her as the healer continued.

"What's that in his hands?" another said.

The sand had polished its metal to a brilliant shine. Emod had somehow dropped his bag of jewels and picked up Rana's copper bust of Mollai. It must have fallen from her bag as she sped away. It took three men to pry it from Emod's dead fingers.

———

When Daniel opened his eyes the air smelled of shampoo. A familiar, floral smell. Rebekah's particular and expensive brand. He was in her apartment, staring up at the lace canopy of her bed. The air was cool and silent, but he sensed he wasn't alone.

"Bek?"

He rose from the bed. He was naked, and there was nothing to put on. He rubbed his eyes, confused. So it had been a dream after all? No, it had felt too real.

Bright light, a summer's sunset, shone through the curtains, turning the room a rosy pink hue. He pushed the curtains aside, and instead of rows of Brooklyn brownstones there was an unending sea of orange sand. Daniel gasped. In the crimson sky, the sun was cracked, like an egg, its molten core dripping to the horizon.

"Hello, Danny."

He spun around. Rebekah stood in the doorway. She wore a gray Mickey Mouse t-shirt, navy jeans, a purple webbed belt, pink slippers. The same outfit she'd worn the morning after he had first stayed at her place.

"I was looking everywhere for you," she said. The light from the cracked sun reflected in her eyes like cinders.

"This is a dream?" he said.

"Of a kind." She stepped closer, glancing at her watch. The sun caught its silver facets, sending sparks up the walls. "It's almost time," she said. "I thought I'd lost you."

"Rebekah," he said. "What's happening? Is any of this real?"

She grabbed his shoulders. "You know I *do* love you, Danny."

He wanted to hold her, to squeeze her, to forget this nightmare ever happened. But he resisted. "And I . . . I love you too, Bek."

She smiled, rows of perfect white teeth. "You don't know how happy that makes me. When the beast stole you from me, I thought I'd never find you again."

"The beast? Caleb?"

She frowned. "Is that what he calls himself now?" She showed her incisors. "The cur."

"Rebekah . . ." He trembled, but he had to ask, no matter how it hurt. "What are you?"

She took his hand, and it was fever hot. "Danny, let me show you what I am."

She smiled, and the cinders in her eyes grew to burn up the room. A bright fire consumed him, but it did not burn, and suddenly he felt as if he was hurtling across vast distances of space and time. Air whooshed by his ears, full of hiss and static and whispers. Then the blinding light ebbed, and he found himself on a parapet attached to a hideous black tower. Infesting its crowded levels were ten thousand arches, buttresses, balconies, and minarets. Spires reached for the night sky like the claws of some huge animal, so that the overall impression was not that he stood on a parapet of some nightmarish palace, but on the side of some enormous, sleeping beast.

Rebekah was here too. She wore a flowing white gown, and gold bands wrapped her head, wrists, and waist. Their golden reflections rippled like water.

He wore clothing too, a crimson robe with floral blue and green filigree, soft and delicate against his bare skin.

"The robe suits you, Danny," she said.

The parapet overlooked a black lake surrounded on three sides by steep and ragged cliffs. It was night, but the sky was bright with a thousand pregnant stars, red as pomegranates.

"Where are we?"

"Sheol," she said, smiling as a hot breeze tousled her hair. "The first Shard to be settled, after the Shattering. This is the palace of

Abbadon. My home, Danny. My *real* home. But it can be ours, the home we always spoke about making."

"Ours? Here?"

She stepped over to the ledge and peered at the lake. The viscous waters gave no reflection, not even of the ruddy stars. "Sheol may seem bleak compared to what you're used to, and I couldn't agree more. Sheol is a wasteland, like all the Shards. We tried to make a home here, to build ourselves a safe place in the Cosmos, but we have few resources. Sheol has never been more than a shadow of Earth."

She approached him. "We survive on scraps that fall to us through the Abyss. Below the city immense power vats harvest the energy that trickles down from Earth. We use it to keep our world alive. Without them, we would wither away."

"I've heard," he said, "that the Shards depend on Earth to survive."

"Then you must know how the Shards suffer. How they cling to the small scrap of life they have been given with all of their being. But it's still never enough. Does any of this sound familiar to you, Danny?"

He stared at her. "Familiar, how?"

"With your work at the Shulman Fund, you helped the weak, the sick, the hungry. This—" she gestured at Sheol with her hand— "is just a projection of my memories. But if you come to the *real* Sheol with me, those barren cliffs will bloom, the seas will thrive, and the twin suns will rise over a new, fertile world. If Ashmedai has told you that you're a Lamed Vavnik, that you sustain worlds, then you know, by your presence alone, life would improve for millions."

"You want me to come here, to live?"

She held out her palm and a band of gold appeared in it, just large enough to fit his head. "In Sheol, I rule alone." She held the gold band before his eyes. It shimmered as if made of liquid. "Remember how much good we did when we worked together? All those people we fed, housed, and healed? Think of it, you and me, human and demon, helping a billion Shards rise from the ashes. We could change the Cosmos forever."

She reached to crown him, but he stepped away.

"What is it?" She seemed hurt. "You helped hundreds on Earth, thousands. Here, in Sheol, you can help *trillions*."

"No more games, Bek. I'm not going back to sleep."

"You are asleep, now. And I'm trying to wake you up!"

"I'm not falling under your spell again." He felt sick. All of the past few months with her, everything was a lie. "I won't let you kill me."

"Kill you? Why in Sheol would I want to kill you?"

"Stop, Bek! Just stop. Your lies don't work anymore."

"Ashmedai has truly poisoned your mind," she said, scowling. "Did he tell you I wished to kill you? Danny, that's just not true! Tell me where you are. I know he's taken you to Gehinnom. Just concentrate on your location, and I will come and fetch you. I'll show you that I'm not here to hurt you, but to give you a chance to be the person you were meant to be. Let me bring you home, to *our* home, to Sheol, and we will forget all this darkness ever happened."

He felt something sharp and hot in his side. His robe by his waist was quickly turned red. "Bek," he said, collapsing against the railing as pain overcame him. "I—"

"Danny, what is it? What's wrong?" Then she saw the blood. "Hurry! Tell me where you are, so I can help you!"

He thought of the desert, the endless waves of sand. Where was he? Somewhere on the Tattered Sea, walking in front of a wave of sand. Rebekah smiled. Then he was traveling again, hurtling across time and space and thrust into a small room that stank of cedar and sweat. He lay on his back, and Caleb was peering down at him, his white eyes huge. Marul was mumbling a spell beside him, while a blue-white mist flowed from her hands into Daniel's side. The pain ebbed, the mist faded, and Marul lowered her hands.

Daniel sat up, and the room spun. He wore only boxers. And to his horror, much of his body hair had fallen off. He was also much skinnier than he remembered.

The room had slatted cedar walls, a low ceiling. Dripping candles burned from corner sconces. Crimson curtains hung before a small window. "Where am I?" he said.

"Inside a palanquin skate," said Caleb.

"A what?"

"A floating conveyance reserved for weddings or respected elders. You should feel special, Daniel. Elizel kicked out a crone for you."

"What happened?"

"Some of the Bedu aren't too keen on us traveling with them," Caleb said. "A few were unsettled by your black cloak, it seems."

"But I took the cloak off. I'm not a Mikulal." His side hurt with every breath. "Not yet, anyway."

"Wearing it was enough," Caleb said.

"A boy stabbed me." Daniel rubbed his wound, which was now covered with pink scar tissue. It was tender and soft.

"It was easy for the children to get close," he said. "And to evade blame. The Bedu are unlikely to punish the child. Meanwhile the true perpetrators stay hidden."

"Disgusting," Marul said. "Using children like that."

Caleb laughed. "If I recall, witch, you used your magic to seduce a small harem of lovers in Shanghai. Were they all of consensual age?"

Marul frowned. "That was a long time ago. I regret that very much."

"Spare me your contrition," Caleb said. "You spent time in a cave and think you've changed, that you've cast out your worst natures? You have only succeeded in denying them. You're no different from these Bedu, who think that by casting out the Mikulalim they make themselves holy. The Mikulalim are aspects of their nature that they deny, and in so doing only strengthen their own darkness."

"What do you mean?" Daniel said. "How are the Mikulalim aspects of the Bedu?"

"Fifteen centuries ago," Caleb said, "there was a Bedu tribe like this one. They made a deal with Azazel, and he cursed them."

"What kind of deal?"

"The Bedu had said, 'Give us knowledge, so that we may know all the tongues of men in all the lands of men, and thus become a mighty nation.' And Azazel said, 'I will grant your request. I will teach you the first language, from which all languages spring, and you shall speak with all men as a native of their lands. And all the days of your life, which I shall extend seventy-fold, you shall hunger for the flesh of men. For as you request, so I do give. You shall truly know *all the tongues of men*.'"

"So he tricked them," Daniel said, "to gain power over them."

"A rather crude trick, if you must know. But my brother, for all his knowledge, was always rather crude."

"Azazel is your brother?"

"We've grown estranged."

"Why do you rule the Mikulalim and not him?"

"Because I won them in a bet," Caleb said.

"What kind of bet?"

"Keep your damned voices down!" Marul said. "Bedu soldiers are just outside!"

Caleb smiled. "The Bedu see the Mikulalim as traitors," Caleb said. "But what they really fear is, if given the same choice, they might make the same deal. The Mikulalim don't fear famines. They can live without food or water for years."

"Would you keep your fucking voices down?" Marul said a little too loudly, and Daniel remembered her plan to out Caleb to the Bedu. She *wanted* Caleb to be heard.

Daniel crawled toward the window, and the floor shifted under him, as if they were on a boat. Black, angry clouds tumbled in the sky, though the air was oddly quiet for all the motion. Was it dark so soon? He examined his wound again. It seemed as if it were weeks old and healing well. Besides a little tenderness, he would never have guessed he'd been stabbed.

"I'm still getting used to all this magic," he said. "Thank you, Marul."

"I've done better," she said. "I'm weak."

"You'd make one hell of a doctor."

"Tried that. In Shanghai, I ran an underground clinic for a year. Didn't end well."

Clouds turned in violent gyres overhead and faintly reflected the orange torchlight from below. Marul gave Daniel a bladder and told him to drink as much as he could.

"When did this storm start? Is it night already? I don't remember seeing any clouds."

"A half hour ago," Caleb said. "It's still daytime, and that's not a natural storm."

"More magic?" Daniel said. And with a pang of dread he remembered Rebekah's plans to come and fetch him. "Did Mashit do this?"

"No," Caleb said. "She is never so subtle. This is Chialdra's work, though I don't yet know why."

Daniel turned to face Caleb, so he could read his expression and sense his hidden motives. "Caleb, why does Mashit want to kill all the Lamed Vav?"

"Because she can."

"But won't she destroy Sheol too? What does she get from all this?"

Caleb wolf-white eyes peered deep into his hindbrain. "She's a shortsighted fool, blinded by passions. Who can understand her convoluted logic? I never could."

But Daniel saw that there was more than Caleb was letting on. He leaned out the window but the air was calm and quiet, despite the incessant motion above. Thousands of tents were arrayed in neat rows. Tall banners proclaimed each house, Timnah, Alvah, Jetheth, Aholibamah, Elah, Pinon, Kenaz, Teman, Mibzar, Magdiel, Iram, and dozen more. Torches lined the makeshift avenues, and curious reflections arced under the roiling sea of clouds.

"Are we under in some kind of dome?" he said.

"Yes," Marul said. "The magicians formed a glass sphere around the camp, above and below us, to protect us from the turbulent storm."

The palanquin skate hovered three feet above the ground, rocking gently. Nearby was a guard of ten soldiers clad in leather and bronze who eyed Daniel warily. Daniel retreated back into the palanquin.

"So we're just waiting?" Daniel said.

"The Synedrium meets as we speak," Caleb said. "The Lords of the Houses are deciding whether or not to toss us into the storm."

"What are our chances?"

Caleb rested his hands on the sill, and the palanquin skate tilted with his weight. "Look at these people, wrestling with an unforgiving desert," he said. "The sand assails them, demons vex them, the cities despise them. They know no peace. Every day is a struggle against annihilation. Only knowledge keeps them alive. But in Gehinnom, knowledge evaporates like water in the sun. What is known today is forgotten tomorrow. Our chances? *Poor*."

Daniel glanced at Marul. If she planned to betray Caleb, it would be after the Synedrium made their decision.

A strong young man in a brown tunic, leather belt, and bracers approached the palanquin, joined by several tired-looking soldiers. He said, "The Synedrium requires your presence." He frowned when he saw Daniel wore only boxers. "But you must clothe yourselves respectably first."

Daniel lifted his blood-soaked cloak from the floor and removed the wedding boutonniere from the pocket. He held the cloak up to the soldier. "Do you happen to have another robe?" He stuck his finger through it. "My last one seems to have developed a hole."

CHAPTER TWENTY

CALEB AND THE OTHERS WALKED TOWARD THE SYNEDRIUM under the stormy sky like men to the gallows. Though it was still daytime, the storm made the desert dark as night, and only the flickering torchlight guided their way. Their escorts whispered amongst themselves. How long had it been since strangers walked with the Bedu like this?

"If they choose to cast us out," Caleb whispered to Daniel, "if they do not respond to my request, I will need you to speak for us. Can you do that?"

"Yes," Daniel said, even though persuasion was foreign to his kind. The power of the Lamed Vav was subtle, never manipulative.

The phalanx of soldiers dividing the Synedrium from the camp stepped aside to let them through. They moved into the circle of Houses, led by their guard.

"Sit on the sand," a soldier said, a boy, pointing with his sword. "Do not speak unless commanded to." Then their armed escorts departed the circle. What happened here wasn't meant for soldiers' crude ears.

Sixty somber- and dour-faced Bedu surrounded them. Weary-eyed, middle-aged men who tugged at gnarled beards. Buxom, stocky women whose embittered eyes accused without trial. The men kept their emotions behind stony facades, but the women spat and scowled. The Synedrium were a bitter bunch.

Everyone stood but for Lord Elizel, upright on his wooden throne. Its finials had been carved into heads of a lion, a goat, a camel, and an ox. They writhed in the firelight. Behind Elizel a wide banner proclaimed, "Chieftain Elizel, Sovereign Lord of the Quog Bedu by the Blessing of the Goddess." The black-bearded Otto stood to his left, glowering at Caleb. To Elizel's right, the camel-eyed Uriel watched stolidly.

Caleb stilled himself with deep breathing. *As the twin suns of Sheol rise above the black cliffs of Abbadon,* he thought, *so I must rise now.* To win their hearts, he had to make his cause theirs.

The storm spun above them, but all eyes were on him. Lord Elizel said, "Beloved Caleb." His words silenced the murmurs and whispers in the crowd. "I've explained to the Body what you've told me, that you need the Bedu's help to travel to the Kuurku, where you seek to prevent the destruction of the Pillars."

"You are correct, Elizel," Caleb said. "Your help would be—"

"Hold your tongue!" Otto spat. "Speak only when commanded to!"

Caleb bowed in apology. He had to win these people to his side, even if it meant pretending to respect their stupid formalities.

"The Synedrium wants to know who you are," Elizel said. The circle tapped their staffs, while nodding and murmuring their assent like a tribe of bleating goats.

Marul glared at Caleb, hatred in her eyes.

"Witch," Caleb whispered. "If you want to live, better hold your tongue. I know of your plan to out me."

She shuddered. "And . . . what *plan* is this?"

"You are as transparent as glass," he said. "If you tell them what I am, I will tell them what you did. Which is worse in their eyes? A demon? Or the betrayer of the Cosmos?"

"Halt your whispering!" Otto shouted.

Caleb bowed again. "Lord, Elizel, my name is Caleb."

Elizel said, "And where do you hail from, Caleb, son of . . . ?"

"I have disowned my progenitor. I am Caleb, and that is all."

"And your origins?"

"Irrelevant."

Elizel sat up. "Not to us."

"I'm sorry, Elizel, but this is a terrible waste of time."

The Synedrium stirred. "You shall address him as your lord!" Otto said. "And you shall answer his question."

"My *lord*," Caleb said. "While you obsess over trivialities, a demon army hunts for Daniel, the Pillar of the Kuurku. On Earth, demons are preparing to destroy another Pillar. If the Pillars are destroyed, Gehinnom will be destroyed too."

"And you, alone, plan to save us all, do you?" Elizel said.

"Not alone, my lord. With your help, the Bedu, the most knowledgeable people on Gehinnom, will ferry us to Earth, which swims in the waters of the Kuurku."

Uriel raised his palm, and Elizel gave him permission to speak. "What you ask," Uriel said, "is impossible. We do not know how to ferry you to the land of Erte."

"No," Caleb said. "But Marul Menacha knows how to create a vessel that can traverse the Great Deep as a boat sails the oceans."

"Let us assume that she knows such a spell," Uriel said. "It would take tremendous power to loft you between the worlds."

"Is it not said that the Bedu shake the sand and sky?"

"We were mighty once," Otto said. He turned an accusing eye at Elizel. "But we have fallen from our glory. Our robes hang ragged. The luster of our gold has tarnished. Above us, this crystal sphere wavers, cracking. Once, we might have crafted this shield with a single mage. Now we need dozens."

The fool plays politics, Caleb thought, *while the Cosmos teeters on the edge!*

Elizel frowned as he twirled his fingers in his white beard. "Enough!" he said. "We are still a strong people."

"Strong as a blade of grass in the wind," said Otto.

Uriel hung his head and said, "I'm afraid it is true, Caleb. The power you ask for does not exist among the Bedu anymore. It does not exist in this world."

"I'm sorry, Caleb," Elizel said. "But you see, we cannot help you. When the storm abates, we will send you off with provisions for three days. May you find your way to Erte, Blessed Mollai help us all."

"Do you want me to talk to them now?" Daniel whispered.

Caleb turned around slowly, taking in the faces of all of these Bedu leaders. Had he misjudged them? All along he had assumed the Bedu had the power he needed, but now, as he gazed into their hateful eyes he saw them for what they were. Cowards, like all humans, afraid to face bitter truths. No, he, Ashmedai, King of Demonkind, would not let these pathetic, stubborn, frail, cravenly humans thwart his grand visions! He would wake them up.

"No, Daniel," he said. "I've a better idea." Then he shouted, "Lord Elizel, there is another place on Gehinnom where the power exists to return us to Earth."

Uriel said, "And where is this?"

"Not where, but *who.*" The circle was silent, waiting. He said, "In the one whom you call the Betrayer."

Like a gaggle of startled birds, the Synedrium gasped and shrieked.

"We do not speak that name in this holy circle!" Elizel said. "May his name be erased!"

"Then your taboos will be your death! Are we not near the ashen wastes of the Jeen? Beyond the black sands in Dudael lies the Abyssal of Lost Hope. Chained at the bottom of that chasm lies—"

"Stop!" Uriel shouted. "Have you not heard our lord as he has commanded you? We do not speak that name in this—"

"*Azazel!*" Caleb shouted.

Their mouths fell open, and they wailed as if their children had been slaughtered. Their faces twisted in horror, contempt. Someone shouted an order and there were sounds of swords sliding from sheaths. Otto yanked out his blade.

"Yes, I've blasphemed," Caleb said as he stood. "And I will blaspheme again! Only by shocking you awake can I make you see. You seal the fate of the Cosmos with your taboos. The name of the Betrayer is barbarous to your ears. He tricked your ancient kin and turned them into flesh-eaters. And though he is bound upside down at the bottom of a chasm in Dudael, he daily plots your torment. Is not this storm above our heads the product of his cruel messenger, Chialdra? Azazel's name is anathema, and for good reason. But Azazel, my lords, is the only one who can help us now. He is the only one on Gehinnom who can give your priests the power to return us to Earth. Hear me! Azazel is the only one who can save the Cosmos now."

"Abomination!" Otto shouted, pointing his blade at Caleb. His voice silenced the crowd. "This man defiles our holy circle! He rides into our camp on the backs of maneaters and brings a horde of demons in his wake. And now, he begs us to ally with our most-hated enemy? Do we not send the scapegoat into the desert to confound him whom we do not name? Hear me, fellow Houses of the Bedu, we have grain and oil to deliver to Blömsnu before the quarter moon. We have not time for a man's obscene delusions! He brings evil into our midst. He and his companions must die!"

A chorus of assent rose among the Synedrium.

"Lords of the desert," Caleb said. "We sit here at your mercy." Daniel and Marul looked up at Caleb as if he'd just signed their death warrant. "We came before this holy circle because we are desperate. We traversed the Tattered Sea because we believe the Bedu would help us. Daniel Fisher is a Pillar of the Kuurku. His kind have buoyed the Kuurku for eons, keeping you and your ancestors safe. Will you cast him out into the desert like your scapegoat? If so, then let it be known for all time that on this day the Quog Bedu let the Cosmos die."

Their murmurs quieted. The only sound was the faint ticking of the storm against their crystal roof, the occasional lick of flame from the smoky torches. Caleb sighed. He was spent. But he just might have convinced them. Daniel stared up at him.

Marul climbed to her feet. "My lords," she began.

"Don't you dare," Caleb said.

"There is something you need to know," she said.

"Witch," Caleb said, grabbing her arm. "Heed my warning!"

"This man with whom you speak with is none other than—"

"Don't!" Caleb said.

"He is—"

"*Ashmedai.*"

But it wasn't Marul who'd spoken his true name. The voice was small, raspy, and came from the far edge of the circle.

The crowd gasped as a grizzled, bloody monster, a walking pile of carrion, shoved its way through the circle, a shiny dagger clutched in its hand. Four soldiers ran up to the beast and formed a shield of swords.

Who is this creature that knows me? Caleb thought. *A soldier of the Legion?* He didn't sense its demon essence, but perhaps that was how it had entered the camp undetected.

Elizel rose from his chair. "Kill that vile demon!"

The creature paused as the soldiers moved in.

"I am Rana Lila," the creature rasped, "Daughter of Ari and Nediva. Born in the city of Azru, which stands no more. And I am no demon."

The knot in Caleb's chest unfurled painfully. How could this bloody creature be Rana?

"She ran in from the storm!" a man shouted. "She is human, and her companion is dead, Lord Elizel!"

"My parents are dead," Rana rasped. "My city destroyed. My sister, missing. All because of him. Caleb. Ashmedai. The *demon*."

"You are delirious," Elizel said, stepping down from his throne. He whispered to a page who ran into the crowd. "Our magicians would have known if Caleb was a demon."

"He is Ashmedai, King of Demonkind."

Elizel looked troubled. Otto, sword outstretched, strode toward Caleb as he nodded to someone in the circle.

Damn her! Caleb thought. *Damn Rana to the lowest Shard! I had them! They were mine!*

"It's time," Rana said, eyes on Caleb, "to rid the world of an evil."

And then she sang.

Oh, such glorious, empyrean symphonies! Her eyes were the twin suns of Sheol beaming over Lake Hali. The Synedrium were the steep black cliffs beside the waters. A wind blew through the curtains as Caleb lay on his bed inside the palace of Abbadon. Thirteen of his most recent children giggled as they played on the floor, their voices ringing down the palace halls. She lay beside him, Mashit, his wife, her smile a thousand bright dawns. Was it possible that, in their unending realm of suffering, they had found happiness together?

And Rana sang on.

They *were* happy, weren't they? So why had he awoken in chains? Why was he dragged like a traitor through the streets in a cage as they spat and threw stones at him? And there, before the whole throng of Sheol, Mashit stripped him of his power in a ceremony

of blood and glass. His children testified against him. Not one—
not one!—came to his defense.

She had poisoned their minds, turned them against him. His
own children! Why? He had given her everything he had!

He fell to his knees, covered his ears. "Stop it! Rana, please stop!"
Rana sang on.

Bobel, my youngest, why do you throw stones at me? Kumeatel, my
yellow-eyed darling, you can ensnare nations with one glance, why
do you spit at my heels? Atrax, mightier than mountains, why do you
turn your back to me? My children, you cast your eyes down before
your father. Now I am a mongrel! Creator, Mother, where have you
gone? Why do you not come when I call for you? In what dark corner
of creation do you hide?

Rana took a breath, and the visions ceased. She ran to Caleb,
dagger raised. "For Azru!" she shouted. "For my parents!" She
lunged at him, but three soldiers tackled her, and her knife fell
from her hands.

"Slaughter them!" Otto commanded. "Slaughter them all!"

"Belay that order!" Elizel said. "Chain them, but do not kill them!"

"You must gag the singer!" Uriel shouted.

The soldiers shoved them all to the ground. A soldier pressed his
sword to Rana's throat. "Sing your demonsong again, and I will cut
off your tongue!" he said.

Rana seethed as she stared at Caleb. As they bound his hands
behind him he said to her, "Take a good look around, Rana. For
this is how the Cosmos dies!"

CHAPTER TWENTY-ONE

PAIN MATTERED LITTLE. REVENGE WAS THE ONLY TRUTH. BUT they had robbed her of that. The soldiers threw Rana onto her back and shoved cotton deep into her mouth, securing it with a muzzle of burlap. She felt like vomiting as the gold button of the sun broke through the parting clouds. White-robed men with dark beards chanted spells at her, tunelessly, like braying goats, and she felt as if a collar was being tightened around her neck. The magicians made their company of soldiers stuff wax into their ears, "Lest the demon witch somehow still sing, even with her gag. Curse Elizel and his orders!" And with their ears stuffed the soldiers looked like crazed, fearful donkeys. They dragged her across the camp as if she were an animal herself. The Bedu cursed and spat at her, flicked her a thousand curses. It would take her a decade to appease Mollai after this.

The sand worried its way into her wounds, and she moaned, but her voice had vanished, collared by their spell. Damn them! Without her voice, she was nothing.

They bound her wrists and ankles in iron cuffs, then affixed the chains to an enormous log. Daniel, Caleb, and Marul were sagging in their chains, when they dragged forth another man, one as bloody as her.

Emod.

He hung limply from his chains, dead. They had stripped him naked, his last dignity removed. His mouth hung open as if his soul had just flown from it.

And that is how I will die, she thought, delirious from pain.

Twelve soldiers, ears waxed and cottoned, kept watch over them. Two magicians in fluttering white robes identified themselves as priests of the Bedu as they approached.

"Stupid demon," one priest said to her in Bedu-Besk while sucking loudly on a prune. "We are the most learned magicians in the world. Did you think you could charm us Bedu with demonsong? Elyam, my friend," he said to the other, "tell the demon what we'll do if it voices the black sound again?"

"We have orders to kill it, Avra," the other said, scratching his beard.

"She's no demon," Marul said. "Under that shredded flesh is a child. You idiots chain a girl!"

"A *demon* girl," said Avra, his beard prune-stained.

"Don't you see that she bleeds like any man?" Marul said. "She's been shredded by the storm. By the Goddess, I beg you to help her!"

"By the Goddess, we curse her!" Avra said, biting into another prune. "Look how her wounds have stopped flowing, even without healers."

And Rana saw that it was true. Her pain had lessened too, and her many wounds had stopped suppurating. Once, a long time ago, she had helped Papa slaughter an ox and accidentally sliced her arm. The cut was deep and bled profusely, and Papa was more worried than she'd ever seen him. He sat by her bed the whole night, praying to the Goddess, even wept. And in the morning, when she awoke and they took off the bandage to examine the wound, only a small nick remained. A week later there wasn't even a scar. Papa had said the Goddess had answered his prayers, and he became devout, for a time. Rana had thought it was the Goddess too. But now she thought that maybe it had been something more.

"No human can pry men's wills with demonsong," Avra said. "Music has always been the indulgence of evil forces." He spat juice onto the ground.

"For a people who pride themselves on knowledge," Marul said, "the only evil is your ignorance. She's no demon!"

"Then what is this chained grotesquery who wields such power?"

Marul stared at Rana, and her gaze held histories within histories. "You fools. She is Gu."

Marul's words lingered in the air. Havig had called her that. So had Grug. Was this the name for the power she wielded?

"A Gu?" Elyam said. He laughed, and Avra almost choked on his prune.

"The ignorance is yours, woman," said Avra. "The Gu designed the great cities in the days of the Twelve Kings, when Asa and Jehoia, in the House of Almon ruled Gehinnom, when the Tattered Sea was a true ocean under parasot of water, and myriad creatures swam here. The Gu Loshn, designed and built Karad, where the Goddess Mollai dwells in divine splendor. The Gu Lider inscribed the Verses of Bethor, which are lovelier than a moon over an oasis spring. And the Gu Oyern built the Obelisk of Shean, which still stands at the shores of the southern seas.

"Their artistry is renowned throughout Gehinnom, even where the skies turn gray and cry. But because we have sinned, Goddess Mollai withdrew the Gu back into her womb. Now the Goddess sits in Karad, waiting for her people to return to righteousness, when she will give birth to the Gu again and return Gehinnom to its splendor. The Gu are long dead. Their overflowing urns have shattered, their great works evaporated. Only hints of their glory remain, and only we, the Bedu, remember them."

"I am not Bedu," Marul said. "And I remember."

"You are confused."

"And you are wrong. She is Gu."

Elyam scowled as he waved his hand dismissively. "The Gu were never female!"

"Men!" Marul cursed. "Always convinced you are the center of the universe! Here you stand in the presence of a Gu, a Pillar, and the King of Demonkind, yet all you can see is your own self-importance. No wonder the Bedu have fallen."

"And what are you?" Avra said, smirking. "The Goddess herself?"

"I am Marul Menacha, The Witch Who Gives Demons Pause."

Avra smiled. "Pause to stop and laugh!" The priests chortled. "The Thirty-Six Pillars are holy beings. Men of great strength who hold up the Kuurku day and night with their might. They are not pale-skinned, shrunken little men who cavort with maneaters." He shook his head. "The Pillars were resplendent even at night. The Gu were exalted by kings! And the King of Demons, crossing the desert like a thief in the night, as if he fears the mouse that sleeps in the dunes. Ha! Liars, liars, the lot of you!"

"And fools, fools, the lot of you!" Marul spat. "The Quog Bedu have changed much."

"And much for the better," Avra said. "Much for the better."

The two priests whispered amongst themselves for a time, and Rana was grateful for the respite. Though her wounds were healing faster than they had any right to, she still suffered with every breath. Blood and drool fell from her mouth as she tried to shift the lumps of cotton aside.

I will not roll over and die like some beast, she thought. *I must escape.*

Caleb was chained at the opposite end of the log. At least she had the solace of knowing that the Bedu would kill him too.

She met his unholy white eyes and his face turned as red as the setting sun. "You stupid, short-sighted, pathetic child!" he said. "The priests are right. Did you think you could bewitch the whole tribe with music? You are powerful, but you know nothing. The Bedu mastered magic a thousand years before you were born! And now everything is ruined. For a song."

"Will you stop whining?" Marul said. "You make my ears hurt."

"Your pain is nothing compared to what you will feel when the Earth shatters. Our bodies will wither and decay, but our souls will live on, tumbling for trillions of torturous years through endless voids. Woe, woe is us."

I have debased Caleb, Rana thought. She had made this demon writhe and sob, and that gave her some small satisfaction.

"Shut your mouth," Avra said. "Your words are poison."

"And yours are the brays of lambs before slaughter," Caleb said.

The clouds were fleeing rapidly, and sun and shadow chased each other along the ground. Emod swung in the wind, chains creaking. If not for Caleb, Emod would be smoking his pipe and smiling at passersby on Bedubroadstreet now. Mama would be singing as she hung the clothes to dry. Papa would be staring out the window at the rising Ukne, cursing so loudly that dust would fall from the ceiling. Her feelings overwhelmed her. Never again would she see them. Their bodies were rotting in the yard, pecked to the bone by scavengers, or eaten by Mikulalim. She shivered at the thought. And Liu, her round face, her glistering brown gem eyes. The sobs came like waves of sand. But she could breach no sound, and her own eyes were too dry to make tears, so she just shuddered in her chains.

"Oh, Rana," Marul said. "I'm sorry. I'm so, so sorry."

Caleb grunted. "Sentiment is the path of fools. While you weep, the Cosmos teeters."

"Says the one who was weeping minutes ago."

Caleb took a deep breath. "We are all broken, in one way or another," he said.

"Some more than others," said Marul.

"All I ever wanted was to make us whole again," said Caleb.

"At whose expense?" Marul said. "Because it's always at someone else's expense, isn't it, Caleb?"

"Would you believe me if I said that this time it's just not true?"

"I would sooner believe a goat doesn't shit.".

Elyam shouted, "Stand tall! Lord Elizel approaches." And the soldiers parted for him.

Lord Elizel's shadow flickered as the last vestiges of cloud whisked before the sun. Suddenly the crystal dome blinked out of existence. The lurking winds, still gusting and strong, tore through the camp, stirring up tornadoes of sand. Banners and tents shuddered in the breeze. Rana grimaced as sand worried more deeply into her wounds.

Elizel's long white hair was tossed about as he said, "Leave us."

"But, my Lord," Avra said. "There is evil among—"

"Leave us!" he said.

Avra and Elyam bowed. "Yes, my lord."

"And take the soldiers with you."

Avra was about to speak when Elyam grabbed his arm.

"Yes, my lord," Avra said, frowning.

As their guard departed, Lord Elizel squinted at Rana, as if he were trying to glimpse the person underneath her shredded skin. He sighed, a sound like a dry wind blowing over ruins. "What a ragged, motley lot you are."

Marul was about to speak, but Elizel raised his hand to stop her.

He ran a hand through his beard, closed his eyes, and sighed. "Prudence says I should slay all of you and cast your ashes into the desert. This is the overwhelming vote of the Synedrium. But I have a niggling doubt. It's crawled into my brain like a sandworm. I can override the Synedrium in times of dire need. And I believe this is such a time.

"One of our far-seers has conveyed to me that a mammoth army approaches from the south. An army of grotesque creatures, odd lights, gargantuan beasts. A demon army, on its way north, to us. General Otto says this is the Legion of First, the army of Sheol.

"I've asked myself, why do they send so great a number for five pathetic souls? The only conclusion is that you are much more than you appear. Perhaps you, Daniel Fisher, are a Pillar. And you, Caleb, are the King of Demonkind. Though how you have all fallen so low is a mystery to me. I was never clever with riddles. So what to do?

"I could cast you into the desert like our scapegoat and let the Legion have you. But that might aid this demon army, which I cannot abide. But neither can I shelter demons, nor put this tribe at risk. So I am forced down the narrow path.

"The shift begins soon. The sands will carry us northeast. If we make haste, catch the right currents, by dusk we will reach the Jeen. We will take you to the edge of the desert of death and forgetting. There you can make your way to Dudael, may the Goddess protect your souls. No sane army would follow you across the Jeen, though I cannot vouch for your own safety once you enter the place where even demons fear to tread."

"The Legion," Caleb said, "is farthest from sane. Lord Elizel, who else but your priests, learned in magic, can perform the spell to bring Daniel and me to the Earth? Without your help, all is lost."

"Yes," Elizel said. "Uriel has told me this may be true. So I've offered my people a choice. Those who wish to follow you into the Jeen to help you may do so. The rest will continue on our way. My message is being conveyed to the houses as we speak. I don't think your chances are good."

"We need ten priests!" Caleb said. "Ten learned magicians! Can you promise us that?"

"I've already given you too much. My people are frightened, and the Bedu do not scare easily. Their trust in me has . . . *wavered*. I cannot ask them for more."

"Perhaps your time with them has ended," Caleb said. "Come with us and make yourself a new history."

Elizel took a deep breath. "My place is here, among my people," he said. "Even if they despise me."

"You're an honorable man, Lord Elizel," Caleb said. "They do not know what kind of leader they have."

"Or perhaps they know all too well," he said. And with those words, he walked away from them, and their guards returned.

"Give us water!" Marul shouted after Elizel. "And a healer for Rana!"

But Elizel kept on walking, until he was just another speck in a thousand moving shapes.

———

This was not Rana's battle, Daniel thought. She didn't ask to be part of this. She looked like Gram after the fire, her body ruined forever. Another casualty, because of him. He hung his head, ashamed. Too many people had been hurt because of him.

The sun approached the horizon. It would set soon, thankfully. His skin was on fire. And as he hung in his chains, he noticed the Bedu weren't packing camp yet. If the Legion was coming, what were they waiting for?

The dead man hung lifeless in his chains, and in the sun his body had begun to bloat. Daniel tried not to pay attention to the rotten smell, because even though it disgusted him, under his revulsion was something else.

Hunger.

He shivered. *I'll never allow myself to eat human flesh!* he thought. *Never.*

Twice, he begged the priests and soldiers to find Rana a doctor or healer or get her some water, but they responded only with mockery or the pointed tip of a sword.

Across the camp a loud horn blew. Like the shofar on Yom Kippur, the note was long and piercing, a call to attention. On that most solemn of Jewish holidays the shofar blast was—in its original intention—meant to ward off the demon Azazel. Yet if all went according to plan, they were going to meet the very same demon! Two more horns joined in, and the soldiers with their padded ears stirred. One tried to remove his cotton, but Avra stopped him.

A few hundred feet away from the log, several white-robed priests carried out two hefty brass bowls. The bowls glimmered in the sun. The priests filled the bowls with different powders in some sacred order, pausing to pray after each new ingredient. They brought torches to the mixture, and it flared up with tall green flames. Columns of black smoke corkscrewed into the sky, and winds brought the scent of molasses, cinnamon, ginger, and a mélange of other spices.

Avra and Elyam fell to their knees, made a triangle with their fingers, and pressed this symbol to their chests and their foreheads. The soldiers kneeled and bowed toward the smoke.

The priests by the censers raised their hands skyward. A colorful bejeweled palanquin skate sparkled as it drifted over the sands. Its doors sprung open, and eight priests emerged from it hefting a large gilded container. The container was even more reflective than the palanquin, second only in brilliance to the sun. The gilded container, rectangular, was mounted on long poles, and as the men turned, squares of reflected light moved across the camp. They spun it several times, as if to dazzle all with its glare. Golden birds adorned its top, wings touching, their chests puffed outward, eyes gazing upward.

Like the cherubim on the Ark of the Covenant, Daniel thought. He felt surreal, as if he were watching a ritual of the ancient Jews as they crossed the desert from Egypt to Israel.

White-robed boys pulled two stubborn goats over to the priests. The priests laid one goat on a wooden block, and with a quick knife blow and a gurgling bleat, it was slaughtered. Blood flowed down the block into two smaller bowls. The priests sprinkled the blood droplets about the sacrificial altar while chanting more prayers.

The slain goat was quickly disemboweled into sections, its entrails placed into one of the censers. The air grew thick with its pleasing odor, not because Daniel hungered for meat, but because of some uncanny reaction in the mixture that made the smoke smell like lilac. The entire camp seemed to grow sleepy and dreamy as they inhaled.

A priest poured goat's blood over the living animal, then screamed as he kicked it. The horns blew a hundred staccato notes as the goat bleated and darted across the camp, terrified. The Bedu leapt out of its way, shouting imprecations, spitting at it, until they forced the animal out of the camp. It sped off into the desert, bloody and free.

"*May our sins be upon it,*" Elyam and Avra said in a language neither Bedu-Besk nor Wul.

In the same language, the whole Bedu throng chanted, "*May her great name be exalted and sanctified in the world which she hath created according to her will. May she bring rain to the faithful, succor to the sick, abundant blessings to the righteous. May her great house shelter the weak and homeless . . .*"

There was so much similarity between their rituals and Judaism, past and present. *Who influenced whom?* he thought. And if the Ark of the Covenant held the Ten Commandments, what was inside the Bedu's holy box?

"Is there no limit to their stupidity?" Caleb said in English, so that only Daniel would understand. "With all this smoke, they might as well draw a map for the Legion and mark our position with a cross."

"Shut your mouth!" Avra snarled. "The splendor of her Holy Corpus is revealed! Be quiet or I'll sever your tongue!"

Avra and Elyam bowed and said more prayers. And when they seemed suitably engrossed, Daniel whispered to Caleb in English, "What's inside their golden ark?"

"Their goddess," Caleb whispered. "Mollai sheds her bodies as a snake sheds skin. Inside that box is one of her discarded vessels."

"Her skin is in the box?"

"A dead body. The Quog Bedu worship a corpse, Daniel. *Es per shemp Bedu.*"

The Bedu bowed and recited their prayers in an inflectionless chant, as if the notion of harmony was anathema to them.

"Look at them," Caleb whispered. "A dead man hangs in chains beside us, and here they pray for succor for the weak. The real curse of humanity is its willful blindness."

Daniel paused. Surely Caleb could see his own irony? "And how are you different?" he whispered. "You've been blind to others' suffering since we began."

"I make no pretense," Caleb said. "I do not say, 'I am holy,' with my left hand while my right murders. Humans claim to be morally superior to demons and all living creatures. But in their hearts, all men are demons."

"Every one has the capacity to do evil," Daniel said. "But also for good. That is the beginning of morality: choosing to do good against one's instincts."

"Morality is a human concept that has no analog in the Cosmos. What does a lion know of morality? A scorpion? If you repress your nature, it resurfaces as perversions. Look how the so-called 'righteous' faiths of Earth have perpetrated so much evil in their attempt to quash it. These Bedu, they profess to be righteous, yet they worship a corpse, slaughter the innocent, and leave the weak to die. And where is their Goddess now as their doom approaches? Mollai cares nothing for the ways of these desert roamers, except when they stop worshipping her."

The horns sounded an overlapping, interminable note. The shining Holy Corpus was carefully returned to the hovering palanquin. The prayers ended with the horns' cessation, and six thousand kneeling Bedu rose. The censers had burned out. The charred goat remains were carefully buried in sand. And in the south, just over the horizon where the air rippled with waves of heat, a small cloud of dust appeared.

The horns sounded seven sharp notes. A pause, then repeated. The camp stirred. The soldiers glanced at each other. A messenger approached and ordered half the soldiers to the southern perimeter, and the two priests whispered concernedly.

"It's the Legion," Daniel said. "Isn't it?"

"Their stupidity has caught up with them," Caleb said.

But it wasn't them, Daniel thought. *It was me. I told Rebekah where I was, in my dream.* "They just want me," Daniel shouted. "Send me out to them! I won't let another person die on account of me."

"If it were my wish alone," Avra said, "you'd already be gone. But we have orders."

With three bracing horn blasts the tribe readied to move. They lifted bags, tightened straps, kicked camels to standing. Goats brayed as shepherds stirred them to wakefulness.

Elyam tightened the belt of his robe and said, "Prepare yourselves for the shift."

"How are we supposed to walk bound to this log?" Marul said.

"You drag it, witch!" Elyam said.

"And drag a dead man with us?"

Avra and Elyam considered this. "I suppose he will only slow you down." He ordered a soldier to release the body. Avoiding the corpse's shredded skin, the soldier carefully unlocked the chains, and the man fell to the sands.

Rana shuddered.

"He needs to be buried," Marul said. "And rites spoken over his grave."

"No time," Elyam said, sipping water.

"Can't you spare him one small prayer?"

With the ram's horn, the Bedu, arrayed in their houses, jerked suddenly forward. "If he was a man of the Goddess, she will see to him."

Rana, kneeling beside the man's body, put a hand to his forehead. Her lips moved soundlessly and she closed her eyes.

"Move!" a soldier said, shoving his sword under Rana's neck. "Or I kill you now."

"Rana!" Marul said. "Stand up!"

Rana slowly climbed to her feet, and together they dragged the log forward. Daniel looked back at the body as they walked, feeling as if he were leaving behind something important. It was difficult to move, made worse by his thirst and the oppressive sun. He was already winded. Marul panted, and Rana could barely stand. How far could they go like this? The Bedu behind them gave the body a wide berth. Even the goats and camels would not approach it.

"One corpse revered," Caleb said. "Another shunned."

A wave of sand two hundred feet high rose behind them. Blood rushed to Daniel's head as it rolled underneath their feet, lifting them skyward. And when it sank, the body lay a thousand feet away, a black speck on the sands. Another dune rolled under them, then a third. At each peak he looked back until he could not see the body anymore.

On the horizon, the dust cloud steadily grew.

CHAPTER TWENTY-TWO

THE SUN STOOPED LIKE AN OLD WOMAN AS CALEB AND THE others dragged the log. Soon she would sleep, never to rise. Avra and Elyam tugged at their beards. Their fingers weaved through the air as they argued the finer points of some esoteric religious doctrine. *The fools ponder the interpretation of a phrase from scripture,* Caleb thought, *while a sword hangs above their heads!*

Soldiers walked beside them, grasping pommels, grinding teeth. Women, shepherds, camelry, children, all stole glances back at the cloud that pursued them furtively, like a hungry mountain cat, waiting for the right moment to pounce.

The Bedu tried to hide their fears. They raised their chins and hauled their cargo like the good, strong traders they presumed to be. They gave Caleb and the others water only when it seemed they would faint without it. And thus the waves thrusted them up and down, moving them toward the desert of black sands and drunken stars. Toward the mad desert, the Jeen.

Rana shuddered with every step. She was just like the power vats under Abbadon—in fact, the Gu were their inspiration. She captured the water of life falling from above in the well of her being. Because of this she healed faster than any normal human. But her wounds were still severe. She still might die.

Rana fell to her knees. They had dragged her a few paces before they stopped. A huge wave of sand approached from the south. They had to keep moving or risk falling behind. Soldiers pointed blades at Rana. "Get up!" they spat, and the tide of Bedu flowed around them as if they were a stone in a rushing river.

"The sands do not abide laggards!" one said.

"Fool! She cannot walk," Caleb said. "She is but one breath from death."

"By the Goddess, heal her," Marul said.

"Please," said Daniel. "If there is a shred of humanity in you, heal her."

"Our Goddess does not abide demons," Avra said.

"If you fools only knew who your Goddess is," said Caleb.

Elyam leaned to his partner and whispered, when Avra frowned and gave a reluctant nod. "Bind the shredded girl to the log. You three can haul her."

It was better than leaving Rana to die. With hand signs Avra signaled the soldiers to bind Rana to the back of the log, and they rushed to obey. Rana's eyes had lost their luster. They were glassy and gazed blindly at the sky. Her lips moved incoherently. When she was secure, Caleb and the others dragged her lacerated body forward again.

"Will you let a Gu die?" Caleb said. "Shall it be written that Avra and Elyam, the greatest fools to ever walk on Gehinnom, let a Gu die because of their own ignorance?"

"She is no Gu," Elyam said over his shoulder, but his voice was small, skeptical. He had to have witnessed her quick healing by now. But even if he suspected he was wrong about her, Caleb realized, his pride would not allow the admission of error.

"Rana, my Little Plum," Marul said, "why did you have to come for me?"

The knot in Caleb's chest tightened. How was it that Rana had breached the walls of his heart? Perhaps this was only the feeling of his hopes fading, his dreams evaporating like smoke. If Rana died, it would be an unquestionable loss, yes, but he would survive. He always had. Yet the world would be such a poorer place without her.

Like a bead of sweat trickling down his back, his spine tingled with a familiar, long-forgotten feeling. How long had it been since he'd felt this sensation? He closed his eyes and remembered the caresses under silken sheets, the callused but gentle hands touching his neck, the soft fur pressed against his thighs. How long had it been since he'd felt a bed as warm?

It is you, Koko, Caleb thought. *You've come.*

Horns blasted, and the people stirred. Ranks of soldiers rushed to the southern flank, where Lord Elizel waited at their helm. A wave of sand hoisted the Bedu up above the desert. The southern horizon was one long and massive cloud of dust. Beyond its murk walked thousands of colored specs, growing closer. The Legion waited.

In the valley below stood a giraffe-shaped demon with a vicious rat's face and spiraling ram's horns, his white fur stark against the orange sand. His pelagic eyes, blue within blue, were bottomless, cold and inviting.

Koko, Caleb thought. *Oh, Kokabiel. How I've missed you!*

Soldiers raised knives, swords, and slingshots. Camelry mounted animals by the hundredfold. They tightened their leather armor and raised bronze shields. They pulled scythes and daggers and powders from their belts. The priests chanted preparatory spells, and children lifted stones for slinging. And all this while they continued to walk north, propelled by the rolling waves.

Once, Kokabiel had been Caleb's most trusted general. No secret did Caleb have that Koko did not share. He remembered the vanilla scent of his fur. The sweet musk of his sex.

But Mashit promised you more, hasn't she? he thought. *And so you shift beds like the suns of Sheol swap positions in the sky.* He couldn't fault Koko for lack of ambition. But Koko had chosen the wrong side, and Caleb would remember this day.

Kokabiel's keen eyes spotted him chained to the log. He bowed his long neck in deference, while the Bedu raised their shields.

Once they had made the stars jealous with the heat of their passions. Was this bow all Caleb would receive for a century or two of bliss? Only for those sweet memories did Caleb bow back to his old lover now.

In a stentorian voice that still stirred Caleb's sex, the demon shouted to the scrambling Bedu, "I am Kokabiel, Second General of the Legion of the First."

Only Second General? Caleb thought. *You disappoint me, Koko.*

"I come with a message," Kokabiel shouted. "Heed it, and you shall live. Give us Ashmedai, the Traitor King, and Daniel Fisher, the Cosmic Pillar, and the Quog Bedu shall live to walk Gehinnom another day. Resist us, and your days end here."

Kokabiel's ocean-blue eyes scanned the Bedu ranks, marking their numbers, their weapons, while his hind leg scraped the sand haphazardly. By the black waters of Lake Hali, was Koko bored? When you've conquered entire Shards, a few thousand humans might seem minuscule by comparison. But the Koko Caleb had known would never let down his guard, not even for a gnat.

"You have until the sun touches the horizon," Kokabiel said. "Tarry a moment longer and you shall be effaced from this land forever, and your name shall be a curse among the living for fifty generations." He strutted away on his towering legs as a sand wave rose to obscure him from view.

Why does the Legion wait? Caleb thought. They could easily march in and take them all. Never in his long rule would he have let the Legion set *terms* with the enemy! They would take what they wanted and destroy the rest. Why was Mashit playing coy?

From the south, a regiment of twenty soldiers rushed down the rolling hill toward Caleb and the others. Square-bearded Otto helmed their rank. A long sword dangled from his belt, its bedizened pommel polished to a vulgar shine. His dented bronze shield was engraved with a lion devouring a lamb, as were his leather bracers and greaves.

"By order of our sovereign, Lord Elizel," General Otto said to the guards, "I am commanded to release the prisoners into the hands of the demon horde at once. Stand aside!" Sweat poured down his face and drizzled from his beard.

"I thought Lord Elizel didn't want to help this demon army?" Caleb said.

"He's changed his mind."

Has he? Caleb thought.

Avra said in a trembling voice, "By all means! I'm happy to be rid of their lot." He lifted a key from around his neck, and Otto's soldiers quickly unlocked their manacles. The ear-stuffed guards watched with bemused interest.

Caleb rubbed his wrists. It felt wonderful to be free of chains. Rana's eyes fluttered as a man tossed her body onto his shoulder. When all of them were unchained, his men ordered the prisoners to disrobe, which was not easy to do while the ground was shifting beneath them. Otto had four of the ear-stuffed soldiers put on their discarded clothes, and when all were dressed, Otto's men chained the soldiers to the log in their place. These new prisoners seemed quite troubled at the turn of events.

"What all this about?" Avra asked.

"Elizel's orders."

"You mean *Lord* Elizel?" Avra said, skeptically.

Otto ignored him and forced Caleb and the others into priests' white habits, even Rana. As they struggled to put the robes on, Avra shook his head and said, "Why does Lord Elizel want us to dress these monsters in our holy linen?"

"Does it surprise you, priest?" Otto said. "Our *lord* has no qualms against taboo."

"This makes no sense at all."

"We live in nonsensical times."

"This is not Lord Elizel's order, is it Otto?" Avra said.

Otto's face grew as red as Sheol's stars. "The Bedu do not aid demons!" he shouted, spittle flying from his lips.

"But this is treason!"

"Yes, and Elizel is the traitor. He betrayed us when he sheltered these abominations. Now I shall set things right."

"No," Avra said. "Lord Elizel must know what you've done."

"For a learned man, Avra, you're a fool." Otto stepped up to Avra, and with a swift jerk, thrusted his sword into Avra's gut. Otto's men grabbed the bleeding man before he fell. Blood poured from his belly and mouth, leaving a red trail behind them in the flowing sands.

"Unplug your ears!" Otto commanded, gesturing to the ear-stuffed soldiers. The soldiers looked at each other concernedly before removing their ear coverings.

"Hear me, valiant of the Bedu!" Otto said.

The soldiers' eyes flitted from Otto to the dying man.

"Elizel has betrayed you. These creatures are demons. They have supped in our tents, defiled our people, and yet Elizel would have us bring them to safety. Treachery is a plague of his house, for did not his father consort with Chialdra? And look to the south! A legion of hell threatens our destruction, but our leader tarries like an old man! The Bedu cannot afford to suffer the whims of a senile codger. Our existence is at stake! Stand with me, brothers, and I shall send these abominations back to the hell from which they came, and after we shall make the Bedu proud again. What say you, men?"

After a few looks at one another for affirmation, the soldiers nodded. "We serve Lord Otto!" one shouted. "Chieftain of the Quog Bedu!" The others joined his salute.

Otto smiled and said to Elyam, "What say *you*, priest?"

"I—I serve Lord Otto," Elyam said, his cheeks wet with tears.

"Good." Then to his men, he said, "Bind the bleeding man to the log. We will make it look as if the prisoners are still bound. We will free these men later, when all is done."

They stripped Avra of his bloody clothes and fastened him to the log, while Elyam winced and averted his eyes. The ruse set, Otto and his men marched Caleb and the others toward the southwestern flank, where the soldiers' ranks were thinnest.

"Are they going to kill us?" Daniel whispered in English.

"No," Caleb said, "Otto wants to hand us over to the Legion."

"Hush!" Otto snapped. "If you so much as fart, I'll slay every one of you!"

The mass of Bedu folk took little notice of them as they walked across the bustling scene. They were but another group of priests and soldiers readying for battle. But the log with the iron chains was another matter. As they walked across the sands people were speaking concernedly about it. Some had noticed the shift of prisoners.

"Who is that new person tied to the log?"

"Have the prisoners changed?"

"Yes, they seem different."

Otto was foolish to think he could deceive the sharp Bedu eye.

Someone shouted as Elyam, who had been walking with them, sprinted away.

"Go!" Otto shouted. "After him! Don't let him go!"

But the stocky priest was unusually agile, aided by magic. Bedu turned to watch the priest as he darted across the camp.

"Damn him!" Otto said. "I should have slain that craven lizard. Never mind. Just go!" His men hastened them toward the flanks, while Otto shouted, "The Bedu do not flee like sparrows! Elizel would have us skip into the Jeen like frightened lambs. But we are lions!"

"Hear, hear!" his men said, tapping swords on shields.

"There will be a signal," Otto said. "It will come from the north with the next dune rising. Wait for the yellow smoke, then march these demons onto open sand. We will cast these monsters out into the desert like the Betrayer's Goat. The demon army will take them back to hell, and we will be hailed as heroes."

His men cheered, when a soldier blurted, "Lord Otto, look!"

Behind them a battalion of five hundred Bedu soldiers was rushing toward them.

"The cursed priest!" Otto said.

Lord Elizel led the charge of five hundred men, his head a white puff of hair surrounded by glint of armor and sword. The air reeked of their sweat carried on the wind.

"Hurry!" Otto shouted. "Make for the slope! Zebu, the signal!"

A soldier raised a black banner with the sigil from Otto's shield, a lion eating a lamb. A column of yellow smoke rose a moment later from the northern flank, and a thousand anxious Bedu turned to look at the new fire.

Otto shouted, "Faster! Hurry!" His soldiers cajoled them forward.

Marul stumbled and fell.

"Get up, whore!" Otto said, yanking her up by the collar of her robe.

She stood, but tripped again.

"What are you doing?" Caleb said. "They're about to set us free!"

"Into the clutches of hell!" Marul said.

"Carry the hag!" Otto ordered, and a soldier bent to lift her.

Lord Elizel and his battalion reached them. Five hundred swords flashed in the sun. A crowd of Bedu civilians circled around the soldiers. Their feet moved like a performance of synchronized dancers, and everyone kept their positions even as the sands rose and fell beneath their feet. For Caleb, for Marul, and for Daniel, it was a constant battle just to stand.

Lord Elizel stepped forward, his armor sagging. "General Otto, by whose order do you conceal and move the prisoners?"

Otto shoved past his men to the front. "By mine alone! For I am the new Chieftain of the Quog Bedu." The crowd gasped. "You have harbored demons. You have disgraced our houses. We will cast these abominations out of our midst. And you shall be tried before the Synedrium and put to sword for treason."

Elizel shook his head woefully. "You were my right-hand, Otto, my most trusted. The only treachery here is yours. Hear me, men of Otto's camp. We greatly outnumber you. Lay down your swords and there will be no punishment against you. You have my word as Chieftain. You shall be forgiven for your transgressions, like a lamb that has drifted from the herd."

"Do you not see our banner?" Otto shouted. "Lions eat lambs! Is forgiveness all you can offer these heroes? How many times did you make unnecessary concessions with weak kingdoms? How many years did we barter like beggars instead of taking what was ours? Once the Bedu were feared. Now children of cities mock us in demonsong!"

The crowd edged closer, murmuring as their numbers grew. They moved in to see, their feet dancing with the ever-shifting sands.

"Hear me, my bedraggled family!" Otto said. "I am Otto ben Zadok, and I shall make our people great again. What has Elizel brought us but struggle, ruin, and disgrace? In the poems we recite to our children we speak of how mighty we are. Once that was true, but today they are lies. We have lost our glory. Because of him!"

"I am imperfect," Elizel said. "As all men are. I make no secret of my flaws, but instead embrace them. For a full generation I have kept the Quog Bedu free from war, disease, and curse. In twenty years our numbers have grown. Most of our children reach adulthood, and our wives no longer fear childbirth. Perhaps I have given up our marauding ways. Perhaps they were meant to be forgotten."

"You'd have us give up our souls!" Otto said. "Beloved Bedu, glimpse this withered man with clear eyes. Do not permit mine to do the seeing. Look! He shelters demons. Look! He cowers from battle. Look! He skitters away like a lizard. Is this the man you want for your lord?"

"The people know who I am," Elizel said.

"Yes," Otto said. "And they tire of it." He unsheathed his sword.

"We raced camels as boys," Elizel said. "We drank palm wine together under the stars. Is this how you wish to end our friendship?"

"Our friendship ended long ago."

Otto swung, and Elizel dove to avoid it. The sword missed his shoulder by a hair. The crowd gasped and pushed closer, while their feet skipped heel over heel, keeping up with the shift. Their swords clanged and clamored as a white-robed priest, jostling for a better view, sidled up to Caleb. With their attention diverted, Caleb grabbed Daniel's hand and whispered in English, "Come on, Daniel. Let's get out of here!"

But a soldier grabbed his shoulder and shoved his blade into his lower back until it pierced flesh. "Move another step," he said with foul breath, "and I'll split you like an ox!"

Daniel and Marul had swords in their backs too, but their guards' were looking at the fight. Rana hung limp on the shoulder of a fourth, her bloody drool staining his back.

"You—" Otto said as he swung "—don't deserve to rule!" Otto's muscles bulged, and his sword flew with ease.

"And you," Elizel said, hopping like a sparrow, "have the loyalty of a scorpion!"

"Your father consorted with demons!" Otto said, tossing his sword from hand to hand. "Cursed blood runs in your veins!" Otto swiped and slashed off Elizel's white beard at the chin, leaving a bloody gash. The crowd gasped and Otto smiled. "And now your blood runs without." He picked up the bloody tuft of hair. "Wisdom is not in the length of one's beard." He chuckled as he tossed the hair away, and the crowd laughed uneasily with him.

"Nor," Elizel said, rubbing his bleeding chin. "In the sharpness of one's sword."

"We were once great!" Otto said, swinging.

"Your failure," Elizel said as he parried, "is not seeing that we still are!"

The hooded priest who had sidled beside Caleb whispered, "He is right. We were once great. I remember it well."

The voice was familiar, and it took Caleb a moment to place it. He turned to face the priest to meet his yellow candleflame eyes.

Hiding under his hood was a familiar, withered face. A smiling face.

Havig.

In the silent language, Havig said, *It's good to see you, my lord. The desert sparrow told us you were with the Bedu, but it took time to find you. Prepare yourself, my lord.*

The swords clanked and clamored, and Elizel bled from several wounds. Otto dripped with sweat, but didn't have a single scratch. The crowd gasped with every swipe and swing. Scattered among them were two dozen hooded priests, their faces shadowed and hidden, except for their eyes, which glowed with faint yellow light. While everyone watched the battle, these hooded priests gazed at Caleb. In unison, they bowed, ever so slightly.

Caleb laughed, and Marul said, "You find this amusing?"

"For more reasons than you know."

Havig slit the throat of his guard and he fell gurgling to the ground. In the same breath the other guards were slain. A few saw the blood and shouted, but most mistook the wails for jeers and kept their eyes on the fight between Elizel and Otto.

"Hurry, my lord!" Havig said. "Put this on." He gave Caleb a silver chain. The Mikulalim sigil shone from its pendant, just like the necklace he had given Rana in Yarrow. "We have enough for all of you."

A ram's horn blew as a dune rolled beneath them to reveal the southern horizon. Kokabiel was galloping toward them, a hundred paces beyond the southern flank. He roared, revealing rows of sharp teeth.

Behind Kokabiel loomed rageful Hemah, tall as twenty men, wrapped in black and red chains that were consumed in flames. The chains dangled in her hands, ready to strike.

Beside her stomped Af, the nine-headed elephant, whose tusks probed like snake tongues. Beside Af ran Abezethibou, the one-winged demon. Beside him, Baalberith the mammoth fly. And Naamah, who carried her harp made from the tendons of the slain. And Roeled, and Ieropael, and Buldumech, and Nefthada. And behind them were ten thousand more, the Legion of the First, the army of Sheol, once Caleb's to command, now charging toward them.

There was a pregnant pause. The Bedu held their breath. A baby cried in the distance.

Kokabiel lifted his neck high and, like a pendulum, swung his head down. His horns slammed into dozens of soldiers. They flew in long arcs and crashed on the sand. The screams began.

Koko broke his own word. This was nothing new. *But why now?* Caleb thought. *Did he think we were going to be slain?*

"Cover the south flank!" Lord Elizel ordered. "Ready the attack spells! Prepare the—"

Otto shoved his sword deep into Elizel's stomach. A woman shrieked.

"Your time has ended," Otto said, twisting the blade.

Elizel whimpered as blood fell from his mouth.

"Today the new Bedu are born!" Otto shouted. He yanked out his sword, holding it up high, while Elizel's bowels spilled onto the sand. Elizel tried futilely to stuff them back in, before he fell forward, dead. The moving sands took him away, and a crowd of people went with him.

"Bastard!" Marul cried. Scores of Bedu bleated like frightened sheep and ran to their fallen leader. In the same moment a dozen soldiers from Elizel's camp rushed Otto. They shredded the traitor in seconds.

The Bedu scattered like birds. At the southern flank the battle had begun. Stones flew and swords clashed with a hundred angry demons.

Penemue, his body densely tattooed with letters, scribed an ancient and terrible word in the sand, and every person who looked upon it collapsed like a sack of grain.

"Come, my lord!" Havig begged, tugging at Caleb. "What are you waiting for?"

"By Sheol, aren't they glorious?" Caleb said.

"And no longer yours to command. Come!"

"Yes, Havig. I think that's wise."

Caleb donned the silver necklace as the Mikulalim took them from the scattered crowd. A Mikulal lofted Rana on his shoulder, and she stared blankly up at the sky.

"Hang on, Rana," Caleb said to her. "Just a little bit longer, and we will be free!" To Havig he said, "How many men do you have?"

"Five hundred, my lord. More on their way."

"Magnificent, Havig."

Rahab, the sea dragon, shot steam from his nostrils, burning the flesh off of those unlucky to greet him. Shemhazai held up a mirrored scepter, entrancing those who gazed into its reflections. As they stared helplessly, he crushed their heads with the scepter's heavy blow.

The Bedu assaulted the invaders with swords, stones, and spells. Fools! They might as well have tried to topple a mountain with a hammer.

Bedu magicians tossed balls of green fire from their hands. Kokabiel swatted the vortices away as if they were gadflies. The balls exploded into sparks like shattered universes.

A gargantuan dune rose in the south, much out of sync with the natural ones. It hoisted five hundred men above the desert. The wave broke suddenly, burying the men under tons of sand, and sending others tumbling to their deaths. The wave rumbled beneath Caleb, and he stumbled as it lofted them high above the desert. From this view, the Legion seemed to cover the whole desert. Tens of thousands of demons, ready for battle. But where was their queen?

As they ran from the fighting, a Bedu soldier shouted to Caleb, "Priest! We need your healing! We have set up a triage by the—" The man saw the Mikulalim, and his mouth fell open.

They strode past him. The ground fell rapidly, and they dove into a valley. Ahead floated the jeweled palanquin skate that held the Holy Corpus of Goddess Mollai. They ran for it as Klothod flew overhead and plucked a screaming woman from the ground and swallowed her whole. Klothod could have plucked Daniel and Caleb just as easily, but Azazel's pendants hid them from their gaze.

Ten soldiers guarded the Holy Corpus, but Caleb had forty Mikulalim. The Bedu threw down their swords and raised their arms.

Havig eyed Caleb. *Let me avenge my brothers*, he said in the silent language.

Caleb nodded, and swiftly the Mikulalim slayed all the guards.

"No!" Daniel cried. "Damn you, Caleb, they surrendered!"

"As did my brothers," Havig said. "But the Bedu let them burn in the sun. Ten for ten. Now the debt is paid." He flung open the palanquin doors and the Holy Corpus blinded them with its gilded reflections. But the Corpus was not alone. Several priests cowered inside like frightened kittens. They smelled of piss and shit as they prayed to their absent god. Elyam quailed with them.

"Mollai protect us!" they said, grasping each other.

Havig lifted his sword and stepped inside.

"Keep the priests alive," Caleb said. "We need them." He counted six as he stepped in, waving Marul and Daniel inside. Daniel looked back at the raging battle, frowned, then climbed inside. The Mikulalim placed Rana on the floor. Her eyes had stopped fluttering. Caleb dared not look at her. He did not want to know if she were dead.

Havig and five Mikulalim joined them in the palanquin, crowding the small space. The Mikulalim closed the doors, plunging them into darkness.

"Woe is us!" Elyam said. "Cursed ones beside the holy Corpus! Oh, Blessed Mollai, forgive us."

Light bloomed in the dark. A lick of red-orange flame floated above Havig's palm as he and the Mikulalim hummed a singsong spell.

"Stop!" Elyam squealed. "Stop your demonsong!" The priests covered their ears. The palanquin skate slammed hard into sand, and everyone stumbled.

The walls became translucent, like smoky glass, as the battle raged outside the walls. They sat on the sands that crept ever closer to the southern flank. Soon they would drift right into the arms of the Legion. Havig closed his palm and the flame winked out.

"Grab hands," Havig said. "You too, priests!"

"I'll not touch an abomination," Elyam whimpered.

"Grab my hand," Havig said, "or the hands of that demon army. Which shall it be?"

"Oh, dear Goddess," Elyam said. Grimacing, he took Havig's hand.

The priests and Mikulalim joined hands in a circle around the Holy Corpus. Havig closed his eyes, and the Mikulalim joined him. The walls buzzed and rattled as they slowly rose from the ground.

But a moment later, they crashed to the sand, and the Holy Corpus slammed against the wall, making a dent.

"Why can't we fly?" Caleb said.

"Not enough power, my lord!" Havig said.

"We cast shields over the Holy Corpus," Elyam said. "We have little power left."

"Your life is in danger and you protect a corpse?" Caleb said. "Marul, can you help?"

Marul was busy removing the gag from Rana's mouth. Rana moved her lips.

Caleb allowed himself a sigh. Rana was alive!

Daniel crouched beside Rana, helping Marul make her more comfortable.

"Marul!" Caleb shouted. "Now or never!" She nodded, then got up to join the circle. They started the spell again. This time they floated a bit higher before they crashed. The battle raged closer. They were less than a minute from the front now.

"We're too heavy," Elyam said. "We don't have enough power."

"Then we lighten the load," Caleb said. He flung open the doors, and the sun shone in. The Mikulalim winced and turned away from the light. With one great heave Caleb shoved the gilded Corpus out the door.

"Goddess, no!" the priests cried as the Holy Corpus tumbled onto the sand, flashing in the sun. The lid slid off to reveal the desiccated corpse inside. Long gray hair, flaky skin, hollow eyes. The body had once belonged to a girl, her mind obliterated so that Mollai could use it for her own pleasure. The priests shrieked as Caleb yanked the doors closed.

"Blasphemy!" one shouted.

"Necessity," Caleb said. "Now try your spell again."

The Mikulalim grabbed hands, but the priests shook their heads.

"Do it or we'll all die!"

Trembling, weeping, the priests joined hands. This time they remained hovering. Slowly, they floated eastward, then south, toward the Legion.

"Fools!" Caleb said. "The other way!"

They wobbled as they turned, zigzagging roughly north. Through the translucent walls the battle continued. To the east, three hundred

Bedu were struck dead by Alath's breath. Fires burned in the south, choking the sky with oily smoke. In the west, Hephesimireth the snake devoured fleeing children by coming up from beneath. The Bedu, a people three millennia old, would not live through the hour.

"*Es per shemp Bedu*," Caleb said.

As they moved from the battle, Havig said, "My lord, I've ordered my men to take the other palanquins and flee in many directions. It will not be easy for them to know which one you are in."

"Havig, you are loyal like none other. You shall be rewarded."

He bowed his head.

"Rana's dying," Daniel said, cradling her head. He gave her water from a bladder. "You're magicians! Can any of you help?"

With a gesture from Caleb, a Mikulal broke the circle. The palanquin tumbled for an instant until they moved to close the gap. The Mikulal showed Caleb a small phial from his belt.

"We expected injuries," he said. "We brought the greyel wine. But we don't have much—"

"Give it to her, now!" Caleb said.

While Daniel held her head, the Mikulal poured the viscous black fluid into her mouth. She blinked and groaned.

"She's been gagged with a spell," the Mikulal said. "But it's fading. She'll need time to recover."

"My brothers and sisters are no more," Elyam said, staring at the receding battle. "My house is dust. The Bedu are no more."

"A true shame," Havig said.

Caleb laughed.

"No, my lord. I am sincere. I regret the Bedu's passing."

"Havig," Caleb said. "You surprise me. Do you really care what happens to the Bedu?"

"A long time ago, my lord," Havig said, "we were kin. I'd always hoped one day we would be kin again."

"Yes," Caleb said, "you and the Bedu would make one large, happy family."

He heard a grunt, and turned. And there stood Rana, diving for him. The sword in her hand—where had it come from?—plunged deep into his belly, and he cried out.

"It's over," she said hoarsely, twisting the blade. "The beast is done."

CHAPTER TWENTY-THREE

RANA TWISTED THE SWORD INSIDE THE DEMON'S BELLY, AND SHE savored the horrified look in his eyes. Havig leaped from the circle, and with a swift motion flung her sword to the floor. He held his blade to her throat.

She lifted her chin and spread her arms wide. "Do it," she said. "*Kill me!*"

"My lord," Havig said, eyes on Rana. "Are you gravely wounded?" The palanquin bobbed as a Mikulal moved to close the broken circle. The tip of Havig's blade pressed hotly against Rana's neck.

Caleb lay on the floor, bleeding, his back against the wall. He held his stomach and gazed at his wound. "The human form is so . . . fragile, Havig." He coughed, and his white priest's habit slowly turned red. He turned to the Mikulal who'd given Rana the greyel wine and said, "How did you let her get your sword, fool?"

"My lord, I—"

"Never mind! Give me your phial. Hurry!"

He ran to Caleb and was about to pour the black syrup into his mouth before Caleb snatched the phial and swallowed it all.

"But, my lord, that's all we have!"

"If I die," Caleb said, "then you're all dead too."

Rana squeezed her fists until she thought her palms might bleed. So damned arrogant! So damned self-righteous! She took a deep breath and prepared to sing him back to hell.

Havig said, "Hum a note, Rana, and I'll make myself a harp from your vocal chords."

She lifted the pendant from her neck and showed it to Havig. "And what of *this*?" Her voice was raspy, remnants from the Bedu spell, the sandstorm. "You gave me this necklace, remember? You *love* my voice."

"I love my king more."

"Why?" Rana said. "You are his chisel. He hammers you for years and tosses you away when you grow dull."

"Lord Ashmedai has given the Mikulalim more than any other."

"You are deluded. He won your people in a bet. He has your mind in a cage. You are his puppets, his dancing dolls!"

Havig threw back his hood, and his hollow eyes glowed like dying suns. "He gives us purpose in a meaningless universe."

"And what a woeful purpose that is."

"Before Lord Ashmedai," Havig said, "we were mere beasts, hiding in shadows, surviving on scraps. The nomads slaughtered us. The cities hunted us. But under Lord Ashmedai's rule, we became a mighty nation, countless in number."

"And how long before your king grows tired of you and throws you into the sun?" She shook her head. "This is useless. You are under a spell. You'll never see." A wave of despair consumed her. "It is *all* useless." She yanked off her chain and threw it to the floor, where it rolled to a stop at Caleb's feet.

"Rana," Caleb said. His wound was deep. Even with the greyel potion he still coughed up blood. "I don't understand why you loathe me so." He wiped fluid from his mouth. "Hear me for a moment. If after, you still want to kill me, I'll order Havig to give you his sword."

"My lord?" Havig said.

"Havig, it is my wish."

Rana stared at him. What clever trick was this?

"You hate me," he said, "because you blame me for all you've lost."

She shuddered. "If not for you, none of this would have happened."

"But *is* it because of me?"

"Who else?"

"Mashit is destroying the Lamed Vav, but I have saved Daniel from her. And I want to protect the other Lamed Vav too. Her actions will destroy Earth and all the Shards. But I want to stop her. The Legion, under Mashit's command, has destroyed Azru. Remember how we fled from your city like a thief? What harm did I wish Azru then? Her minions murdered your parents. But I hid from your parents in your studio. I am not the one whom you should hate!"

"But the Legion followed you!" she said. "You knew they'd come after you, after Daniel. You brought them here. And for that you carry the blame."

"If we must cast blame, then let's gaze more deeply at the facts. Has your beloved Marul Menacha told you yet why I imprisoned her?"

"Because you're a cruel demon."

"If only it were that simple. I imprisoned her, Rana, because she betrayed all of us. The Lamed Vav have remained hidden for millennia—"

"Caleb!" Marul said. "Please, I beg you. Don't."

Marul gave Rana such a weighted, pained look that Rana had to turn away.

"How do you think Mashit knows where to find the Lamed Vav?" Caleb said. "Many years ago, a powerful, aging witch lived on Earth in a city called Shanghai. There she discovered a secret that few have ever known. She found the names of the Hidden Righteous Ones, the Pillars of the Kuurku, the Lamed Vav. She knew how valuable this information was, and so she offered the list to demons in exchange for permanent youth."

Marul had closed her eyes. Why wasn't she denying this? Why wasn't Marul accusing Caleb of lies?

"Yes, that witch was Marul Menacha," Caleb said. "If we must cast blame, one should look no further than your beloved friend. She sold out the Cosmos for the promise of immortality. She gave Mashit the names of the Lamed Vav—only six names—and promised the others when her youth was restored. But her rank stupidity has put the whole Cosmos in danger. To protect us all, I hid Marul away in the cave, and I told Mashit that her delusional fantasies would get us all killed. And for this act I was stripped of my throne, tortured publically, drained of power, and exiled from Sheol."

Rana was trembling. Marul still had not denied any of this. "Marul," she said, "tell me he speaks a bushel of lies."

Many moments passed. "I was getting old," Marul said, her voice small. "My back ached, my feet hurt, my eyes were growing poor. My powers were fading with my body. I was searching for ways to help Gehinnom, and I thought if I extended my life, I could continue the search indefinitely."

"Do not mock Rana with more falsehoods," Caleb said. "You'd given up your quest years before you made the offer to Mashit. You were using magic to seduce, and little else. You wanted to stay young only to continue indulging your perversions."

"I knew I was weak even then," Marul said. "Corrupted. I thought if I were in a young body again, just as how the Goddess changes each time she takes on a new body, I might find the strength to help Gehinnom. I thought I could be a goddess too."

"You were a goddess," Rana said. "To me."

"I know."

"Look at me," Rana said. "Open your damn eyes and look at me!"

Marul's sullen gaze found Rana. The corners of her mouth curved down with infinities of regret. But her eyes glimmered with the same warmth Rana had once coveted more than her own mother.

"Did you know this would happen?" Rana said as she gestured toward the desert, the decimated cities, the teetering Cosmos. "Did you know that everyone would suffer if you told Mashit how to find the Lamed Vav? That my parents would die? That I might die? That we all might soon die?"

She shook her head. "No! I never planned to give her all the names. *Only six.*"

"Killing six," Caleb said, "is enough to collapse the Kuurku and destroy Earth."

"Great Giver of Rain . . ." Rana said as she stumbled back against the wall.

"Rana, in my years locked in that cave I did nothing but think," she said. "I have seen the errors of my ways ten thousand times."

"But it's too late," said Rana. "You've already told Mashit. Dear Goddess, I thought you were somebody else."

Marul sighed, a distant wind across a forgotten plain. "Rana, I had always wanted to be that woman. But you were too smart. I knew that if I stayed too long, you would discover who I was. That's why I always left, after a time. Better to have a beautiful fantasy than a bleak truth."

"There, Rana, do you see?" Caleb said, coughing blood into a rag.

"Yes," Rana said, sliding to the floor. "I see it all."

With a nod from Caleb, Havig sheathed his sword and rejoined the circle, and the palanquin sped on with renewed certainty. Caleb's wound still bled, while her abrasions sloughed off like dead skin. Underneath were fresh, baby-like patches of new skin. It reminded her of Liu. How many parasot away was her sister now, in body or in spirit?

They traveled over a thousand dunes, while the priests murmured and the wind tumbled over endless seas of dust. The sun touched the horizon, and the sky turned as red as molten glass. Every so often, she gazed at Marul, hoping this was some kind of cruel joke.

My parents, she thought, *are dead because of her!*

A long time ago Rana would leap with joy whenever Marul sprang unannounced into her house bearing gifts from far-off kingdoms. Marul would regale her and her parents with tales of handsome princes, queens who ruled by magic, and violent demons older than time. And after a meal of laughter and suspense, Marul and Rana would walk along the twilit streets of Azru, where under Marul's careful eye every crevice blossomed with mysteries.

"Do you see that curved sigil there?" Marul said as they rounded Seamstress Row one moonless night, when the stars were as numerous as grains of sand. "That sandworn one, carved into the cornerstone? That's the mark of Beor, a king who ruled this city when it was called Dinhabah."

"I've never heard of Beor."

"You wouldn't. No monuments remain to testify of his rule."

"Then how do you know of him?" Rana said.

"It's wise to ask, Little Plum. An old and dangerous demon showed me him in a vision."

"Were you scared?"

Marul straightened her neck. "Ha! I do not fear demons."

Rana's heart burned with the fire of the stars. *One day,* she thought, *I'll be as fearless as Marul. I'll conquer demons and travel to other worlds.*

"Was Beor a great king?" she said.

"One of the greatest."

"Greater than King Umer?"

"Umer is a pebble to Beor's mountain. Beor was one of the greatest kings ever to rule, and his name was renowned from the frigid empires of the north to the boiling seas in the south."

Rana's heart grew troubled. "But if Beor was so great, why doesn't anyone remember him?"

"Because it was a long time ago."

"How long?"

"Seventy-four years."

"But that's not a very long time."

"On Gehinnom, it's an eternity."

"Did Beor have a big palace?"

"Enormous."

"Where is it?"

"It's gone."

"Gone to where?"

"It's just—" she waved her hand as if waving away smoke. "Gone."

"But how can something so big just . . . *vanish*?"

Marul sighed. "I'm afraid, Rana, that time has its way with us all."

Rana stopped mid-stride. Hadn't Papa said the same thing?

"What's wrong, Little Plum?" said Marul.

"I don't like how things can just disappear like that." Could the sculptures, the paintings, the instruments in her studio vanish like King Beor's palace?

"I'm sorry. I shouldn't tell you such things."

Rana swallowed her fear. She would be brave like the great Marul Menacha, The Witch Who Gives Demons Pause, the woman who traveled to other worlds in vessels of light and learned secrets from fearsome monsters. "When I am older," she said, "I will build a monument so big it will last forever."

"A palace?"

"No, a statue. Of you, Marul."

Marul's cheeks blushed. "I'm flattered, Rana. Very flattered. No one wants to be forgotten. No one wants to die. Me especially." Marul gazed longingly at the stars, as if she had left something behind in the heavens. "Come, it's late. Your mother will be getting worried."

The next morning, like King Beor and his enormous palace, Marul vanished. Rana longed for her return, but Marul never came back, and soon Rana's parents hinted that it was better to assume the witch was dead, that a demon had finally bested her. And Rana had listened to them and had even carved Marul a tombstone. Later, in a fit of anger, she'd smashed it.

And yet here she sits, Rana thought, *back from the dead. How did I miss her true form?* Like the hucksters on Bedubroadstreet, Marul had won her confidence, only to rob her.

"Don't judge her too harshly," Caleb said, holding his belly. He looked even paler than before. "She was as blind to her nature as you were to yours."

"And what is my nature?"

"You are Gu."

"I've heard as much. What exactly does that mean?"

"Your Priests of Mollai never told you?"

"I didn't spend much time in the temples."

"In ancient Bedu-Besk, a 'Gu' is an overflowing water jar. As Earth's energy drips into the Great Deep, some of that energy collects in basins, pools, oases. You are such an oasis, Rana. You overflow with life. Have you ever considered where your creativity comes from?"

When she was young, her neighbor, Yrma, once told Rana her parents had no money to buy her a doll. So Rana made one out of beads, cloth, and string. Yrma loved it so much, she carried the doll everywhere. But Yrma's parents thought the doll looked too much like their daughter, that its eyes were too keen, it's shape too human. They said to Rana's parents, "No human child can sew and stitch with such uncanny skill. Your child is a demon!" They burned the effigy, accused Rana of devilwork, and forbade Yrma ever to see Rana again.

Day after day, whenever Rana passed Yrma on the street, her friend scurried away with a look of terror in her eyes. The next year, Yrma and her parents left for Ektu El. She heard they died in a sandstorm on the way.

When Rana had grown older and girls her age were sneaking off to get drunk and meet boys at the fermentaries, she worked nights in her studio, carving busts out of wood, smelting metal into pins and charms, and painting strange vistas that haunted her dreams.

She had often wondered, *Why does this fire burn in me and not others? Am I a demon?* But the question soon became irrelevant. *I must create*, she had thought, *and that is enough.* Art was her only friend. Art, and Marul.

And now? Rana turned to Marul. "You knew I was a Gu, back then?"

Marul nodded.

Rana felt her belly grow hot. "So was anything between us real? Why did you visit me? Was I just a step on your path to goddess-hood?"

"At first," Marul said, "your Gu-nature fascinated me. But I came to love you, Rana." Her voice was small. "I still do."

"You've made clear how much that love means."

Marul sighed. Her eyes were dark and baggy. Her lips quivered. "Can you forgive an old woman her mistakes?"

"You want *my* forgiveness? You betrayed all of existence! My forgiveness means nothing."

"It means everything to me."

"Then for that alone you won't have it."

Marul shuddered. The palanquin shook with the force of her tears. Rana had to look away from the despicable sight.

Caleb gave Rana a pitying look. Was this an affectation, or did he feel genuine pity? A demon could not feel pity, could he?

"What happened to Grug?" Marul said, after a time. "Is he safe in Yarrow?"

"I'm sorry," Havig said. "Grug is dead."

"What?" Marul's voice cracked, and the palanquin heaved. "*Dead?* Grug? Oh, Grug. How? How did he die?"

"Killed," Rana said. "By pillagers."

"You were there?"

"Yes," Rana said. "And I gave them what they deserved."

"What do you mean?"

"She sang to them," Caleb said. "Didn't you, Rana? You weaved melodies through their minds, as you tried to do with the Bedu." He was staring at her.

"Yes," she said. "And while they were entranced, Emod slaughtered them all."

"Oh, Rana," Marul said. "You used your powers to kill? The child I knew would never have done that."

"Then it seems we both have mistaken the other for someone else."

Daniel had been sitting quietly against the wall, and he abruptly stood. His cheeks were hollow, and dark circles ringed his eyes. "So it was you!" he shouted to Marul. He bared his teeth, a threatening sight, and if it wasn't for his pale skin, Rana might have thought him a Mikulal. "If not for you, I'd be back on Earth, Rana would be with her parents, and the Bedu would still be alive." His face grew red with rage. "Say something, Marul! Don't you have anything at all to say?"

"I thought it wasn't in a Lamed Vavnik's nature to judge?" Marul said quietly.

"How can I not judge?" Daniel said. "You've ruined it for all." He scanned the frightened Bedu faces, the hollow-eyed Mikulalim. His eyes swept over Caleb, and when his gaze landed on Rana, he said, "I've witnessed so much pain on this world. And I've been told the other Shards are even worse. What an utter tragedy. The Cosmos is broken, but I'm going to put it all back together. Not only the Earth, but I'm going to mend all the Shards."

"*Humpty Dumpty,*" Marul said. "What you speak is impossible."

"What do you know?" said Rana. "You gave up trying to help Gehinnom so you could stay young and keep fucking."

Marul closed her eyes, and Daniel shook his head. "After we save the other Lamed Vav," he said. "I'll devote the rest of my life to helping the Shards. I can't go back to Earth knowing how many suffer."

"Daniel," Caleb said, "you and I share the same goal. We want to make a better world for all."

"The difference is," Daniel said, "that I won't kill in order to do that."

"Hear, hear," announced Elyam, who had been sitting quietly in the circle. "I will help the Pillar return to the Kuurku. But I will not stand beside demons, nor aide in their quest, no matter how noble it seems. Demons always betray." He stared at Caleb.

"Hush, father!" another priest said. Untamed goat-hairs sprouted from his chin. He looked younger than Rana.

"Zimri, you'll stand beside your father," Elyam said. "As all the Bedu will." He scanned the ranks of his brethren, and they returned his gaze with alternating looks of skepticism and agreement. "We will loft the Pillar back to the land of Erte, but without demon help."

"My dear Elyam," said Caleb, "I wish there were another way. But the Betrayer is the only one who can help us now. You may choose not to help us. And thus you choose to let Gehinnom die. Think on it. We'll reach Dudael soon."

Elyam frowned and said no more, and they flew onward. Through the translucent walls, dunes wrestled beneath them. The sun was a huge cinder on the horizon, and the palanquin's shadow stretched across the desert, all the way back to Rana's childhood of naive hopes and unfulfilled dreams. An immense dune rose in the north, and the palanquin ascended its steep bank. And when they crested it, Rana gasped at the immense vista beyond.

A desert dark as coal and smooth as molten glass stretched to the horizon. The ground slanted askew, and the sands seemed to writhe at the corners of her vision. Though the air still held the heat of the day, warmth fled from her body as if she were fevered. She shivered and knew they had crossed into the Jeen, the demented desert, where even the hated demons of Fintas Miel dared not tread.

"This morning I was a high priest of the Quog Bedu," Elyam said, "and now I cross into the black desert with maneaters and demons. Goddess help us all."

"Your goddess," Caleb said, "can't even help herself."

The sun set, and the Mikulalim removed their hoods. Rana opened the palanquin doors, and a cool wind whipped through the interior. It reeked of soot, as if a hundred cities had burnt to the ground. She remembered this smell. It had been on Chialdra as she swooped low over her and on the traders who'd come into

Azru from the deep desert. The air carried whispers of far-off places. They were tenuous and perhaps imagined. She heard a woman crying over her stillborn child. A boy begging a pet lizard he accidentally crushed to come back to life. An old man cursing the Goddess for giving him a hideous, disfiguring disease.

She sat on the edge and dangled her legs over the dark sands. This place reeked of death. Not just death, but the stillness that lay beyond it.

She shivered as a million stars trembled and awoke in the sky. Collectively they seemed brighter than the sun, yet only a faint flicker reached the sands. The sky was immense, unfathomable. It pressed down upon everything with a tremendous, ineffable weight. She had trouble breathing. Over long minutes the stars wandered in strange courses, stumbling about like drunken men. Bits of ash blew into her eyes, and she hugged herself to keep warm. Her dead skin blew away in the wind. Underneath was something new, different, unrecognizable.

Who would she be now? Who *could* she be?

Caleb approached her. He grabbed the roof with one hand while his other cradled his bandaged stomach. Blood seeped through the white strips of cloth. His hair fluttered in the breeze. "Stunning, isn't it?"

"That's not what I would call it."

He sat down beside her. "No? What would the Gu call it then?"

"A waste."

"Yes." He nodded. "Eternity rests its weary head here. The Jeen is a place of annihilation. The opposite of what you are."

She shivered as the stars wiggled mindlessly about.

"You're cold," he said. "Havig, do we have a coat for her?"

"No," she said. "I don't want to be covered. I don't want to hide anymore."

Caleb considered her. "Your wounds are healing well. Unlike mine. That was quite a jab." He smiled, revealing canines stained with blood and greyel potion.

They passed over a gargantuan skeleton of some eight-legged beast, its spine half-buried in the sand. Even its ancient carcass seemed an affront to the emptiness.

"There's something very wrong about this place," she said.

"The Abyss tugs more strongly in the Jeen. What you sense is but a taste of the hell we'll experience when the Earth shatters and we wither for eons in the Great Deep."

"I left my sister back in Azru."

"So you've said."

"Her name is Liu. Emod saw a baby outside my house after the attack."

"And you want to go back for Liu."

"Yes."

"Rana, we have to move forward before we can go back. We must save all before we can save one. You do understand, don't you?"

Rana closed her eyes. All she could see was Liu's face. Slowly, she nodded.

"Good. I *need* you. In some ways I need you more than any of them." He leaned in and whispered, "You have a power, Rana, that could help us all. You're a font of creation. Like the Creator who fashioned us, you've built worlds. And you and I, we can build another."

"What do you mean, *another*?" She looked into his eyes, and the feeling arose in her again, the same feeling she'd had in Yarrow, when Caleb had put his hands on her shoulders. A warmth, a comfort in his presence. And now she understood why. Caleb knew her like none other. In his presence she was fully accepted for who she was, without fear.

He smiled. "Another universe."

The palanquin heaved, and Caleb and Rana nearly tumbled out the door. Caleb grabbed her shoulder, pulled her in, and shouted back to the circle, "What's happened?"

"We're exhausted!" Marul said. "We're losing control."

Like an unruly bull, the palanquin would not be tamed.

"We need rest!" Marul said.

"There's no time!" Caleb shouted.

"We can hardly keep this box in the air," Marul said, "and you want us to loft you to Earth? Caleb, please!"

"My lord," Havig said. "A rest would do us well. My brothers are exhausted."

"We go on!"

"If I don't rest soon," Marul said. "I'm going to pass out. Who will build your Merkavah if I am unconscious?"

"Are you mad?" Elyam said. "You want to set down here, in the Jeen?" The priests stole glances at each other as if to confirm that this was indeed a real possibility.

Caleb considered and said, "We rest for ten minutes and not an instant more!"

Against the priests' protests, the palanquin drifted down. Rana moved away from the door, away from the black sands. They settled with a thud that stopped much too quickly, as if eaten by something. The sands were impossibly flat, and there wasn't a single dune under the sky of deranged stars.

Caleb stepped onto the sands. His footprints seemed to defile the emptiness. Daniel walked after him and looked bewilderingly up at the sky. Starlight turned his face a sickly white. The Mikulalim disembarked one by one and checked each other for wounds. The priests remained inside and huddled in the far corner. The desert seemed to eat their voices, and everyone had to speak up to be heard.

Though the ground was still, she felt as if they were spinning on the rim of a gargantuan whirlpool, the sky a gulf that would digest their souls over eons. She wanted to close the doors and cower in the corner with the priests. But she challenged her fear, because only by facing it would she find the strength to continue.

She held her breath and stepped onto the sand. The ground shifted beneath her, as if uncomfortable with her presence. The grains were as fine as ash, and in the starlight seemed faintly blue. The sooty odor grew stronger the more she sniffed.

Elyam reached forward and said, "We'll be in here," then he yanked the doors closed.

The Jeen was the flattest expanse Rana had ever seen. But up close, millions of undulating lines wiggled across its surface, as if an army of tiny snakes had slithered through here. The air murmured horrid sounds, and it seemed as if the drunken stars were humming in a key high above her range of hearing.

No, not humming, she thought. *The stars are screaming.*

A shooting star arced across the sky. She gasped as the desert turned green with its light. The star turned sharply and vanished over the horizon.

"That was no meteor," Caleb said. "It was a scout."

"Did they see us?" Daniel said.

"Let's hope not. I knew it was foolish to set down here."

Marul pushed the black sand into a heap, laid her head upon it, and closed her eyes.

"How can you rest here?" Rana said.

"Perhaps for her," Caleb said, "annihilation is comfort."

"Annihilation is the greatest of comforts," a voice said. It was as insubstantial as air.

Everyone spun toward the voice, but there was nothing to see. The wind whistled as it blew over the palanquin.

"Who said that?" Rana shouted, but her voice had the volume of a whisper.

"No one said that." The disembodied voice came from a different location, but there was nothing there either.

"Where are you?" Rana shouted. "*Who* are you?"

"Show your face!" Havig said as the Mikulalim unsheathed their swords.

"We have no face," the voice said. It came from atop the palanquin. Then from behind Daniel, it said, "And we have no place."

Rana said, "Only cowards taunt with riddles while they hide."

"Hide?" the voice said, now beside Caleb. "How can we hide when there is nothing to conceal? You see us as we are. It is you who hide flesh under clothes, organs under flesh, secrets under all. You adorn yourselves with layers of concealment."

"I've had enough of riddles!" Rana said. She would give this dreadful Jeen a taste of its sorely needed life. She would show these creatures who their master really was.

And then she sang.

As the first note left her lips, twelve tornadoes of ash formed around the palanquin, twisting into the sky. The wind wrestled with the funnels, trying to tear them apart. But Rana sang on, and the wind abated, admitting defeat. Marul opened her eyes and stared at the stars. The Mikulalim's mouths hung open. Daniel and Caleb's pupils grew as wide as cities. She felt as if she had been struck like a bell; her body rung.

Suddenly exhausted—she had been through much today— she ended her song. Her body buzzed. Her hair stood on end.

The black desert quickly subdued and devoured her last note. Everyone blinked and awoke. And when the winds abated, and the tornadoes blew away, twelve naked and hairless figures encircled them. Their bodies were basalt-colored, gray-white, and lacking any sexual organs. Their enormous eyes were black as oil and reflectionless. The last of Rana's abrasions had blown away with her music. Her skin was fully healed.

The creature closest to Rana grimaced as it examined its hand, as if the notion of form was repugnant to it.

"What perversion in hell are you?" Havig said to the figure.

The creature let its arm drift back to its side. The movement seemed hollow of will, making the hair stand on the back of Rana's neck.

"We are the no-things of the desert beyond form," it said. "We are the sunderers of cities and the demise of civilizations. We have been called annihilation, destruction, death, entropy. But we have no name. For who remains to name us?" It turned to Rana, affixing its hideous black eyes on her. "Your music has weaved us into flesh and form."

Havig said, "So that we can see you as we tear your flesh apart!" He slashed at the no-thing and his blade plunged deep into its shoulder. But the no-thing didn't bleed. Instead it considered the wound as one might consider a mote of dust. It exhaled, a sound of ancient cities crumbling to dust.

Havig yanked his sword out of its shoulder and struck again, but this time his blade shattered into a thousand pieces. He gasped and tossed the hilt to the ground.

The no-thing turned to Rana and said, "We knew a minstrel like you, once. She sang one of our brothers into form."

Rana gazed into its lightless eyes and felt as if she were looking at all of history spread across eternity, her life but one infinitesimal point along an endless plane.

"Cities are futile constructions, where humans hedge against eternity. Our brother followed this minstrel to one such city and tried to dwell in the world of form with her. He had forgotten that all is forever empty. So we reminded him. We erased her city from existence. And we erased the minstrel too. We hoped he would return to us, but his mind was poisoned with form.

Now he wanders the desert beyond the Jeen, pining for his lost world. We cannot abide your kind. You are a curse that must be erased."

It reached for Rana, and she screamed, but Caleb yanked her away before it could touch her. "Being of emptiness," Caleb said, "I am Ashmedai, King of Demonkind."

"Names are pointless. All is dust."

"Do you know who I am?"

"Tales are lofted on the wind. We know of your reign on the Klippoth of Sheol, where twin suns burn in a fractured sky. We know how demonkind once bowed down to you. And we know how your rule has come to an end, as all things end. But we follow no kings and have no master except emptiness." It reached for Rana again, and Caleb pulled her further away.

"I can give you wealth beyond imagining!" he said. "My store-houses are renowned across all the Shards for the volume of their gold."

"Wealth is useless to us. We have nothing and we need nothing."

"And what about power? I can give you power beyond your conceptions."

"Power is transient. Even the brilliance of an exploding star fades."

"Then what do you want?"

"We want only peace. Peace and silence." The creatures moved closer, surrounding them.

"Then let us leave in peace!" Caleb said. "Everyone, into the palanquin!"

"You have already disturbed us," the creature said. "You have made impressions in the sand. They must be smoothed." It reached for Caleb.

"Wait!" Caleb said, retreating. "If you destroy us then you will disturb your stillness even more. We are trying to save Gehinnom from destruction. If we fail, you'll tumble in a tumultuous chaos for eons!"

"We know of your quest and of the coming catastrophe. We have no interest in it, because eventually all shall come to rest again."

"*Eventually*?" Caleb said, exasperated. "After trillions of years! Would your people give up your peace now to suffer eons of torment?"

A brisk wind kicked up and faded, and the eaves of the palanquin babbled like muttering crones. The no-things paused, considering.

"No," it said. "We would not. But you have disturbed us. We cannot let you pass without recompense. To restore our peace, one among you must be erased."

A shiver trickled down Rana's spine. *Erased?*

Havig threw open the palanquin doors. "My lord, take one of the Bedu." The priests huddled in the back, terrified.

"They will not suffice," the no-thing said. "They make but a ripple in the waters of history. Their world-lines are small."

"World-lines?" Havig said.

"Footprints in sand," the no-thing said. "Impressions beings of form leave."

"And how do you erase them?" Havig said.

"Whatever we touch is erased from this world. It will be as if they never were. And all their works shall become dust."

"*Everything* they've ever done?" Daniel said.

"Every imprint shall be smoothed. Every crease in time made flat."

Daniel stepped forward. Rana sensed something awful was about to happen as Daniel said, "Then take Marul! Erase her! This woman, *here.*"

"Daniel!" Rana said.

"She's the root of our problems," Daniel said. "If she vanishes, all her sins will be undone." He faced Rana and said, "Rana, your parents, Azru, the other Lamed Vav. Everything begins and ends with Marul. We can undo all her damage."

"Is this true?" Rana said, her heart pounding like an army at the city gates. She loathed herself as she said, "Would my parents come back if Marul was erased?"

"No," Marul said, shaking her head. She climbed to her feet. "What is sundered cannot be made whole. What has been given cannot be taken back. I would be erased from this world, but the damage I've done would linger. Mashit will still know the names. The dead will still be dead. The only difference will be that I will fade from your memories like ripples in a pond, until it's as if I've never existed."

"You know us well," the no-thing said.

Marul stood, a disheveled, gray, broken thing. "A long time ago I came to the Jeen, seeking the no-things. I wanted to learn how to manipulate the flow of time. You let me come and go in peace then. Why not let us go again now?"

"No. You had two twins with you," the no-thing said. "A boy and girl, the bastard children of a powerful king, who had hidden these children from his queen, because she would have killed them for fear they might one day usurp his throne. From city to city he shuffled these children, until you promised him you would take them to the safest of hiding places. You offered their histories to us, and in return we told you the secret of the now and the endless."

Marul hung her head and looked ill. "Dear Goddess, I don't remember them."

"Not even their father remembers them."

Marul trembled. "I've caused so much suffering."

"All existence is suffering," the no-thing said.

"No," she said, turning to Rana. "Sometimes existence is beautiful." She stepped toward the no-thing. "You can touch me. I offer my history to you."

"No!" Caleb said. "Without you, we cannot get back to Earth!"

"Who else but me?" Marul said.

"Havig!" Caleb ordered. "Give yourself to them, now!"

Havig gave Caleb a bitter, mournful look. "Yes," he said softly. "Yes, my lord." He stepped toward the no-thing, but Marul leaped in front of him. Rana screamed, Caleb jumped for her, but they were too late. Marul touched the no-thing's shoulder.

"Marul!" Rana shrieked.

Marul gasped, grabbed her hand, and stepped back.

Caleb shouted, "You stupid witch!"

Marul held her hand, and stumbled backwards. Everyone backed away from her, as if she might erase them too.

"It is done," the no-thing said. "Her histories have already begun to unravel. By dawn it shall be as if she never was. The price paid, we will leave you in peace."

That's it? Rana thought. *Just one touch to unravel a lifetime? Even a life as long and knotted as Marul's?* Rana reeled at the horror of it.

The twelve no-things backed away. With each step, flesh from their bodies flaked off like wax shavings. They blew away in the wind, until there was nothing left but sand and stars.

Marul looked queasy. She put a hand to her belly. Rana helped her sit on the palanquin's doorway. Marul's hands were frigid in her own.

"Water!" Rana shouted.

Havig gave her a bladder.

Marul took a few tentative sips and coughed.

"Slow," Rana said. "Slow."

Marul touched a cold finger to Rana's cheek. "My Little Plum," Marul said. "This place is full of death, but you! You are so full of life." She ran a hand through Rana's hair. "You've no idea how beautiful you are right now. You have stars in your hair."

"Marul," Rana said, trying not to cry. "You shouldn't have done that."

"Yes," she said. "I should have."

They entwined their fingers together, as they did so many times on their twilight walks through the city.

"You stupid, selfish witch!" Caleb spat. "You've doomed us all. Again!"

"Stop whining," said Marul. "Azazel will show you how to build a Merkavah, and much more besides. You only needed me because you didn't want to ask him."

"My brother is a great unknown. It would not surprise me if he'd let the Cosmos die just to spite me."

"It's all one big happy demon family," Marul sneered.

"Everyone," Caleb said, "into the palanquin! We're leaving now!"

As everyone climbed inside, Rana said to Marul, "I won't ever forget you!"

"Yes, Rana, you will."

"But I'm Gu. I overflow with the force of life. Maybe I can save you."

Marul smiled. "Look at you! How you cry out to the void, 'I am here!' But you must let me go, before the universe yanks me from you."

They climbed in with the others, and though the air was rancid with sweat and blood, she preferred the interior to the yawning gulf of the Jeen.

Havig had left a space for Marul in the circle, but she shook her head. "I'd be more hindrance than help. I'm too weak now."

Instead Marul sat with Rana against the wall, and they held hands. Daniel sat on the other side. Perhaps he had been right—maybe Marul deserved to die—but she could not look him in the eyes. The priests, eager to flee the Jeen, joined hands with the Mikulalim, and the palanquin rose again. Soon they were speeding over the black desert.

Caleb said, "Faster! Fly faster! Our witch will vanish before dawn."

"We're flying as fast as we can, my lord," said Havig.

Rana twirled her fingers in Marul's gray hair. It was covered with so much grease it looked black. "Your hair used to be as brown as tea," she said. "One day you came to my house with a head of gray hair."

"I was traveling in the spiritual realms," Marul said. "I got too close to the Pardes, the Heavenly Orchard. Its guard Kaspiel nearly obliterated my soul. Rana, I'll tell you, there are far worse fates than gray hair."

"Do you remember that night we walked up Ramswool Row and a one-eyed thief tried to rob us?"

"I held out my hand and told him his mother had asked me to give him what I held inside it. But there was nothing in my hand."

"But he dropped his knife anyway," Rana said, "and ran away sobbing."

"I wonder what he thought I held."

"Do you remember the morning when I walked into my studio and found you staring into a chunk of blue glass. Inside were thousands of tiny dancing people. I hadn't seen you in months and the first thing you said was, 'Rana, come look into another universe!'"

"Yes," Marul said. "Delightful people, those Enuus, but cook they cannot!"

"Do you remember how you made the sun turn green for my tenth birthday?"

"It was your twelfth, because I brought you twelve pink diamonds."

Rana's stomach turned, because Marul was right. How could such a memory disappear? Where had it gone? She closed her eyes and tried to recall every moment with Marul, how sunlight had played across Marul's eyes one morning, the honey-wine smell of her clothes, the way she put finger to lip and looked to the sky when she pondered. She would not let the universe rob these memories from her. Not now, not ever.

A brass finial had broken off the Holy Corpus and was rolling about the floor. Rana picked it up, turned it over in her hands, and set her gaze on the slats of wood lining the walls.

They were far too empty.

CHAPTER TWENTY-FOUR

RANA AND MARUL REVIEWED A LIFETIME OF SHARED MEMORIES, and Daniel listened to every word. Eventually the women fell quiet, their minds lost in the past. Rana had been nervously scratching words into the floor with a shiny metal object for a while now.

The Mikulalim sat with closed eyes, and Caleb stared out the translucent walls. The Bedu seemed nervous, tired. But the boy priest, Zimri, was giving Daniel angry, accusing looks.

Marul gasped and said. "What's that, there? In the east?"

Everyone opened their eyes and looked, when the moving sands slowed to a crawl. The winds stopped. Everyone froze, eyes unblinking, still as mannequins.

"At last," Marul said. "Now we can speak." Her voice was muffled, close. Her palms were clasped just as they had been in the Bedu tent.

"What the hell?" Daniel said. "You stopped time again?"

Marul nodded and gave him a wan smile. "The no-things taught me mastery over time, and now they've taken the last of my time from me. Daniel, I'm a plucked note that fades."

Why would she want to speak with him, alone? Revenge, perhaps, for what he'd done? He got to his feet. "Marul, I *had* to choose you. You brought this on everyone."

"Calm yourself, Daniel. I would've made the same choice if I were in your shoes. Well, in fact, I did."

Caleb was frozen in a grimace, holding his belly, and Zimri was staring-daggers at where Daniel had been sitting. Rana was frozen too, but the Gu seemed more alive than any other, like a plant, imperceptibly turning toward the light. "Then why are we here?" Daniel said.

"Because I wish to tell you a secret."

"A secret?"

"Don't be a fool, Daniel. *The* secret. Who the Lamed Vav are, and how you can return to Earth without Caleb or Azazel."

"*Without* them?"

"You've seen Caleb's nature, Daniel. He may want to save the Earth as much as you, but he has no qualms about killing to achieve his goals. And you were right. I've been no better. But you must believe me when I say I wish to cause no more harm."

"And you must understand how difficult it is to trust anything you say now."

"You *have* to trust me, Daniel. The future depends on it. I will teach you how make a Merkavah to travel across the Great Deep to Earth."

"I'm no magician."

"Aren't you? Your presence sustains worlds, and that's more magical than anything I've ever done. And anyway, the spell is not complex, just exacting. I'll teach it to you."

"Now?"

"When else? I'll be dust before dawn. I'm using the last of my energy to cast this spell. We have twenty minutes here, maybe less."

"You want me to go back to Earth, alone?"

"You can hide the other Lamed Vav. I'll give you their names. After, you can return to the Shards and help them too, if that's your wish."

He considered her. Quick, wise, conniving. She must have been formidable in her day. "How did you find the Lamed Vav in the first place?"

"Simple," she said. "I cheated."

"You cheated?"

"I stole their names."

"Stole? From whom?"

"Who else? Our Creator."

"*God?*"

She beamed proudly, and even though she'd be dead in hours, she seemed decades younger. He saw glimmers of the beautiful, dangerous woman she once had been.

"You stole the names from God? How the hell did you do that?"

"When you've lived as many lives as I have, what at first blush seems impossible proves later only to be extremely difficult."

"But *God?* How did you steal the names from God?"

"I was deep into the heavenly realms—worlds of spirit—evading angels who guard primordial secrets. I made my way, gate by gate, into the Pardes, the Heavenly Orchard, where the secret of secrets is kept. I found a list, whereupon thirty-six names were written. I had memorized only six when the angel Kaspiel found me and nearly obliterated my soul."

"And that's when you returned with gray hair?"

She nodded. "And that's when I returned with gray hair."

"So you never had all thirty-six names?"

"No, but Mashit and Caleb think I do. That lie has kept me alive. But come, Daniel, our time is short. Let me teach you how to build a Merkavah. Let me tell you the names of the Lamed Vav. Ready yourself."

He wasn't ready, but she didn't pause. And so she began the lesson of lessons. Marul explained that to build a Merkavah one needed immense power. "To sail across the Great Deep safely, one must generate the energy of a small supernova."

"But there's no such thing as a small supernova."

"Exactly my point."

And the source of this energy? "Besides the Bedu, Azazel is the only one on Gehinnom who wields such power. If he decides to help you, Azazel will give Caleb his power in the form of an object. Look for a necklace, a ring, a belt, an amulet. It will be something physical, I'm certain. You must wrest this object from him."

"Wrest it? From a demon?"

"By any means necessary."

This was going to be much harder than he had imagined.

"You will need ten spellcasters," she said.

"Like a minyan?" he said.

"Like a minyan. A person of basic intelligence will do. It's the power that's the most important. You have enough people here." She gestured at the Bedu and Mikulalim frozen in their circle, while her green eyes peered into his.

"The spell itself," she said, "it's based on the sephirot. Draw the ten divine emanations and their twenty-two lines in the ground." She demonstrated by drawing the figure in the sawdust, the same one that had been painted on the floor of her prison, the same figure that had hung on Gram's wall.

"Write the names of the sephirot inside the circles like so, and label the connecting lines with their proper letters. Place a spell-caster inside each sephirah. You, Daniel, must stand in the lower-most sephirah, in Malchut."

"Why there?"

"Because creating a Merkavah is much like creating a small universe. That's what Malchut—Kingdom—really means. In order to traverse the Great Deep you'll be creating a bubble universe to carry you safely through."

Daniel took a deep breath and rubbed his temples.

"Are you all right?" she said.

"This is a lot to take in."

"Learn fast, Daniel! There will be no second lesson."

She instructed him on the words of the spell, variations on the Tetragrammaton, the four-letter the Hebrew name of God. Yud, Hey, Vav, Hey. "The pattern is important. For each sephirah it is subtly different."

Over and over, he repeated the spell back to her, and she corrected him many times. As he recited the spell and their ten variations, a strange energy tickled his skin. His senses grew sharp, and he could see the tiny grains of wood deep within Rana's shavings and he could see the microscopic flecks of brown in Marul's eyes. The Holy Name, he sensed, was power itself.

"And now the names. You'll have to find the surviving Lamed Vav, before another is killed. Thankfully, they can't all be killed at once."

"Why not?"

"Because when a Lamed Vav dies, another is born somewhere in the world, and thus hidden from Mashit again. To kill one permanently, to remove a Lamed Vav from the Earth forever, one has to perform a very complex ritual."

"Like the weird stuff Rebekah—Mashit—did at my wedding?"

"Yes, that *weird* stuff. Preparing that ritual takes time, hence why we're still alive."

"Marul," he said. "I saw her, Rebekah. In a dream."

She squinted at him. "When?"

"Twice. Once when we left Yarrow, and again when I was stabbed. She showed me Sheol. She wants me to rule beside her." He realized he was grasping the wedding boutonniere, the shriveled remnant of it, in his pocket.

"And are you tempted by her offer?"

"She told me she wants to help the Shards. But she's just like Caleb. I see that now. She'll kill whoever gets in her way. But what I don't understand is *why*, if she says she wants to help the Shards, is she bringing death upon everyone, including herself?"

Marul shook her head. "All I know is that she's killed three Lamed Vav, and if you don't stop her from killing again . . . the world vanishes like me."

He sighed and nodded.

"Enough small talk! We've only minutes left. I must teach you the names!"

And it was here, in the palanquin, as the black sands crept forward an inch per hour, where the wind paused and the stars slept, that Marul revealed the secret of secrets, six names of the Hidden Righteous Ones, the Tzadikim Nistarim, the Lamed Vav.

"They are Paula Baumgarten, Sunil Pranadchandr, Maya Dorje, Pandate Romsaitong, Baaba Lankandia, and you, Daniel Fisher."

The palanquin seemed to shudder as she spoke each name.

"Not all Jewish?" he said. "Not all men?"

She wrinkled her nose. "The Lamed Vav can be anyone, male or female, of any place, religion, or creed. Now, repeat them back to me."

"Paula . . . ?"

"*Baumgarten*! You'll have to do better, Daniel! Again!"

They rehearsed the names, ten, twenty, fifty times. She had him recite the spell again, and the names, and the spell, over and over. He felt as if he were cramming for the ultimate test, to live or to die! But even after a hundred repetitions he wasn't sure he had everything memorized.

"If you disappear," he said, "will I remember any of this?"

"For the sake of all, let's hope you do." She gazed at her hands, shivered, then looked up at him. Was she contemplating her imminent demise? "You must find the Lamed Vav quickly," she said. "They could be anywhere, and there might be people with identical names who are not Lamed Vav."

"So how will I know if the person I find is a true Lamed Vavnik?"

"You'll know, when you meet them. As I knew you." She stared at him.

"Marul," he said. "I was wrong to ask you to die."

She shook her head. "No, you were sustaining the universe, as you always have. Daniel, my power is waning. Return to your seat. And one more thing. Call it a personal favor. You may consider it my dying wish. If you do remember me, after I'm dust, and Rana has forgotten, do not remind her. I've given her enough grief for one lifetime. Let her forget me." Her pupils, sharp as needles, gazed at Rana. "It's funny, you know? I wanted to live forever, and now no one will remember me."

"She'll remember you."

"Better if she forgets."

He resumed his position, back into the heat of Zimri's stare.

"Ready?" she said. "Here goes."

First came the wind, a faint whoosh that became a roar. The sands stuttered and slid forward again. The palanquin rocked, and the stars resumed their drunken courses as everyone looked east.

"What is it?" said Caleb. "What do you see, witch?"

"I saw a shooting star," said Marul.

"I was looking east," Havig said, eyes on her. "And I saw nothing."

The sephirot that Marul had drawn in the sawdust remained at her feet. He stared at her until she looked down and quickly brushed it away. "I saw a light," she said.

Havig squinted at her, and his candleflame eyes seemed to brighten.

"You see the demise of your own mind," Caleb said. "Keep your observations to yourself, witch. We've had enough of them for nine eternities."

"Don't worry," she said. "I'll be out of your hair soon enough."

Rana frowned and went back to work on the floor.

Everyone fell quiet again, and Daniel felt the weight of his task press upon him. The names, the intricacies of the spell, whirled in his mind. Then he remembered.

He was still cursed.

If he went back to Earth, would the curse vanish? Or would he remain half-Mikulal? Marul had said that once he tasted human flesh, the quickening would be complete. He'd be a Mikulal forever.

But it was Azazel's curse, the same demon who they were going to see. Maybe Azazel could remove it, because Daniel couldn't go back to Earth, hungering for dead flesh, shunning the sun, withering like a corpse, and hope to be a Lamed Vavnik too.

Marul and Rana shared more memories, while Rana carved their words into the floor in an elegant script. Her talent was beyond comparison. And when the floorboards grew crowded with her writing, she began carving on the walls.

"You defile this holy place," Elyam said, his eyes bloodshot.

"No," said Marul, "she's making it holy again."

Rana's letters were mesmerizingly beautiful and perfect, as finely crafted as if they had been done by machine and not by hand. They outdid the floral elegance of the Bedu prayers scrawled over the palanquin walls. And this done in haste using a broken gold fixture as an impromptu awl.

What could she do, Daniel wondered, *with proper tools and the freedom of time?* But in life one never had the right tools or enough time.

The palanquin rocked as they flew through turbulence, and his stomach heaved. Rana had worked every available surface of the palanquin. She had carved around their bodies and the decorations on the walls. There was a Daniel-shaped gap behind him, and he shifted to let her fill it in. She wrote a sentence over Caleb's head as the demon watched, fascinated. "We bought tapestries on Bedubroadstreet from the gold-toothed man." She carved another around the arc of Daniel's thigh. "We boiled chickpeas you brought from Ektu El and both got sick." On the opposite wall, underneath a prayer to Mollai, she wrote, "We climbed the Timnah Tower and watched red-tipped blackbirds circle before the setting sun."

She carved on.

A gust of wind howled through the open door and she paused. She looked up, as if to confirm a memory, then went back to work.

The stars grew tired and stopped their incessant wandering. The black sands of the Jeen brightened steadily into a sulfur yellow. Stones reached up from the ground like fat black fingers. A scattering of troubled shrubs and wiry trees struggled for life. It was the first sign of vegetation he'd seen outside of Azru.

"Dudael, at last," Caleb said. "Soon now."

They passed over campfires glowing outside a small stone city, where strange people huddled around feeble flames. In the east, the ruins of some ancient palace rose in silhouette before the stars. A giant bird sat atop one of the crumbling ramparts and watched them pass.

The palanquin creaked and groaned like a sea galley as they flew. The wood sounded as if it were under great duress. With a sudden loud screech, one of the doors snapped off, tumbling away, taking a piece of the wall with it.

Shocked by the sound, the circle was broken. Daniel held on as the palanquin hurtled toward the sands.

"Hands!" Havig screamed. "Close the circle!"

They quickly joined hands again, and the vessel righted. The wind tore at the opening, jostling them wildly.

"Did we hit something?" Caleb shouted.

"No," Marul said. "The no-things stood on the roof. Everything they touch becomes dust."

Rana looked down at her scratchings, at the walls, at Marul. Then she bent over and continued.

"Just a little farther," Caleb said. "The Mountains of Darkness are near."

Marul ran her fingers over Rana's letters. "Queen Atepsh's portrait?"

Rana said, "A man on Bedubroadstreet tried to sell us a painting he swore was a portrait of Queen Atepsh, painted by her royal artist."

Marul squinted. "Did we buy it?"

Rana squinted. "No, Marul. It was a painting of you. I gave it to Emod, who'd sold it to the street dealer."

"Oh."

"Remember how the dealer hemmed and hawed as he tried to take back his lies?"

Marul paused a beat. "Of course."

Rana's eyes glimmered. "Don't lie to me. You're forgetting."

Marul frowned. "You have to let me go, Rana."

"Why?"

"Because all I've done is drag you into darkness, when your nature is light."

Rana hung her head. The carving stopped. "All those beautiful moments that we shared, Marul, they weren't yours alone. They were mine too. They still are." She bent over and went back to work.

Daniel let the scratching lull him into a trance. It had been forever since he'd slept. He was dozing off when there came a sudden bang. The roof tore off and flapped away into the wind. A dozen sentences had gone with it. The wind howled, the stars twirled madly above, and sawdust from Rana's carvings tornadoed out the gaping hole.

"My lord!" Havig shouted. "We must set down!"

Caleb got to his feet. "No, the Abyssal is just—"

The remaining half-door slammed against the frame and bounced away. A portion of the wall went with it too. Rana screamed. The priests uttered prayers to their Goddess, and even the stolid Mikulalim looked terrified. Daniel held the wall, searching for purchase among its arabesques.

"We need to set down!" Havig said.

"Not yet," shouted Caleb. "Just a little farther! We're almost there."

"*Yes, my lord,*" Havig said through gritted teeth.

Memories broke off as they sped on. There went a gilded plank with prayers to Mollai. There went a description of Marul's elephant tattoo. There went a golden sconce and its candle. There went a twilit walk with Marul, when Azru's sparrows sang their evening song.

Everyone huddled close to the circle as the palanquin shrunk, until they all rode on a few knife-edged timbers and a scrap of wall held together by will alone. They corkscrewed through the air under a canopy of stars, too many riders on a broken magic carpet.

From nowhere, huge onyx mountains appeared to the east and west. It was as if the mountains had lain hidden behind thick fog. But the air was sharp and clear.

"The Mountains of Darkness!" Caleb shouted over the wind. "The Abyssal is close. Keep going!"

"We won't make it, my lord!" Havig said.

"We'll make it! Just keep us in the air!"

The mountain peaks were irregular and sharp, like animal teeth, and it seemed as if they were flying right into the mouth of an enormous beast. The cliffs reflected starlight, and the mountains glimmered and writhed as they flew, as if they were made of molten black glass. Dark stones and sulfur-colored sand speckled the wide valley below, and here and there rose crooked skeletons of unhealthy joshua trees.

Caleb pointed north, where an immense fissure split the earth. At its widest span it was more than a mile across, but its edges walked a jagged course, so that in places it looked as if one could leap to the other side. Its canyon walls were so dark they were practically invisible.

"There!" Caleb said. "The Abyssal of Lost Hope! My brother lies at the bottom."

A gale blew sand off the top of a dune at the fissure's edge, and the yellow dust tumbled down into the abyss, vanishing into its shadows.

"My lord," Havig said, "shall we set down by the edge?"

"No," Caleb said. "Take us inside!"

Havig took a deep breath. "My lord, we're flying on damned scraps!"

"Then on damned scraps we fly!"

The last wall tore away with a loud screech, leaving nothing of their vessel but a few ragged boards. The wind tore at their hair and everyone grabbed onto the circle. Daniel grasped the belt of a Mikulal, holding on for life.

"Keep going!" Caleb shouted. "Keep going! We're almost—"

The floor suddenly disintegrated to dust, and everyone was flung high into the chill air.

Everything went still and silent as terror consumed him. The others floated around him, astronauts in zero-g. A spray of dust glittered behind them like a comet.

The priests' faces were stricken with terror. The Mikulalim flailed, grabbing for each other. Caleb reached for Rana, who stared back at the comet's tail. Above them all, the stars shined fever bright. The mountains loomed, sublime.

Marul is saving us! Daniel thought. *She cast a time-slowing spell. We won't die!*

Suddenly came screams and rushing wind. Time had *not* stopped. They had merely been in freefall. The ground came rushing toward him. He slammed hard into sand, tumbled, smacked his arm into stone, flew into the air, and crashed onto his back.

He gasped and could not catch his breath. Then came the pain, evil, foul throbs in his right arm. There was so much adrenaline in his body that he didn't notice he was throwing up until he had vomited a third time. He slowly became aware of other moans and cries. He heard Caleb's voice. And Havig was calling for Daniel.

He sat up as Havig came to him. Havig appeared unharmed. "Are you hurt?"

Daniel, shuddering, said, "My arm's broken." His voice cracked with fear.

"I'll be back," Havig said. He left Daniel and turned over two bodies. The dead priests's bodies were broken and torn, but they hadn't bled much. On a crop of nearby stone lay a Mikulal. His dark blood dribbled down the sides.

Havig approached Caleb, "My lord, are you hurt?"

Caleb coughed up a volume of blood. He was covered with abrasions. "Fires of Abbadon! Madness of Barsafael!" He spat up blood. "How many hurt? How many dead? Is Rana alive?"

Everyone turned when they heard Rana's voice.

"*Marul?*" Rana shouted. She ran around the crash site, shouting, "Marul? Marul?"

"My son, Dranub, is dead," Havig said. He paused, waiting for Caleb. But the demon said nothing. "And two priests," Havig said. "Daniel has a broken arm. The others are bruised but otherwise unharmed."

"We were lucky most of us landed on sand," Caleb said.

Havig glanced at his dead son, Dranub. "*Lucky*, my lord?"

A shower of glittering dust snowed down upon them. It smelled of cedar, sawdust, and soot. "Is this ash," Caleb said, "all that remains of our palanquin?"

"Marul?" Rana shouted. "Where are you? *Where are you?*"

Rana rubbed the ashen snow between her fingers, sniffed it, tasted it. Suddenly something shifted in her aspect. She shuddered, then turned her face up to the snow and closed her eyes.

Marul is gone, Daniel thought. *She's become dust.*

Columns of winking ash snowed on Rana's hair, and Rana let the memories fall. As the ash blew into his eyes, Daniel felt sick with pain.

I will not let Marul die in vain, he thought. *I will cast this spell and get back to Earth.* He looked at Caleb. *Without him.*

Rana was murmuring, "Marul Menacha, The Witch Who Gives Demons Pause. Eyes as green as Ketef, the summer star. A nose like a mountain and a smile like the sun. Marul Menacha, The Witch Who Gives Demons Pause. Eyes as green as Ketef . . ."

Elyam approached one of the dead Bedu. Zimri, Elyam's son, was alive and huddling with the other priests, a look of shock on all their faces. Elyam put a hand on the dead man's head and whispered a prayer. He turned to Daniel. "He was a good man. An honest man."

Daniel didn't know what to say. "I'm sorry."

"Shall it all be for naught?" Elyam said. He gave Daniel an accusing look. He approached the second body and prayed over it too.

Daniel held his throbbing arm. The priests huddled together, murmuring. The Mikulalim surrounded their dead kinsman, Dranub, Havig's son. Would they eat his body as was their custom, even Havig, his father?

"Beside the Abyssal," Caleb said to Havig, "that expanse of flat sand." He pointed to a shallow depression beside the chasm edge. "That's where we cast our spell. With the witch dead, my brother is the only one left who can show us how to make the Merkavah."

"And the quorum of ten?" said Havig. His words had become heavy, slow. "I count only nine. Four Bedu and five Mikulalim."

"I will be the tenth," Caleb said.

"Yes, my lord."

No, Daniel thought, *I cannot let that happen.* He had to get back to Earth without Caleb.

"Havig," Caleb said, "do you have the powder?"

Havig patted a satchel at his belt. "Yes, my lord."

Caleb snatched it, then turned to the great fissure and shouted, "*I summon thee, Azazel, from the black depths. I call forth the ancient one from his slumber and demand conference.*"

The words were not in Wul. They sounded vaguely Hebrew. Perhaps Aramaic.

The sound of his voice echoed through the valley, winded its way through folds of rock, and up the steep mountain cliffs. Sand whorled at the fissure's edge as Caleb's voice thundered over it. The mountains regurgitated the sound, and the echoes came back distorted, perhaps with new words added, others missing.

The desert was quiet, but Daniel sensed that a vile, ancient force had just awakened. At the Abyssal's edge, something skittered. A shadow leaped from rock to rock.

"The Black Guide comes," Caleb said, holding his ribs.

A four-legged creature leaped onto a nearby stone. As large as a bear, its silhouette rose before the stars. It had the body of a jaguar, with two tails, and its fur was as dark as the cliffs. On its dragon-like head, its long mane was braided and well tended. Its eyes were large, dark, almond-shaped. A line of yellow drool hung from its lips.

The beast peered down at them as its twin tails whipped about.

"You woke me from my sleep," the animal droned. A female voice, seductive, sly, measured. But her words were oddly disheveled, as if she had spoken them out of order and they had fallen into place only as an afterthought. She yawned, revealing sharp rows of golden teeth. She sniffed the air. "My dreams were foul, but you are fouler."

"Messenger of the Bound One," Caleb said, "take us to Azazel."

The cat yawned. Her hot breath reeked of meat. "The Bound One shall not be disturbed by a rabble of fools." She lowered her head to examine the party. Drool splattered on the stone and a drop landed on Daniel's arm. It burned like acid and he struggled to wipe it off.

"What a bloody lot, you are," the Guide said. "You make me hungry. Why not offer those corpses to me? Maybe I'll let you flee with your skin."

"Do you not recognize me?" Caleb said.

"I recognize a fool when I see one." She raised herself up and bared her teeth, hissed. "Your wounds smell delicious."

She leaped for him, but he threw the gray powder from Havig's satchel into her face. She froze, sneezed, and phlegm exploded from her mouth. The stones smoked where the phlegm had landed. She mewled like a cat in heat. "What is this foul-smelling dust, and why do I feel so . . ." She yawned. ". . . so sleepy?"

"You inhale the ashes of a cock, slaughtered in Azazel's name. You are compelled to take us to your master."

"Damn you!" she said. "I was looking forward to a good meal."

She quickly adopted the body language of a friendly house cat. Daniel half-expected her to start purring. "Very well. You win this round, but I cannot carry all of you. The Merkavah will fit only four, including myself."

"The *Merkavah*?" Caleb said, stirring. "You can craft one?"

"How else shall we descend to the Bound One? To walk the stair would take days!"

"Can you craft a Merkavah to take us to Earth?"

The Guide snickered and more drool fell. "If only! It has been so long since I've traveled to Earth. I used to be worshipped as a goddess there, you know? I would give one of my tails to go back, but my master needs me here. No," she said, shaking her head mournfully, "the Merkavah I create is small, fragile. Not strong enough to traverse the Great Deep. Only strong enough to float down into the dark before popping like a soap bubble."

Daniel winced at the Guide's odor. She clearly knew little of soap.

Caleb frowned. "These two, Daniel and Rana, will come with me."

"Come with you where?" said Rana.

"Down the Abyssal. To see my brother, Azazel."

"Why do you need me?" Rana said.

"I don't *need* you. I want you. You are a Gu, Rana. You gush with the force of creation. Your creativity has caused great upheaval in your life. But who has ever shown you what you truly are? Come down the Abyssal with me, and I'll show you what you're capable of." He held out his hand.

Rana's lips mouthed her mantra again. *Marul Menacha, The Witch Who Gives Demons Pause. Eyes as green as Ketef.* She looked at the dead bodies. The glittering snow had ceased. Ash twinkled from her hair like diamond dust. Her lips stopped moving.

"I want to know," she said, stepping forward. "Show me what I am."

Caleb smiled as he led her to his side. He turned to Daniel, "Come, Daniel, and we'll have Azazel remove your curse."

Daniel wanted his curse removed so much that he trembled. But if he went down the Abyssal with Caleb, he wouldn't have time to prepare the spell. And if Caleb came back to Earth with him, how many more would die? It had to stop, here. He had to go on alone.

"No," Daniel said. "I'm staying here."

"Staying?" Caleb said. "What in Abbadon for? Do you want to remain cursed?"

"I'm staying *here*."

Caleb leaned forward, cradling his wound. The cuts on his face bled. "Why?"

"Because I'm done with you, Caleb."

"Do you forget?" Caleb said, snarling. "If not for me, you'd be dead! You *owe* me, Daniel!"

"I owe you nothing."

"You need me to get home!"

"Then I'll wait here for you. I'm not going down there."

Caleb's face turned bright red. "Don't be stupid! If you're cursed you might not be able to uphold worlds any more. You may no longer be a Pillar!"

"I'm *not* coming," Daniel said, backing away from him. "And that is final."

"You chose this place, here, to become proud?" Caleb said, flaring his nostrils. "Daniel, I *need* you."

"My lord," Havig said, stepping forward. "We know our own kind. Daniel is not a Mikulal. He's still very much a Lamed Vavnik. We sense his sustaining power even now. Go see Lord Azazel. I am sure he will give you something to cure Daniel, which you can bring back with you. Lord Azazel is, after all, all-knowing and wise.

I'll keep watch over Daniel. He will be here when you return from below. You have my word."

Caleb examined them, a suspicious look in his eyes. Gritting his jaw, he shook his head. "I hope you're right, Havig. For the sake of the Cosmos, I hope what you say is true! And what a great shame, Daniel, that you'll never see the majesties below. Make sure you are here when I return, or we all die." He turned to the Black Guide. "All right, cat, let's go. I need respite from these fools."

The Guide took her time finding the right spot before sitting on her haunches. "The Merkavah mustn't be rushed." She closed her eyes, and her disordered syllables tumbled into sequence. "Ye. Ye. Ye. Ye. He. Ye. Ye. He. Va. Ye . . ."

It was much like the spell Marul had taught him, but the phrasing was a bit different, and he feared he might conflate the two and forget the original. He wanted to cover his ears, but that would have tipped off Caleb he was up to something. He had no choice. He had to listen.

"That pattern," Rana said. "I've seen it before, in a dream."

Daniel knew it too. In Gram's books, the Tetragrammaton, the four-letter name of God, arrayed in a Fibonacci pyramid, the source of the Golden Ratio that was woven into nature in the spiral of nautilus shells and the blossoms of sunflowers. The Greeks had used it in their architecture, and thousands of mathematicians across history had delved into its secrets.

The Guide held out her sharp-clawed paw, pad up. A point of light appeared above it, blossomed into a golden pyramid. Its facets sparked and glimmered as it turned.

The Guide raised her other paw, and a second pyramid formed above it, inverted and spinning in the opposite direction. Their facets blinded like mirrors in sunlight, and as Daniel looked into the light he longed for something lost. The light promised an impossible comfort that would eradicate all fears forever. It shone like a primordial home.

The Guide brought her two paws together. A flash of light exploded in all directions, climbed over the mountains, and tumbled into the chasm. The two pyramids had merged into a star. A ghostly sphere formed around the Guide, and the star expanded to fill it. A thousand polygons turned inside it, spinning into dijointed dimensions, whirring in occult rhythms, a clock of cosmic gears.

"Step beside me," the Guide said.

Taking Rana's hand, Caleb took his place beside the Guide. The gears moved through their bodies unimpeded, and Rana's mouth hung open as she reached out for the spinning parts.

As the sphere hardened it gave a faint reflection. Rana rapped on it and it rang like glass. She stared wide-eyed as the Merkavah rose from the ground and floated away toward the Abyssal. Shadows leaped from the stones as the vessel receded, a bright star above the sands. Then the Merkavah slipped down into the fissure, taking the light with it.

Daniel blinked away the spots in his vision. He was consumed with a feeling of dread as the weight of his task pressed upon him. He looked at the nine men, Mikulalim and Bedu, broken all. He'd have to convince these sworn enemies to work together, against Caleb, and help him cast the spell and get him home. A spell he could barely remember.

There was much work to do.

CHAPTER TWENTY-FIVE

CALEB FLOATED DOWN INTO THE DARK WITH RANA AT HIS SIDE. How long had it been since he'd visited this Abyssal of Lost Hope? A millennium? Two? It had changed little in all that time. The Guide steered their Merkavah using verbal helices, cosmic ratios. Rana stared, her pupils wider than the chasm. She had wounded him gravely, and he was slowly bleeding out. But if he had his way, all would be healed soon.

Golden light from their vessel shined onto the wrinkled walls, and thousands of albino bats scattered from their light. Armies of yellow spiders scurried further into the darkness. A ragged strip of stars tore across the sky above the chasm, shrinking quickly as they fell.

An impenetrable gulf yawned beneath them, as dark as the Great Deep. The murky air smelled of sulfur and tears. The dust of eons slept uneasily here. Rana trembled beside him as she stared down.

They passed caves that opened into large chambers, where precious gems curled over emerald walls. On curving parapets and balustrades of gold, torches spat blood-red flames. Crowded on their edges, a crowd of lanky beings watched them fall. Tall, hairless men puffed pipes from lipless faces. Five women, breasts as large as melons, dangled their feet over the edge as they plucked tendon-strung psalteries. Their music echoed discordantly from the walls. "Who are they?" Rana whispered, but her voice echoed loudly across the space.

The musicians paused and gave her scornful looks. She had ruined the performance. Caleb waited until they had descend another dozen stories before he said, "Those were the Nephilim, a hybrid of human and demon. They once covered the Earth. This is their last refuge."

The broken music resumed as they fell, until it slowly faded. They passed a cavern brilliant with gold. Moans spilled from its wide mouth.

"Mielbok lives there," Caleb said, "son of Baalberith, Master of Flies, and his servant, Atleiu." Rana stared into the cavern, as if she could discern its secrets.

An arch of amber stone framed another cave. Purple light pooled on a terrace. "There is the home of Obyzouth the Limbless, who speaks the language of rocks." And of a dark cavern, its insides thick with fog, Caleb said, "And that is one of the many homes of Astaroth, who knows how to impart life to dead matter. But that is all I shall speak of him, for to say more would endanger us."

They fell into a realm crowded with eyries. Huge featherless yellow birds roosted on black eggs. Their nests were fashioned from leather and bone and had been built on jutting stones. Their red eyes were like huge drops of blood.

"Lorbria!" Rana exclaimed. "My pet bird . . . she was one of them!"

"The Children of Ziz," Caleb said, "a bird whose wings span continents. They adore Mikulalim music." Their blood-red eyes twinkled in Merkavah-light as they fell.

Deep below, glowing filaments reached across the chasm, sinews of light binding the walls together. As they fell toward them, the filaments grew to mammoth proportions. Their huge arcs of fire spanned the gap, and at each end, wide tunnels led to deeper caverns. The bridges roared, deafening as they burned.

"The Bridges of Fire," Caleb said. They descended through their hot webwork, and though a billion fiery tongues licked hungrily at the air, their shapes remained fixed. The Guide weaved a steady course between the dancing flames. One touch and they would be ash. Caleb wiped sweat from his brow.

"How," Rana said, resplendent in the firelight, "how do you build a bridge of fire?"

"Anything is possible, Rana, with the right knowledge."

"But how do the flames stay together?"

"By will. All is will. You are used to thinking in human terms, in stone and mortar. But you will do so much more. Compared to what you can do, The Bridges of Fire are child's play."

The Bridges receded above them, and their roar ebbed. They had descended into darkness for many minutes, when a faint light appeared. Phosphorescent blue mold clung to the walls, and the air here was humid, almost tropical. Dew dripped from the many cracks. A blue rainbow arced across the mist, winking as they fell. On one wall a giant effigy of the demon Agchonion had been carved in the Assyrian style, helmeted and with spear. Lesser demons crowded his leather boots. Above his head was a cracked egg, and a thousand terrified figures poured out. Agchonion treaded on a shell fragment—a Shard—victorious.

"Goddess, it's fifty stories tall," Rana said.

"One should not mention her name in this place."

Rana didn't seem to hear. "How did they carve such a large effigy all the way down here?"

"Piddling stuff, Rana. Amateur. You will do so much more."

"You keep saying that. So what *can* I do?"

"What was your job in Azru?"

"I was a mason."

"An apprentice?"

She nodded.

"What a travesty! How many buildings did you design?"

She considered for a moment. "Thousands."

"And how many of these designs did you actually get to build?"

"Well, none."

"You were always building another's design?"

She looked across the chasm. "I added highlights, when I could."

"What a waste! Here you were dreaming up cities that touch heaven, monuments that would last for nine eternities, but you were only allowed to build brothels for a fat king and outhouses for his overfed guests. They denied you your dreams."

"What do you know of my dreams?"

"Everything, because I share them. Rana, I want to build something that lasts for nine eternities too, something that touches heaven. Something far greater than any city. You and I can build it. Together."

She squinted at him, her eyes scintillating in the Merkavah-light. "I don't understand. What can we build that's greater than a city?"

He paused. "A universe."

Her breath had become quick and sharp, and blood vessels were pumping at her temples. She was about to speak, when the Black Guide said, "Prepare yourselves. We're arriving at the master's house."

Below them a mirrored floor stretched like a silver sea toward dark horizons. They fell toward their own brilliant reflection like two atoms about to collide. A gargantuan ziggurat came into view, squeezed between the cliff walls.

Built from titanic basalt blocks, the ziggurat's levels were each several stories tall, but shadows obscured its full dimensions. A steep terrace led up to a large entranceway, which flickered with faint green light. There were no guards outside, for who would be fool enough to enter the Lair of Azazel without invitation?

They would.

He coughed up blood. The pain had worsened. He had little time left. They touched the mirrored floor and their fragile Merkavah exploded in a shower of light. Sparks corkscrewed into obscure dimensions and vanished. The faint green light from the entrance was the only illumination. Their shadows reached into dark corners, where unseen things tittered and laughed. Perhaps they knew something he didn't.

"Come," the Guide said. Her voice returned from the distant walls in tatters. Water dripped loudly into pools, stirring up the dust of centuries. Something large splashed nearby as the Guide scampered up the steep steps. She paused to wave them on before leaping inside.

The steps were slick and treacherous. He offered his hand to Rana, but she was too enamored with the architecture to notice him.

Through a stone arch they entered an enormous antechamber. Walls leaned at malicious angles, and thousands of circular portals pockmarked the chamber, as if they had entered the den of a burrowing creature. In some way, Azazel was such an animal. The tunnels led off in oblique directions, intersecting at impossible angles. A hundred stone stairways crisscrossed angrily overhead, and the mirrored floor multiplied everything infinitely.

In the center a green flame burned in a stone bowl, and its shifting light made the walls shiver. Rana stumbled, and he grew dizzy.

The Guide snickered. "One of these doors leads to the master. The others to madness." She picked gristle from her teeth with a sharp claw.

"So?" Caleb said. "Which door is it?"

"Well," she said. "The ashes you blew at me were quite old."

"Which is the door, fool?"

She strutted closer, and he noticed a bloody carcass in the corner. "Your spell is wearing off, and I'm hungry."

He pushed Rana behind him. "Feral creature! Don't you recognize me?"

The Guide guffawed, and the tunnels regurgitated her laughs in maddening waves. "Ha! You should have seen your face! I was just having fun. It's so quiet here. Not to worry. Your spell still compels. It always does, as long as that is his wish. This way!"

Rana grew timid as they followed the Guide up one of the stone stairs to a tunnel mouth indistinguishable from the others. "The entrance changes every hour to confound his enemies," she said. "Sometimes I forget which one too. Now, hearken! At a fork of two, head left. A fork of three, head right." She scratched her head. "Or is fork of two, head right?"

"Which is it?"

"Give me a moment. Ah, yes. Like I said at the beginning. A fork of two, head right."

"But you said 'left,'" Rana said.

"Did I?"

"Enough games you wretch!" Caleb said. "Show us the way, Baast, or I'll ask Azazel to feed your mind to mad Barsafael."

A tremor rippled through her. "How do you know my ancient name?"

"Because I am Ashmedai, fool, brother of your master."

Her tongue fell out of her mouth as recognition shuddered through her. She crawled over to him and fawned at his feet. "Oh, forgive me. Forgive me! I didn't recognize you. I—"

"Get away from me! Just tell us the way."

"I was just playing. You know! Just a game to—"

"Tell us the damned way!"

"Go left. Always turn left. To reach the Bound One, always go left, like Gevurah, the judging hand."

"You are a worm, Baast."

She gazed meekly at them. "You'll tell my master I escorted you well? It was just a game, you know? A little fun, to pass the time?"

"I hope you enjoyed that meal," Caleb said. "It was likely your last."

Baast whimpered as they entered the circular tunnel. As they walked, her mewling lingered, and her voice seemed to come from all directions.

The air grew chilly as they walked. "Hard to believe that fool was once worshipped on Earth," he said. "Humans built cities for her."

"They built cities for fools on Gehinnom too," Rana said.

"How true."

A dim yellow light illuminated their way, reflecting from the stone walls, its source unseen. They reached the first fork, where three tunnels diverged, and they went left. At the next fork they went left again. They turned, and turned again in maddening spirals, as if they were tying a knot that would never unravel.

"What did you mean before," she said, "about building a universe?"

"Gehinnom is broken."

"Yes," she said. "Marul said that." Then, she added, "Marul Menacha, The Witch Who Gives Demons Pause. Eyes green as Ketef, the summer star. I don't know why that's stuck in my head, like a song."

"Gehinnom rests on a cracked foundation, Rana, as all the Shards do. Because of that, everything that is born there is transient, fleeting."

"It's horrible," she said. "I hate it. *I hate it!*" Her voice raced down the tunnel and marched back a dozen times.

"You hate it because it's anathema to your essence. But what if there were a universe with a solid foundation? Where things lingered forever?"

"Earth, you mean."

"No, I'm not speaking of Earth. We are like scavengers, Rana, waiting for scraps to fall. Our lot is foul, but it doesn't have to be. We can give every miserable soul in the Shards a chance to be whole."

"How?"

"Daniel's universe will collapse when enough Pillars die. If we send Daniel back to Earth, it would give us more time, and we might stop Mashit from killing another. But that would only preserve the status quo. Earth would continue while the Shards suffer unremittingly. But if there were another universe, a *new* universe, not dependent on Earth, we could make a home there."

She stared at him. "A new universe? Is that even possible?"

"As I said, Rana, *everything* is possible, given enough will. The Merkavah—the vessel that will ferry us across the Great Deep—is a small universe of its own. Instead of using the power to send Daniel home, we can use it to force the Merkavah to grow."

"To grow? How?"

"Like a bellows that blows air into a fire, we will use Azazel's power to expand the Merkavah into a fully realized universe, with planets and moons and stars. But this new universe will be fragile, like a newborn child. So we will need to hold its walls firm. We will need the help of one who sustains worlds."

A look of recognition flashed in her eyes. "You mean Daniel?"

"Yes, the Pillar, Daniel Fisher, will sustain our new universe."

"But we only have one Pillar. The Earth had thirty-six."

"Good! You're already thinking like an architect. Our universe won't be as large as Earth's. For our purposes, one Pillar will suffice. For now."

"But where will the ground come from? The air? The sun and the stars? Do they just appear? Who makes them?"

He smiled at her inquisitive nature. "Nothing comes into being without will. This is why I have sought you. All those beautiful worlds you've dreamt of, all those glorious vistas that haunted your dreams, you can make them real. You've always been an architect, but you have been denied the power to build your great designs. Today you won't be building yet another brothel, tower, palace, or even a city. Today you'll be building a universe."

Rana was shaking. "You are joking?"

"I've never been more serious. You can build any world you desire. Maybe flowers bloom in your footprints. Maybe children are born with music instead of blood. Maybe in your world, no one will ever go hungry, no one will ever suffer."

"Liu," she said. "Could I bring my sister? If we find her?"

"You can bring whomever you want. Once our universe is built, I will rescue as many as I can before the Shards wither."

For a long moment, she stared at him. "Is this true? Can I make a world where my sister will never suffer, where no one will ever suffer again?"

"That has been my goal from the beginning."

She seemed to look inward, then smiled wryly as she turned and marched down the tunnel. "Let's go, Caleb. Let's go!"

He wanted to dance and laugh. Rana, the most beautiful creature in all the Shards would build a universe for him. For *all*. His heart fluttered, whether from loss of blood, or for her, he didn't know or care. At last, his eons of suffering would end.

The tunnel opened into an enormous chamber, a cavernous space so vast its extremities were lost in shadow. Columns split the basalt walls into wide sections, and the interstices crawled with byzantine arabesques. Half a million names, written in Aramaic, had been carved into the walls, each name a slave to his brother. All the Mikulalim were listed here, and some names were older than Gehinnom.

Against the wall, a naked man hung upside down, strung between two wide columns. Gleaming silver chains bound his wrists and ankles and pulled his limbs taut. His beard concealed his face, and it had grown so long that it covered the floor like a hairy gray sea.

The ground beside him was filled with large polyhedrons, a giant's playpen of colorful shapes. An emerald dodecahedron refracted solutions to obscure mathematical proofs. A spiky yellow ditrigonal icosidodecahedron sparked with maddening artistic inspiration. Through self-referencing twists of a Klein bottle, a thousand paradoxes wavered on the edge of non-existence. The distorted orange contortions of a Gordian Knot revealed the occult laws of metaphysics.

Here lay the knowledge of eons made solid, like vapor frozen into snow.

Rana moved toward the Gordian Knot, toward the secret knowledge flickering inside its facets. He tapped her shoulder, and she blinked awake from her trance. He gestured toward the chained figure as they walked, their footfalls rousing the slumbering eons. A thousand eyes watched them from a triambic icosahedron that promised self-knowledge beyond all ken.

They paused at the shoreline of the gray hair, twenty paces from his brother. A drop fell from the darkness above, splashed into a stone pool, and water trickled over the edge toward the shadows beyond.

"It's been too long," his brother said gravely, as if the dust of long-dead stars spoke through him. A tuft of hair by his face wiggled as he spoke.

"Have you been well, brother?" Caleb said.

"Other than the fact I must defecate upside down until the end of time, I cannot complain. My servants see that I am well cared for." He took a slow breath. "I thought you'd be here sooner, brother. I've been expecting you for weeks."

"Your servant, Baast, didn't seem to know I was coming."

"When, dear Ashey, have I ever made things easy for you?"

If he wanted to spar, then spar they would. "My brother, have you heard? Raphael shares his bed with Seket, the Golden One."

"What do I care of that wench? I have my playthings to keep me occupied."

"Yes," Caleb said. "It's obvious you have such raucous company." Caleb let the silence speak for itself. "Still, to think the great Azazel does nothing while the woman whom he pledged to marry before the assembled host of Abbadon now shares her bed with the man who chained him down in this dark chasm. People say that Azazel's power isn't as great as it once was."

"My power is greater than it has ever been," he said. "And what do I care of Seket?" Dust shook loose from the walls with the volume of his voice. "She has forsaken me, and therefore she is ash. I might say the same of you, Ashey. When was the last time you visited, brother? The dripping water has dug canyons since your last visit."

"I've been busy."

"So I've heard. Stripped of power, exiled from Sheol. Did they cut off your cock too?"

"Mine is quite healthy, I assure you. And don't be crass. I've brought a guest."

"Yes, and you haven't introduced me."

"You don't know who she is? I'm disappointed, brother."

"She is Rana Lila, Gu of Gehinnom, whose magnificent works make my imprisonment almost bearable. But I prefer formal introductions."

"Azazel, meet Rana."

"It's quite an honor to meet you, Rana. Please forgive my brother's rudeness. He and I are unrefined creatures, born from ashes."

"We are all born from ashes," she said.

"Ah," said Azazel. "She has wit too. Rana, what do you think of my little brother? Please don't be shy. I want to hear a Gu's thoughts on him."

She glanced at Caleb, and he gestured for her to go ahead. "He's determined," she said. "Smart, brutal. Cold. But I'm starting to understand him."

"Oh? Please go on."

"He's been suffering for ages. If I were in his shoes I might be doing the same thing."

"Determined, brutal, cold, seeking a way of out of a personal hell. Yes, that sounds like little Ashey. But smart? Hardly. While he stumbles through the Shards like a drunkard, I survive by what I offer others."

"Knowledge," Rana says.

"And wise too, this Gu. Yes, I have collected universes of knowledge in my Codices. Yet my brother would have me abandon them. Has he explained his plan to you?"

"He wants me to design a new universe for everyone to live in."

"I'm offended, brother," Azazel said, "that you didn't approach me first."

"Are you surprised?" Caleb said. "You have the taste of a Sumerian priest."

"And you the tact of a Roman Centurion. Rana, tell us, what do you think of this plan?"

"It's absurd. Insane. But—"

"But you worry you might create a world as broken as this one."

"No!" she said, stunned. She stood up straight. "I know whatever I build will be perfect."

Azazel smiled. "And confident too! Modesty is, after all, so unbecoming in a Gu. Tell me Rana, have you thought about my brother's role in this new world?"

"His role?"

"After this world is built, where will Ashey sit? On a gilded throne? Because I for one do not wish to be his subject."

"I was the greatest king Sheol ever had," Caleb said. "The people adored me!"

Azazel laughed and his whole body shook repulsively. "Greater than Abbadon? You ruled always in his shadow, even after his death. Brother, they shamed you and cast you out."

"Because they were fed lies! Because the nature of the Shards is impermanence! Nothing lingers, not even kings! Yet still I ruled for longer than Great Abbadon himself! That is how much they adored me."

Rana turned to him, a grave look on her face. "You want to be king over this new world?"

"This new world will need a leader, a wise, strong, and caring leader. I won't rule by threats or deception. My subjects will give me their fealty because I will have given them what the Creator could not. A life without suffering. And I won't rule alone. You and I, Rana, could rule together. Think of it, Rana Lila, a Gu, born on a Shard, who becomes the queen of a universe. A universe she designed! You would rule over a world where you have the power to create anything you want, a world free from suffering, for all eternity."

She stared at him, as if he were mad. Perhaps he was, but he also knew there was a part of her that wanted this more than air.

"Brother," Caleb said, "when the Earth shatters, and the waters of this Shard dry up, your bonds will break. Then I will rescue you from this prison. I will save *all* who wish to come with me. You've done many wretched things to me, brother, and still I will save you. I will make you a prince over worlds, and you shall rule without chains. The three of us shall stand firm as the world around us shatters."

"*Si fractus illabatur orbis, impavidum ferient ruinae,*" Azazel said. "'If the broken world should fall to pieces, the ruins would strike him undismayed.'"

"There will be time for poetry later. You know what I've come for."

His brother sighed. "I have foreseen the end. In a few hours, in the city of Bahavnagar, India, the demon Af will cleave the Lamed Vavnik, Sunil Pranadchandr, from Earth's universe using a gross perversion of a Hindu wedding ritual. With this cleaving of a Pillar, the Earth will collapse. Its life force will flood down onto the Shards in a splendid torrent. But soon the waters will cease, and we will wither away in agony for a trilion, trillion years. And to think that I distrust you to such a degree, Ashey, that I have considered succumbing to this fate instead of helping you."

"The distrust is mutual. But now we must put that aside. Despite all that you've done, you are still my brother. I swear by the waters of Lake Hali, by the Seal of Great Abbadon, and the twin suns of Sheol, by the very blood that unites us, that I will not abandon you, Azazel!"

"Your vow is worth less than dust."

"In the new world," Caleb said, "there will be no dust."

"Brother, one thing I have learned in my long existence is that, wherever you go, there is *always* dust."

———

The sands were as yellow as turmeric. Daniel held his throbbing right arm and looked at their troubled faces. The priests hovered over their dead brothers, trembling. The Mikulal corpse dripped black ichor down the stones, while the others huddled beside him, looking hungry. How would he get these sworn enemies to work together?

He needed ten men to perform Marul's spell. Ten men to get him home. He heard Gram's voice, as loud and present as if she had whispered in his ear. *Nayn rabonim kenen keyn minyen nit makhn ober tsen shusters yo.* Nine rabbis can't make a minyan but ten shoemakers can. In other words, you make do with what you have.

The Mikulalim and the Bedu shared a common ancestor. Perhaps there was a scrap of ancestral memory in them now that he might use. But first he would have to convince the Mikulalim not to eat their dead, because how could he get the Bedu to trust the Cursed Men if they committed that abomination here, in front of their eyes?

Holding his broken arm, trying his best to ignore the pain, Daniel approached the Mikulalim. *I want to speak with you in your own tongue,* he thought to them, projecting his thoughts as he had learned from Junal. *Can you hear me?*

Havig stepped forward. *You might have removed your curse if you'd gone down to Lord Azazel,* Havig thought. His words crashed into Daniel's head like thunder. *Yet you chose to remain. Why? Have you come to accept what you are?*

Daniel wasn't quite sure what he was now, nor what he would be. *I've come to ask you a great favor,* he thought.

You want us to refrain from eating Dranub.

How did you know?

Your thoughts leak like a broken barrel, Havig thought. *We sensed Marul's magic in the palanquin. And we saw the Tree of Life drawn in the sawdust.*

Daniel inhaled sharply. What would they do to him for betraying their king?

The Gu Rana was right, Havig said. *Lord Ashmedai uses us as his tools. But he doesn't wait until we dull before he throws us away.* Havig glanced at the dead Mikulal. *Dranub was my only child, heir to the throne of Yarrow.* Daniel's mind filled with a vision of a Mikulal woman holding a shriveled babe, wet and bloody from birth, and an overwhelming sense of melancholy as Havig, the father, contemplated the horrid life his child would lead as a Cursed Man.

My son, Havig continued, *was born with Azazel's Curse. And he died with it. Never was he a whole man. But Dranub to Lord Ashmedai was nothing more than an unlucky fool.*

But you are different, Havig said. *We've watched you. You mourn every death. You loathe his ways. If our will was our own, we would serve you.*

Chills ran down Daniel's spine as he remembered Rebekah's promise to make him king over Sheol and all the Shards. And now the Mikulalim wanted him to rule them too? *No,* he said. *I'll be no one's king.*

You are a king who wears no crown, who demands no subjects. Therefore you are the only one worthy of ruling.

I don't want to rule, Daniel said. *I just want to get back to Earth.* He paused. Aloud he said, "Without your king."

The Mikulalim glanced at each other.

When we saw the mark on the floor, Havig said, *we guessed your plan. We have discussed it amongst ourselves. We will help you return to Earth, without Lord Ashmedai. But know this. We cannot openly defy him. If he demands it, we must act. We have no choice. Our will is not our own.*

Your chains are invisible, Daniel said, *but strong. Once I'm sure the Lamed Vav are safe, I'll return to Gehinnom to free you from your curse. All of you. I promise.*

Make no promises you cannot keep, but do what you must to save the Earth, Lord Fisher.

Please. I'm no one's lord.

On the contrary. The Cosmos owes its existence to you.

Daniel sighed. Why was everyone so obsessed with rulers and kings? Why did everyone need a master to bow down to? Kings and queens were the cause of most of the world's problems. But how else could he get these people to work together if not by leading them?

The Mikulalim would help him now. But what about the Bedu? His arm throbbed as he said, "Elyam, let me help you bury the bodies."

"Bury?" Elyam said, his voice cracking with emotion. "Tell me, Pillar, to whom shall our prayers go?"

"To the Goddess," Daniel said.

"And where is our Great Mollai today? Our families have been slaughtered, our holy relics defiled. She has forsaken us."

"So why were you just praying to her?"

He paused. "An old habit."

"Let's at least give your honored fallen a proper burial."

"Would the Pillar have us bury our brothers beside the Betrayer himself?" He gestured at the Abyssal. "They will have no rest in the world to come. Beasts will disturb their bodies here."

"We'll burn them," said Havig. "And their ashes will scatter in the winds."

Elyam looked repulsed by Havig's every gesture. "With what fire? We've no kindling."

"We can weave fire from air," Havig said.

Elyam paused to consider this. "Through demonsong, no doubt."

"Let's cremate the bodies," Daniel said. "All three of them." *What better way,* he thought, *to unite two peoples than with a shared ritual.*

"What do you mean, *three*?" said Zimri, Elyam's son.

"The Mikulal and two Bedu," Daniel said. "Together as one."

Elyam nodded. "This is fitting. Let the high be brought low. Let the holy burn beside abominations. Nothing matters anymore."

"Father," Zimri said. "Have you lost your mind? They are servants of demons. They would defile these holy men."

"But don't you share a common ancestor?" Daniel said. "A long time ago, weren't the Bedu and Mikulalim one people?"

Zimri approached Daniel. His eyes—blue as an autumn sky—sparked with rage. "I heard the demon Caleb. Of course you would side with abominations. You *are* one."

"I have been given the curse," Daniel said. "That's true. But I'm not fully a Mikulal yet. I'm half-human. In a way, I'm both of you."

"You're nothing like us," Zimri said.

"Son," Elyam said, stepping in front of Zimri. "This wretched day has shown us that all things end. Let our enemies burn together with our friends. Perhaps their ashes will forge a new friendship in the corridors of eternity. I've had enough of battles."

"You're mad, father," Zimri said.

"Perhaps. But on the other side of madness lies clarity."

The fuming Zimri stepped aside to let the Mikulalim carry Dranub's body over. They laid him beside the priests, then spoke their spell, a sequence of harsh words. The bodies quickly ignited. Red flames leaped from their skin. Everyone stepped back as a column of smoke twirled toward the stars.

Havig hung his head, his eyes glistening. "Farewell, my son."

"He was your son?" Zimri said.

Havig nodded. "I was given a choice. Eat the cursed flesh and become a Mikulal, or die on the battlefield with ten thousand of my brethren. I took the coward's path, and so suffered this fate.

But Dranub had no such choice. He was born with our curse. And all his life he remained a slave to a demon, with no taste of what it was like to be free."

"You mean you don't want to be . . . as you are?"

Havig turned to Zimri. "I would give my right eye to remove this curse."

"So why didn't you go down with Caleb?"

"Because neither Lords Azazel nor Ashmedai allows us to. It's part of our curse. They prefer us as their playthings, their puppets. This is who we are and who we ever shall be."

A light glimmered in Zimri's eyes as he heard these words. "I always thought your kind chose to be the way you are. That you chose to live in shadows and eat men."

"You wouldn't be the first to think so, nor will you be the last. Sometimes, we are just given a foul lot."

As they watched the bodies burn, Daniel said, "What were their names? These men?"

"Abner ben Zamir," said Elyam. "He knew the Books of Tobai by heart, every stanza and verse, and ever since his wife died in childbirth he wrote hundreds of poems about her."

Another priest, his white sideburns overgrown, said, "He is— he *was* Shallam ben Ori. He didn't speak much. But when he did, everyone listened. With one sentence he could silence the House. He was the wisest man I ever knew. I'll miss him dearly." The priest hung his head.

"Tell me *your* names," Daniel said. "I want to know you all."

The Mikulalim introduced themselves. There was Havig, King of Yarrow, and Dnoma, with his harelip. And there was Prelg, with cheekbones as high as mountains. And there was Lamu with a missing eye. Krieg was short and stooped.

And of the priests, there was the boy, Zimri, and Elyam, his father. And Ahazia, who was stocky and wheezy. And Baasha, who had one brown and one green eye.

Daniel said, "Their deaths weren't meaningless. Listen to me, we don't have much time. Caleb and Rana will return soon, and I need your help. Every one of you."

In the east, the sky had begun to brighten, as they all turned to face him.

CHAPTER TWENTY-SIX

What could I build, Rana wondered, *if the only limits were my imagination?* Perhaps a world where rains came at dawn to swathe a thousand rainbows across the sky. Or one where every tree bore gigantic star-shaped fruits, and every field brought forth ten thousand bushels of grain. Or a world where she and Liu spent their days making art instead of breaking their backs for fat kings, where famine, war, drought, plague, earthquake, fire—all things to fear had been erased like that woman . . . what was her name?

Marul, The Witch Who . . . The witch? Who?

In this new world, Rana thought, *I'll rule with a kind hand. I'll make every day a holiday and every night a feast. I'll turn every sorrow into joy.*

But she couldn't have Caleb controlling everyone like he controlled the Mikulalim. *When I create this new world,* she thought, *I'll make it so that neither Caleb nor Azazel, nor any demon, has more power than anyone else. They can thrash and roar all they want, but they will be as impotent as lambs.*

"I want to see you with my own eyes," Azazel said. His voice was soothing and tender, so that when he spoke she longed to move closer to him. "The Sefer Yetzirah, the Codex of Formation, sits behind you, Rana," he said. "That red hypercube. Place your hands gently, gently inside it."

She stared into its shifting visage, where a thousand unnamable structures flickered across its oddly angled surface. "What will happen?"

"You will receive a precious gift."

The cube was translucent, ruby-red. A rectangular brick floated in its center, roughly hewn. It seemed as if this was the first brick ever excised from stone. She felt a kinship with it, as if the brick co-existed deep within her heart, the foundation of all her creativity. She took a steadying breath and reached for its surface. It was pliant, like viscous oil, and comfortably warm. As her hands vanished into the cube, a river of thoughts flooded her mind.

She stood in a smith's forge. Hammers pealed against metal. Sparks flew. The air smelled of molten iron. Heat from the furnace blasted her skin as men poured glowing metal into molds. They hammered the cooling shapes into tools, unaware of her presence as they worked, as if she were a ghost. Her perception was acute. She noticed every hammer stroke, every curve of mold, every subtlety of technique, until she felt as if she were no longer learning from them, but directing them, a spirit whispering instructions in their ears.

Then she found herself on a long, narrow boat, sailing up a river. A dozen rows of dark-skinned oarsmen propelled the boat forward as sweat dripped down their backs. A taskmaster rode them severely with a whip. Huge blocks of limestone rested on the deck, dusty from a recent quarry.

The boat docked on a sandy shore, and with skeins of ropes and tangles of pulleys, the oarsmen heaved the stones onto logs of wood, which they used as wheels. In this fashion they rolled the limestone blocks a great distance across a desert. On the horizon a huge ziggurat was being built. Using a webwork of kites and pulleys to augment their strength, the slaves hauled the stones up its steep banks. They placed the new stones at the top, one of hundreds, and hundreds more to go.

From the summit she gazed across the magnificent city. Its stony walls were etched with curious glyphs and figures of gods and beasts painted in bright colors. Tall trees with huge feather-like leaves sprouted in the streets. To the east and west loomed two giant pyramids, and she suddenly realized that this was not a ziggurat, but the unfinished third and largest pyramid. A sarcophagus for a king still a boy. She watched them build until she knew their well-guarded secrets, like how to cut stone using fire, wood, and water, and how to calculate the angle of the sun, so that, at a certain time of year, it penetrated the stone layers into the central chamber, where the boy king would one day spend eternity.

Then she found herself in an underground tunnel, the air cool and damp. Pale-skinned men with large, curving noses tunneled into white rock. As they moved forward, hour by hour, day by day, week by week, they set stones in arches over their heads. They dug the tunnel toward a distant river. And when they were done, flows of human excrement washed into the tunnels from the city above, a city decorated with immense, ornate columns and limestone statues of muscled gods, a city of fanfare and trade, while underneath them their filth flowed out to sea.

Then she was high above a great city, higher even than the DanBaer, standing on a mammoth metal skeleton. Men with yellow hats directed giant metal arms strung with wires. The wires hauled heavy bars of metal into the sky. The power of lightning itself was conducted through thin metal filaments and called to action with the push of a lever. They used locking rods and a tool that spit fire to melt the metal into place. She watched the tower rise, week by week, story by story, on an island with so many towers that at night their glowing windows outshone the stars. People flew above the city inside winged metal cylinders that rumbled louder than thunder, moving faster than the tides of the Tattered Sea.

Then she hung below an enormous and resplendent aqua ball that filled three-quarters of the sky. The ball was blinding against the sea of all-consuming black beneath her. She drifted beside three people who floated inside white, bulky suits, their faces hidden behind curved mirror plates. They positioned a mammoth metal cylinder into place against the superstructure. Flat gold panels reflected sunlight, storing its energy for later. Gray tubes and spikes of metal bristled from the superstructure like spines on a cactus.

The cylinder they positioned weighed more than a house, but with the barest touch they moved it left and right. A shadow swallowed the orb above her as the sun set behind its curved horizon.

White lamps on the superstructure cast stark shadows as the people worked. A spray of lights on the orb spun into view, the lights of a city a great distance away.

The black expanse yawned beneath her. Or was it above? Up and down had lost meaning. The sky was filled with innumerable stars. True stars.

This blue orb is a world, she thought, *and its people know how to build houses in the sky. Now I know, too.*

Her mind filled with complex tables of numbers that these folk stored in machines using bits of static and lightning. The machines could think faster than any person, but were stupider than a goat. And she knew that even though they floated as if they were in a womb, they were falling, forever falling toward the great blue world that kept leaping out of their way.

Then she was reclining beside a group of purple-skinned beings. Not demons, nor humans, but of another race. They resembled large, wingless birds, and they used a machine that made matter forget itself and collapse to birth a new sun from an ancient cloud of gas. She listened to the secrets their machine whispered to matter, when the beings sensed her presence and invited her on a billion-year journey across the universe to the oldest star, where their god dwelled in a castle made of light. But before she could answer she was whisked away.

In a vessel shaped like a mirrored ball, she and silent white beings, as skinny as twigs and with a thousand long limbs, moved through immense gulfs of space without moving at all. She learned from them that space was pliant, like clay, that it had no intrinsic substance, but was formed by relationships between strings of energy that danced within it.

Then she was in a room full of children—human boys and girls—who were playing with toys on a floor as girders of sunlight split the room. A girl who resembled Liu stacked toy bricks into a widening spiral structure. Rana had dreamt this dream many times, but she could never build this shape without failure, except that one time on the DanBaer, beside Daniel and the demon dog, where it had stood without falling.

The girl smiled and offered Rana her toy tools. A hammer, small, orange, and soft. The other a chisel, thin, green, and hollow. A hammer and a chisel, the most basic of tools. But with them she could build a whole universe.

The dreams ended. She was back in Azazel's lair. She gasped and withdrew her hands from the Codex. In one hand she held a chisel, a real chisel, it's blade mirror sharp. In the other, a large iron hammer, heavy, covered in rust. Her body shook. She had just absorbed lifetimes of knowledge. All of it was still fresh in her mind. She could now write out the mathematical representation of a satellite in an elliptical orbit around a planet or build a bridge that could support a stampede of elephants. But much of it, like the secret the purple beings had whispered to matter, and the substance of space itself would take time to process. Some things, she knew, she would never remember.

"Astounding," Azazel said. "Isn't it?"

Her mouth was dry. "What did I just see?"

"History," he said. "Everything you have just witnessed has happened, somewhere in the Cosmos. These colorful shapes are my Seforim Daat, my Codices of Knowledge. For millennia, the knowledge contained here has brought back countless civilizations from ruin. Every time a world crumbles to ashes, I am here to help it rise again. But there will be no more worlds but the one you create, Rana. The others will wither like dead leaves in autumn."

Rana examined the tools in her hands. "What are these for?"

"Bring them to me," he said.

She wished she had chalk and a board, a canvas to scribble down her ideas; they were coming so fast. She saw a thousand cities swimming in the skies above a planet. And a doorway one entered in one place and exited a thousand planets away. The ideas would not stop. She paused before his sea of gray hair. It spilled in a waterfall from his face.

"Don't be afraid, Rana. Come closer."

She took a tentative step onto his hair. It was soft, cotton-like, and she resisted the urge to fall to the ground and wrap herself in its warm blanket. From where had this feeling come? She checked herself. Her heart thrummed. Her breathing was heavy. Her cheeks were flush. She was in love, but with whom? She let slip a laugh as she realized the truth. She was in love with creation itself.

"Laugh, my dear. For knowledge *is* joyous. Now, push aside this ancient hair from my face."

She paused before his body. Even upside down he looked taller than Caleb. Stronger too. Curly hair spread over his chest like wild, dark grasses. His flaccid penis hung to his belly. He had no navel. As she stared at him, her arousal grew. She felt energized, like the metal filaments in her dream. Every motion made her ache for caress. With a shaking hand, she parted the canopy of Azazel's hair.

It was softer than wool. Underneath its shadow rested a young, beautiful face, with rosy cheeks and plump lips. His eyes were the color of new leaves sprouting in King Jallifex's gardens. Almost the same color of her eyes, what was her name, that woman, who used to come and visit. Marie something . . .

She had a sudden urge to bend down and kiss his plump lips.

"You are more beautiful than I imagined," he said, and her cheeks grew hot.

"Why are you chained?" she said.

"For the crime of giving knowledge without wisdom. Some believe that knowledge should be sequestered away, that knowledge is dangerous. It *can* be dangerous, that is certain, but only to those in power. To those who are slaves, knowledge is freedom."

"Who chained you?"

"A malach called Raphael."

"A bystander?"

"An *angel*."

"Is an angel a type of demon?"

"The most dangerous kind."

Caleb stepped forward. "Enough chatter. Time is short, brother."

Azazel blinked. A tear rolled down his cheek into the folds of gray. "I never thought I'd say this, but I will miss this place."

He closed his eyes. Then he groaned as if under a great internal struggle. His voice echoed from unseen walls, greatly amplified. His cheeks grew red, and she felt a blast of heat from him as if she stood before a furnace. A blister appeared on his forehead above his left eye and began to grow. From under the tangle of hair rose a small curving horn, like a ram's. As it grew it made sounds like tearing leather and chattering stones. Rainbows twirled angrily around its length. The horn spiraled out of his head, until it was twice as large as her arm.

He opened his eyes. The color had drained from them. They were as gray as his beard. His face had withered, and he looked like an old man.

"Take your tools," he said. His voice had become frail, aged. "Cut free this horn. All of my power is contained within it. My life is in your hands now."

Trembling, she took a deep breath. She leaned in and took an exploratory chip at the horn's base. It was as hard as granite.

"I trust the Gu won't cut off my nose."

It took nine hard raps to free the horn, and he winced with each one. She placed the tools on a small stone pedestal and lifted the heavy horn. As she lifted it, its immense power seemed to flow into her arm, up her shoulder. When it reached her head she gasped.

"There," he said, with a brittle sigh. "It is done. You hold in your hands the Horn of Azazel, all of my power. You hold in your hands our fate."

"I will not betray you," Caleb said. "I will come back for you, brother."

"So you vow," Azazel said. "But we shall see. Now go, and let me rest. I will sleep the sleep of eons."

"Brother, wait, you still need to teach me the spell to create the Merkavah."

"I won't be teaching you," said Azazel.

"But without the spell all this is moot!"

"Brother, I have given Rana the spell."

"You did what?"

Rana searched her memories and there it was. A figure of ten circles connected by twenty-two lines. The sephirot, the Tree of Life. She knew it intimately, now. She had seen it before. In a cave, somewhere. She had a vision of an old woman, her greasy hair hanging to her shoulder, weeping on the floor of a candlelit prison. The vision terrified her. But Rana couldn't remember who this woman was.

Syllables of some ancient tongue were fresh on her lips. *Hebrew*, the language that Daniel had spoken of on the DanBaer cliffs. They had gone there for something she couldn't seem to remember now.

"But why Rana?" Caleb said.

"So I can guarantee that Rana builds this new world and not you."

Caleb scowled. "Conniving to the last."

"Did you expect anything less?"

"And what about Daniel Fisher, the Lamed Vavnik. He has your curse. Can you undo that too?"

"My, brother, you ask for much. Use the Horn. It has the power to heal him and much more besides."

"Good," Caleb said. "We need to get back to the surface. I hope there is another way besides your pathetic Baast."

"Behind you are eleven chambers. Enter the one framed with the tallest arch. My servant Chialdra lives there. Show her my Horn, and she will obey you till the end of time."

"The end of time is hours from now," Caleb said.

The mention of Chialdra's name didn't scare Rana. And why should it? With this new power she wielded, she could do anything. What was a demon bird compared to the power to build worlds?

"I owe you much brother," Caleb said.

Azazel closed his eyes. "Yes, Ashey, you do." His slow breaths sounded like long-dead spirits sighing in abandoned halls. Rana felt sorry for him, forced to dwell here for all eternity. She squeezed the Horn in her hands and knew that it contained the power to create a universe.

And she alone held it.

CHAPTER
TWENTY-SEVEN

DANIEL STOOD ON THE EDGE OF THE CHASM AND PEERED DOWN into the dark. The Abyssal of Lost Hope was immense. It was at least a mile to the other side, and its edge twisted a crooked course into the bordering mountains, as if a great hand had chiseled the planet in two here. A hot wind blew up from the depths like an old man's fevered breath. He couldn't see the bottom, and he shivered as he stepped back from the ledge.

Caleb had chosen this spot to perform the spell for good reason. The yellow sands were flat, devoid of stones. There were five Mikulalim, four priests, and him. That made ten.

Nine rabbis can't make a minyan but ten shoemakers can.

He helped them draw the sephirot in the sands. Ten wide circles, the ten divine emanations. Keter, Chokmah, Binah, Chesed, Gevurah, Tiferet, Netsach, Hod, Yesod, Malchut. He sensed their power as he drew each one. He showed them how to connect the sephirot with twenty-two lines, one for each letter of the Hebrew alphabet. Though the ambient light was weak, the sephirot seemed to glow.

Elyam corrected a mistake in the sephirot, and Daniel said to him, "You know the Tree of Life?"

"Intimately," Elyam said. "All Bedu magic are permutations of it."

Daniel carefully taught each man his portion of the spell and hoped he remembered the parts correctly. The Black Guide's spell had confused him. But these men were adept learners. Magic came easily to them, Bedu and Mikulal alike.

"From whom did you learn this spell?" Elyam said.

"Marul taught it to me."

"Who?"

Had even their memories of her become dust? "A woman who tried to be a god." He walked to the Abyssal edge and Elyam followed. "Now she isn't even a memory."

Elyam kicked sand over the edge and watched it fall. "Will this be our fate too?" he said. "To tumble forever into the Abyss?"

Havig joined them, and his expression was dour. Solemnly, he said, "The Lamed Vav will sustain us, as they always have."

"'He will slake your thirst in parched places, and give strength to your bones,'" Elyam said. "'You shall be like a watered garden, like a spring whose waters do not fail.'"

"I've heard that before," Daniel said.

Baasha, the priest with one brown and one green eye, approached them and said, "'A man from your midst shall rebuild the ancient ruins. He shall restore foundations laid long ago.'"

The wheezy priest Ahazia said, "'And he shall be called Repairer of the Fallen Walls, Restorer of Lanes for Habitation.'"

"That's from Isaiah," Daniel said. "I remember it now."

"It is Yeshayahu," said Elyam, "from the Fourth Book of Tobai."

"What does the source matter?" Baasha said. "Truth is truth."

"But *is* it truth?" said Elyam. "We've studied the holy books. They promised salvation for the righteous, but it has brought us only ruin. Daniel, *will* you repair the fallen walls? *Will* you restore the foundations laid long ago?"

What could he say to that? "I will try."

Elyam closed his eyes. "As must we all. This artifact that holds a demon's power, you've no idea its shape or size?"

Daniel shook his head. "Marul said it might be a necklace, or an amulet, or a ring. Something physical."

"Who is Marul?" said Havig.

Only moments before, Havig had mentioned her name. She was slipping from their minds like sand through fingers. Would he forget her too? And if so, what did that mean for the spell? "We have to get this object from Caleb," he said.

"And how do we do that?" said Zimri. "Do you slide on the ring? Clasp the necklace? Is there an incantation? A gesture? Do we use pyromancy? Chronomancy? Astrology? Do we have to wait for an alignment of the stars?"

They all looked expectantly at Daniel.

"I don't know," he said. "I have no idea how these things work."

The boy shook his head and glanced at his father. "And this is the one who will save the Cosmos?"

"I'm doing my best," Daniel said. "I didn't choose this path."

"None of us chose this path, Pillar," said Zimri. "Nevertheless, it is laid out before us. Will you leads us into the abyss, or into heaven?"

The boy was right. He needed to lead them into confidence, not doubts, no matter his own thoughts. He straightened himself. "Havig, what's the extent of Caleb's power over you? Have you tested its limits? Could you lie to him?"

"Lie, no. But obfuscate, perhaps."

"What if you asked him to hold the artifact for safekeeping?"

"If he senses something is awry and orders me to speak, I must tell him what I know."

"Then we won't give him the time to think. Zimri, you must ask Caleb as many questions as you can to keep him off balance."

"I suppose I can do that," the boy said.

"All of you must do the same," Daniel said. "Do your best to distract Caleb, so he doesn't notice what we're doing. Elyam, tell Caleb you knew enough about this Merkavah spell to prepare the Tree of Life on the sands. He might even thank you for your forethought."

"Yes," Elyam said. "That's good. Very good!"

"Then this is our plan," Daniel said. "Does everyone know what they need to do?"

They all nodded, but none looked overly optimistic.

Daniel recited the names of the Lamed Vav to himself. Paula Baumgarten, Sunil Pranadchandr, Maya Dorje, Pandate Romsaitong, Baaba Lankandia. Daniel Fisher. "After I've seen to the safety of the Pillars," he said, "I'll find a way back to Gehinnom. I'll find a way to help the Bedu and the Mikulalim. This won't be the last time you see me."

"You're a good man," Elyam said, putting his hand on Daniel's shoulder. "Men like you are far too rare."

Daniel sensed the desperation in Elyam's voice, a despair echoed in Havig's gaze. All of them shared the look, the same great hope that their lot would improve, that their forsaken world could be made into something beautiful. And Daniel would be the one to save them. He had seen this look in the eyes of the homeless on Earth, the desperate who begged for help. They looked at him then and now as if he were a god, with the power of life and death.

But I'm no savior, he thought. *I'm just someone who tries to help others.* And perhaps that was all a Lamed Vavnik ever was.

Elyam gazed at the brightening sky. The eastern mountains glimmered, as if a fire burned behind them. "Even this bleak place has beauty," Elyam said. "We take each breath for granted. We forget the splendor of things. It's only when confronted with our end do we see the value in the trivial." He withdrew his foot from his sandal. "The feeling of toes in sand." He looked at Zimri. "Sharing morning tea with my son." He turned east. "The majesty of a sunrise."

A thousand shades of blue belted the sky, brightening to orange as they extended eastward, toward the approaching sun. He gazed at the Tree of Life in the sand, each circle a divine aspect of creation.

How strange, Daniel thought, *to stand on the cusp of eternity.*

"Look!" Ahazia shouted, sharply wheezing. "What in Goddess's name is that?" Everyone turned. Deep in the southern valley a dusty cloud was forming, and within its swirling murk a thousand horrid shapes marched closer. A moment later the rumble came, like a stampede, whose volume steadily grew.

———

Rana and Caleb crossed the cavernous chamber, leaving Azazel to his slumber. As they approached the great archways that framed the enormous shadowed halls, her mind considered their weight distribution, the mathematical solutions to their design. But even with all her new knowledge, their structure defied explanation. By all accounts their arrangement was impossible.

She stared in awe as they headed for the tallest arch.

She clasped the Horn of Azazel and its power thundered through her. She felt as if she were being refashioned from granite, the hardest stone, made invincible. If she had been confident about her plan before, now she had become intrepid. Gehinnom was in ruin. Its kingdoms shattered. But she would make a new world, one brimming with food, wealth, and most of all love, because why shouldn't this world overflow with love too?

And isn't lovemaking, she thought, *the ultimate act of creation? Two bodies joining to form a new life?*

They crossed under the arch and she grew flush. The distant walls were lost in shadow. She and Caleb were, for the moment, alone. She turned to him, and his eyes were bright as moons. "Caleb," she said, her voice vibrating with energy, "I . . ."

He moved toward her. "What is it, Rana?"

She pushed him against the wall, and he let her move him. For the first time, she felt more powerful than him. His eyes, once domineering, seemed to cower from her, and only now did she glimpse the being under his stony external shell. Caleb, at heart, was a frightened boy, spurned by his mother—the Creator—cast into darkness, forever searching for a path back to the light.

"Why did you choose me to build your new world?" she said.

"Because you are magnificent," he said.

"I don't fear you anymore."

"I never wanted you to."

She pressed her lips to his, a test. He seemed shocked at first, but then he pressed back with a force that surprised her. His lips were warm, soft, probing, and gentle. He was shivering. They both were. She pulled back to see his face. His pupils had dilated into caverns.

She freed him from his Bedu robe. He helped her out of hers. Naked, she pressed him to the ground. He lay on his back, staring up at her. A melody came like sweet wine to her lips, and she was overcome with an urge to sing. And as she did she swept his mind away, obliterated him through music.

In this new world, she thought, *you will be a lamb. Harmless and docile.* She focused her gaze, her music upon him. The Horn, still in her hand, amplified her song and her power. *You will help others and not harm them,* she thought as she sang. *You will be a force for good.*

Music flowed from her, washing his will away.

He was hard as she mounted him, and she was as slippery as oil. How good it felt to be filled. She moaned and arched her spine. His eyes rolled back into his head. He reached for her, tried to pull her toward him, but she pressed him down. He would not command her ever again. She lifted the Horn of Azazel high as the acoustics of the enormous chamber turned her song into a symphony. The Pedestal of Lamentation had nothing on this.

Her voice woke the sleeping centuries to wakefulness. She rode his shuddering body, not permitting him release. Palaces of pleasure filled her, and she lost herself in bliss. It was too much for him, and with a scream his dam broke. A sky of light flooded her vision.

Ecstasy consumed her. *I am a goddess!* she thought. The pleasure came and came and came, until she didn't recognize herself within it anymore.

After what felt like a long time, she became aware of her panting. Her vision returned. There were tears on his cheeks. She collapsed onto his chest in a blissful haze, shuddering, fluid dripping from her. She wouldn't spoil the moment with words. She only wanted to sustain this feeling forever.

Something shuffled behind them. A large creature shambled across the stone floor. She jumped off of Caleb as an enormous black eagle limped into the light. Its topaz eyes blinked and considered them as it moved closer.

Chialdra, the demon bird, wheezed as she came for them, beak spread wide. "I heard such beautiful music," cawed Chialdra. She sniffed, cocked her head. "And I said to myself, 'I know this voice that sweetens this dead air with empyrean sounds.'"

Naked, they both stood as Chialdra spread her wings.

"The Crooner!" Chialdra screeched. "How do you still live? How did you survive my sandstorm? And you, demon, with your prick still twitching like a morning worm, I know you. We've met before, but your shape has changed."

"I'm sorry about your leg," said Caleb, his voice hoarse as if he had just awakened from slumber. Perhaps he had, in a way. "But you would have hurt Rana, and I couldn't allow that."

"You are the mongrel who did this to me?" Chialdra said. Her leg was covered in suppurating scabs. "I vowed to destroy you. How is it that you arrived in my den? Does my master know you are here?" Chialdra spread her wings and opened her mouth to reveal hundreds of sharp teeth.

Rana lifted the Horn of Azazel and shouted, "Be still, Chialdra! This is the Horn of Azazel, which he has given us."

Chialdra's eyes focused on the Horn as Rana's voice echoed through the unseen halls. Chialdra closed her wings and turned her head, as if terrified of the Horn.

"Take us to the surface," Rana said, power coursing through her.

Chialdra turned and offered them a wing to climb upon. "Demeaned, crippled, left to fester," she said. "What a foul lot I have!"

Caleb handed Rana her robe and began to dress himself. "Your lot will change," he said. "A new kingdom will rise from the ashes. You can come with us, if you wish." He stepped onto Chialdra's wing and offered Rana a hand.

It was firm and warm as she took it. They climbed onto Chialdra's shoulders. Caleb grabbed a tuft of feathers, and Rana crossed her arms around his waist, the Horn locked in her grasp between them.

"And what will be different in this new kingdom?" Chialdra said. "I will be a slave under a different master."

"I will give you what all creatures ultimately want."

"Riches? Power?"

"An end to suffering."

Chialdra huffed. "You mean death!" She laughed bitterly as she readied for flight.

"No," said Caleb. "I mean the life we've all been denied."

Chialdra leaped, and they were airborne. It was wonderful and terrifying, and Rana tightened her clasp around Caleb's waist as the bird flapped. They flew into a wide columnar chimney in the ceiling, and darkness enveloped them.

She grew dizzy as Chialdra sped upward into unseen caverns. Wind tore at her face and hair. They burst from the ziggurat's roof, into light as feeble as a candle. The Lair of Azazel had aged like its master. The bricks were worn, misplaced, pitted.

The mirrored floor had become dull, scratched, dirtied with dust.

Chialdra flew faster, and the ziggurat shrunk behind them. The wind in her face cooled her racing thoughts. *All of Gehinnom*, she thought, *will wither when the next Lamed Vavnik is killed. Killed!*

One man will die, she thought, *so that millions can live without suffering*. She might carry on with that stain on her conscience, but how many people would die when Earth shattered? She trembled like the Araatz, beyond the DanBaer. *Does that make me*, she thought, *no better than Caleb? No better than a demon?* The Horn of Azazel thrummed in her hands, as if uncomfortable with her ambivalent thoughts.

"You mustn't tell Daniel of our plan," Caleb shouted over the wind. "He'll try to stop us. Later, when we're safely in our new world, he'll come to see that your creation is better than any that has come before. Because you have built it, Rana, it will be perfect."

"Caleb," she shouted. "I'm scared."

"There's nothing to fear." They flew past caves spilling scattered light onto the Abyssal walls. "You've done this a thousand times, in your imagination. Now you will do it for real. Here you are, flying on the back of a demon, the Horn of Azazel in your hands, about to create a new universe! Marul thought you weren't strong. If only that witch could see you now!"

"Who?" Rana said. "Who is Marul?"

"No one," Caleb said. "No one at all."

Rana felt an odd emptiness gnawing inside her chest. "But you still haven't told me *how* I do it." They darted through the Bridges of Fire, and the searing heat came and went. "How do I build this new world? With brick and mortar? Hammer and nail?"

Caleb's hair whipped in the wind as he looked over his shoulder at her. "I'm surprised the Gu Rana hasn't guessed by now."

"No! Tell me!"

"Rana, my dear, to create a new world, you have to sing!"

———

Daniel and the others gazed into the southern valley where whorls of multicolored shapes were kicking up a giant cloud of dust. The air rumbled with distant thunder. "Goddess protect us," Prelg said, his cheekbones as sharp as mountain peaks. "They come to devour us."

"Go to your circles!" Daniel shouted. "Hurry! Begin your spells."

"But we don't have the power," Elyam said.

"Then pray it arrives soon!"

They took their positions in the Tree of Life, and the demons charged into the valley as the ten began the spell. They chanted the syllables of the Tetragrammaton, Ye, He, Va, He, in spiraling Fibonacci sequences. Each chant was subtly different from the others, part of a greater whole, a spiral within spirals.

His spine tingled. His hair stood on end. Their hairs were rising too. It looked as if they were hanging upside down from the desert floor. The mob of horrid creatures thundered closer. A green, four-legged horse with an ostrich's head waggled its long neck. Red sparks raced down the body of a gigantic millipede. A huge bat with an octopus's beak swooped low over the demon ranks. A giant, naked man, green as slime, hobbled forward on legs five stories tall.

The ground shook and the mountains thundered with their echoes as the cloud of dust filled the sky, red and angry in the pre-dawn light. The purple hair of a voluptuous woman waved like a sea anemone. A jackal barked, its white scales as nacreous as seashells.

There were so many vulgar forms that Daniel felt sick with terror. But he continued the spell, and the others, watching him, continued too.

Closer flew green-winged apes and pterodactyls with goats' heads. Closer crawled spiders with human faces and rats as large as rhinos. Closer came the ten thousand demons. Daniel chanted louder to fight his fear.

A hundred feet from him, the Legion abruptly stopped. The line of monsters huffed and panted. The swirling dust fell with a soft hiss as the echoing thunder of their approach slowly faded from the mountains. Daniel had stopped his spell without realizing it, and so had the others. Their hair drifted back down to their heads with the dust.

A yellow elephant, an amorphous blob of ink, a knife-limbed wolf, and a thousand other monstrosities peered down at them with a mixture of malice, bitterness, confusion, curiosity. Colorful mists of condensation puffed from panting mouths. Oily drool splattered on stones. Belches, flatulence, and gurgles befouled the air.

Why did they pause? He began the spell again, and the Mikulalim joined him, but not the Bedu. Baasha cowered low. Ahazia had shut his eyes. Elyam was praying, while Zimri stared in wide-eyed horror at the multitude.

A huge giraffe with white fur, spiraling ram's horns and a vicious rat's face stepped from the throng. Its eyes, the blue of the deepest oceans, scanned the assemblage. Kokabiel, Second General of the Legion.

"Stop your ritual," Kokabiel said.

Daniel continued, and he hoped the Bedu would join him, that maybe Caleb would arrive with his magic object this very moment. But the giraffe demon leaned forward, and with a powerful exhalation, blew them all to the ground. Daniel gasped, the wind knocked out of him.

Kokabiel said, "Now rise for her majesty."

Daniel spit sand from his mouth as hoof and claw and foot parted for an approaching procession. Four gray wolves, large as horses, led the pack, their eyes milky and blind. A group of imps hopped and giggled like mischievous children behind the wolves. They smacked tambourines and played disturbing melodies on flutes of bone. Stout, hairy hobgoblins walked behind the imps. They held up long wooden poles whose tops burned with bright phosphorescent flames. The hobgoblins swung the poles toward the crowd, and demons barked and leaped back.

Four deathly pale women followed next, naked, though their thick hair, candy-apple red, wrapped their bodies like wool dresses. Their webbed feet squished as they walked over the sand, and their long tails snapped behind them as they walked. The women hefted the thick poles of an elaborate throne. It was covered in sparkling jewels, silver ornament, and ivory filigree. Upon its elevated chair sat a smiling woman.

Her hair was so dark it seemed blue, her eyes were an autumn forest, and her freckles on her porcelain skin were like a sky full of stars.

Rebekah, Mashit. Queen of Demonkind.

Her body glowed faintly blue, like ancient sea ice lit by moonlight, as the red-haired women lowered her throne to the ground. Her silver shoes were bedecked with many mirrors, and when she stepped onto the sand her sharp heels did not sink. Her white satin dress fluttered behind her in the breeze from the Abyssal, but hobgoblins made sure it never touched the ground. A wide belt hugged her waist, and its oversized crystal facets, like diamond chips, winked brightly as she walked. Her large buckle, the Hebrew letter Ayin, shined with its own illumination. She was a moon goddess, luminous, full of mystery, fallen to earth to walk among mortals. Daniel trembled at the sight of her.

"Rise for your queen!" Kokabiel shouted. His voice was heavy with magic, and Daniel found his legs rising against his will. It was a horrid, sickening sensation, perhaps what the Mikulalim felt every day. When everyone had stood, Rebekah said, "Now, now, Koko. Calm yourself. That's no way to open a dialog, and we've a lot to talk about, Danny and me."

The sound of her voice stirred him. Daniel hadn't seen her—not while awake—since the wedding. She fixed her gaze on him. Her eyes burned, as if he were looking into the nuclear heart of a star. His breath caught, and he knew this power had always burned there, hidden from him by magic. How many times had she had used her powers to cajole him when words failed to persuade? How far down had she invaded his mind? Her eyes scoured his mind now, probing for answers, but a wall he didn't know he had possessed until this instant blocked her.

She waved Kokabiel away, and he bowed and retreated. Then she approached Daniel. "I've missed you, Danny."

She blinked, and the burning star cooled. Suddenly she was a demon no longer. Standing before him was the Rebekah he had known. The human. His sweetheart. "I've missed you too, Bek," he said.

He heard a gasp from the Bedu.

"You don't look well," she said.

"I've felt better."

"We both have." She circled him, examining his body as if he were a statue, and he remembered the wedding, where she made only five circles, instead of seven. These were for the five days of creation, before the arrival of man. The hobgoblins cursed quietly as they struggled to keep her dress above the sand. And as she moved, her belt flashed like distant suns.

"Ashmedai has poisoned your mind," she said. "If only you had stayed with me, none of this would have happened."

His hand had slid into his pocket, and he pulled out the shriveled remnant of the boutonniere.

"Is that what I think it is?" she said.

"I've held onto it," he said, "because I wanted to believe this was all a nightmare, that I'd wake up and have a laugh. But I'm awake now, Rebekah."

"Do you remember that day we went to Coney Island? We walked the boardwalk, rode the Wonder Wheel and Cyclone, and then it started to rain. You said, 'Don't worry, Bek, it'll pass.' But it rained all day. We waited under the awning of the Fun House for the storm to pass, and I said, 'The day is ruined.' And you said—"

"I said, 'No day is ever ruined with you.'"

"Well, Danny," she said, blinking at him. "Here I am."

"I said those words to an illusion," he said.

"You said them to me."

"I said it to Rebekah. You are Mashit."

"You can still call me 'Bek' if you like. You can call me whatever you want." She turned and said to the crowd of demons, "Vostiel, bring me the vestments."

A pea-skinned hobgoblin with a brass ring between his nostrils emerged from the throng carrying a plush pillow. Draped across it was the crimson robe with floral blue and green filigree, the one he had been wearing in the dream. On the robe sat a bejeweled crown.

"I don't want to be king," he said. "Not in Sheol, or anywhere."

"But you *do* want to help the suffering, don't you? Think of what you and I could do, together, Danny."

"I have. And that's what scares me."

She offered her hand to him. "No one else has to die, Danny. Come with me, and together we can end the suffering of the Shards. From the throne of Abbadon, you and I will rule the Cosmos doing what we've always done, helping those in need."

"I'm sorry, Bek."

"Danny, please. I love you."

He felt as if someone was squeezing his chest, tighter and tighter. "You have a funny way of showing it."

"I've scoured the Cosmos looking for you. Is that not love?"

"If you love me so much, why try and kill me?"

She seethed. "Is that what the *cur* told you?"

"I know you are killing the Lamed Vav."

She grimaced and took a deep breath. "The cur has fed you many lies, Danny. I've no desire to *kill* the Lamed Vav. I have not harmed a single one."

"Stop it, Bek. I know you've already killed three. I saw their fragments raining down over the desert with my own eyes."

"Yes, you saw fragments, but they weren't from a Lamed Vavnik. Why would I destroy so precious a thing? When you chisel a jewel from stone, you must chip the surrounding rock away. *These* are the fragments you saw." She pointed to her waist, turning her hips left and right, and her crystal belt flashed like oil in moonlight. "This belt I wear is made from those same fragments, a gift from General Kokabiel. What you saw streaking across the sky was not a dead Lamed Vavnik, but the mortar that had fastened them to the Earth."

"If the Lamed Vav are not dead, then where are they?"

"The are in Sheol. In Abbadon. Maya Dorje, Paula Baumgarten, and Baaba Lankandia are alive and well there."

Daniel's head spun as he recognized the names. "The Lamed Vav aren't dead? Why bring them to Sheol?"

She smiled, and it brought him back months, to when they'd first met and laughed at everything, because everything then had been beautiful. "Soon my servant Af will free Sunil Pranadchandr from Earth. With his removal, Earth will shatter. Its waters of life will gush out."

"And everyone on Earth and all the Shards will wither and die."

"Not exactly. With four Lamed Vav in Sheol, our Shard will not wither. We will persist as the Earth has persisted. And, with the help of the Lamed Vav, Sheol will grow."

Daniel opened his eyes wide. "While everyone else withers."

"The Shards will not wither in a day. As they dry up, Sheol will offer a helping hand. We will become the source of the waters, as Earth has been the source for eons. In the cosmic hierarchy, Sheol will take Earth's place at the pinnacle. Our sustaining waters will flow down to Earth and the Shards. Sheol will finally have what has been denied us since the beginning of time, the freedom that comes from abundance."

She swept her gaze over the Bedu, the Mikulalim. "Hear me, people of Gehinnom. No one has to die. You may come with us to Sheol, where you will be our honored guests. But if you choose to stay, then you shall wither here. And when the waters dry up, you'll have nine eternities to contemplate your mistake." She turned to Daniel and held out her hand, "So, Danny, will you come with me? Will you help me build a new Cosmos?"

An enormous black eagle darted from the Abyssal. The horde gasped and shouted at the sight of it. Daniel recognized the glittering topaz eyes, those elephantine wings. Caleb and Rana clung to Chialdra's feathery neck.

Chialdra circled the demon ranks, and the Legion sprung to action. Arms reached for potions. Weapons were drawn, amulets lifted. Lips muttered the first lines of dark spells. But Mashit cut them short with a raised hand. "Hold your positions! Do not attack!"

The eagle circled the ranks, cawing, "I am ashes! You've led me to my demise!"

"Shut your damned screeching!" Caleb shouted. With a great whoosh of air Chialdra thudded to rest on the sand beside the Tree of Life. Daniel blinked dust away. The bird stood on one healthy leg. The other, badly infected, bent crookedly. Caleb and Rana climbed from her wing. Rana held a large curving horn, like an enormous shofar. Her hair was windblown, and she kept adjusting her dirtied robe as if it didn't quite fit.

The horn! Daniel thought. *This is the object of power.* He snuck a glance at Havig and Elyam. Both gave him a curt nod.

"I didn't expect a welcoming party!" Caleb said. His voice was hoarser, smokier than Daniel remembered, the voice of someone who had awakened from a long sleep.

Rebekah scowled as she examined Caleb. His bandages were red with blood, and his robe, like Rana's, was filthy.

"I was told Great Ashmedai bleeds," Rebekah said, "but I did not believe it."

"Why does my blood surprise you?" said Caleb. "For you draw it so easily. You should have killed me when you had the chance."

"Death is too easy," she said. "Exile has duration. Suffering is prolonged. When the Shards wither, I'll enjoy your pleas for mercy."

"Why, Mashit? Why would you destroy what we had?"

"What we *had*? We had nothing."

"We had a family," Caleb said, stepping closer. "We had a palace full of children. We had love."

Rebekah—Mashit—gazed at Daniel. "You don't know what love is."

"And you do?" Caleb said. "Your love is as fickle as Sheol's stars. Daniel, whatever this bitch has promised you, she'll not give it. Come with me, and I'll show you what true happiness is."

"Is the cur still obsessed with his childish fantasy?" Mashit said. "A little universe to call his own? Let me guess, the Gu will build this new world for you. Tell me, Rana, what has the cur promised? Are you content to let a mongrel be your master?"

"What are you talking about?" Daniel said.

"He hasn't told you?" Mashit said.

"No."

"Centuries ago, one of Ashmedai's astrologers came to his court and laid out plans for cosmogenesis, how to create a new universe. The astrologer had all the pieces worked out, except one. How to prevent this new universe from collapsing. The only things known to sustain universes were the Lamed Vav, except we didn't know who or where these Lamed Vav were."

"And now you do," Daniel said. "We were never going to go back to Earth, Caleb, were we? You want to use me to sustain this new world of yours."

"Yes," Caleb said. "You will be its Pillar, and Rana its architect."

"Did you know of this, Rana?" Daniel said.

Her cheeks were flushed and she wouldn't meet his gaze. "I've only just learned of his plan," she said. "But you haven't lived in this hell, Daniel. You don't know what it's like. This is our chance to make things right!"

"It may be right for some," he said, "and hell for others."

"Ashey, my dear," Mashit said. "This dream of yours is nothing more than a childish fantasy. Come home to Sheol, and I'll see you're well taken care of. There's a stone house on the cliffs by the lake that would be a perfect place to retire."

Caleb coughed, and blood pooled in the corners of his mouth. "So I can be your trophy? So your guests can drink wine on your balcony as you point to the cliffs and say, 'There lives Ashmedai, once King of Demonkind, now a sad little hermit.'? Never."

"There are worse fates," Mashit said. She raised her arm, and the Legion rose to readiness.

"You forget," Caleb said. "We carry the Horn of Azazel. Do you know how much power it holds?"

Rana seemed dwarfed by the throng, uncertain in her new role as demon ally. Daniel was surprised and disappointed with her. Hours ago she had tried to kill Caleb. Now she wanted to build a universe with him? What had happened down in the Abyssal? Was she under a compulsion, or did she really believe this was the best path? Either way, he still had to snatch the Horn from her.

"We outnumber you ten thousand to one," said Mashit.

"You'd kill us easily," Caleb said, "but not before the Horn destroyed half your Legion, and you as well."

"Then let us end this peaceably."

"The time for peace is long gone."

Mashit ran a finger down the edge of a facet on her belt, up and down, as if it were a knife blade. "Perhaps we can come to an arrangement," she said.

Caleb approached Mashit, unblinking, his eyes bloodshot. "Why should you care if I create a new universe? Why pursue me across this barren world? You can have Sheol and the throne of Abbadon. I don't care about that anymore. Sheol has forsaken me, and so I have forsaken it. Leave the Pillar with me and go build your happy kingdom."

"He is coming with me," she said. "Isn't that right, Danny?"

A crystalline sound suddenly rang through the air, a loud wind chime of glass parts. Rebekah reached between her breasts and pulled out a silver pocket watch that dangled from a chain about her neck. She pressed the clasp, and the face popped open. A clockwork mechanism blossomed in the air, a huge flower of gears and light. The spinning movement hovered above the case, flashing as the gears ticked quickly forward. Seven luminous hands marked the time, racing wildly.

"It's almost time," she said. "Sunil Pranadchandr will be cleaved from the Earth in moments. Af will carry him across the Great Deep to Sheol, and the Earth will crumble." She snapped the watch closed and the gears of light dripped away. "Daniel, it's time for you to choose. Come with me to Sheol, and we'll do what we've always done together, help the suffering. But this time without human limitations. All the resources in the Cosmos will be ours."

"No," said Caleb. "You'll be her slave, and when she grows bored with you—and she will—she'll crush you. If you come with me, Daniel, you won't need to heal the suffering anymore. We will dwell in a world without suffering of any kind. All your loved ones can come too. And all the people on Earth, all those who suffer in the Shards, will be welcome. You know in your heart my solution is the best, Daniel."

Caleb shouted at the Legion, "And what do you lot wish for, my demons? You've lived so long as husks, do you even know what you lack? Suffering has been your most intimate friend. But in our new world, all suffering shall be forgotten."

He turned to the men standing on the Tree of Life. "Priests of the Quog Bedu, your centuries of wandering, waiting for redemption, ends today. Daniel, Rana, and I are the redeemers you have been praying for. And my Mikulalim servants, so faithful and true, you will shed your morbid curse and live as whole men, released from my yoke. Hear me, Legion of the First, army of Sheol, let us perform the spell. All may come with us, if you so choose." He turned to Mashit. "Everyone else can rot in Sheol."

Mashit grabbed Daniel's forearm. Her hand was hot, and her sharp nails dug into his skin. "Danny is coming with me!"

Caleb grabbed Daniel's other arm. "Bitch, he's coming with me!"

"Let the Pillar decide," Rana said. Her voice was small, but it silenced everyone. "Let Daniel choose."

The Legion stilled their breaths. The air itself seemed to await his answer. Daniel thought he heard dew dripping down the mountains, miles away.

He said nothing for a long moment. Everyone stared at him, human, cursed man, Gu and demon. Finally he took a deep breath and said, "You both want to make things better for others, and I see great hope in that. But you've trampled on everyone who has stood in your path. If you had come to me and asked, 'Will you help us make a better world?' I would have said 'yes' without hesitation. But look at how much death follows in your wakes. Where is your empathy? Where are your hearts?" He pulled free of their hands. "I'm sorry, but I choose neither."

The sun breached the mountain peak, and a wave of light raced across the yellow sands. The air cracked with a thunderclap so loud it sounded as if the mountain had split and fallen asunder. At the zenith, a light brighter than the rising sun shone down, and from its center, long fingers of light reached outward.

Daniel suddenly longed for something missing he could not fully comprehend, the wound of an ineffable loss, a hole never to be filled. He had felt this when the fragments had fallen from the sky. But another Lamed Vavnik had not been killed this time. Sunil Pranadchandr had been cleaved from Earth like a gem from stone and was now on his way down to Sheol.

Globules of light formed in the sky, as if he were traveling through a dense cluster of stars. The size of grapefruits and basketballs, they birthed solar systems of smaller globules. As Mashit looked up at the sky her belt flashed beams of yellow light into the throng.

Another crack split the air. He thought it might have shattered his eardrums. But it was only the extreme heightening of his senses. The sounds of fleas leaping from one fur-backed demon to another thundered in his ears. A drop of sweat fell from a demon's nose to crash onto the sand louder than colliding trains. Each sound was intense, personal, terrifying.

Screeches and wails tore the air, as if a trillion people were crying. At the zenith, the fingers of light had formed a spiral. It quickly widened, spreading to fill half the sky, and the million stars and their solar systems rained down.

The globs of light stuck to sand and skin like viscous drops of oil. One marble-sized sphere touched Daniel's arm and his heart expanded with a delicious, unutterable joy.

He was nine, awake early on Saturday morning. He snuck through the house, past his sleeping parents, and ran outside. The robins sang morning hymns. The wind was sleeping in. He sat on the grass and peered at a purple hyacinth, trembling awake from its winter slumber. The sweet scent of cut grass filled the air. The sun was warm, and his heart was full. This was what paradise was like.

All the demons turned their mouths to the sky to drink in the rain. As they swallowed the golden balls the demons grew.

Caleb tore off his robe. Naked, blood spilled from his belly. But as he expanded his bandages tore off. His wound shrunk quickly and vanished. The blood flaked away. His two legs split into four. His head split too, and split again, so that he soon had four heads, one of an ox, one of a ram, one of a goat, and one of a man. This last still bore Caleb's face. Black wings, slick and rubbery, sprouted from his spine. All his mouths screamed.

Waves of joy washed through Daniel. Joy and memories. Mommy wrapping him in warm blankets to set him down for bed. Daddy gazing down into Daniel's crib. A wall of fire, ancient holy words drawn in flames, his parents standing beyond, holding hands, gazing at him. A dream, or perhaps a memory.

The Horn! he thought. *I have to get the Horn!*

Rana had fallen to her knees, spasming in seizures. The Horn of Azazel lay beside her, flashing colors as it soaked up the glowing rain. The Bedu sobbed and the Mikulalim moaned.

Havig's body swelled, and his hollow eyes filled with vitreous fluid. His muscles grew thick and strong. He was no longer a corpse, but a man. He laughed hysterically as his Mikulalim brothers changed too.

Daniel watched his own body grow strong again too. Azazel's curse held no sway against this rain. The sky split open as if it were made of glass. Girders of white light shined through the jagged cracks. Plants sprung up where the bright rays touched the ground. A hundred species of cacti sprouted from the yellow sands, hurtling through years of growth in seconds. Their sharp spines wiggled in small spirals as they turned toward the sky.

The cracks in the dome widened. The girders of light grew brighter. Trees sprouted where the light touched the ground, from seedlings to adults in seconds. Japanese maples and tulip poplars and patchwork sycamores rose from the dust. The light itself was the seed.

The leafy canopy spread over their heads, shading the ground from the sky.

A blue cornflower blossomed fifty feet wide and spat a mist of pollen that spun through the air like a flock of turning birds. On the edge of the Abyssal, beyond the tangle of plants, moss grew in florescent green clumps. A million tiny white flowers opened on it in grotesque waves.

The Horn! Daniel thought. *Where is the Horn?*

A throng of tall, thin people climbed over the Abyssal edge, singing as they tasted the rain. A cloud floated across the Abyssal, and a joy of rainbows made love in the shifting light.

I have to do something! Daniel thought. *Remember! Remember!*

He was a spermatozoon, flagellating through warm liquid, hungering with his entire being for the privilege of joining with the egg. He merged with it, in love, a wedding of chemical customs and genetic rituals. He danced to molecular music, joying out cells by the billions, manifesting love into human form.

And he was a human baby thrust out into the world of light and pain, and he was the baby grown into an adult woman, and he was her baby, and her baby's baby, and so on, for countless generations. And he was the cries of all newborns, and the joy of all mothers. He twirled in dervishes with the spirals of DNA, and he raced photons down to lower atomic orbits, where even at the quantum level the quarks were making love.

Daniel opened his eyes. He was on his knees, convulsing. Demons danced all around him, as a hundred thousand plants reached for the sky.

He wanted to drown in this blissful rain. But the Earth was crumbling. He blinked, and behind his lids every atom exulted with life.

Mashit spread her arms wide as she grew. Her belt snapped off with a spark and impaled a tree. Her two legs became four, and her head split twice into four heads, one of a goat, a pig, a scorpion, and a woman. She spread large black wings behind her.

All the demons were changing.

Caleb's wings grew translucent, shining like glass. His four heads merged into a single head again. It had Caleb's face, though younger and rounder. A cherub. His body was man again, but three times his normal size. He had lost his sexual organ. There was only smooth skin. His body was hairless except for long white strands raining from his head. He floated off the ground, arching his back, his hair hanging to his ankles.

Mashit underwent an identical change. She was a beautiful androgyne with a child's face, her hair raven black. Mashit and Caleb shuddered as they met gazes. Rays of white light shot from their eyes and mouths, connecting them with tunnels of light. Pulled by a great force, they sped toward each other. The air hummed a high-pitched note, a glass bell struck by the hand of God. Their clear wings flapped like newly emerged butterflies drying in the sun.

Two more androgynes floated from the throng, beams of light bridging their faces. They drifted between Caleb and Mashit, forming a foursome. Their beams of light made a cross, like the spokes of a wheel, and the four demons spun about its axis.

This quartering happened throughout the Legion. In a choreographed dance, thousands of androgynes coalesced into four-member troupes. They spun, their eyes and mouths connected with columns of light. All of them turning, wheels within wheels, like Ezekiel's divine vision.

I must get the Horn! Daniel thought. *I must get to Rana!*

She turned to face him, as if anticipating his gaze. Her face exploded with light as blue as an autumn sky, and he realized that he was emitting light too. It connected them, and as her light shined into his mind he felt himself filled with her memories.

They floated above the ground and drifted toward each other. Daniel was Rana, drawing a woman's face on the floor of a stone house with a piece of charcoal. Mama's face.

Oh, Mama, how I miss you!

Mama and Papa, their skin shaved like wood in the courtyard behind the house.

Both dead because of me!

Rana's thoughts poured into him, and his into her.

Daniel, a boy, eating dinner in the back yard with Mommy and Daddy, a bumblebee buzzing past, legs heavy with pollen.

What a stupendous little creature! Rana thought.

Rana, on top of the DanBaer, Papa showing her the proper way to hold a chisel. But she knows already. She has a mason's instinct. "Time is the greatest of all masons," Papa says. "She lifts mountains and grinds them to dust, and the strongest men and the richest kings always succumb to her hand."

Oh, Papa!

Danny, in bed as the house erupts in flames. Gram bursting through the doorway like a demon herself to carry him to safety. Gram, starting a prayer she will never finish, "*Shma yisroayl, adonai elo—*"

Little Liu—Goddess!—Little Bean, her eyes glistering brown gems. Her giggle!

Daniel, in the palanquin as Marul freezes time to show him the secret of the six names and the spell to get Daniel home before she vanishes forever.

"Marul!" Rana screamed. "How could I forget Marul?" A life of memories, washed away! Rana devoured his memories of her. All those histories she had carved into the palanquin walls, turned to dust.

Marul sold out the Cosmos, Daniel thought. *And I wanted her to die for it.*

She was my only true friend, Rana thought. *But she lied to me and betrayed us all.*

I must get the Horn, Daniel thought. *And get back to Earth.*

But we can make a new world, Rana thought. *Without suffering.*

Zimri and Elyam, bound together with tendons of light, drifted between Rana and Daniel. The four spun slowly clockwise.

And the four became Rana as she lay with Caleb and they were the bliss of orgasm as he released himself into her.

I have no words! thought Elyam. *Is this love or blasphemy?*

Is there a difference? thought Zimri.

Elyam, standing over the body of his infant son, Ruach, dead of malnutrition. Another famine to devastate the Bedu, the fourth in five years. Elyam had been faithful, devout! What did poor Ruach do to deserve this fate?

Zimri, watching his mother die from dehydration, wishing there was something he could do, crying out to Mollai for help. Hearing only the desert wind.

Rana, in her bed on a moonless night, realizing that if she stayed in Azru she would never be anything other than a slave to King Jallifex.

Zimri, vowing never to marry, never to love, for love never lasted. Zimri, mourning a boy he had loved and made love to, once, who was killed by marauders for a silver necklace.

For a drop of silver, Zimri thought, *I lost the only one I ever loved.*

I never knew, Elyam thought, *what you felt for him.*

I had forgotten, Zimri thought, *what Mother looked like.*

Daniel, letting his father wrap phylacteries around his forearm one sunny morning. Daniel, embarrassed after prayers, running off to play. Daniel, watching his father pray every morning, alone, wrapped in leather, until his death.

Daniel, beside Gram, chanting the Mourners Kaddish over his parents' graves.

Daniel, thinking of the homeless huddled on street corners, begging for money, food, anything to lessen their suffering. Millions walking past in their rich clothes and expensive jewelry heading back to their warm homes, ignoring those who slept in the gutter, even cursing them for their debased state, as if it was their fault.

Rana, building a copper bust of Mollai for Mama. Mama, just this once, happy with Rana's art. Rana hoping Mama would be happy forever.

Daniel, in Gram's front yard, the summer after the fire. Gram, uncovered, her face like a monster as she sits beside him. "Did you know," says Gram, "that beside every blade of grass is an angel that whispers, 'Grow, grow.'"

Daniel, imagining his parents as small angels, whispering to all the blades of grass in his yard, in every yard, in all the world.

But the angels do not whisper here, Elyam thought.

We are given only half of what we need to live, thought Zimri.

Less, thought Rana.

It's not fair, thought Daniel. *You shouldn't have to suffer like this.*

Even Earth suffers, thought Zimri. *You cannot escape despair. The Cosmos is rife with it.*

What can we do? Elyam thought.

Make a new world, thought Rana. And they all saw a pearlescent sun, golden fields of wheat, warm rains, and peace, peace, peace everywhere. Rana's perfect dream.

As one they thought, *This could work! We could really make a better world!*

But what happens to this world? Zimri thought. *And all its people?*

And Earth? Daniel thought. *And its billions?*

We would be no better than the Creator, Elyam thought.

Who smashes her creations because they're imperfect, Zimri thought.

A mediocre artist abandons her works, Rana thought, *because she sees her own imperfections reflected in them. But a great artist knows that all art is perfect, even with its flaws, from the child's scribble to the adept's masterpiece. All is precious.*

If we let the Shards die we are no better than the Creator, Elyam thought.

We must be better than God, Daniel thought.

We must do better than God, they all thought.

We shall be the ones to rebuild the ancient ruins, thought Elyam.

And restore the foundations laid long ago, thought Zimri.

We will provide what God has not provided, thought Daniel.

We have to get Daniel home.

The light that bound them broke, and they fell to the ground. Rana picked up the Horn of Azazel, which had grown along with the demons to be nearly as tall as her.

The globules of ecstasy rained down upon them as he and Rana ran over to the spinning foursome of Ahazia, Dnoma, Krieg and Lamu. He pulled them apart. Full of life, reborn, young again, they were barely recognizable as the people he had known. They rubbed their faces, bewildered, as he shouted, "The spell!"

He shouted until they understood. They took their positions at the Tree of Life. Ivy had grown around the circles in sculpted curves. Burdock and clover blanketed the ground inside the sephirot, forming perfect circles. In each sephirah grew a rose bush in riotous bloom, each bush birthing flowers in a different hue of the rainbow.

Daniel searched the spinning bodies for the other spellcasters. Rana found Havig, Prelg, Baasha, and a creature that might once have been a hobgoblin floating in a foursome and she yanked them apart.

"The spell!" Daniel shouted, pulling them toward the Tree of Life. The Mikulalim and the priest ran toward the sephirot. But the once-hobgoblin snatched the Horn from Rana's hands and sprinted into the forest.

"No!" Daniel screamed.

"I'll get it!" Rana shouted, sprinting after the creature. "Start your spell!"

She vanished into the shadow of the jungle as he took his place at Malchut. He stood beside a rose bush of bright red blossoms, its sharp thorns pricking his arm.

"Begin!" he said.

They chanted the first syllables, and their voices rose above the din as power coursed through them. Their hair rose, and his skin felt electrified.

A sphere, like tinted-red glass, suddenly appeared around him. One appeared around each of the spellcasters, each the same color as their local rose bush. Flowers, stems, trunk, and leaves were cleanly severed where the sphere's surface had intersected their growth. The glowing rain splattered and rolled down the spheres' curving surfaces. Random lightning sparked between the the spheres, linking the sephirot with twenty-two lines of power.

On the surface of each sphere, mammoth conflagrations were reflected that did not exist in the external world. In Daniel's hands, two pyramids appeared, one upright, the other inverted, just as had happened for the Black Guide. The Merkavah was forming. But where was the Horn?

In the writhing throng of plants and demons the hobgoblin expertly avoided Rana. He leaped over roots, ducked under shrubs, spun around the bowers of a tree. He dove into the spinning four-some of Mashit, Caleb, and two others and pulled them apart. The four demons collapsed onto the ground. The Horn skidded to a halt several feet away.

Rana ran for the Horn, but Mashit, fifteen feet tall, swatted her aside. She snatched Rana by the collar of her robe like cat grabbing the scruff of a kitten. Rana flailed as Mashit bent over and reached for the Horn. But Caleb kicked Mashit in the face. She fell back, and Caleb caught Rana before she hit the ground. He placed her down before charging after Mashit.

The Horn tumbled into a cluster of morning glory, where its vines and purple flowers quickly covered it.

Rana ran for the Horn, but Mashit reached it first. She tried to grab Rana again, but Caleb tackled her. The two wrestled, trampling flowers, bushes, grass. They slammed into trees, shaking down a rain of seedlings that immediately sprouted into young trees. The two rolled on top of the Horn, pressing it deeper into the tangle.

Zimri's sphere wavered. Ahazia's wavered too. Daniel felt weak, and his sphere was beginning to fade too. They needed the Horn, now. The two pyramids grew to fill his sphere. And clockwork mechanisms spun madly around him, gears turning into obscure dimensions, while rose thorns pressed into his back.

Mashit tossed Caleb a dozen feet into a sequoia. The trunk split and came crashing down. Rana leaped out of the way. Caleb dove for Mashit, and they tumbled into a foursome of floating demons, breaking their union. The demons blinked, confused. Rana tore madly at the vines until she freed the Horn. She ran toward Daniel with the Horn held above her head, leaping around a thicket, over knotted roots, and under shady bowers.

Mashit saw Rana with the Horn and screamed. Her crystal belt was impaled in the trunk of an oak tree. She pulled it out and flung the wire strap toward Rana like a whip. It wrapped around the Horn, and Mashit yanked it free of Rana's hands. The Horn flew into a thicket of forsythia, its yellow blooms turning like a startled flock of birds.

Rana and Mashit raced for the Horn.

Daniel was focused on the spell, when something sharp bit into his leg. He skipped a syllable, and his sphere wavered. Mashit's belt had wrapped his ankle, and one of the crystal facets dug into his skin. Blood spilled from the wound.

The pain was intense, but he continued the spell.

"Don't leave me, Danny!" Mashit wailed as she tugged on the belt's wire strap, pulling herself closer. He fell to the ground of the Merkavah, but kept chanting as she pulled. "Please, Danny! I love you!"

She pulled, and he pressed against the Merkavah wall. The crystal cut all the way to bone as he screamed each syllable of the spell.

Rana, the Horn in her hand, ran up to Mashit, and with a powerful swing slammed the Horn into Mashit's face. Mashit screamed and flew backwards hundreds of feet.

The tension released from his ankle, but the pain now worsened as blood poured from him. He grew dizzy, sick. Rana ran to him with the Horn, when Caleb came up behind her. He scooped her up in his enormous hands.

He pried the Horn of Azazel from her, and she screamed.

No! Daniel thought.

Caleb strode over and placed Rana gently down inside the Merkavah, beside Daniel and the rose bush. "I can't fit!" Caleb shouted. "No! Damn you all, I can't fit!"

Caleb looked over his shoulder, and Mashit was sprinting toward them. "It would have been beautiful, Rana," he said. "I know your world would have been perfect." Then Caleb—Ashmedai, King of Demonkind—lifted the Horn of Azazel to his lips and blew.

The Sound!

Every atom in the Cosmos seemed to awake and take heed. A note like none other, a note in every key. A note made from all other notes. The demons stopped their manic dance. The four-somes split apart. Every cell in every plant paused its mad growth to ponder the triumphant sound. Caleb blew the Horn of Azazel, and up the Mervakah flew.

Mashit leaped onto Caleb, knocking him over. The note ended, but she was too late. The Merkavah rushed upward like a satellite on its way to orbit, pushing Daniel and Rana to the floor. Mashit's belt still clung around his ankle, and blood pooled on the floor of the Merkavah. A thousand multidimensional gears spun around them, and a dozen new blooms opened on the rose bush.

Rana pressed her face to the transparent wall. "Liu!" she screamed. "Liuuuuuu!"

They sped skyward.

CHAPTER TWENTY-EIGHT

RANA SCREAMED. "WHAT'S HAPPENING TO THE WORLD?"

The desert of Dudael had vanished under a tangled green tapestry. A rainbow palette of enormous flowers blossomed from the receding landscape. If only she had paint and a canvas, so she could capture this scene before it was lost. They rose higher than birds.

"Liu!" she screamed. "Liuuuuuu!"

The Jeen, the mad desert, was desert no more. Tall, knotted fungi and twisting white sprouts climbed from the peaty ground. What did the horrid no-things think of all this new life? Did they too fatten and grow?

Marul! she thought. *I remember you! Look at what you've done! All this is because of you! But still I love you, and I don't care if that's wrong.*

Where the Tattered Sea had been, a great blue sea glimmered— a real sea of so much water. More than Rana had ever seen. Light cascaded over violet waves, while nacreous creatures, as large as cities, breached the waters and splashed down, stirring up clouds of foam and mist.

The Merkavah rose, and the horizon bent like a bow. *The world is bending,* she thought, *about to break.* And she remembered her vision in Azazel's lair, when she had floated above the blue world, the sky bent like it was just now.

Daniel had collapsed to the bottom of the Merkavah. His blood pooled on the floor of their sphere. Mashit's belt had cut deeply into him, and its crystal glowed with hoary light. Beside them a thorny bush was sprouting large red flowers, and the air grew dense with their sweet fragrance.

Daniel was shivering. She crouched down and they held each other as the sky darkened from blue to black. How fast were they moving? Faster than the tides of the Tattered Sea. Faster than a diving hawk. They hurtled toward a crack in the sky, where rays of brilliant light shone through. It looked as if there was nothing at all on the other side.

Daniel said weakly, "Rana, you'd better hold on. I think this might—"

And then they were nothing.

She wanted to scream, but she no longer had a mouth to scream, or even a body. Everything had become dark, silent, and still. She floated in an infinitely vast and empty sea, impossibly cold, impossibly devoid of light. This sea would never change in a thousand eternities. It mocked all notions of time and space.

And she hated this place with all her being.

Daniel floated beside her, a point of light, a spark from a fire. Beautiful in his singularity. She was a spark too. The Merkavah's physical form had vanished, but she felt its presence as a rushing wind guiding them across this horrid black gulf.

They floated for ten thousand lifetimes, and their journey had only begun. The chasms of space and time that opened beneath her and the vast distances they crossed maddened her. But perhaps they had only been traveling for an instant, and only covered a distance no greater than the width of an eyelash.

In the everlasting silence came a sound from far away, drawing nearer, century by slow century, like a rush of escaping air, or a waterfall. They approached a sphere of a deep violet color, like the sky after a sunset. Its sides were cracked, like a broken egg, and golden globules floated from it, drifting into the great abyss to splash onto the Shards like they had on Gehinnom, stirring up new life.

They hurtled toward the broken sphere and entered one of the infinitesimal cracks. And then they were physical again, alive inside the Merkavah's spherical shell. She gasped at the sudden sensation of form, of time and space, and her mind reeled at her memories of the infinite emptiness. They plunged toward a blue orb, the one she had seen in her vision.

"Earth!" Daniel said. "Oh, how beautiful you are, my lovely Earth!"

They plunged through layers of clouds toward an island bounded by two rivers. In the south was an enormous ocean, blue and gleaming, and to the north and west spread a great continent crowded with cities and patches of green land. Huge metal towers filled the island, except for its center, a large rectangle of forest in the midst of the city. Small lakes reflected sunlight as they plunged toward the ground.

As they sped for the forest they held each other. "Oh Goddess!" Rana said. She closed her eyes as they slammed into the ground. The Merkavah bounced, rolled, and bounced again. As they tumbled end over end, the bush's thorns sliced her. Daniel's blood splattered onto her face. On and on they rolled, until eventually the Merkavah came to rest.

They were covered in blood. Mostly his. The spinning gears vanished. The spherical shell popped an instant later, and they fell a handbreadth to the ground. Daniel gasped.

She sat up. She was covered with small cuts. The bush lay beside them, still blooming. They were on a field of grass. Smooth black paths curved nearby. Majestic trees surrounded them on all sides. In the distance, people in strange clothing were staring at them.

"I'm on Earth," she said. "I'm on another world!"

She stood. Nearby, a stone tower and two parapets overlooked a small pond. Some distance away, much larger metal towers peeked above the line of trees. Their details were intricate, clever, and she wished she could see them up close. The air smelled different from Gehinnom. Here it was heavy, full of moisture. It carried scents of soil and the sweet exhalations of trees. Within it all, she smelled something noxious and burning.

Daniel groaned and sat up. The crystal belt still wrapped his leg. He grunted as she helped him yank it out. The cut was deep, life-threatening. He had bandaged her, when the thief had cut her in Azru. That seemed so long ago now. Now it was her turn. She tore a scrap of her robe and used it to wrap his leg. But he needed a healer.

"Rana," he said weakly. "Look! You're glowing."

She gasped, because her body glowed as if she were a piece of molten iron removed from the furnace.

"Help me stand up," he said.

He grimaced as she helped him to his feet. The sun, red as embers, reflected off the glass-walled towers. The light made the city look as if it were aflame. The sky was sulfur-yellow, like the sands of Dudael.

"Something's wrong with the sky," Daniel said. "The sun is too dim." He sniffed the air. "And can you feel that?"

"Feel what?"

"The air is much too thin, like were on a mountain."

A bough from a nearby tree fell and splintered to pieces. Nearby, a loud creature wailed, and the sound echoed down the city's wide avenues. "What's that awful sound?"

"Sirens," he said. "Emergency vehicles."

Columns of smoke appeared above the tree line. The ground trembled violently, and they both stumbled and fell. Windows popped from their frames and plunged to the ground to shatter with loud crashes. A crack in the ground split the grassy field in half. The crack widened, while the grass quickly died as if a painter was daubing the landscape with an invisible brown brush.

Two dozen blue-gray birds suddenly fell from the sky, dead. "Your world," she said. "It's still broken!"

"I don't understand," Daniel said. "Sunil is gone, but I'm back! I sustain worlds. I'm a Lamed Vavnik!"

"But are you? Still?"

He stared at her. "What are you saying?"

"Maybe Gehinnom changed you. Maybe you're not the same person who left. Daniel, maybe you're not a Lamed Vavnik anymore."

A wave of despair spread over his face. He slouched forward, looking as if he might pass out. "All of this to get me home, and there's nothing at all I can do? I can't accept that! God," he screamed, "I'm here! I'm back! Why won't you listen to me? Stop letting the Earth fall apart!"

The sky turned as red as a smoldering fire. The temperature dropped, and the cold air nipped at her skin. The wind gusted, sour with ash and smoke. Strange, frightened people ran across the field, shouting and crying.

Mashit's belt lay on the grass. Light pulsed in waves through its crystal facets. Though the grasses were dead, around the belt the grasses were green and thriving. She wiped blood from the belt and picked it up. Her tired, worried face was reflected back at her.

"Rana," he said. "Your feet!"

To her shock, the grasses were still green and thriving where she stood. She took a step, and where she had been, the grasses remained bright and alive. And new shoots sprouted where she stood now. She took a few more steps, and wherever she went the grasses burst back to life.

"It's you," Daniel said, eyes wide. "You're the Gu."

"What do you mean?" she said. "Why is this happening?"

"You're a Gu. A receptacle," he said. "You catch the life force as it rains down. And it just rained *torrents* on Gehinnom. Torrents of life, Rana! And you've been filled with it."

Rana slowly nodded, because she understood, perhaps for the first time, who and what she was. "If I am a receptacle for life, then I need to give it back. She fastened Mashit's belt around her waist, and its rays shone toward the dying trees. And where the light hit dead matter, new leaves unfurled. The grasses doubled their growth, twisting around her calves. Life flourished wherever she stepped.

"How?" he said. "How can you give it back?"

Caleb's words echoed in her mind. "To heal the world," Daniel, "I have to sing."

And then she did.

She called to the shattered sky and beckoned the dying sun. She serenaded the dead grasses and becalmed the frightened people. She sang, and her music filled a million holes.

She walked, and flowers blossomed in her footsteps. The sun grew hot, bright, and yellow-white. A circle of blue burst from the sun to erase the sallow sky. The field exploded anew with life in a mad attestation of green.

Like a healing scar, the crack in the ground sealed shut. The trees celebrated with a new set of leaves. Brightly colored insects circled Rana's head. She was so tired. She needed to sleep. But the ground was still frightened and trembling. The mortar had not yet set. If she stopped singing, the world would crumble again.

She had to give more. In order to save the world, she had to give *everything*.

Daniel stared at her, shaking his head, as if he understood what she was about to do. His eyes pleaded with her, and a hint of their former mental bond leaked through.

Please don't, Daniel thought to her. *Please don't, Rana!*

But she had to. She had to fill the Earth with music. She filled the Earth with herself. With song she sanctified the trees and their curling leaves. Her melody exalted the skies and their tumbling clouds. With vibrations she blessed the dirt and their hungry worms. Her notes praised the sun for its loving warmth.

She fell to her knees, trembling. "Goddess . . ." She was so tired. More tired than she'd ever been. She could sleep for an eon and it wouldn't be enough. She turned to Daniel and said, "Your Earth is so beautiful."

"Rana," he said. "Rana, no . . ."

She felt airy and insubstantial. Her heart was fluttering erratically. "Daniel, if you ever find my sister, Liu, tell her that I'm sorry. I'm so, so sorry."

She curled forward, unable to hold herself upright. The blades of grass grew tall before her eyes. She remembered Daniel's memory, what his grandmother had told him: "Beside every blade of grass is an angel that whispers, 'Grow, grow.'"

Insects crawled between the grass blades. In the dirt beneath her wiggled grubs and worms. And tiny things, too small to see, ate the dead matter, turned it into food so that the grasses could live again. And beneath the dirt slept mountains of granite, and beneath the granite, molten rock as hot as a furnace. And on the other side of the world, the lava hardened to stone, the stone softened to dirt. The dirt fed the grass, and the grass exhaled the sky. Beyond the sky spread an immensity of stars, all spinning in an expanse so vast the light from distant suns burning for millions of years had not yet reached the Earth. And all of this directly beneath her feet. It would survive for another day.

She leaned forward, kissed a single blade of grass, and whispered, "Grow, grow, grow . . ."

One moment, Rana was there bent over, and the next she was gone. Daniel watched her vanish like smoke in the wind. This spot, here on the Great Lawn of Central Park, before the Delacorte Theater and Belvedere Castle, would be trampled on by thousands of people. They would run across this spot to catch a ball or fly their kite, or they would sprawl upon it while picnicking in the grass.

And not a single one, he thought, *will know that this is the spot where the Gu Rana Lila saved the world.*

Sirens wailed. Screams echoed down Manhattan's avenues. But the sky was blue again. The wind had calmed, and the ground had become still. Fires still burned. People were hurt and suffering and needed help. But these were human, not cosmic problems.

Rana had, like a sponge, collected enormous amounts of energy as it fell on Gehinnom. And she had given all of it back. But that wasn't quite enough. Too much had already been lost. To save the Earth and the Cosmos, she had to give all of herself too.

A blade of grass grew where Rana had been, three times as tall as the others. All that remained to mark her passing from this world.

A cardinal chirped hesitantly, as if testing the air. Two long whoops, then five short chips. Others joined in. From the trees came a chorus of birdsong, of rejoicing.

"Remember," he said to the birds and the plants and the sky. "Remember what Rana Lila did here today." The air answered him with a humid breeze that turned over the leaves and made the trees bow.

His leg was healed. Not even a scar. His broken arm too. Her song had sealed his cracks as well.

I'm home, he thought. *I'm finally home.* But the sun was burning his skin, as it had in the desert. He could not linger here. But he knew where he needed to go.

He headed out of the park and walked down Central Park West, keeping to the shadow of buildings. The traffic lights blinked red. Many weren't working at all. Cars had crashed, and police and ambulances raced down the avenues. People were frightened, rushing home. They glanced at Daniel in his bloody robe, the hood over his face, but had more personal concerns.

An earthquake? A nuclear blast? A meteor strike? They all wondered.

Theories were shouted into cell phones or blasted from street vendor radios, as people huddled around to listen. He kept walking. He turned east on 59th Street and hurried over the Queensboro Bridge. The sun turned overhead he walked the shoulder of the Long Island Expressway while cars honked and drivers cursed the heavy traffic. The sun had begun to go down when a man in a pickup, stopped in the traffic, rolled down his window and said, "Hey, buddy, you need help?"

"I don't suppose you're headed to Babylon?" Daniel said.

"Lindenhurst, actually, but I could take you there. You hurt?"

"I'm all right," Daniel said, getting in the cab. "Thanks."

"Crazy fucking day, huh?" the man said. He was in his late fifties, of African and Hispanic genes. He hadn't shaved in days, and his beard was as white as the headlights of oncoming traffic. His ashtray was overflowing with cigarettes. "Mind if I smoke?"

"Only if you don't give me one."

The man laughed. So they smoked and drove east, while the man on the radio went on about the "Event." The driver said to Daniel, "They first said it was a terrorist attack, and now they're saying this Event happened all over the world. They're saying it's a solar flare or a nearby supernova, something astronomical. The sky changed color. Did you see that shit?"

"Yeah," he said. "I did."

"You a priest or something?"

"No."

"What's with the robe?"

"This is borrowed."

The man looked Daniel up and down. "You sure you ain't hurt? Where'd all that blood come from? I could take you to the hospital."

"I'm just fine, thanks. I really just want to check on my grand-mother in Babylon."

The man nodded, cigarette dangling precariously from his lips. "I'm going to check on my daughter too. Her phone isn't working."

The highways were crowded with cars and emergency vehicles. The traffic was slow and exhausting, but they made it to Suffolk County in less than three hours. Daniel directed the man through

Babylon's suburban neighborhoods. Gram's house, the house he had grown up in, stood as it always had. But it seemed a lot older, a lot more tired, even though the bushes and lawn were still neatly trimmed, a point of pride for Gram. He felt like crying at the sight of it.

The man put the car in park

"I'm sorry," Daniel said. "I've lost my wallet. I've nothing to give you. Can I give you my phone number, so I can send you some money?"

"Not necessary. You just make sure your family's okay. I don't want your money."

"All right, thank you," Daniel said. "Hey, I never got your name?"

The man lit up a cigarette and smiled. "I'm Raphael." Then he yanked the door closed and drove off.

Daniel stood out front, afraid to go in, and worked up his courage. The door was open, and it creaked as he stepped inside. He moved slowly, afraid to disturb the dust of old memories.

He crossed the foyer and heard a buzzing sound. It resolved into the voices of TV newscasters going on about the Event.

"A massive dip in solar output, coupled with a curious drop in global air pressure . . ." He entered the living room. Gram sat in her favorite chair, remote in hand.

"You know the rules, Danny," she said. "Take off your shoes before coming into the house." She turned to face him, and her blue eyes shone.

"Gram," he said, his voice cracking. "Oh, Gram . . ." He ran to her, and suddenly he was the ten-year-old boy who'd scraped his knee or fallen off his bike or lost his parents in a fire. He squeezed her tight. "Is this real? Am I really home?"

"Home?" she said. They released, and she looked him up and down. "Where the hell've you been, Danny? I've been worried sick."

His eyes watered. He tried to speak, but no words seemed right.

She looked askew at him. "Your friend Christopher has been calling me every day since you left, to check up on me, see if I need anything or if I've heard from you. He doesn't seem to remember the dog leaping onto the bimah and turning into that white-haired man. No one does. No one, except me."

He shivered. "Gram . . ."

The newscasters rattled on annoyingly, and she muted the TV. "Where did you go, Danny? Are you hurt?" She looked tenderly at him. "You look like hell. What are you wearing? Tell me, Danny. Where have you been?"

He looked at the TV. Scenes of the Event flashed from all over the world, fires burning, crashed cars, scenes of destruction, interspersed with endless talking heads.

"A lot of deaths," Gram said. "It's awful. A third of Suffolk lost power. It went off here for a few minutes, but we seem to be doing okay now."

She was trembling, and he took her hand. "It's over now, Gram."

"Is it?" She stared at him.

The truth was, he wasn't sure. Four Lamed Vav were now in Sheol. And Mashit and Caleb were still alive, thrashing below him in the Shards. He knew they would not give up their plans, ever. Demons were the most single-minded of creatures.

On the wall, above the unused piano was an illustration of the Tree of Life. Beside it was a picture of him, nine years old, and his parents.

"Gram?"

"Yes?"

"When you were in the hospital . . ."

She looked warily at him. "Yes?"

"You told me that one shabbes eve, as the sun was going down, my crib—"

"Your crib's shadow made a menorah on the wall, with seven little flames."

"And you thought this was a sign that I was a—"

"Danny! *Genug.*" Enough.

"You knew what I was, Gram. You've always known."

She frowned and looked at the TV. "I don't know what you're talking about."

He nodded. "Yeah. I thought so."

She took her glasses off and placed her frames on the table beside her chair, rubbed her eyes, then sighed deeply. "I kept your room just as you've left it. Why don't you have a shower, change into some fresh clothes, and then you can tell me all about where you've been."

He was hungry, so damned hungry. The sun still burned his skin. His hands were thin, the sinews tight as guitar strings. His grasp of languages was still as acute as it had been on Gehinnom. That damned curse still boiled in his veins. And he wasn't a Lamed Vavnik anymore.

"Gram," he said, "do you have any brisket?"

"Brisket? You're eating meat again?" She shook her head. "What's happened to you?"

"I woke up."

She nodded, as if all was understood. "Just so you know, Danny, you can stay here as long as you like. As long as you need to get yourself better."

"Thank you," he said. "But only just for a little while, Gram. Only for one night, maybe two. The world is still broken. People still suffer. There's still so much work I have to do."

ACKNOWLEDGMENTS

IF IT TAKES A VILLAGE TO RAISE A CHILD, IT TOOK A UNIVERSE TO produce this book. *King of Shards* wouldn't exist without the help and support of countless people.

To Stephen and Judith, my parents, for giving me this blessed life with so many opportunities to thrive. To Sondra and Liz, my sisters, to Gary, my cousin, and to Adam and James, my brothers-in-law, for their constant encouragement. To my in-laws, Stephen and Anne, Didi Semko, Julie and Joe, Steven and Betina, for warmly welcoming me into their family, and for their support.

To Ellen Datlow, my partner in crime, for her friendship and unending support. To Richard Bowes, for his kindness, wisdom, and friendship.

To the folks of Altered Fluid. To Mercurio David Rivera for his humor, friendship, and good-natured evilness. To Devin Poore and Rajan Khanna for the beer, always for the beer. To Paul M. Berger for his private tours of the Museum of Natural History. To all the past and present members of Altered Fluid, the best damned writing group in the world, including Kristine Dikeman, E.C. Myers, Lilah Wild, Richard Bowes, Alaya Dawn Johnson, Sam J. Miller, N.K. Jemisin, Greer Woodward, Tom Crosshill, K. Tempest Bradford, Danielle Friedman, James Trimarco, James Thomas, Alyssa Wong, Lee Thomas, and Lauren McLaughlin. Thank you for reading early drafts of this novel and for your always-brilliant critiques of my fiction. You have all helped me grow tremendously as a writer.

To Alice K. Turner, may her memory be a blessing, for introducing me to the writing world through her class at the New School. To Joe Salvatore for showing me grammar is not only fun, but sexy.

To Ellen Datlow, John Joseph Adams, Neil Clarke, Scott H. Andrews, Jody Lynn Nye, Michael Brotherton, JoSelle Vanderhooft, Darin Bradley, Sean Wallace, Rachel Swirsky, John Klima and all the editors who have published my fiction.

To Kate Baker, Stefan Rudnicki, and Scott H. Andrews for their spectacular podcast narrations of my fiction.

To Ekaterina Sedia for the experience of publishing *Paper Cities*, which won the World Fantasy Award. To Gavin Grant and Kelly Link, for innumerable things, but especially for their support of *Sybil's Garage* and my earlier endeavors into the world of publishing.

To Jonathan Kravetz and Jonathan Armstrong, my lunch buddies, for their friendship and conversation.

To Michael Harriot, my agent, for his patience and dedication.

To Darin Bradley, my editor, for his sharp eyes, keen insight, and all his hard work making sure *King of Shards* is the best novel it possibly could be.

And greatest of all thanks to my one and only, my wife, Christine. You are my rock and the love of my life. A joy shared with you is infinitely more joyous. If every man is a universe, then you are the Pillar of mine.

You are all a part of this book, and I am forever grateful.

Matthew Kressel is a multiple Nebula Award-nominated writer and World Fantasy Award-nominated editor. He's published dozens of short stories in venues such as *Clarkesworld*, *Lightspeed*, *io9.com*, and elsewhere. He co-hosts the Fantastic Fiction at KGB reading series in Manhattan alongside veteran editor Ellen Datlow. He is a long-time member of the Manhattan-based Altered Fluid writing group, is an amateur Yiddishist, and knows more than one should ever need to know about the film *Blade Runner*. When he's not writing, he builds websites and writes software for businesses small and large. He lives in New York City with his wife.

CPSIA information can be obtained at www.ICGtesting.com
Printed in the USA
LVOW04s0539180915

454621LV00002B/2/P